West End Murders

REVIEWS FOR *Murder in the Monashees* by Roy Innes

THE MIDWEST BOOK REVIEW:
"Written in a straightforward manner, Roy Innes obeys all the rules in turning out the perfect mystery. The murderer is there in the background; pertinent clues abound; and the police have their problems tracking their man. He includes a captivating love story, his characters are ordinary people just trying to get by, and the killer has a human face. There is no shortage of action, and the book reads easily and has a refreshing twist. Innes is a mystery talent who should keep cranking out his product. An excellent read!"

PEACE RIVER RECORD GAZETTE:
"Roy Innes vividly evokes the colourful characters of Bear Creek and the killer that lurks among them in their once safe, rustic community. A page-turner from beginning to finally crafted end, *Murder in the Monashees* is one of life's great pleasures, a good bedside read."

THE PACIFIC RIM REVIEW OF BOOKS:
"He's good at all the details of the police procedural and the book unfolds in a convincing and realistic manner. Innes also populates the novel with a host of fascinating minor characters, many of whom function as both red herrings and colourful background. *Murder in the Monashees* is a terrific first novel and first rate mystery. Even the ending is as unconventional as it is riveting."

West End Murders

Roy Innes

To Nicki and
George

Enjoy

Roy Innes

247 8868

NeWest Press

Library and Archives Canada Cataloguing in Publication

Innes, Roy, 1939-

West End murders / Roy Innes.

ISBN 978-1-897126-27-1

I.Title.

PS8617.N545W48 2008   C813'.6   C2007-906527-9

Editor for the Board: Don Kerr
Cover and interior design: Natalie Olsen
Cover illustration: Natalie Olsen
Author photo: Lynne Young

NeWest Press acknowledges the support of the Canada Council for the Arts, the Alberta Foundation for the Arts, and the
Edmonton Arts Council for our publishing program. We also ac-
knowledge the financial support of the Government of Canada
through the Book Publishing Industry Development Program
(BPIDP).

NeWest Press
201–8540–109 Street
Edmonton, Alberta T6G 1E6
(780) 432-9427
newestpress.com

No bison were harmed in the making of this book.
We are committed to protecting the environment and to the
responsible use of natural resources. This book is printed
on 100% recycled, ancient forest-friendly paper.

1 2 3 4 5 11 10 09 08

printed and bound in Canada

1

It was a typical domestic scene, late night, wife upstairs reading in bed and her husband in the den below playing a computer game. But the game this husband played was quite different.

"Den" was probably a misnomer for the outsized room, furnished like a posh British men's club complete with a full-sized billiard table. The computer station was ensconced in a huge armoire which, when closed, hid the very latest high-tech equipment and two shelves of reference books, all computer and software related, save for one very odd exception: a copy of James Joyce's *Ulysses*.

But it was that very book the man pulled off the shelf while he waited for his computer to load. The screen lit up and demanded a password. He glanced at his desk calendar and confirmed the date.

"Second day of the fifth month."

He opened the copy of Ulysses, turned to page twenty-five and ran his finger down to the last full sentence. Leaning forward, he spoke into a microphone connected to the computer and recited the first letter of each word, followed by the number of letters the word contained.

"T–three –L–four–s–eight–o–two–T–three–P–four."

Not until the welcome screen blinked off and his desktop icons appeared did he place his hand on the mouse.

He watched the clock at the bottom of his screen tick off the seconds, and at the precise moment of midnight double-clicked the chat line icon. In less than thirty seconds, five other individuals came online to join him. He was delighted; no one was absent, despite the hour. Central got it going.

Excellent, he thought. I'm first for a change. He began to type.

FIVE-SIXTHS ACCOMPLISHED. NO PROBLEMS. COMPLETION DATE AS PLANNED. GAAAWU.

GAAAWU (God and America are with us) had been his suggestion as a sign-off and he'd been pleased when they'd all accepted it.

Only one of the reports was negative.

PLAN A ABORTED. PLAN B REQUIRES OVERSEAS HELP. PROCEED? GAAAWU

Central replied: PROCEED.

The other two were positive.

CLIENT APPREHENSIVE BUT EVERYTHING IN PLACE FOR CLOSING THE DEAL. GAAAWU

And

CUBAN VENTURE GOING SWIMMINGLY. NO RIPPLES. GAAAWU.

Central terminated the session.

REPORT PROBLEMS ONLY TO SS1. WILL NOTIFY RE NEXT CONFERENCE. GAAAWU

He logged off and sat back, watching the screensaver come on, a three dimensional aquarium complete with bubbles and sound.

SS1 was the secure site in Washington, D.C.; he'd set it up himself. Central was so computer illiterate it was a joke, but he was their leader and so far he'd done a good job. It was odd, though, that Central hadn't commented on the Washington operation. Perhaps he assumed everyone would understand that there was no holding back the VV (Vietnam Vets) contingent after the desecration of the memorial.

"Don't you get enough of that thing at work?"

He jumped at the sound of his wife's voice. She'd come downstairs to the den.

"For heaven's sake, turn it off and come to bed. It's after midnight."

8

He relaxed and smiled.

"Yes dear," he said and shut down the computer.

But sleep came slowly. The troops were deployed and his unit was poised to strike again, this time at the primary target: the biggest prize. America was on its way to being born again and he was one of the six making it happen.

Onward Christian so-oh-ldiers, marching as to war, with the cross of Je-ee-sus....

"Don't cry, son," his father had said, lashing him again and again. "What you and Billy did was wrong. Boys don't do that with boys. God is guiding my hand and when it's over, you'll be a Christian again. Sing. Sing it out."

The speeds of approaching vehicles flashed on the dashboard radar, but Corporal Blakemore parked his police cruiser and paid little attention to them. He looked up instead at the Monashee Mountains that towered above the highway. The green was becoming more uniform now as the lighter colours of spring faded into summer. Trout were biting in the streams; deer were budding new antlers; grouse sat on nests incubating the latest hatch. He loved this wild country and dreaded leaving, but he loved his wife more and it was his turn to make a life change.

His decision had sparked an immediate bonus: Barbara's enthusiasm in bed improved remarkably and she became her old, cheerful self again. He attributed most of her unhappiness to their inability to produce a child, but deep

9

down he knew that despite a real effort on her part, she'd never been happy with small-town life.

He took one last forlorn look at the mountains and then returned his attention to the highway. His mood lifted when a familiar sight appeared at the far end of the stretch he was monitoring.

Two cars sped towards him side by side, neither driver willing to give way. He knew even before he could see the license plates that the car to his left was from Saskatchewan. Born and raised in BC, Blakemore could never understand the rage that came over Wheat Province natives when another vehicle tried to pass them. The radar had them clocked at one hundred thirty km/h. He flipped on his red-blue flashing lights and stepped out of the cruiser.

He was fearful for a moment that the two drivers were so locked in their rolling combat they weren't going to stop, but they finally saw him and, just as he'd suspected, the stubborn car had Saskatchewan plates. Both vehicles pulled over, Saskatchewan maintaining his lead right to the shoulder of the road.

The driver's face glowed beet red when Blakemore walked over to him and the colour wasn't from prairie sunburn or road rage; the cause was sitting beside him: a very angry woman.

"You crazy old fool," she screamed. "Are you trying to get us killed? I hope the officer throws the book at you. I've a good mind to get on the train and go right back home."

He was probably in his early seventies, certainly old enough to know better, but Blakemore didn't bother with a lecture. He couldn't get a word in anyway; the woman never ceased her diatribe. He simply wrote out the ticket and handed it over. The man drove off without saying a word.

The second driver was more prepared, a younger man alone in a pickup with BC plates.

"Officer," he said, his voice pleading. "I've been following that guy for fifty K. He floors it on the straight sections and then slows to a friggin' crawl around every curve. It's the traffic behind me that's scary. Twice I've been damn near rear-ended and I couldn't drop back because there was no room to pull in. Everyone else was trying to get past the bugger, too."

It was a familiar refrain, but the logo on the young man's baseball hat drew Blakemore's sympathy: "ROCK CREEK ROD AND GUN." There was great mule deer hunting in Rock Creek. He wrote out a warning and told the man not to be so impatient.

"The guy's an old fart and I've scared the piss out of him. He'll have to find a washroom soon."

Blakemore felt better. It was his last day on the job and he needed to cheer up. Barbara deserved it. They weren't actually leaving Bear Creek for another week, lots of time for more lovemaking before he had to face the big metropolis.

3

Twilight approached as a solitary runner moved along the Stanley Park seawall. The man's stolid expression implied a brain set in neutral, but Bruce Leighton was deep in thought.

He felt like a carpenter with so much paraphernalia clipped to the belt of his running shorts: cellphone, ID pouch, and that stupid pepper spray his partner insisted he get.

"If you must run in that big, dark Stanley Park at all hours, you need protection."

Bruce smiled, recalling the admonishment. But the nagging, he knew, was based on love, and Chris did have a point. The park had become risky for a lone runner. The recent murders made that all too clear.

He tried to throw off the negative thoughts that had crept into his head and blunted his runner's high, but the deaths were too close to him; he'd known the four victims well.

Two of the men, Jason and Dwayne, preferred to train off the beaten track and used the park's forest trails, a mistake in Bruce's opinion. The seawall, in contrast, was exposed and usually crowded with walkers, cyclists, runners, rollerbladers, dog-walkers, and the like. So what if one had to do two or three laps on pavement to get in the miles? At least it was safe. He was convinced that muggers were responsible for both Jason and Dwayne's deaths, despite the police refusing to give out much in the way of details.

Roger and Frank's murders were more disturbing: killed in their own apartment. Word leaked to a *Star* reporter that it was "an execution-type slaying," both victims shot in the back of the head. Bruce could think of no reason the two would be "executed." That was gangland stuff. Roger and Frank ran a flower shop and he just knew they weren't into drugs or anything like that. It made no sense.

He liked to finish his run at dusk, and with Daylight Saving Time that wasn't until eight o'clock. He was running well, without pain or shortness of breath, and the rhythmic slap-slap of his Nikes on the pavement, the smell of the sea, and the fragrance of park blossoms gradually swept away his worries. He felt almost ethereal, moving on another plane and with a rare treat this evening: a stretch of seawall to himself. Even the dog-walkers had left, the impending darkness drawing people away from this distant point on the wall back to the warm lights and the safety of their urban dwellings.

Rounding a curve, Bruce saw the Brockton Point lighthouse come into view, one quarter the size of a real lighthouse but an important navigational beacon nonetheless. A simple passageway extended through its base, allowing continuation of the pedestrian walk. The opening, however, was narrow, prompting park custodians to install iron railings at both entrances, encouraging cyclists to dismount and walk their bikes through. That, of course, was a challenge to some, particularly the mountain bike enthusiasts to whom dismounting for any barrier was tantamount to surrender.

Not wanting to break his stride, he was annoyed to see one of those stubborn individuals approaching the lighthouse from the other side, barely moving as he tried to manoeuvre his bike around the barrier. Realizing he was going to have to stop and let the testosterone-burdened jerk come through, Bruce decided a little act of aggression on his part was in order. If he sprinted right up to the man, the fellow would be forced to dismount, a small victory for the runner.

But a second bicycle appeared, behind Bruce. Its rider had pulled onto the seawall moments before and was approaching quickly, soundlessly, and just as Bruce reached the lighthouse, the gap was closed. The cyclist dismounted and rushed forward, a pistol in his hand. Bruce was so intent on his confrontation with the first rider, he heard nothing. In fact, all anyone could have heard was a soft thump when the nine mm slug traveled a scant twelve inches from the tip of the silencer to the base of Bruce's skull.

His body never reached the pavement. The two men grasped him as he fell, carried his lifeless form the few feet to the edge of the seawall, and heaved it over; the splash, like the shot, was muffled by the sound of the surf crashing against the stone wall. The entire incident took exactly five seconds from shot to splash. The two assailants remounted their bicycles and rode together at a casual pace until they reached an access road and then turned off, disappearing into the failing light.

Inspector Mark Coswell didn't care that everyone told him living in Vancouver's Chinatown was un-befitting a senior officer in the RCMP. He liked the neighbourhood. It had history. For over a hundred years it was a first home for immigrants—Italians, Portuguese, Indians, and Chinese — most moving to better environs when they could afford it.

His building, erected in the late 1800s, was once a rooming house for migrant workers. Pictures in the city archives showed the stark wooden structure with half-curtained windows, a large veranda in front strewn with lines of drying laundry, and shabbily dressed individuals sitting on the stoop.

One hundred years later, forward-thinking architects converted the old structure into modern apartment units and awaited the rush of genteel purchasers. But the architects' vision was too optimistic; Chinatown's slum reputation dashed their commercial dreams. The units didn't sell until the prices plummeted to the break-even point, allowing individuals like Coswell to buy them for a song.

The apartment was pristine when he moved in, but in no time he'd applied his own personal touch, transforming the interior into a mess. He blamed his over-indulgent mother for his being such a sloppy housekeeper. She'd always picked up after him and adulthood had not altered his carelessness. Clothes were strewn about, magazines spilled off the coffee table, and dust-balls blew about every time the door opened. His bed was never made and dresser drawers were left pulled out in his neverending search for clean clothes. Towels littered the bathroom and he made no effort to put away his shaving materials. The stains in the sink would have made a lesser man shudder.

The only tidy room was the kitchen, but that was only because he barely used it, eating out for almost all his meals.

Once a month, though, Iris Chew came in and cleaned house. Coswell tried never to be there when she did. He left her money in an envelope on the kitchen table. Iris spoke little English but her reproachful looks were anything but inscrutable.

Rare for him, he'd slept in. Perhaps it was the image of Iris the day before, slaving away cleaning up his apartment, that had done it. He was exhausted for her.

It took him a little longer than usual to get going. Everything was put away so neatly that he had to go looking in drawers and cabinets until he found what he wanted. It was so much easier to simply eyeball his wardrobe thrown over chair backs and have all his shaving stuff laid out on the sink.

He had to hurry; the morning was starting off with a bang at RCMP headquarters.

Coswell hadn't been in his superior's office more than a few minutes before he became royally pissed off. Chief Inspector Ward was on his high horse again and Coswell, as usual, was assigned the role of pooper-scooper.

"I've just had a meeting with Mayor Schmidt," Ward thundered, "which rhymes with shit and that's exactly what I got, for a full ten minutes, no less. He wants to know in detail why we're not making any progress in the West End murders investigation."

"We're just consulting on those cases," Coswell argued. "The West End is Vancouver City Police territory."

"I know that," Ward snapped. "But the Mayor pointed out to me that the RCMP receives considerable funds from city coffers, and he wants action for his bucks. Now what the hell is the problem? Why aren't we getting anywhere?"

"It's tough working with local police," Coswell said, annoyed at the whine creeping into his voice. "A lot of them resent our noses stuck into what they consider their territory."

"Well, I want you to stick your nose and everything else you've got into this investigation and bugger the locals. Now what do you need to solve these cases?"

Coswell jerked to attention (as much as he could on the rock-hard chair in front of Ward's desk).

"First," he said. "I need to be named Chief Investigating Officer and that means seniority over the Vancouver Police detectives."

"Okay, I'll get the Mayor to clear that with his police chief."

"Second," Coswell continued. "I want the Vancouver General Hospital to handle all the lab stuff. Peter Mueller is one of the best forensic pathologists in Canada and has the backing of the main labs in Ottawa, which the city crew doesn't have."

"Tricky, but I'll arrange it. The city coroner will probably be happy to get some of this grief off his back anyway. The number of stiffs he handles on a daily basis is plenty without adding the ones from the West End."

"And finally," Coswell said. "I want two ranking officers as assistants — corporals at the least."

"That's tougher. You know the situation: lots of constables, but most of the higher ranks are commanding outposts in the boonies. I'll see what I can do, though."

He got up, and Coswell had to admit that the Chief Inspector was an impressive sight at full stretch: six-four, ramrod-straight, with piercing blue eyes that caused men to cringe. He was always in uniform, immaculate from his military-cut grey hair to his spit-and-polished boots.

Coswell, on the other hand, barely met the height requirements at five-nine, carried twenty pounds excess weight, and hated wearing his uniform (it was often conveniently "at the cleaners"). He also detested wearing a jacket and tie, preferring loose-fitting slacks, a polo shirt, a dark blue nylon windbreaker, and an RCMP baseball hat to cover his balding head. Personal comfort aside, he reasoned that his attire coordinated better with the casual dress worn by the city police detectives, thereby improving his rapport with them.

Chief Ward was not of like mind.

"You realize you're an embarrassment to the force in that get-up," he said. "I know you're too fat to get into your uniform, but for Christ's sake spend some money and buy yourself a decent suit."

"Right, sir," Coswell lied. "I've been meaning to do that but I've just been so busy...."

Ward waved him off.

"Dismissed. But I want a daily report from you. Next one's at 0730 tomorrow, right here. Got it?"

Coswell got it. He had less than twenty-four hours to bring a spark of happiness into his boss' life.

***
***

Certain that Ward wasn't about to get any action out of the Mayor for a couple of hours, Coswell decided to ease the stressful start to his day by doing breakfast at The Dutch House of Pancakes on Main Street, a block from RCMP headquarters.

Normally he avoided this outlet, frequented by RCMP administrative staff and personnel from adjacent car dealerships, but at eight-thirty he expected most of the breakfast crowd to be gone and it was too early for coffee break.

He pushed open the fake Dutch doors, painted a royal blue, and went inside. He ignored the "Wait to be Seated" sign and headed for a secluded corner beside the kitchen where he knew he'd get the best service, the waiters forced to look him straight in the eye whenever they picked up an order.

The place was almost deserted but, to his dismay, someone was already seated in the secluded corner wolfing down one of the trademark pancakes. The man had his back to him, but there was something familiar in the broad shoulders and the way he attacked the food. Curious, Coswell approached and then his heart sank when a face from the past turned and looked right at him: Corporal Paul Blakemore, his Kootenay nemesis.

"Top of the morning to you, Inspector," Blakemore said. "Fancy meeting you so soon. Barbara and I just moved in on the weekend. Have a seat."

Reluctantly, Coswell joined him.

Memories flooded into his mind. Some years back, he and Blakemore worked together briefly on a multiple murder case in Bear Creek, a hick town in the southeast corner of the province, the corporal's posting at the time. The inspector was sent from Vancouver to take over the investigation, a blow to Blakemore's small town ego. There'd been a messy end to the case; the perp got away and the inspector took most of the heat for it. As a result, when the forced alliance came to an end their parting was mutually appreciated.

"You've been transferred to Vancouver?" Coswell blurted, knowing that Blakemore, with his redneck, backwoods, straight-from-the-shoulder cop mentality was ideally suited to a rural posting; in the city he'd be a disaster. Some ignorant bureaucrat at RCMP headquarters in Ottawa must have made the decision, but Blakemore's accepting the move surprised Coswell. As a corporal, Blakemore had some choice in the matter.

"Not transferred," Blakemore explained. "Posted. My three years are up in Bear Creek and I have to move."

"To the city?"

"Yeah," Blakemore said. "My wife, Barbara, finally got her way. She wants me to buck for sergeant and, as you well know, that means accepting any posting, anywhere."

"But, Vancouver?" Coswell was still unable to accept the fact that Blakemore was going to work in his city. A horrible thought occurred to him.

"What division have you been assigned to?"

"Homicide."

Oh, lovely, Coswell thought, me and Smokey the Bear again. Ward's answer to my corporal request, no doubt.

Was the old tyrant getting back at them both for losing the Monashee killer?

The waitress arrived and poured him a coffee. He disregarded the menu she handed him.

"I'll have the strawberry and banana pancake with two eggs, easy over and four strips of bacon ... and I want extra maple syrup. Two pitchers, please; they're small."

"Jeez. You won't be able to move after all that," Blakemore said.

Coswell eyed the pancake and egg remnants on the corporal's plate.

"Look who's talking."

"I had ham instead of bacon, less fat; my eggs were poached, not fried. I'm watching my weight," Blakemore replied.

"You've got a lot to watch, I notice."

Blakemore changed the subject.

"You might be interested to know there's been a bit of an exodus from Bear Creek since you were there. I'm the last to leave. Ernie, my partner, handed in his resignation and left last year; Doc Benson moved out even before that to specialize and Heather McTavish followed him. Some big newspaper offered her a job."

Ah, the feisty Bear Creek *Bulletin* reporter. A pain in the corporal's considerable backside, Coswell remembered.

"But the weirdest thing," Blakemore continued, "is that they all ended up here in Vancouver. I got a postcard from Ernie telling me his father died and left him a chunk of money. He's bought an art gallery in the West End."

"I didn't know about Ernie, but I have bumped into Heather and Zachary Benson. She's a crime reporter for the *Vancouver Star*; he's doing a forensic pathology residency at the General Hospital."

There was a moment of awkward silence, broken by Blakemore.

"I've been reading about those West End murders. Interesting."

Coswell's mind raced. What in God's name was he going to do with this rube? No way did he want Blakemore panting over his shoulder, particularly in the West End investigation. That called for top men accustomed to police procedures in a big city.

Suddenly, it came to him — he knew exactly what to do with Paul Blakemore.

"I take it you're killing time till you meet with Chief Inspector Ward this morning?"

"Right — at nine o'clock. I gather he meets all new staff personally. Sounds like an okay boss."

A benign smile appeared on Coswell's face.

"Tell you what. I don't have much on this morning, so why don't I go with you and introduce you to the Chief?"

"That's kind of you," Blakemore said. But he was no fool. Beneficence from the inspector, particularly towards him, suggested an ulterior motive.

Coswell's food arrived: a giant Dutch pancake, fourteen inches across, with six banana slices radiating from a generous blob of strawberries plunked in the middle, the whole thing coated with powdered sugar. The eggs and bacon came on a separate plate with two pitchers of dark maple syrup set alongside.

He scraped the strawberries away from the centre and slid the eggs and bacon into their place. Finally, he poured both pitchers of syrup in concentric circles from the edge of the eggs to the rim of the plate. He then ate the entire mess in three minutes, washing it down with coffee.

"That feels better," he said. "Now let's go meet the Chief."

Jane Taylor, Chief Inspector Ward's secretary, was a remarkable woman. She'd risen to her position from the typing pool many years back and held it through a series of chief inspectors, the latest being Ward. Unlike many of her ilk, who take on a self-importance directly proportional to their boss' status, Jane kept a good rapport with everyone she dealt with, from the lowly constable to the Mayor himself. She did have favourites, though, and Coswell was one of them.

"I didn't expect to see you again until tomorrow morning, Inspector," she said when the two mounties came into the office. "Couldn't stay away from the cozy ambiance, eh?"

She knew he was plotting something, likely at the expense of the new corporal, but she held her tongue.

"Paul Blakemore and I worked together a while back and I thought it might give him a leg-up if I personally introduced him to the Chief Inspector."

Jane almost laughed at the charade.

She flicked on the intercom to Ward's inner office.

"Corporal Blakemore's here ... with a friend. Shall I send them in?"

"A friend?"

Silence for a moment, then the intercom clicked off. Seconds later the Chief Inspector emerged from his office, but Coswell was ready. Grasping Blakemore by the arm, he pulled him forward and began speaking at a staccato pace.

"Inspector Ward, sir, I'd like to introduce Paul Blakemore. We go a long way back, Paul and I. We've just had breakfast together and I started to get an idea that I think will give us a big boost in the West End cases. Perhaps we could discuss it all together, because it does involve Paul."

Blakemore looked as stunned as Ward, but had extended his hand. Ward gave it a perfunctory shake.

Jane, standing beside her desk, amused by the performance, decided to interject, a touch of mischief in her voice.

"There's nothing in the appointment book until nine-thirty, sir. You do have time."

Ward turned on his heel and called back over his shoulder, "All right, Coswell, but it had better be good."

They followed him into the office. Coswell remained standing, but gestured for Blakemore to sit in a single chair in front of the Chief's Inspector's desk. Ward settled into his own seat and leaned forward, mustache bristling.

"Well. Out with it."

Coswell took a deep breath and began:

"The four men murdered were all gay, as you know. City cops are not popular in the gay community and I think witnesses are clamming up on them, so I'm suggesting a plant — an undercover man to dig out information for us. Paul, here, used to live in the West End and knows his way around. Also, he's been away long enough now that no one's likely to remember him. How long has it been, Paul?"

"Twenty years," Blakemore said. "But how did you know I used to live there?"

"Ernie told me. In fact, if my memory serves me correctly, he mentioned you actually grew up in the West End."

Coswell had no grounds to question his memory. Even though some time had passed since the Monashee murders, his recollections of the people and events there were crystal clear. Ernie was one of the good ones.

"To go on," Coswell said. "We could set Paul up in a dummy job of some sort, maybe a bouncer at one the clubs down there, and get him an apartment close by. I just know it'll work. What do you think, sir?"

A furrow deepened on Ward's brow. He wondered at Coswell's motives and a glance at Blakemore's puzzled expression reinforced his suspicion. After a few moments, however, he made the decision.

"All right," he said. "But Blakemore here counts as one of your corporals. You'll get one more if I can find someone, but most likely a couple of constables will have to do, so allow for it. Now off you go and work out the details. Welcome to Vancouver, Corporal Blakemore."

Coswell was delighted. As they left, he waggled his fingers at Jane.

"This is just great," he said.

He felt a twinge of guilt, knowing that the undercover role he'd just created could mean Blakemore being separated from his wife for a time. But then he reasoned that Blakemore was probably moping around the house, missing his outback lifestyle and being a general pain in the ass to his wife, Barbara. Coswell liked Barbara; she deserved a holiday from her big husband.

"We're going downtown," Coswell said, leading Blakemore to one of the RCMP marked cars in the lot. He got into the driver's seat and motioned the corporal to the passenger side.

Blakemore relaxed with Coswell at the wheel, knowing it would take him a while to get used to city traffic again. The Vancouver drivers were a lot more aggressive than he remembered. He was amazed at how often vehicles cut in front of the squad car, despite the RCMP insignia on the doors and the familiar red and blue light bar on the roof.

None of this appeared to bother Coswell who casually

navigated the vehicle through the busy streets, oblivious to the agitated drivers around him and not missing a beat in his one-sided conversation with Blakemore.

"In a nutshell, this case involves four murders—two separate ones in Stanley Park and a double in a West End apartment building. All the victims were gay and probably knew one another, but it's who they were that's added to the fuss—city VIPs of the highest order, hence the Mayor getting all hot and bothered about it. The details are in a mountain of police reports you'll have the dubious pleasure of reviewing later this morning."

***
***

The intersection of Hastings and Main has been the centre of the infamous Vancouver downtown Eastside for decades. The sidewalks are crowded with drunks, druggies, prostitutes and paupers. One doesn't go half a block without seeing the familiar blue and white cruisers either parked or driving slowly, the two officers inside on the lookout for trouble. They never have to go far to find it.

Coswell pulled into an alley and then turned down a ramp into an underground parking lot directly below the station.

"A heads-up for you, Paul," he said when they got out of the squad car. "I've just been put in charge of the West End investigation by the Mayor. You can imagine, I'm sure, how our city colleagues are going to take that. We've been barely tolerated as consultants; being made their bosses is really going to bite their asses."

Coswell's prediction was true. The atmosphere when they entered the squad room was decidedly cool. Numerous plainclothes and uniformed officers sat at desks in a huge open area appearing busy at their tasks. They barely glanced at the two Mounties. A tall, thin, dyspeptic individual, shirtsleeves rolled up and tie askew, emerged from a glassed-in office, on the door of which was stenciled, "Inspector Marsden."

Coswell took the initiative.

"Good morning, Bob. I want you to meet Corporal Paul Blakemore, a new and welcome addition to our homicide unit. He's come down from the interior to help us out."

Marsden gave Blakemore a curt nod and spoke directly to Coswell.

"Good morning, Inspector. I've just informed my men of the Mayor's decision to put you in command of the West End investigation. You will, of course, have our complete cooperation."

He led them into his office and waved them to chairs positioned in front of his desk while he settled himself into a big swivel chair behind it.

"We'll get a private office set up for you momentarily. We've not had time yet to adjust to the change in command."

"No problem," Coswell said. "I'll need that soon — the office and the adjustment. I've got some new ideas for the investigation and I want them instituted without delay."

Coswell's intimidation tactics irritated Marsden who, as a full inspector in the Vancouver City Police Force, was used to giving orders, not taking them. He leaned forward, pressed an intercom button, and spoke into it.

"Sergeant Burns — my office — now."

The intercom, connected to a loudspeaker, broadcasted the message to the entire outer office.

One of the officers seated there, a large man wearing a suit that barely contained his bulk, rose slowly from his desk and made his way to the office. The entire process appeared to give him pain, but the expression on his pock-marked face was stoical.

"Bring yourself a chair and shut the door," Marsden said.

The detective did as he was told, eventually setting his chair in a corner, as far away from Coswell as he could get.

Marsden ignored the manoeuvre.

"Detective Sergeant Burns will be your liaison with our department. I suggest you use him to pass on your orders rather than deal directly with the men yourself."

Burns' body language was not reassuring, especially to Paul Blakemore whose undercover role would involve both chains of command and who hoped the liaison would work, since it was his ass that was on the front line, not Burns' or Coswell's.

"I'll try it that way," Coswell said, eyeing the sergeant. "Providing it is efficient."

"It will be."

Despite the fact all three men were looking at him, Burns showed no reaction. He returned their collective gaze with unblinking eyes.

"Now I *am* looking forward to your new ideas," Marsden continued. "We'd all like these cases solved as quickly as possible. None of us enjoy the flak from above or the bad-mouthing in the local rags."

"Right," Coswell said. "Here's what we're going to do."

While the inspector reiterated the plan he'd outlined to Ward earlier, Blakemore's anxiety was replaced with something that almost approached enthusiasm. He could, with any sort of luck, become the linchpin in this investigation, a real boost up the promotional ladder.

"I've thought of the ideal job for him," Coswell went on. "A meter reader. The Mayor's office could arrange that easily enough. He'll drive one of those little Jeeps with the Hydro insignia on it—blends in everywhere and with a clipboard in his hand, he can get into any building in the West End."

"My detectives can get in anywhere, too," Marsden argued, "and they're not all that conspicuous."

"Paul will have an advantage. First of all, he's going to live down there. An apartment's to be rented for him. He'll soon establish himself as a neighbourhood fixture; he's good at that. He'll be making contacts day and night. I expect significant information from him in just a few days."

Blakemore gulped.

Heather McTavish counted her blessings. The jump from small-town newspaper reporter to number two on the *Vancouver Star's* crime beat was a big one, but Harold Frayley, after an initial hiccup, made the transition a dream. Frayley, the *Star's* multiple award-winning journalist, had the personality of a badger. He was reputed to eat underlings for lunch, but four-foot-eleven Heather of the flaming red hair was no push-over. Her first day in the newsroom began abruptly when she was summoned into his office.

"Your job," he'd said, "is to make sure there are fresh batteries in my recorder every day and my copy gets to the editor on time. Oh, and I like my coffee black, French Roast, which you get across the street at The Bistro."

She'd fired right back. "That's a weak sentence, using 'which' like that. There should have been a full stop after

'French Roast,' followed by a new sentence beginning with 'That'—comma—'you get across the street at The Bistro'. It gives much better emphasis to your chauvinistic comment and implies I'm so stupid that I need explicit directions."

His eyes widened. She continued.

"I'm a published author with a bestseller that's in every bookstore in the country. The stuff you've written is in landfill somewhere or stacked beside the holes in a thousand outdoor privies. Now get off the pot and give me a decent assignment."

They were buddies from that moment on.

Even her love life was convenient. She and Zachary Benson, who was in his last year of a forensic pathology residency at the Vancouver General Hospital, worked equally long hours, and so neither felt abandoned by the other at any time.

She was jolted from her reverie by Frayley, who burst out of his office and hurried over to her desk in the news room.

"Let's roll, Babe," he said. "They've just fished a body out of English Bay, a jogger with his brains blown out. I think the West End Murders have just reached number five."

Being so short, Heather was sensitive to diminutive-type words, but chose to interpret Frayley's pet name for her as meaning hot, vivacious, or downright stunning. She grabbed her purse, notebook, and recorder, and followed him out the door.

Despite the *Vancouver Star* logo plastered all over the car, they couldn't get any farther than the public parking lot in Stanley Park. The police had Prospect Point entirely cordoned off with yellow crime scene tape. Uniformed cops blocked all vehicular access. Heather was pleased that her small hand-held recorder weighed a fraction of the clunky thing that Frayley insisted on using, and the comfortable

Nike runners she wore were a distinct advantage over her partner's stiff English leather oxfords.

Frayley was puffing and wincing in pain when they finally made it to the Prospect Point lighthouse, a good quarter of a mile away. Two checkpoints on route delayed them only seconds. The policemen recognized Frayley and waved them on.

She arrived first on the scene. Coswell greeted her.

"Ah, Heather, my dear, so nice to see you," and when Frayley chugged up moments later, added, "I see you brought your ugly friend."

Recognizing that her boss was too out of breath to reply, Heather seized the opportunity to start the questions.

"Who's the victim? And who found the body?"

"A kayaker out for an early morning paddle. He spotted the body wedged between the seawall and a big rock at low tide," Coswell replied. "But I can't give you the victim's name until next of kin's been notified."

Frayley, his breathing back to normal, jumped into the conversation.

"I see the coroner's wagon's gone and no sign of a kayaker, so I guess that just leaves you to give us some information. Was he shot in the back of the head, like the others?"

Coswell frowned.

"How did you know he was shot?"

"Sources."

Heather knew the source: a driver for the city coroner's office who was a wannabe mystery writer, desperate to be published. Frayley had set him up nicely by reading some of his stuff and offering encouragement. The man would do anything Frayley asked, even at the risk of losing his job.

"I'll be looking into that," Coswell said. "There's enough panic in the West End about these murders as it is without someone leaking information to the press."

"I don't know what it is about you cops," Heather said. "The victim's dead with a hole in his head just like the others. How long do you think that's going to be hushed up and why should it be? The public deserves to know that the West End's not a safe place with a killer lurking about, who, by the way, doesn't seem to be slowing down any, despite all the police assigned there."

"And where the hell's Marsden, or at least Igor, his sergeant?" Frayley said. "I smell a story in this."

"Have a heart, you two," Coswell said. "You act like a couple of pit bulls going after the postman."

Coswell admired the reporters; they had a dedication to their jobs equal to his own and he had a particular soft spot for Heather, who'd been the key in cornering the Monashee murderer. As well, in her book *The Making of a Killer*, which recounted the affair, Coswell and his RCMP colleagues were cast in a good light. It helped defuse some of the criticism directed their way when the killer fled to the United States.

"Okay," he said. "This poor bugger is number five. I can't give you his name yet, but he's gay, just like the others."

He paused for a moment, and then sighed — might as well tell it all. If he knew the Mayor, it would probably end up on the six o'clock TV news anyway.

"You're right again about the significance of my being the only ranking officer here today. There's been a change of command. The Mayor's arranged for me to head up the West End Murders investigation."

Frayley gave a harsh laugh.

"When the team's doing bad, fire the coach," he said. "Typical."

Satisfied that their probing had gotten results, the two reporters eased off.

"Well, from our point of view," Heather said, "it'll be a nice change to get a different source of police information. We were getting a bit bored with Inspector Marsden's 'The Department is following up a number of leads.' What leads? Do you really have any?"

"None that have gotten us anywhere," Coswell admitted. "All five of the victims were upstanding citizens, loved by one and all, it seems. Our working hypothesis is a hate crime — the ultimate gay-bashing, in other words. Lord knows, there's a ton of that mentality around, but we haven't been able to put a finger on anyone."

The hate theory was old news, and the veteran reporter wasn't buying it.

"What's your off-the-record theory, Coswell?" Frayley asked. "I know you. You'll have one, I'm sure."

Coswell hesitated. Frayley's assurances aside, he knew that loose lips around reporters was a bad idea, off the record or no.

"When I've got something to back it up, I promise you'll be the first to know. In the meantime, I'll get the victim's identity to you as soon as I'm allowed to release it. That's the best I can do for now."

Heather looked ready to pounce, but Frayley stopped her with a glance.

"We'll remember that promise," he said, and then to Heather, "Let's go, Babe. We've got enough for today's edition. I'm sure we'll have a name to print before it goes to press."

Coswell watched the two leave. Heather paused for a

moment, studying the scene. He was afraid she might question him further, but she just frowned and hurried after her partner.

***
***

Paul Blakemore, despite his reputation for being thick-skinned, was feeling decidedly uncomfortable as he pored over the reports Sergeant Burns had produced for him. They were using the office Marsden relegated to Coswell, a small room originally used for interrogations. The feeling of claustrophobia was slightly alleviated by the replacement of the one-way glass with a clear pane that afforded a view into the general squad room. The furnishings were sparse: a steel table, filing cabinet and three metal chairs. A light fixture dangled from the ceiling but the bulb was missing, which left a small lamp on the table as the only reading light.

Blakemore's forty-year-old eyes were feeling the strain, and the presence of Burns sitting with his chair tilted back against a wall didn't help. The man spoke only when absolutely necessary, mostly remaining silent like a fat Buddha, minus the smile. When Coswell finally breezed in, Blakemore was more than a little relieved.

"Well. Got the case solved yet?" the inspector said. He glanced around the room and then focused on Burns. "And what the hell are you doing, sitting there like a bump on a log?"

"Obeying orders," Burns said. "I'm to gofer anything you two want and that's what I've done. Those are all the records we have on the West End cases."

Coswell knew it was time to set Burns straight. The man had a chip on his shoulder that needed flicking off.

"I'm going to tell you something, Sergeant. Either you're a professional policeman with some pride and dedication to your job or you're some prima donna with her nose out of joint. If the former fits, you're with us and I expect you to jump in with both feet. If you're the latter, then get your sorry ass out of here and send in a clerk who can do all the gofering we need, probably a lot more cheerfully than you. Now what's it going to be?"

Burns tried to hold the inspector's gaze, but couldn't. He looked down at his feet.

"What do you want me to do?"

Coswell took the advantage. He'd dealt with men like this before. Hammer them down, then lift them up.

"You were the main man in the trenches on this one, Burns. I've noticed how Marsden depends on you. Now, on this table is a pile of paper. I want you to sum it up and tell us what you think is going on."

Burns straightened up.

"There are five now, all gay men, and identical shots to the back of the head from close range with the same gun, a nine mm. Three were killed in separate incidents, including the latest, and two were murdered together in their apartment. The only sign of struggle in the whole bunch was on one of the apartment victims. According to our pathologist, hair was forcibly pulled from his scalp."

"And what do you glean from this?"

"I'd say that there are two killers, working in tandem— one distracts the victim and the other shoots him. It's unlikely that all three of the Stanley Park vics would have ignored someone coming up behind them. The apartment killings, in my opinion, definitely required two men. Both victims had to be immobilized at the same time and I think that one, hearing his buddy shot, tried to pull away and his assailant held him till the guy with the gun could shoot him too."

Blakemore, happy to see the change in Burns, joined the discussion.

"I noticed that no shell casings were found at any of the scenes. How sure are you that the same gun killed all five? I thought slug identification was iffy."

"It can be," Burns agreed. "But there were enough rifling marks in every case to confirm the fact. Nine MM: same gun."

"Good choice for a killer," Coswell said. "Lots of them around, and nine MM ammunition's easy to get. Hell, even the Vancouver Police use it in their Glocks."

Burns continued his assessment.

"As you know Inspector, forensics came up blank on just about everything. Foot-printing was useless. The victims were all caught on hard-packed trails and dumped right alongside. The bodies were found within hours, maybe even minutes of their deaths but we couldn't find a single soul that heard or saw a thing."

He paused to let his words sink in. The city police had not been sitting on their duffs.

"I think the shooter's using a silencer," he went on. "A nine mm makes a big bang. Someone would have heard it. This isn't New York; Vancouverites get involved."

"Nothing in the apartment?" Blakemore said. "No revelations from forensics?"

"Nope. Not a thing. There were indentations in the carpet, but useless for any sort of identification."

It was time to sum up.

"It would appear then," Coswell said. "That we're dealing with pros. If that is the case, I think our best chance at catching them will be by logic and old-fashioned policing."

Doctor Paul Mueller, Chief of Forensic Pathology at the Vancouver General Hospital, watched as his resident, Zachary Benson, completed the autopsy on Bruce Leighton. Despite the high profile of the case, Mueller had total confidence in Benson. Before returning to complete his residency the young man, working as a GP, had done an outstanding job as acting coroner in the Monashee cases.

"Nothing, again, Doctor Mueller," Zachary said. "Healthy, 47-year-old male; cause of death, a nine mm soft-point lead slug through the foramen magnum transecting the brain stem. He didn't feel a thing."

"No signs of trauma elsewhere?"

"None, and no needle tracks or nasal mucosal abnormalities to indicate drug use. I've sent blood for analysis but I'm sure it'll come back negative."

"In short, then," Mueller concluded. "We're going to be a disappointment to our men in blue."

"I don't think they were expecting much," Zachary said. "Especially after the downtown forensic boys drew a blank on the apartment killings. It's too bad we weren't in on that one. Maybe we could have found something."

"Maybe we can. This bundle I'm holding is from Inspector Coswell: complete files on all the West End victims. He's asked us to study them, which we'll do over a cup of coffee in my office. Bring me your results on Leighton. I'll sign them off there."

✦✦✦
✦✦✦

Mueller's office displayed a wonderful combination of the business of his profession and his escape from it. A huge, solid oak desk with comfortable chairs on either side took up a full third of the room. Aside from a telephone and a gold-plated pen holder, the surface of the desk was surprisingly free of clutter. x-ray view boxes were mounted behind the desk. Diplomas and awards hung randomly on one wall, but on the others, framed portraits of composers and posters of opera performances prevailed. A complete sound system installed in a glass cabinet rounded out the decor.

Mueller poured two cups of coffee from a machine hidden in a roll-top cabinet, and handed one to Zachary along with half the files. They studied these for almost twenty minutes before the veteran pathologist set down his bundle and broke the silence.

"The victims do follow a physical pattern," he began. "All five extremely fit. Three were runners, probably at a marathon level I'd say, judging by how little subcutaneous fat they had. The two from the apartment were much different, though. Big, sharply-defined muscles — body-builder physiques."

"Right," Zachary agreed. "Which might explain the head shots. Given a chance, any of these men could have run away or put up one helluva good fight. That means the killer or killers acted fast. I'll bet even the two in the apartment were shot within minutes of the killers gaining entrance and didn't have enough time to realize what was going to happen to them."

"The killers must be in pretty good shape themselves," Mueller added. "I don't see any overweight Mafiosa hitmen taking these five down so easily."

"Yes," Zachary said, holding up a photo. "Aside from this one, who's had some scalp hair pulled out, there isn't a sign of a struggle on any of them."

"Did you notice whether or not that victim's hair was analyzed?" Mueller asked.

Zachary re-read the file quickly.

"No it wasn't. But what would that show? The assailants were likely pros wearing disposable gloves."

"I know it's a long shot," Mueller said, "but maybe the killer's grasp was strong enough to break the gloves and release some skin particles or even knuckle hair."

"I guess the city guys didn't think of that and I can tell you it's too late to do anything about it now. The body was released to relatives two weeks ago. They had him cremated."

Mueller sighed. "Well, as I said in the beginning, we're going to be a big disappointment to Inspector Coswell, but maybe we can help on the next one."

"You think there'll be a next one?" Zachary said.

"No doubt. I get the impression our police colleagues aren't even close to catching the murderers. If the killers are of the hate variety, they're having too much fun to stop."

★★★
★★★

Coswell was beginning to regret his decision to let Burns question Leighton's roommate, Chris Reikel. He'd reasoned that giving the responsibility to the dour sergeant would help keep him on side. Unfortunately, Reikel couldn't stop crying, from the moment he identified his lover's body in the morgue until they returned him to the apartment in the West End where the two cohabited.

"He looked so frail lying on that awful steel table," Chris

blurted between sobs. "My Bruce — gone. What will I do?"

Coswell could see the sergeant's patience slipping; the emotional diarrhea was getting to him.

"What did you do?" Burns asked. "When he was alive, I mean. Did you work for him?"

"Yes," Chris said. "I ran his household and did it very well, thank you. He'd have been lost without me."

"Right. And what, exactly, was your boss' occupation? I understand he was in retail clothing or something like that."

"He was a designer, for heaven's sake," Chris shot back. "One of the best on the Pacific Coast. But you, of course, would be unlikely to know that."

He punctuated his remark with a disgusted glance at the sergeant's ill-fitting suit.

Coswell interrupted. Animosity wasn't going to get them anywhere.

"Mr. Leighton specialized in men's fashions," he said. "I wish I could afford just one of his creations but not on a policeman's salary, I'm afraid."

Burns looked at him, wondering where that fact came from. If anything, Coswell was the dress slob.

The answer was "Googling." Five minutes on the internet gave a mass of information on Bruce Leighton: his life history, his years with Armani, and the international awards the man received for his designs. Burns needed to move into the twenty-first century.

Mollified, Chris settled down with Coswell doing the questioning and supplied as much information as he could. Unfortunately his answers produced nothing in the way of leads. It appeared that Bruce Leighton had reached the pinnacle of success without stepping on anyone's face.

Even his love life appeared stable.

"We hardly ever argued, Bruce and I, and there was none of that ugly jealousy that just spoils everything," Chris said.

Coswell wondered at the unsolicited assertion. Jealousy, he suspected, often ran just below the surface in many a gay relationship and when male hormones exploded, the results could be lethal.

Burns was looking bored. Coswell decided to let him back in.

"Sergeant. Do you have any questions you want to ask at this point?"

Burns paused for a moment, and then doggedly began a pattern of interrogation, honed over many years on the force. First, he reversed his bad start with Chris.

"We are sorry for your loss," he said. "But I'm sure you want your friend's killers caught and punished."

Chris closed his eyes and nodded.

"We're looking for a pattern," Burns said. "And if we can find one, then two things will happen: the murderers will be identified, and even more important, we'll prevent any more killings."

"Yes, yes," Chris said. "There can't be any more. This is all too horrible."

Coswell leaned back in his chair. Burns was no slouch. In just a few sentences he had Chris' full co-operation.

"I think the killers knew a lot about your boss, his being gay and his running habit. The ambush was carefully planned. They predicted exactly where Bruce Leighton could be intercepted and killed with no risk to themselves. Where do you think they could have gotten that information?"

"His being gay is general knowledge in this city. He's had lots of press, TV and all that. He wasn't afraid to show affection in public either, especially in the West End bars. We

40

were envied for that."

He paused for a moment, thinking, and then said, "I can imagine how some uptight straights would consider that obscene. I'll bet if you look in the back of a gay bar somewhere, you'll find Bruce's killers lurking and stewing in their own bile."

Coswell knew that possibility had already been considered, and there'd been extensive canvassing of just those bars.

"As for his running," Chris continued. "He's enrolled in the downtown YMCA marathon clinic. This is the third year he's done that, the poor man. He developed knee problems the first two years and never managed to run in the actual race, but this year he was so sure he'd be able to compete."

Sobs again. Burns waited patiently this time.

"Did he always run alone like that? I thought those marathon clinics were a group thing."

"They are. But the groups get together only on Sundays. Marathoners, for some strange reason, prefer to train alone. Bruce, too, although he knew how I frowned on the habit."

While Burns labouriously wrote down the long list of Leighton's friends and business associates that Chris gave him, Coswell made a mental note to check out the YMCA as a possible lead. Jason Collins and Dwayne Wright, the first two West End murder victims, were runners as well and that aspect of the men's lives hadn't been delved into.

"May we look through Mr. Leighton's effects?" Burns asked. "An appointment book or a diary might give us useful information."

Coswell noted Burns' continuing gloves-on approach. In a murder investigation the police had every right to examine the victim's quarters without asking.

"Help yourself," Chris said. "But Bruce, the darling, never

brought his work home with him and he didn't keep a diary. You'll have to go to his office to check on business appointments."

He got up and went over to a small table in the entrance foyer. On it was an ornate box containing a stack of business cards. He took one out and handed it to Burns, who quickly glanced at it.

"His office is a houseboat?"

"Yes," replied Chris. "Isn't that just the sweetest? He rents the whole thing and it's all there — secretaries, designers, cutting rooms, tailors — everything to create Bruce Leighton masterpieces. Orders come in from all over the world."

"He supplies the whole world in men's fashions from a houseboat?" Burns said.

"No, silly. Factories do that for him. Bruce creates the mould."

"Or did create," he added and then broke down again. He buried his face in his hands and sobbed, stopping only for a moment to utter a final, heart-rending lament.

"We were going to be married in June."

Coswell and Burns beat a quiet retreat, pausing for a moment to leave cards with their names and cellphone numbers on the hall table.

***

Paul Blakemore sat at a table in The Wheatsheaf, a Denman Street bakery, scanning the morning paper and sipping a cup of coffee. He was bracing himself for a day of squeezing in and out of the midget Japanese jeep issued to Pacific Hydro meter readers, when a seductive voice came from across the table.

"Hi, handsome. Care for some company?"

Startled, Blakemore looked up.

Leaning over with an enormous grin on his face was former Constable Ernie Downs.

"Ernie, you son-of-a-bitch. I was going to look you up, but you found me first — great."

He got up and extended his hand but Ernie engulfed him in a hug that took his breath away. Somewhat nonplussed, Blakemore stammered, "And I love you too."

Ernie laughed—a big, open laugh. The uptight, closet gay constable, scared of his own shadow in Bear Creek, was obviously a new man in the city; Blakemore was happy for him.

"What are you doing in that Hydro uniform?" Ernie said. "Did the Force give you the boot? They obviously didn't write you a good reference if this is the best job you could get."

Blakemore glanced around and in a hushed voice said, "I'm undercover, Ernie, assigned to this West End murder affair."

Ernie's smile disappeared. He pulled back a chair, sat down and leaned forward, his face inches from Blakemore's.

"Those men were all friends of mine," he said. "Can you tell me how close you guys are to catching the killer? Every one of those victims was a good man and there's no reason why any of them should've been murdered."

"They think it's a gay-hate thing," Blakemore replied.

Ernie's jaw clenched and his eyes hardened.

"I want to help," he said. "I'm a civilian now but I know this West End crowd and I'm one of them. Your disguise is good, but there are a quarter of a million people living here and only a stroke of incredible luck will get you on the right track. How about it? Are we a team again?"

"Hell, yeah," Blakemore said, and then remembered that

he was under a whole new command. "But I should run it through Coswell first."

Ernie almost choked. "No way. You and Coswell? That's a hoot."

"He's the C.O. on this case, Ernie, with seniority over everyone including the city police."

"Even so, since when did you start worrying about protocol?" Ernie said, the grin returning.

"I know, I know," Blakemore moaned. "I've become a pussy cat, or pussy-whipped to be more exact. Barbara really wants me to get promoted to sergeant and I promised I'd give it a shot."

"It's about time," Ernie said. "Barbara's too much a class act to be stuck in the bush forever."

Domestic issues over, Ernie returned to his proposal.

"While you get the okay from Coswell, I'll start working right away on my own."

His enthusiasm built.

"You know, Paul, you're going to be a godsend. The city cops are chasing their tails on this and they have zero rapport with the gay crowd. You'll be our man, and I can make sure you get in where you need to. Let's meet here again tomorrow, okay?"

Blakemore nodded. Ernie stood up, blew a kiss, and headed out the door.

Only one person appeared to notice this exchange, a customer waiting for his coffee order at the bar, a tall, athletic man who stared intently in their direction. He wore a helmet, wrap-around sunglasses (the frames decorated with stars and stripes), cycling togs and a satchel slung over his back—one of the dozens of downtown Vancouver bike messengers who blend seamlessly into the background.

He quickly averted his gaze when Blakemore looked in his direction.

***
***

Burns, surprised once again when Coswell rushed ahead of him to get behind the wheel of the cruiser, was enjoying the sights of Granville Island from the passenger's seat. Typical in the immediate forenoon, the traffic was almost at a standstill while shoppers vied for parking spots. The huge market, along with dozens of specialty shops and numerous restaurants, drew hordes of people to the island every day of the week.

Parking was not a problem for Coswell. He pulled the cruiser up to a fire hydrant adjacent to the houseboat dock, confident that the RCMP logo guaranteed the vehicle would be left alone.

Berth twelve, Burrard Inlet, was the address of one of a string of picturesque houseboats loved by their inhabitants and admired by visitors. Coswell was not among those admirers. Motion sickness plagued him in all varieties of moving conveyances, trains, helicopters, airplanes, boats, even cars. He hated anything that rocked or swayed, on land, sea or air. He could abort a motion attack if he were at the controls of any of these, but not when he was a helpless passenger.

Leighton's houseboat stood out from the others, not by size (local restrictions dictated they all be the same in that regard) but by virtue of its colour. It was painted bright pink with rich, dark maroon trim. Fringes of greenery suggested a roof garden and wisteria blossomed in purple cascades. A brass plaque beside the door was inscribed with BRUCE LEIGHTON FASHIONS and below it a small sign read, "Welcome. Please come in."

The front office was tiny. A wrought-iron coat rack and an umbrella stand were positioned to the side, along with two plush chairs. The receptionist's desk and a wall of file cabinets behind it filled the rest of the space. A young man sat at the desk. He rose when the two policemen entered and greeted them with a prepared smile, obviously having observed the cruiser parked on the dock.

"Ah. Our brave men in blue," he said. "Come to investigate Bruce's death, I presume? I'm Brian Foulds, the office manager. We just got the news a couple of hours ago."

Burns nodded but said nothing, waiting for Coswell to either take the lead or indicate that he should. A passing boat settled the question, its wake causing the building to rock ever so slightly, unnoticed by the other two but affecting Coswell's stomach like a bad oyster. He turned to look out the window, hoping that if he fixed his gaze on a stationary object, it would stem the wave of nausea sweeping upward to his throat, but it was too late.

"Go ahead, Burns," he said. "I've just remembered an urgent call I have to make to headquarters. I'll meet you back at the cruiser."

He waved off Foulds' offer to let him use one of the phones on the desk and bolted for the door.

"Damn, damn, damn," Coswell cursed as he gulped the fresh air and let the solid ground settle his nausea. He returned to the cruiser and sat inside for a moment before he picked up the car phone and punched in headquarters' number. Jane answered.

"Well, aren't I surprised to hear from you," she said. "But it's a good thing you called. There's been a change of time and venue for tomorrow morning's meeting. Chief

Inspector Ward is playing golf with Mayor Schmidt at the Balmoral Golf Club. They're teeing off at eight am and you and Corporal Blakemore are to make up the foursome. A cart and clubs will be rented for you."

"You've got to be kidding," Coswell said. "I don't know if Blakemore even golfs and I haven't swung a club in years. Is this Ward's idea of a safe place for a meet? Blakemore and I'll stand out like sore thumbs. Besides, golf takes too long. It's a terrible waste of time."

"Chief Ward wants to assure the Mayor that the West End cases will be solved soon. He feels that having you and Corporal Blakemore there in a friendly atmosphere will go a long way towards giving that assurance."

"Bullshit. I know for a fact that Ward's a golf nut and so's the Mayor. They'll use any excuse to play and I'll bet there's a sizable wager involved."

"Tsk, tsk," Jane said. "What a suspicious mind you have. They're playing nine holes which, I gather, only takes a couple of hours. Relax and enjoy. It'll be good for you to go out somewhere green and listen to the birds sing."

"Right," he said. "I prefer the British system — meeting in a smoky pub over a pint of ale, a wedge of Stilton, a basket of crusty bread and Phil Collins blaring from the speakers. But never mind. Blakemore and I'll be there."

Coswell made two more calls, one to Paul Mueller to hear the disappointing forensic results and the second to Blakemore who, in the privacy of the little Hydro car, related his meeting with Ernie Downs.

"Great news," Coswell said. "Ernie was a bright light in that Monashee thing. Keep this liaison under your hat, though. There are probably a hundred no-nos that'll come from above if they know a civilian is involved in the front lines. By the way—do you golf?"

Burns was taking too long and Coswell was getting hungry. The mention of food in his conversation with Jane stimulated his appetite, the nausea now completely abated. He rang the sergeant's cellphone.

"Lunchtime," he announced, when Burns answered. "I'll rush over and get us a table at Bridges before it fills up. We'll sit upstairs. See you there when you're done."

Before Burns could reply, the connection was broken. Frowning, the sergeant returned the cellphone to his pocket and continued interviewing Leighton's manager.

Bridges' Restaurant, painted a gaudy yellow, gains its name from its location between the two major bridges over Burrard Inlet, the Granville Street Bridge and the old Burrard Bridge. The restaurant's upper floor is surrounded by windows that give a magnificent view of the busy inlet, and to the west, English Bay and the beginning of Stanley Park. Coswell was early enough to get a window seat facing the park, the very site of the West End murders.

By the time Burns arrived and made his way to Coswell's choice of tables, the inspector was on his second plate of hors-d'euvres and three quarters of the way through a very large glass of white wine. Burns sat down and accepted the menu Coswell handed him. If Burns thought the inspector would be eager to hear the results of his interrogation and the inspection of the Leighton office, he was wrong. Lunch was the priority.

"I'm having the grilled filet of Ahi tuna with Shiitake Miso, charred leeks, cucumber Sunamono and yam tempura. I like to eat a light lunch and Japanese is the way to go, but order what you want. The Force is picking up the tab."

A pretty young waitress arrived at tableside on cue, her bare midriff dotted with a flashing ring stuck in her navel.

"I'll have a double cheeseburger and a Diet Coke," Burns said to her.

"Good choice," she replied and hurried off to the kitchen with the order.

Coswell sighed.

"Burns. You didn't even look at the menu. I'm surprised they even have such a thing as a bloody cheeseburger here. Look at all those wonderful dishes. You're missing a real treat. And what's with the Diet Coke? At least have a decent glass of wine. This Chardonnay's wonderful. A Burrowing Owl, 2003."

"I like plain," Burns said. "And I don't drink alcohol on duty."

Coswell was surprised. He wouldn't have picked the sergeant to be so self-righteous, but then reasoned maybe Burns was trying to show him up. Fat chance of that; a little alcohol midday settled the brain and lifted the spirit.

"You're a fun guy, Burns," he said. "Okay, let's get down to business. What did you find out in that floating dollhouse?"

"The manager was the only person in the place," Burns replied. "I presume the rest of the staff took the day off to recover from the shock of losing the Golden Goose."

He paused for a moment to remove his suit jacket and hang it over the back of his chair, the heat overcoming his sense of decorum.

"This is another dead end, I'm afraid," he continued. "The business was flourishing, there were no disgruntled clients, and not a hint of extortion from protection thugs ... nothing. I have a Xerox copy of his appointment calendar for three months back and three ahead. You can check it over but I don't see anything suspicious."

Coswell quickly scanned the loose pages.

"What are all these notations in the corner every second or third day?"

"Those are the distances he planned to run as part of his marathon training."

"Jesus, these people must be insane. Look at the day he was murdered—twenty K. That's twelve miles. No wonder they're so skinny. It must burn a million calories doing that."

"And that's less than halfway in a marathon."

"I wonder what's holding my order up," Coswell complained. "I hope they're not waiting till your burger's ready. All this talk of exercise is making me famished."

"I think the point to notice," Burns said, "is the regularity of his runs. His schedule would be an assassin's dream. Stake out a good spot, watch him go by a few times, then bingo, nail him at your leisure."

"I agree," Coswell said. "And that applies to the first two murdered as well, but what about the two in the apartment? They break the pattern."

He was silent for a moment before continuing.

"Unless these killings aren't random and there's an actual hit list. If that's the case, we have to look for a motive. What do all these men have in common? You've mentioned that they're all high-profile gays, but if you're a gay basher, why concentrate on the upper crust? Why not any gay?"

Burns shrugged. "Beats me," he said.

Their food orders arrived and they dug into them with gusto. Burns regretted not ordering a bigger meal and he really would have liked an ice cold mug of beer. Inspector

Marsden's admonition to uphold the dignity of the city police force was becoming a pain in the butt.

***
***

Frayley drummed his fingers on the desk, annoying Heather. They sat across from one another in Frayley's office at the *Star*. Heather's copy for the day lay on the desk between them and the senior reporter had just read it over. He was gazing out the window at the concrete wall of an adjacent building, his mind apparently in neutral.

"Well?" Heather said at last. "Do I give this to the press boy or no? You don't look exactly thrilled by the piece."

Frayley turned his gaze to her and mercifully stopped drumming his fingers.

"It's okay, Heather."

"Only 'okay'? Thanks a lot. What's your suggestion for making it better?"

"Heather, Babe," he said. "I just know there's a blockbuster happening here and we're on the outside looking in. We need more than innuendos in our columns. We need shocking facts. To that end, I've thought of a plan."

Heather perked up. This guy didn't win a Webster Award by being a hack.

"We need to split up," he said. "My face is too well known to do any undercover type journalism but you, my red-headed beauty, are new on the scene. You'll be perfect."

"Perfect for what?"

"Getting the inside dope right on the victims' home turf — the West End. I've got a feeling the denizens there would open up to you, your being petite and wholesome-looking and all that."

Frayley tilted back in his chair and clasped his hands

behind his head, warming to his own brilliance.

"In fact, the more I think about this, the better I like it. I'll keep up with the in-your-face interviews of the police while you sneak around the back. Get some personal stuff. Who were these guys, really, and what's been the impact on the lives of their friends and colleagues? Does the gay on the street have some suggestion who the killers might be? Questions like that."

Heather liked the idea, too. She'd be out from under Frayley's shadow and have the opportunity to gather material that might move her up the recognition ladder at the *Star*.

"I'm in," she said. "Let's go for it. I'll start tomorrow morning.

The Balmoral is one of Vancouver's most exclusive private golf courses. Its membership reflects the Who's Who of the city. The Mayor and the Chief Inspector of the RCMP fit in naturally, but Coswell and Blakemore were a different matter. They'd arrived at the club early, hoping to regain some semblance of golf swings that were never all that great. Blakemore had played the least; the availability of affordable courses in his youth was almost non-existent, but he was a good athlete and had developed a reasonable game by playing the dirt greens course adjacent to the RCMP training centre in Regina. Coswell, on the other hand, had every opportunity. Among his father's Okanagan landholdings was an eighteen-hole golf course, but all the private lessons had been in vain; Coswell was an inveterate hacker.

The young professional on duty eyed the pair when they arrived. Coswell was dressed appropriately in a golf shirt and lightweight pants, although the colours were abominable, the shirt a lime green and the trousers bright red, fashionable in the eighties. Blakemore, however, in his Nike runners, skateboarder's shorts and a sweatshirt with the Canucks' logo on the front created an awkward situation.

It was dealt with smoothly. The young man consulted a list in front of him.

"Yes. Here you are. Guests of Mayor Schmidt and Chief Inspector Ward."

He looked up at Blakemore.

"I see you've just been out jogging, but you're early and you have lots of time to change."

"Change?" said Blakemore.

"The Club's dress code, I'm afraid, forbids cargo pants, and shirts without a collar. But not to worry if you've forgotten your golf togs. We'll have something to fit you, I'm sure. Extra large shirt and 36 waist?"

He beckoned with his finger to a young lady who'd been placing price tags on merchandise. She hurried over.

"Cargo pants?" said Blakemore.

"For Christ's sake, go put on what she gives you," Coswell said.

As Blakemore followed the girl to the changing room, Coswell muttered to the young pro, "You just can't take the farm out of these backwoods types."

***
***

A speaker blared: "On the first tee, Mayor Schmidt's foursome."

Blakemore gazed longingly at the half-bucket of free

balls he hadn't yet blasted out onto the range. The loaner clubs were a complete set of Pings and he was enjoying the luxury of hitting with them. His Regina clubs had been a mixed bag of cast-offs abandoned by previous boot camp graduates.

Coswell gave up hitting practice balls ten minutes after getting to the range, frustrated by spraying shots left and right. He'd moved to the putting green, hoping to get at least some feel for that part of the game. The loudspeaker startled them both.

They obeyed the summons and headed for the first tee. Their two hosts were already there. Schmidt and Ward, like most serious golfers, got down to business at once. Introductions were terse, the wagers quickly decided.

"Usual with us," Ward said to the Mayor, "and the same on the team. We'll play a four-ball and toss a tee to see who gets who. No strokes."

Coswell and Blakemore sensed the intense competition and shuddered to think what "the usual" might be.

"Who's with me?" the Mayor said, tossing a tee into the air. Coswell prayed it would point to him. Ward, he was sure, would be the partner from hell. His wish was granted: Schmidt and Coswell vs Blakemore and Ward.

"Go ahead," the Mayor said to Coswell. "You lead us off."

Now that the teams were decided, Ward's attention shifted to Coswell's attire.

"For heaven's sake, Coswell," he said. "Where did you find that get-up? If you had a yellow belt you could masquerade as a stop light. You should take an example from the Corporal here. That's how a golfer should dress."

Blakemore grinned at Coswell. The girl in the pro shop had dressed him well—black microfibre pants and a red-striped golf shirt à la Tiger Woods.

Coswell teed up his ball on the longest damn tee he'd ever seen, but the face of the loaner driver was so huge that somehow it all looked okay. Since his only desire was to land somewhere on the fairway, he barely swung at the ball and, to his surprise, watched as it came to a rest in the middle of the fairway, 200 yards out. He stepped off the tee box with an air of nonchalance that belied his quaking knees. He was particularly pleased to see Ward raise one eyebrow.

The Mayor lined up and, with a polished swing grooved by hours of private lessons, drove his ball fifty yards past Coswell's, also centre fairway.

Ward nodded to Blakemore.

"Let's see what you've got, boy."

Blakemore stuck a tee in the ground, the tremor in his hand barely noticeable while he steadied the ball on it. When he'd taken his stance, he hovered the head of his driver behind the ball for a moment and then drew it back slowly until he'd made a full shoulder turn. Everything looked good ... until the downswing.

The club descended steeply, propelled by what could only be described as a total body spasm. The head plowed into the sod eight inches before the ball, dug out a black furrow, and would have gone completely under the ball if it weren't for the huge club face. The tiniest margin made contact resulting in a pop-up of Titan proportions.

"Jeez," the Mayor said. "That must have gone two hundred yards ... straight up."

It did, however, drop on the fairway, just past the ladies' tee markers.

His partner wasn't so fortunate. Ward, likely shaken by

Blakemore's performance, hit a drive that looked fine until near the end of its flight, when it developed a vicious slice and disappeared into the trees lining the fairway. At least two loud cracks could be heard as golf ball met tree bark.

"Shit!" was Ward's terse assessment of the team's less than favourable start.

"We're off," the Mayor said, grinning from ear to ear. "Hop in, partner. These two haven't a hope in hell. We're in the money." He actually sang the last sentence.

Blakemore walked to his ball, barely forty-five paces ahead. Ward drove up in the cart.

"For Christ's sake, calm down," he said to Blakemore. "Here's a five-iron. Just bunt the damn thing ahead. It's going to take you two clubs to get to the green anyway."

Blakemore did just that. In fact, he hit the ball so flush it made that wonderful "click" sound that only the pros create with regularity. The ball flew 180 yards, leaving only another 180 to the green. He was back in the game.

Coswell hit next and continued his "chickenshit" (Ward's end-of-the-match assessment) method of concentrating on staying out of trouble by making short, half power swings at the ball. He advanced it 150 yards to leave himself an easy pitch to the green.

Ward was next, but finding his ball turned out to be more of a chore than he expected. Although trees are a major part of the Balmoral's rough, underbrush is simply not allowed and the greenskeepers strip it out the second it appears. Lost balls are rare. Trees, however, sometimes do weird and wonderful things to the flight of a golf ball and Ward's was nowhere to be seen, despite all four men searching for it.

"My, but that five-minute search rule goes by fast, doesn't

it?" the Mayor said at last. "Are you going to go back and hit another or just give up a point?"

Ward stomped back to his cart with Blakemore rushing behind to catch up. When they returned to the fairway and looked back towards the first tee, two men were standing there, clubs in hand, their body language spelling out annoyance at being delayed by the ball searching.

"All right," he said when the Mayor walked up. "I should have hit a provisional ball. Those two back there look like they're in a big hurry. I'll concede a point."

He turned to Blakemore.

"It's all up to you now," he said.

Coswell watched with amusement. He felt the odds of another perfect five-iron were slim to zero and he was right. The pressure of carrying his team caused Blakemore to spasm again, hitting down on the ball and driving it forward in a screaming slice. It started well left, however, and by the time it curved across the entire fairway, it was a long ways up, almost to the green. But, alas, it kept going and disappeared into the rough. A tremendous crack resounded, and then, miraculously, the ball reappeared in a graceful arc, landing on the right front of the green and rolling to within three feet of the hole.

"Jesus H. Christ," the Mayor said. "Would you look at that horseshit luck. Does your mother do spells?"

The Mayor's swing this time wasn't quite as elegant as his drive, hurried perhaps by his anxiety to land his shot on the green and two-putt to at least tie Blakemore. He pulled it left and plugged in a green-side bunker. Coswell skulled his shot onto the green twenty feet from the hole. He and the Mayor both made fives. Blakemore tapped his putt in for a four.

"No blood," Ward said. "Your partner beats me but my

man's four beats you. It's a brand new game."

They walked off the green and hadn't yet reached their carts when — thud! — a ball landed where they'd been standing moments before. Ward looked back in time to see the ball-striker, barely 200 yards away, casually return his club to the bag.

"Bastard!" he said. "That twosome behind us. They'll be on our tail all the way round and obviously impatient as hell. We'll let them through on the next hole. I don't want anyone bitter and twisted hitting into me like that."

They waited at the next tee, sitting in their carts parked just off the path. The wait wasn't long. A high-pitched whine announced the approach of a cart driven at full speed. It screeched to a stop, inches behind Ward and Blakemore. The Chief Inspector got out, stretched to his full six feet four inches, and glared at the two men. If they were awed, remorseful or anything else, their sunglasses hid all expression.

"Too bad you haven't got two friends to make up a foursome so you could play a round at the same speed as the rest of us," Ward said. "But play through. I don't want to hear any more balls land that close to us."

There were no apologies; neither of the two men spoke. They pulled out their drivers, hit excellent shots and then returned to their cart, driving off without a sign of thanks.

"Assholes," Ward said, his remark drowned out by the noise of the cart's motor as it sped past.

Ward's anger amused Coswell. He knew it was wasted on characters like that, probably a couple of successful business psychopaths. The stars and stripes on the sunglass frames one of them wore screamed USA all the way.

Blakemore stared at the two as they moved up the fairway,

his brow furrowed.

"What?" Coswell said to him.

"I'm getting a déjà vu on one of those guys. I think I've seen the driver before but at the moment I can't remember where."

Coswell shrugged. "Well, you're not likely to see him again. I don't think they travel in our circles."

The Mayor interrupted their conversation.

"Now's a good time, I'd say, for you to bring me up to date on your investigation, Inspector Coswell. Ward tells me you're making progress."

Coswell dreaded this, but he was prepared.

"Yes we are. Corporal Blakemore is established undercover now, living in the West End, and has a virtual twenty-four hour watch on the community. We expect a break-through any time now."

"I certainly hope so," the Mayor said. "We've had more than enough sensational press on all of this, especially with our very important visitor arriving in just two weeks' time. A series of gay murder victims, as you can imagine, does not sit well with his security people."

Coswell looked at Ward.

"The Mayor of San Francisco," Ward said. "He's coming here to attend a Pacific Coast Conference on Urban Renewal," and then, addressing Mayor Schmidt, explained, "Security is being handled by special units. Inspector Coswell is strictly homicide and therefore not involved."

"Five prominent Vancouver gay citizens have been murdered in the last month. The Mayor of San Francisco is gay," Schmidt said. "Ergo, Inspector Coswell needs to be informed, if for no other reason than to emphasize the necessity of apprehending these West End killers ASAP."

Seeing Ward blush gave Coswell some pleasure, but it

was quickly overridden by a chill down his spine. Knocking off the Mayor of San Francisco would really give the killers a charge. Getting to their target would be a formidable task, but the efficiency they'd demonstrated to date made an assassination a real possibility. Suddenly he felt pressure and it wasn't from the golf game.

The two golfers ahead had hit their second shots and were moving quickly away.

Coswell teed off first again and played his usual safe bunt to the middle of the fairway, this time getting barely over 150 yards, but he didn't care. He had much greater concerns than the silly golf contest. The Mayor, however, was a man who could change his focus like a chameleon changes its colour. Having dispensed with business, winning the morning's golf match appeared to be his number one priority. He crushed a drive 100 yards past Coswell's ball and turned to Ward with a grin.

"Take that, you tight-ass old bugger."

The rest of the round see-sawed back and forth, with Blakemore having flashes of brilliance interspersed with awful miss-hits. The team match ended up tied, much to Coswell and Blakemore's relief. The "usual" turned out to be fifty dollars. The Mayor and Ward also halved their individual match and so all ended well, so well that the Mayor suggested a rematch in a week's time.

"Hopefully you'll have the killers apprehended by then," he said to Coswell. "I'll look forward to hearing the details."

He turned to Ward.

"Sorry, I can't stay. But please take the men up to the lounge and have lunch on me. I was hoping to use your money to pay for it but the city coffers can handle it, I'm sure."

Ward rolled his eyes. The Mayor was well aware that

the Chief Inspector was so ethically squeaky clean that he would pay out of his own pocket rather than accept any sort of questionable funding, even for something as small as a post-game lunch.

Coswell and Blakemore headed back to the proshop to return the rented clubs and the borrowed clothing. To their surprise, Ward followed them rather than going directly to the members' locker room. The reason soon became apparent. The Chief hadn't forgotten the two rude characters who had played through them. He confronted the young pro and related the incident at the second tee.

"Who, may I ask, were those two bozos?" he said. "And how did they get tee times? I'd like to know the name of the member who signed them in."

"I'm surprised at their behaviour," the young man said. "They actually presented a letter of introduction from the Governor of California's office in Sacramento. It was quite genuine. Mr. Roberts himself checked it."

"Ah, Huey Roberts, our revered club manager — Scotland's gift to Balmoral. He'd be impressed by the official seal, I'm sure."

"Do you want me to speak to the two men?" the pro said, a pained expression on his face.

"No. I'll mention it to Huey myself when I see him. Assholes are assholes, Governor's letter or no. We don't need them here."

Feeling better having vented his spleen, Ward told Coswell and Blakemore to come up to the lounge when they were through in the shop and he'd make good on the lunch offer. He turned and walked briskly to the locker room, completely oblivious to the danger his diatribe was to create for Paul Blakemore. Unknown to them, the young pro took it upon himself to reprimand the impatient duo, when they came in from their round, for hitting into "Chief Inspector Ward's foursome."

Long periods of waiting didn't bother Burns; they were just part of the job. Since Coswell hadn't given him anything specific to do, he sat at his desk gazing out a window, one of the perks of being a senior staff member in both rank and years of service. Most of his colleagues shared desks in the middle of the common office with views only of one another.

The scenery wasn't much from Burns' window. In fact, all he could see was the back parking lot where the blue and whites came and went, but on this occasion there was a bit more colour. The bike patrol, with their yellow cycling attire and black helmets, were marshalling in the yard, receiving orders from a uniformed corporal. Burns admired the men fit enough to pedal their mountain bikes through the streets and alleys discouraging car thieves, muggers and drug pushers. They patrolled from the downtown area right into Stanley Park.

As he watched, an uncomfortable thought began to grow in his mind. Unlike the RCMP, who stressed academic standards in their applicants, the city police, by and large, chose men who were physically endowed with strength and athleticism. Burns himself had been an outstanding lineman for his high school football team and played for a district team when he graduated. The locker rooms and the postgame pubs formed their hard, redneck attitudes, with none of the college-boy airs of their RCMP counter-parts. The subject of gays came up often in the downtown force, but usually in a derisive sense or as a source of bad jokes. Any member who showed some tolerance risked ostracism.

He couldn't help wondering: were some of his colleagues intolerant to a pathological degree? The murder weapon in all the West End cases could have been a city police issue Glock. He continued to stare down at the yellow clad figures, watching them ride off in pairs to their assignments, but his meditation came to an abrupt halt when Coswell burst through the squad room doors and headed to his office, motioning for Burns to follow.

"How was the golf game?" Burns asked, not that he gave a damn, but wished it noted that he'd been hard at work while the inspector played.

"A total waste of time," Coswell said. "Especially having Blakemore there. He could've had a whole morning of West End snooping. Now you and I have to get a move on to make up for lost time. We're going to check out this YMCA connection right bloody now."

The fact that Coswell had stayed for a wonderful lunch at the Balmoral went unmentioned. Burns hadn't yet eaten his and was obviously not going to. His stomach grumbled.

***

The Downtown Vancouver YMCA is an institution beloved by its members and a total enigma to visitors accustomed to more luxurious amenities. There are no frills; the building is small, ancient, and jammed. Members patiently scribble their names on waiting lists to use various apparatus, and are under strict time constraints when they do. Despite all this, membership flourishes. The provincial law courts, a major city hospital, the Howe Street business district, hotels, and most of all the entire residential West End, are within a few blocks of the Y, hence its popularity. Suggestions that the old building be torn down and a larger, more modern structure built are squelched by members who simply can't contemplate surviving a shutdown of any duration.

Coswell and Burns arrived at twelve-thirty, the peak of the lunch-hour rush. Flashing their badges at the front reception desk had considerably less than the usual effect. Two individuals ran the station, one a short, intense young woman who ignored them while she handled telephones that never seemed to stop ringing. The other was an older man, wearing reading glasses halfway down his nose, attempting to deal with a queue of impatient people on a limited lunch break.

"Down the hall to your right," the man said. "Third door's Mr. Leblanc, our personnel officer. He's the only one not so busy right now. Try him."

Coswell decided to follow the suggestion rather than pull rank; the line-up intimidated even him.

Leblanc was in his office and, to Coswell's relief, welcomed them.

"We'd like to see more policemen come here. Not on business, of course, but as participants in our programs. We have quite a number of firemen members, and frankly I'm puzzled as to why there's so few of your colleagues on our rolls."

Burns leapt to their defense.

"We actually have quite good facilities at the station: exercise equipment, boxing ring, gymnasium, whatever. We're into sports, too, soccer, basketball, hockey. Lots of charity tournaments."

Yeah, right, Coswell said to himself. Those were the rookies, straight out of training. The most exercise the senior guys like Burns got was walking to their squad cars (Coswell conveniently ignoring the fact that he and the senior RCMP people were no better).

"Well, we do have a few policemen in our marathon program and we're delighted to have them."

"That, in fact, is why we're here," Coswell said. "About your marathon program, that is."

Leblanc eyed the two unfit, overweight officers and couldn't hide a look of surprise. Coswell caught the look and laughed.

"Right. Burns and I should sign up, but we're actually investigating the murders of three men who were part of that program."

"Yes, I read about them," Leblanc said. "I only knew one of them well — Bruce Leighton. Such a loss. The man was so enthusiastic and encouraging to the other runners. He'll be sorely missed."

Ignoring the saintly image, Coswell persisted in his questioning.

"Did you ever hear any instance of anger or frustration directed towards him ... or to the other runner victims, Jason Collins and Dwayne Wright?"

"No, absolutely nothing. The marathon clinic is just one big, happy family and I mean that sincerely. Everyone is so supportive of one another."

Coswell wondered at that. Some of those runs, he suspected, took hours and there had to be pain involved. Tedium and pain made for irritation and irritation led to anger ... but murder?

Burns interjected.

"We'll want a complete list of clinic participants. We'd also appreciate your looking up two other names for us: Roger Trent and Frank Gofton. They're a couple of body builders who might have been Y members as well."

"Those names aren't familiar to me," Leblanc said, "I lean towards the running group myself, but our weight room is heavily used and the members there probably know one another. Lord knows, they spend inordinate hours pumping iron together."

There was a slight air of disdain in that statement.

"We'd also like a list of people who've joined the Y most recently," Coswell said, "particularly those new to the marathon clinic and the weight room."

"I'll have one of our membership people do that for you this afternoon."

"Much appreciated. Now I'd like a tour of the place, the weight room and anywhere the marathon people hang out."

It turned out that the marathon people spent very little time in the actual building other than to change and shower. Pre- and post-run stretches were done outside. The weight room was a different matter. After descending two long flights of iron stairs, they reached a locked door. Leblanc punched a series of numbers on a keypad and the lock released.

A cacophony of grunts, clanks and shouts of "one more, one more" met them when they entered the room. The smell of sweat was overwhelming; token cooling was supplied by two giant floor fans that sucked hot air through open windows and blew it over the wet bodies. Two instructors dressed in blue sweat pants and T-shirts with STAFF stenciled on the back circulated from station to station, giving advice. Leblanc called one over and introduced him.

"Officers, this is Chuck, our day man in charge down here. I'll leave you with him while I go back upstairs and collect the information you wanted."

From the neck up Chuck looked about forty-five with grey, closely-cropped hair and crow's feet a foot deep. But from there down he had the body of a twenty year old: tight, bulging biceps and a chest that was obscenely large. His wrists were taped and his hands covered with rosin. He was grinning from ear to ear.

"Don't see twinkletoes Leblanc down here very often," he said. "You guys must be VIPs. Did I hear 'officers?'"

On reflex Burns reached for his wallet, but Chuck stopped him.

"No need to flash the tin," he said. "It might make some of today's attendees a mite nervous. We're kind of a half-way house sometimes for cons who want to keep up the bodies they built in stir. Cm'on into my office. You can't hear yourself think in this place."

The office appeared to be a converted closet, windowless, and with the door closed, stifling. Both officers, wearing jackets, began to perspire almost immediately, sweat running down their chests, soaking their shirts.

"Jeez," Coswell said. "A guy could suffocate in this place. Why don't you have a fan at least?"

"Usually I leave the door open, but it's privater this way and you can hear better."

The man had a point, but Coswell planned to conduct the interview in record time before he passed out.

"Roger Trent and Frank Gofton. What can you tell us about them?"

"I knew them well," Chuck said. "They were regulars here and real serious about their programs. It was a big surprise to hear they were gay but then I'm no good at that, recognizin' gays, that is. They worked out together but a lot of the guys do, spottin' one another and the like."

"We're particularly interested in their interaction with others in the weight room. Any sign of animosity, that sort of thing," Burns said.

"Nope, but there ain't a lot of chit-chat down here. People concentrate on their workouts."

"What about new members in the last two or three weeks, two men in particular, probably working out together as well?" Coswell asked.

"Not new. A lot of Y members from other cities drop in, us being so handy to the downtown hotels, but, yeah, now that you mention it, there were two guys here almost every day 'bout a week or two ago. Americans from California, I think. Haven't seen them lately, though."

"Can you describe them to us?" Burns said. "Anything different about them?"

Chuck laughed. "Were they gay, do you mean? Can't tell you that but they were friendly enough. Come to think of it, they hit it off with Frank and Roger so maybe they were gay."

Coswell's pulse began to quicken.

"Did you hear any of the conversation? Any talk about meeting after the workouts?"

"Nothin' I recall. But then I'm real busy with the members. They're always askin' for advice and I have to keep an eye out for accidents, weights slippin' and things like that. Don't pay much attention to small talk."

"We'd like to get an accurate description of the two men," Burns said. "In fact, we'd really appreciate your coming down to the station and working with our police artist."

"You're kiddin'."

"No, he's not," Coswell said. "You may be the first real break we've had in these cases. What time are you off duty? We'll send an officer down to escort you."

The look in Coswell's eyes cut off any argument.

"Five o'clock," Chuck answered, with little enthusiasm.

Coswell was first out the door, climbed the metal stairs with uncharacteristic speed, pushed open the first exit door he came to, and stepped outside to gulp in the fresh air. Burns wasn't far behind.

It took only a minute or two for Coswell to recover from the heat before he started rattling off orders to Burns.

"I have to meet with Blakemore in fifteen minutes at the Pacific Hydro building across the street. I want you to go back inside and milk that Leblanc guy for all he's worth. Who were those two guys? They must have signed in somewhere. Get home addresses and anything else you can dig out. Have every attendant notified that we want to be informed the minute the two reappear anywhere in the building, but not to spook them. You know the routine. We'll meet back at the cruiser at 1700 hours. Bring Chuck. We might as well drive him to the station. Got all that?"

"Yessir," Burns said, almost saluting.

***
***

The cafeteria of the Pacific Hydro building was disproportionately large for the number of people who used it. In its early years there were few adjacent eateries and staff rarely left the building for lunch or coffee breaks. With the more recent proliferation of coffee shops and restaurants in the downtown area, "doing lunch" became common. The Hydro building virtually emptied during breaks and the employees spilled out onto the streets, leaving their huge, sterile cafeteria behind.

Mid-afternoon, Blakemore, nursing a coffee and a large cinnamon roll, was the only occupant in the whole room. The skeleton crew on duty was at work in the kitchen area.

"Help yourself," he said to Coswell, who'd just come through the doors and looked around, perplexed at the lack of humanity in the place. "The coffee's a bit stale but the rolls are still good. It's free right now. In an hour or so they throw it all out."

"I don't know how you can be filling your face with Ward's lunch still sitting on your gut," Coswell said, but poured himself a coffee and grabbed a cinnamon role identical to Blakemore's.

"No willpower," Blakemore said.

Between bites, Coswell related the YMCA lead that he and Burns had picked up.

"I've thought of a plan," he said. "It's a new role for you."

Blakemore set his coffee down.

"And what might that be?"

"We're going to set you up as an out-of-town Y member who's just moved to Vancouver and wants to get in with a marathon training program. Don't worry, I'll arrange for your runs to be short-circuited so you don't have a heart attack. You'll start out, though, at the Y and run to Stanley Park. Do you think you can handle that? It's not very far. I've driven it a thousand times."

"You want me to be bait for these guys? Why? I'm not gay."

"I'm coming to that."

He took a swallow of coffee to wash down the last of his roll before continuing.

"I'd like you to spend as much time as you can with Ernie

and be visible in as many places as possible. Ernie said he wanted to help, and since he's a high profile member of the gay community, our killers might put you in the same category."

"That sounds like a risky venture to me and I emphasize, to *me*. How the hell am I going to avoid being whacked if this pair decides to take me out, especially when I'm running along with my tongue hanging out?"

"We'll set up a route for you, a short one so we can conceal men along the way. You won't be out of anyone's sight, I can assure you. As well, you'll be armed, flak-vested, and we're going to get you one of those cyclist's little rear view mirrors that clips onto a hat. You'll be able to see anyone sneaking up on you from behind. What do you think?"

Blakemore was less than enthusiastic.

"The flak vest's a waste of time. Too bulky, and these guys do head shots anyway. I have a much safer suggestion. Why don't you just stake out the Y and nab them as soon as they show up?"

"We're not sure that the two California weight lifters are our men," Coswell said, "and we don't have enough on them to do any more than questioning. But if we nail them in the park in the act of attempted murder, we've got them good. In short, the West End cases could be solved, the Mayor'll be happy, Chief Inspector Ward will pat us on the backs and you're sure to get a promotion."

Blakemore thought it over for a moment, and then, with a sigh, agreed.

"You sure know how to sweet talk a guy," he said. "I'll discuss it with Ernie. We're meeting around five at his shop."

Heather McTavish knew that Ernie Downs ran an art gallery in the West End and had meant to drop in on him ever since she arrived in Vancouver, but never seemed to have the time. She felt a bit guilty, since this visit was really part of her new assignment, but she looked forward nonetheless to seeing her favourite Bear Creek Mountie. She wasn't prepared, however, as she pushed open the glass doors, for the sight of not one but *two* Bear Creek Mounties deep in conversation.

"Paul Blakemore," she said. "What bomb went off that blew you out of your rural nirvana? You're sure as hell the last person I expected to see here."

Blakemore groaned.

"Oh God. Heather McTavish. That's all I need right now."

Ernie rushed over, pulled her quickly into the shop, locked the door, and switched on the CLOSED sign.

"Heather, so good to see you," he said. "In fact, so good that I'm going to shut down a little early so we can have a good three-way reminiscing. You and Paul go into my studio in the back and I'll join you after I douse the lights and lock the till."

Heather, surprised at being whisked from the gallery to the back room, obeyed. She was sure that she had read "Hours 10 till 6 weekdays" on the front door and since it was just past five, Ernie's "a little early" was an understatement. Although there weren't any customers in the shop when she came in, catching the late-shopping hotel crowd had to be important to art gallery businesses.

The studio was large, brilliantly lit by natural light streaming from huge skylights in the roof and windows in a south-facing wall. A couple of easels, positioned near the wall to take full advantage of the light, held unfinished paintings. One corner of the room was set up as a generous seating area with leather chairs positioned around a glass coffee table. Art journals were strewn about. Floor-to-ceiling shelves crammed with canvasses, painting supplies and framing materials took up most of the remaining space.

Heather and Blakemore had barely sat down when Ernie rejoined them. He walked over to an antique sideboard towering behind the chairs and swung open the doors to reveal a wine storage unit complete with a temperature-controlled cooler for the whites. Wine glasses appeared in a unique drop-down holder. He drew out a bottle of champagne, popped the cork and filled three beautifully etched flutes, leaving just the right proportion of foam to liquid. After handing one to each of his guests, he held his glass up in a toast.

"To the Bear Creek Triumvirate," he said. "Long may it flourish."

Ernie was the only one who drank to his own toast.

"She's going to blow my cover, sure as God made little green apples," Blakemore said.

Heather laughed out loud.

"Same old Paul Blakemore," she said, her eyes twinkling. "A horse's ass to the end."

She lifted her glass in his direction, took a sip of the champagne and then peered at him over the rim.

"What's this 'cover' all about? Do I smell a story?"

Blakemore scowled.

"Now, now, you two," Ernie said. "We all need to be together on this thing."

"Thing?" said Heather, raising her eyebrows.

Ernie looked at Blakemore.

"Ah, hell," Blakemore said. "You might as well tell her the whole plan. Coswell's okaying this on his own. Ward and the brass don't know anything about it. Maybe you can persuade her not to blab it all over."

Heather shot him a disgusted look but held her tongue and listened to Ernie outline the strategy.

"Oh, boy," she said when he finished. "Sounds dangerous to me. Of course I'm not going to add to the risk by printing any of this, but, in return, I want you to promise that I'll have the exclusive when everything goes down."

"You have our word. Doesn't she, Paul?" Ernie said.

Blakemore nodded, but showed none of Ernie's enthusiasm. His past experiences with Heather and the newspaper world were not pleasant memories. She'd hounded him unmercifully during the Bear Creek cases.

On this occasion, however, Heather did show mercy. She quickly finished her glass of champagne and got up to leave. Ernie made a feeble objection but she waved him off.

"You two need to work out your plan and you'll do that a lot better without me around."

On the walk back to her car, she debated with herself whether or not she should let Frayley in on the potential scoop.

***
***

Coswell was disappointed to see that Chuck, so confident in his YMCA weight room, became totally intimidated in the downtown police station. The descriptions he gave to the police artist were almost useless. The resultant figures were so nebulous they could have been almost any males between the ages of twenty-five and forty. It was no use having him go through mug shots after that performance, so Coswell let him go with a reminder to call if he saw the two suspects again.

Watching Chuck leave, Coswell couldn't help but wonder if the man might have been on the wrong side of the law at some time. He made a mental note to run a check on him.

Burns' interview with the YMCA personnel officer, Leblanc, also proved to be a disappointment. The two suspects weren't Y members. They came as drop-ins and paid a daily fee, their names not recorded.

Burns was making noises about being well over his eight-hour shift.

"Okay, okay," Coswell said. "We'll call it a day, but don't turn your cellphone off. If something comes up, I want to be able to reach you."

"Right," Burns replied, wishing this liaison would come to an end and he could get back to a normal Vancouver Police Department routine.

Coswell watched the big man lumber out of the office and felt a twinge of guilt.

Burns was making the best of the situation and deserved a bit more consideration. He'd start on that tomorrow.

***
***

Unfortunately, tomorrow didn't come soon enough. A call came through from Blakemore. He was so agitated, Coswell had difficulty understanding him.

"Would you believe? They tried to whack Ernie! Burns was right. There are two of them, on bikes."

"Slow down," Coswell said. "Give me the details."

"I had the Hydro vehicle parked behind Ernie's gallery. We'd just finished our meeting. I offered to drive him to his car but he said it was in a lot just at the end of the alley and since I was parked facing in the opposite direction, there was no point."

He paused for a second to catch his breath.

"I no sooner got the key in the ignition when this guy on a bike whips past me. He went by so fast I couldn't get a clear look at his face but I picked him up in the rear view mirror. I also saw Ernie, who was maybe fifty meters away, and a second man on a bike pedaling slowly towards him from the other end of the alley."

"Christ," said Coswell. "What did you do?"

"I leaned on the horn. Ernie turned around, saw the guy coming towards him and hit the ground. I barrelled out of the jeep and started hollering. The slow guy spun his bike around and the two of them turned tail."

"What did you holler?" Coswell asked.

"Not 'Halt, Police' if that's what you're worried about, but I damn near did. It's Ernie we're talking about here."

Coswell persisted. "Did you pull your sidearm?"

"I did. But neither of them saw it. They'd already turned around."

"Did you see a weapon on either of them?"

"Negative. It all happened too fast."

"Damn," Coswell said. "The whole thing could have been nothing and you just scared the shit out of two innocent people."

"I'll bet the farm on this," Blakemore said. "Ernie was in real danger, I'm sure of it. I think those were our suspects."

Coswell knew Blakemore was right. Everything fit. Ernie was a high-profile gay and the modus operandi would easily explain the Stanley Park murders. He needed Burns.

"Where's Ernie right now?" he asked Blakemore.

"He's gone back into the gallery. ex-RCMP or no, the man was shaken up. I'm calling you from my car."

"Go back in and stay with him," Coswell said. "I'm calling Burns. He'll get a uniform to take your place. Don't listen to any objections from Ernie, by the way. We don't want to lose him."

Coswell's concern wasn't solely personal. This was the first time the killers had missed. They were starting to make mistakes. Ernie could be the turning point in the case.

"When you're relieved," Coswell continued. "Come down to the station. You, me and Burns are going to finalize the trap to snare those two bastards."

***
***

Sergeant Burns was not a happy man. The inspector's call reached him just as he'd sat down to cabbage rolls with sour cream, a mug of lager and the companionship of his loving wife, Ruth.

Now he sat across from Coswell fighting the gas built up in his stomach from bolting his supper. He tried to concentrate.

"Could be our suspects. But just as likely it could be nothing. Did Blakemore call the station for backup?"

"No," Coswell replied, with a sigh. "He didn't mention that. I guess everything happened so fast, by the time he thought of it, it was too late. His first concern, of course, was Ernie's well-being."

"Right." Burns barely hid his disgust. An all-units call would have been the first thing he'd have done under the same circumstances.

"I know, I know," Coswell said, reading the sergeant's thoughts. "But give the guy a break. We really haven't set up a sharp line of communication with the Vancouver Police for him. Calling me was the natural thing for him to do...and you, of course, were off duty."

Burns wasted no time getting an officer over to Ernie's gallery to free up Blakemore, who drove immediately to the main precinct and rushed into Coswell's office, his adrenalin still flowing.

"Man, but this city is light years from rural policing. Thirty seconds in one dinky alley has more action than a whole day in Bear Creek ... good evening, Burns."

He looked at both men and was dismayed to see that neither appeared terribly excited about the alley scene.

"You're not still doubting this was a murder attempt, are you?"

Burns said nothing; Coswell answered.

"Calm down. You're an experienced policeman and you know damn well that you've jumped to a conclusion. But let's assume you're right. What suggestions do you have to catch these two, now that they're long gone?"

Blakemore, deflated, admitted he couldn't think of one.

"Okay," Coswell said. "Let's look on the bright side. If Ernie truly is in their grand plan, they'll likely try again and we can be ready for them. But what's even better is your association with Ernie. If you become a target, we've really got it made."

While Blakemore absorbed this, Burns spoke up.

"You're suggesting that the West End victims are all on a list, not wackos killing at random?"

"Yes. Ernie would have been the sixth high-profile gay and that's just too much of a coincidence. There's a pattern here and a motive that we need to search for, but we're running out of time. Don't forget the San Francisco mayor's visit."

"You said you had a plan," Blakemore said.

"No. I said you, Burns, and I will work out a plan. Now start thinking. So far we only have the one I've suggested, the runner in the park ploy. Do either of you have anything better?"

Neither had anything better and so the trap was set.

It was Friday. They'd get Leblanc, the YMCA personnel man, to introduce Blakemore to the marathon group on Sunday, and Monday would be his first solo training run. That gave adequate time for Burns to organize his men: an armed policeman every hundred metres along Blakemore's route.

Coswell, satisfied that the details of the plan were clear, dismissed his two officers. Burns was officially off duty for the weekend. Blakemore, however, was stuck in his undercover role but had arranged to meet Ernie later that evening for drinks at a local gay bar. Coswell remained at his desk, by all appearances still mulling over the cases. In reality he was contemplating which of Vancouver's fine restaurants would give him a late dinner reservation.

***
***

"Need a lift?"

Blakemore was surprised when Burns offered to drive him to the Hydro jeep parked a few blocks away. The sergeant's annoyance at him for failing to issue an APB in the alley incident was patently obvious.

"Thanks," he said, "But I'd better protect my cover. Besides, I'm training for a marathon, remember?"

Burns nodded, but there was something on his mind. Blakemore waited.

"What were the two cyclists in the alley wearing?"

"Nothing distinctive that I can remember. Why?"

"Just curious," Burns said, then turned and headed to the staff parking lot.

Pope's Vicinage, a tiny restaurant tucked away in Vancouver's trendy Kitsilano district, is one of the city's most notable eating establishments. Getting a table there on short notice is almost impossible, but Coswell, by virtue of his considerable patronage, managed to book a table for one. There was really no such thing as a table for one, but for a special customer, Iain Pope had his staff set a place crammed into the narrow corridor beside the kitchen.

Coswell was ushered to his seat by the hostess, Nina, a divine brunette. As he followed her up a short flight of stairs to a tiny mezzanine, one of the diners below drew his attention. Facing away from him, at a table with eight of Vancouver's beautiful people, sat Mayor Schmidt.

Coswell was glad he'd be out of their sight. The attack on Ernie wasn't something he wished to make known yet, particularly to the Mayor and especially since he'd decided not to inform Chief Inspector Ward. He moved his chair so his back was to the lower level. Nina noticed the manoeuvre.

"I get peopled out myself sometimes, too," she said, "and a little privacy is a good thing. Mr. Pope will probably stop by though."

"Iain Pope is never an intrusion, Nina. We talk about food and wine. Very therapeutic. Speaking of wine, do you still have some of the Tinhorn Creek Pinot Gris? A glass of that would neutralize a great deal of my stress."

Nina laughed. "I wish my boyfriend was as easy to satisfy as you."

"Your boyfriend is a lucky man. You by his side should be all the satisfaction he needs."

"Oh, pshaw," she said, and hurried off to fetch his glass of wine.

He liked Nina. "Oh, pshaw" was so quaint.

He'd barely opened the menu when he felt a hand on his shoulder. It was the Mayor. The washrooms were on the mezzanine level.

"Good evening, Inspector. Making up for the pub food old ramrod Ward bought you for lunch? I've got to take a quick whiz but I'll come back and sit with you for a moment. I see you haven't ordered yet."

Coswell was not happy. A conversation with the Mayor wasn't the "memorable" he'd had in mind for this meal. He tried to look cheerful when Schmidt returned but he could feel his facial muscles strain.

"Anything new to report?" the Mayor said. Somehow he'd found a chair to pull over and jammed it uncomfortably close.

"We believe we have two suspects," Coswell replied, but before he could elaborate, the Mayor cut him off.

"Terrific," he said. "You don't know how relieved I am to hear that. Maybe those San Francisco security people will give my staff some peace. Your suspects are in custody, I presume?"

"Not quite," Coswell replied. "But we expect to nab them within the next few days."

A deep frown replaced the look of joy, but only for a moment.

"I'm sure you will."

With that, the Mayor abruptly got to his feet, his consternation apparently gone as quickly as it had come.

"Well, must get back to my guests. Good work, Inspector. I think this sorry matter is about to end and I'm sure San Francisco's Mayor Gryndon will be quite safe in our fair city thanks to you and your fine men."

Coswell's immediate impression had labelled Schmidt a complete airhead, but then he realized he was nothing of the sort. The man who'd risen to the highest political office in the third largest city in Canada had just given him an ultimatum.

He finished his Pinot Gris in a single gulp.

Nina noticed his empty glass.

"My, but that went down quickly," she said. "Would you like another?"

He sighed. "No, I'd better get something on my stomach first."

***
***

The anger was almost choking him. He couldn't believe that those two imbeciles had taken it upon themselves to go after some gay on their own just because of a single incident. Everything had been going so smoothly. He'd supplied the weapons, the list, the plans. All they had to do was follow instructions.

Getting the information was a breeze. Canadians were so primitive and so trusting in the new cyber world. They put the most amazing details online for the whole world to see, especially the government agencies, at all levels. The Federal Gun Registry website was an absolute candy store. Even his lowliest office gofer could hack into that system in minutes.

No, those two brainless jocks had to go. Thank God their leader at least had a modicum of intelligence and would ensure that the mission got back on course. The man's insistence that they talk by phone was a bit unsettling, but the phone booth was secure; he was certain of that.

It was equally unsettling that the gay they tried to kill had a boyfriend who could be an undercover cop. He wondered if he should report this to Central but quickly dismissed the thought. The group was ultra sensitive to the possibility of discovery and would probably order his operation shut down. He was determined to avoid that at all costs.

***
***

Years of interviewing and probing into people's personal lives gave Harold Frayley an uncanny ability to read minds. Heather was holding out on him. She'd been a bit too cheery when she got back to the office from her afternoon of prowling the West End, and her copy was little more than a rehash of events to date.

He pushed the copy back to her after giving it a quick once-over.

"Maybe my idea wasn't so hot after all," he said. "That's pretty wimpy stuff. Is that all you could get out of a whole afternoon down there?"

Heather blushed. No use trying to pull one over on the old fox. She relented and related the whole encounter with Ernie and Paul Blakemore.

"You were going to tell me about this, weren't you?" Frayley said when she finished.

She blushed again.

"Of course. But I just wanted to flesh it out some before I presented to you. Right now it's just a promise from Ernie and Blakemore to keep me informed, nothing we can put into print."

"Never, never keep anything back from me," Frayley said, "And let me decide whether or not something should be printed. We're not dealing with the War Office here. We can damn well report anything we want."

"Even if it endangers lives?"

"We don't have to name names. How about 'Undercover Police Closing In On West End Killer?' That's not going to endanger anyone, and the public, especially the gay community, will sure as hell be glad to hear that some progress is being made."

"Coswell would have a fit if he saw that as a headline. It'd be the end of any cooperation with us, I'm damn sure."

Frayley tilted back in his chair, stared up at the ceiling and began drumming his fingers on the desk. Heather fumed.

"Well?" she said, finally breaking the silence.

"Well, what?"

"You know damn well what. You're ignoring me."

"Like you ignored me, eh?"

"Oh, for Christ's sake. That's the first time and obviously the last. Get over it. Now, what are we going to do?"

Frayley smiled, enjoying his small triumph. In truth, he didn't have a plan but he wasn't going to admit it.

"I'd like to hear from the young and the restless first. What do *you* think we should do? I wouldn't want to put your precious Mounties at risk."

"All right," Heather said. "I'm going to stick like a barnacle to Ernie because I've always had a good rapport with him. That sure as hell isn't the case with Blakemore, but I do have to respect the fact that the man's working under cover. What I'll do is feed whatever information I get to you and you can have that in mind when you're pumping Coswell."

She paused for a moment. Another idea came to her.

"That might, by the way, make an interesting slant to write about: the official version of an investigation versus the in-the-trenches one."

"Not bad thinking, for a rookie," Frayley said. "Okay, we'll run with it. I'm meeting Coswell later today. We'll reconvene here at five and compare notes."

Back at her desk, Heather rummaged through her purse, found Ernie's business card and dialed the gallery number. After the third ring, she heard a peculiar double click and, assuming it indicated a switch to an answering machine, was about to hang up when Ernie's voice came on the line.

"Hello."

Hello?—not answering with the gallery's name or even his own—how peculiar. And the tone was questioning, worried, not Ernie's usual cheery welcome.

"It's Heather, Ernie. What's up? You sound like you're expecting the prophet of doom."

"Sorry," he said. "I was just getting ready to leave."

Funny answer. Maybe Blakemore was still there. But no, he'd said 'I was just getting ready....' She decided to take the initiative.

"Zachary's working night shift at the hospital so I'm free for dinner. How about it? We'll talk about the murders so I can put it on my expense account and I won't take 'no' for an answer. Where should we meet?"

He hesitated for a moment before answering.

"It might not be wise for you to be with me right now, Heather. I'd better take a rain check."

"Oh, right," she said. "That statement just made our dinner date for tonight a sure thing. I'll track you down anyway so you'd better say yes."

Ernie laughed.

"Make it my place then. You'll ruin my reputation if I'm seen out in public with a beautiful woman. I'll come by your office in ten minutes. I drive a big, gas-guzzling black Suburban. I need the hauling space for art stuff."

***
***

Heather was astounded when she saw Ernie's West End apartment, the penthouse in a high-rise overlooking Stanley Park and Coal Harbour. The elevator went non-stop from underground garage to penthouse. The automatic doors opened to a small waiting area and a single, solid oak door beside which was a security keypad. Ernie punched in a series of numbers and the door opened. They stepped into a large foyer with a vaulted ceiling thirty feet up. From it hung a magnificent crystal chandelier.

"That's some security system," Heather said. "I guess you never have to worry about being mugged in this place."

"That's for sure. There's also a concierge inside the main entrance, but the cheapest apartment in this complex goes for three quarters of a mil, so top security's a given."

"Three quarters of a million! Then what's your apartment worth? The art business must be a lot more lucrative than I thought."

"I wish," Ernie said, "but it's not mine. The owner's an American who bought it still in the blueprint stage and when our dollar was only worth sixty-five cents US It was a steal."

Heather calculated. Even at sixty-five cents on the dollar, dropping over a half million north of the US border meant someone had a lot of bucks to play with.

"He comes up a few times a year for some R and R and to

visit friends, which include me. He doesn't like to leave it unoccupied, so he convinced me to house-sit it for him. It didn't take much convincing, I can tell you. I feel a little silly sometimes though, rattling around in a three thousand square foot penthouse."

"What a deal," Heather said. "Is he a big movie star or something?"

"Close, but I can't tell you. He stays incognito for the most part when he's in Vancouver."

"But known in the gay community, I'll bet."

"Oh, you're *such* a newshound, Heather," he said.

"Yeah. You'd better not tell me. Snooping's a knee-jerk thing with me, I'm afraid."

Ernie told her to make herself comfortable while he busied himself in the kitchen, pausing briefly to hand her a glass of ice-cold champagne.

"I could really get used to this champagne habit of yours, Ernie," she said, "It's so civilized."

Glass in hand, she moved nonchalantly about the huge living room, inspecting the art-work, much of which was gay erotica. There was a baby grand piano set up on a small mezzanine. She rifled through the magazines on the teak coffee table and was disappointed to see that all the periodicals had Ernie's name on them, no clue as to who the rich benefactor was. She looked for photographs around the room but there were none. A peek into the bedrooms was tempting, but Ernie hadn't offered her a tour. Instead he suggested she step out onto the balcony and enjoy the magnificent view.

It was indeed magnificent. Ernie's building was much newer than most along the Beach Avenue strip and towered above the others, dwarfing the adjacent Sylvia Hotel. She'd read in a brochure that up until 1958 the Sylvia was the tallest structure in Vancouver's West End, but now its mere eight stories were a long way down from the twenty-fifth floor balcony she was standing on.

The view across English Bay to Stanley Park was unobstructed and the luxury developments to the north were blocks away, but when she turned around and looked east, the great urban mass of the West End loomed before her. Most of the buildings were even taller than Ernie's and densely packed. They were blocks away, too, but the uphill slope made them seem closer. Suddenly she felt tiny and insignificant. At four foot-eleven that feeling came to her often, but not quite with this magnitude. She turned and went back inside where the aroma of Ernie's cooking permeated the room.

"Oh, that smells divine," she said, declining a top-up of her drink. "The afternoon coffee and this champagne have got my kidneys all excited. Would it be crude of me to ask where the ladies' room is?"

Ernie chuckled. "Not much call for a ladies' room, but there's a bathroom just to your left up the stairs. You'll probably have to put the seat down."

She climbed the plush-carpeted stairs and found the bathroom. It was spotless, with thick peach-coloured towels neatly stacked everywhere and a wonderful fragrance from potpourri jars filled with dried flower petals. The seat was down.

When she returned and descended the staircase, Heather could see Ernie getting ready to plate their dinner. Stainless steel dominated the kitchen décor, but one incongruous item drew her attention: a cork board on the wall adjacent to the counter. Messages were pinned on it and, to Heather's great interest, a number of photographs. She gazed surreptitiously over Ernie's shoulder while he ladled out the stir-fry and she spotted a familiar face in a photo of three men, drinks in hand, lounging on the very balcony she'd just left.

Grinning back at her was the Mayor of San Francisco, no doubt about it; she'd seen his face a hundred times on various North American news services. If the Mayor of San Francisco were the mysterious owner of the penthouse, then Ernie, by association, was indeed, to use Coswell's expression, a "high profile gay" and a likely target for the West End killers.

She didn't look away fast enough. Ernie caught her gaze. He turned and saw the object of her focus.

"No. None of those three is the owner. But you're getting closer. Actually, the person who took the photo is the owner," he said, and after glancing over the rest of the photos, added, "And he's not in any of the others either."

Heather blushed.

"I told you I was a snoop."

She became serious.

"Ernie, I'm worried about you. When I phoned you at the gallery, the tone of your voice, plus the innuendo about being unsafe company, makes me think something bad's happened and you're in danger. And that double click I heard when I dialed? A bugged phone, I'll bet. Am I right about all this?"

He hesitated for a moment and then poured out the whole alley incident.

"Sergeant Burns did put a tap on my phone and one of his men is sitting in an unmarked car out on the street. I have twenty-four-hour police protection."

"Good. That makes me feel a lot better," Heather said. "Now when's Coswell going to spring this trap of his using Blakemore as bait?"

"Monday evening. It's all set up."

And Heather planned to be close by, but first she had to get more details.

Coswell was the answer, but unfortunately he was also the problem. Tracking him down would require teamwork; she needed Frayley.

***

Monday couldn't arrive any too soon for Coswell. He spent the weekend dodging calls from Heather and receiving bad news from the men on duty. Burns' surveillance crew informed him of Heather's evening with Ernie and suspected she'd dragged a lot of sensitive information out of him. Blakemore called in and reported that the two Californian suspects hadn't been spotted at the Y on either Saturday or Sunday. He also managed to get in how much pain he suffered during and after his run with the marathon group. The only good news was that there hadn't been another killing.

Monday didn't start off well, either. Burns was late for work and didn't arrive at the precinct till almost nine.

"Family crisis this morning," he said, pre-empting Coswell's reprimand. "Did you get my message that I'd be late?"

"No, and whoever you gave the message to needs to learn a lesson in priorities. Are you going to do it or shall I?"

"I'll speak to her," Burns said. "She's a pretty busy lady during shift change."

"Next time, call me on my cellphone. I don't have family crises. Now let's get down to business. Is the sting set up? I want to hear every detail."

Burns outlined the plan and assured Coswell that every precaution had been taken to guarantee Blakemore's safety. The inspector thought it over for a minute.

"That's not good enough. All your men are on foot. I realize that even unmarked police cars could spook these guys but you've forgotten a resource we do have."

"What's that?" Burns said.

"The bike squad. I want them scattered liberally about the route ... out of uniform, of course. They can give chase a helluva lot better than your foot patrol."

Burns winced. He should have thought of that himself and wondered if he hadn't subconsciously suppressed the idea. He still had a nagging feeling that a couple of the bike squad members could be the perps and he'd done nothing to act on that suspicion.

"I'll arrange it," he told Coswell.

"All right, then. Now where do you suggest the two of us be located when all this goes down?"

"The Ferguson Point Teahouse. It's just off the seawall and at that time of evening there'll be plenty of cars in the parking lot, so ours will blend in, no problem. Also, it's just seconds from there to where we think the two will try to take Blakemore: on the stretch leading to Siwash Rock. That's almost a full kilometre of straightaway where they can keep him in view and have plenty of opportunity to pop in and out of the forest."

While Coswell mulled this over, Burns added a comment, his mind seemingly triggered by mention of the famous landmark.

"Pauline Johnson, the Indian poetess, used to sit up on top of Siwash Rock and write her poems, you know."

"You're full of surprises, Burns," Coswell said. "Retaining

that tidbit of cultural trivia from your school days impresses me. Next you'll be telling me you go to coffeehouse readings, smoke pot and have deep intellectual thoughts."

"Not often," Burns replied.

"Good. I don't want you going soft on me. Now, we have almost eight hours before Blakemore hits the trail. Which lead do you think we should pursue to make use of that time?"

Burns shrugged his shoulders.

"We really don't have a decent lead," he said. "I guess Leighton's probably our best bet; the rest of them have already been investigated to the hilt."

"Well, somehow we need to find a vital connection between all of the victims. Catching these two bike guys isn't enough. Pinning a murder rap on them will be damn near impossible unless they sing, and I don't think they will. Get us a motive, though, and we stand a much better chance."

Burns felt obliged to defend his city police colleagues.

"We did find the connection. They're all gay and they knew one another, nothing else. We even tapped our sources in the drug scene and not one of the victims was either a buyer or a seller."

"All right then," Coswell said. "We'll check out the social angle. Let's go talk to Ernie. I've got a feeling he can put us on to something."

***
***

Unfortunately, this feeling also put something onto them: Heather McTavish. She was waiting outside Ernie's gallery ten minutes before the shop was due to open.

"Shit, she's such a midget," Coswell said when he and Burns got out of the squad car. "I didn't see her behind the pedestrian traffic. Now we're in for it. She's spotted us."

"Well, well," Heather said, rushing over to them. "The elusive Inspector Coswell and the implacable Sergeant Burns."

"We're having a bit of trouble with messages getting through to our new office," Coswell said. "The problem's being worked on."

"Did I say I was trying to reach you?" she said, a bemused expression on her freckled face.

"All right, Heather. You caught me, but I want to keep the press away at the moment. We have a delicate operation in progress and I don't want to risk any leaks."

"Just when are you going to let us in on what's happening? If we have to write from guesses, Lord knows what'll end up on the printed page."

Coswell was beginning to understand Blakemore's aversion to Heather and her bulldog attitude.

"You're a tough cookie, Heather, and I think you know lots more than you should already, but we'll go in together and have a chat with Ernie. Your source, I presume?"

"Don't give him a bad time. He trusts me, probably a lot more than he does you."

At precisely ten AM the gallery door was unlocked and the three were admitted, but not by Ernie. Instead, a cherubic young man with a ponytail greeted them.

"Mr. Downs won't be in this morning," he said in reply to Coswell's enquiry. "He called me to fill in for him. I do that from time to time. It's a nice break from my hours in front of an easel."

Coswell noticed the frayed collar on the man's shirt and the skinny tie that was at least five years out of style; both screamed starving artist.

"Is he at his apartment?" Heather asked.

"I don't think so. He said he was meeting a friend this morning, but he didn't say where."

Burns spun on his heel and disappeared out the door. Heather glanced at Coswell. He looked worried. She edged toward the front window and saw Burns dive into the squad car. In a blink, he had a radio receiver up to his ear.

She heard Coswell thank Ernie's stand-in for the information and when he turned to leave, she was right behind him.

"May I say who called?" the young man said, but received no reply as his first visitors of the morning disappeared out the front door.

"It's okay," Burns said, stepping back out of the car when Coswell and Heather approached. "My boys still have him. He's drinking coffee with Blakemore at the Wheatsheaf Bakery on Denman. But would you believe? The man actually walked there from his apartment in the West End. Ten blocks. How the hell can we protect someone who does that? He should be going everywhere in his car."

"I'll get Blakemore to speak to him, but keep your boys back," Coswell said. "I don't want them spotted."

***

Paul Blakemore munched on his fresh-out-of-the-oven morning pastry and washed it down with a surprisingly excellent coffee dispensed from a thermos. He was feeling no guilt about the pastry, confident that his Stanley Park running assignment opened the door to a few extra calories. Ernie wasn't due to meet him for another fifteen minutes, so he leaned back and enjoyed the ambience of the place.

He loved everything about bakeries, the smells, the racks filled with breads, pies and pastries, and the no-nonsense exchange at the counter: make up your mind fast, order what you want, pay for it and leave, or, if you must, sit down. Bakeries were busy places, and the customers for the most part were equally busy people anxious to get on with their day. The few tables at the front were sufficient to accommodate those who actually ate their purchases on site.

He recalled the mornings at his old haunt in Bear Creek. The coffee crowd there was a boisterous bunch. Everyone knew everyone and conversation flowed, but this was pleasant, too — sitting in total anonymity, people-watching, letting his mind go limp, putting off worry over his role in Coswell's upcoming sting.

He was so deep into his reverie that he almost missed them.

They'd ridden up and leaned their bikes against the building. As they entered and Blakemore looked lazily in their direction, something about them tugged at his memory. They both had on wrap-around sunglasses, but the frames of the pair the lead man wore were decorated with stars and stripes. Slowly it came into focus — these were the two jerks who played through during the golf match with Ward and the Mayor!

The moment the first rider saw Blakemore looking at him, he stopped, turned to his companion and spoke a few words. In seconds they retreated, returned to their bikes and sped off. Blakemore half rose from his seat, struggling to grasp the significance of the encounter and when he did, it was too late. They were gone.

Ernie arrived a few minutes later and was taken aback by Blakemore's urgent wave beckoning him directly to his table.

"What?" Ernie said. "You look like you've just seen a ghost."

"Did you get a look at those two that just left?"

Ernie shook his head. Blakemore sighed and settled back in his chair.

"Grab a coffee, Ernie," he said, "And then come and let me tell you about some disturbing thoughts I've just had."

Ernie returned with his coffee and sat down. He waited for his ex-partner to give out his revelations.

"This will be the third time I've seen one of those two cycle guys," Blakemore began. "When you and I first met here, he was over there at the counter watching us. I remember him turning away real quick when I looked at him."

He continued.

"The second time he was with his buddy."

Blakemore related the golf match incident.

"No way do bike messenger guys get into the Balmoral Golf and Country Club unless they stole the letter of introduction and even then, the cost of club rental and carts would be prohibitive."

He paused, waiting for a reaction.

"So?" Ernie said.

Blakemore smiled, enjoying his own performance.

"Think about it. Two Californians, expensive golf course, personalities like snakes ... these guys are not simple bike messengers. I think our two suspects just pedaled away from here and they're professional hit men."

"My God," Ernie said. "That's a quantum leap of reasoning. It sounds too bizarre."

"Does it? Aren't all those West End murders just as bizarre?"

Ernie nodded. He shuddered to think that he might have

just brushed by the men who'd come after him in the alley.

"You know what's unnerving, Paul?" he said. "I think your cover's blown. Why else would they about face when they saw you just now?"

"Good question. Maybe they just want to stay unnoticed."

"Perhaps," Ernie said.

Blakemore thought for a moment.

"Damn. You could be right. Now what do we do?"

"Call Coswell."

***
***

Heather announced she was off to the Wheatsheaf and planned to corner Ernie and Blakemore before they left. Coswell admonished her again not to interfere in a police operation, pointing out that he and Burns were staying well away from the bakery to maintain Blakemore's cover. She waved him off, saying she didn't smack of police in any way and had already established an innocent friendship with Ernie. In her own words she was "no threat to anyone." Coswell just shook his head and let her go.

"I'd have shown her who's a threat," Burns said after she'd gone. "My speech about interference with police procedure would have had a lot more punch."

"Just listen and learn," Coswell said. He pulled out his cellphone. The vibrate function had gone off while they were in the gallery. Blakemore needed to talk or perhaps set up a meeting.

The conversation was brief. Coswell listened to Blakemore's report and then responded:

"My office, right away and tell Ernie not to give out anything to Heather McTavish, who, by the way, will be rolling into the Wheatsheaf any minute now. Hopefully she can't find parking so you can get the hell out of there before she arrives. Ernie can keep her occupied while we get down to business — police business."

***
***

Burns and Coswell had barely sat down at the Main Street precinct office when Blakemore walked in. He'd squeezed the little Hydro car into a parking space less than a block away.

On the ride to the station, Coswell outlined the bakery incident to Burns, but the sergeant saved his comments until Blakemore was present.

"This is the second time you've neglected to bring our men in to chase down those guys," he said. "Why didn't you put out an immediate APB? I thought we'd cleared that up after the last one."

Blakemore squirmed.

"Sorry," he said. "I guess I should have, but I'm still not used to big city procedures. In Bear Creek we didn't get into situations like that and what's routine for you isn't for me. It won't happen again, though. I'm not that slow a learner."

Burns didn't comment further.

"All right," Coswell said. "There've been mistakes on both sides. Your city boys, Burns, haven't exactly been rocket scientists either. Paul here at least got us all headed in what looks like the right direction. Now let's put some thought into this and make a decision. Do we go ahead with the seawall thing or no?"

Blakemore shrugged his shoulders. Burns looked at the ceiling.

"I can see you two are going to be a big help. All right, I'll make the decision. It's on."

He picked up a pencil and began tapping it on the desk,

suddenly deep in thought. Burns and Blakemore waited. The tapping stopped.

"Yes, we'll go ahead with it," he said. "And do you know why?"

They shook their heads.

"Because I think our bicycle boys will soldier on regardless. They're not the brightest pennies in the jar and they proved that at the golf course. Can you tell me how?"

"That's easy," Burns said. "It broke their cover."

"Right. But that's only part of it. Their mistake was bigger than that."

Enjoying the puzzled looks in his direction, Coswell reached for the desk phone and buzzed the switchboard.

"Get me the pro shop at the Balmoral Golf and Country Club on the phone, please."

Blakemore had a flash of insight.

"Fingerprints!" he said.

Coswell remembered the name of the young pro, Derron, on duty the day of the golf game and asked to speak directly to him. Derron had no problem recalling the two men and was more than pleased to co-operate. They had not left a good impression.

"Handle the sign-in card by the edges," Coswell told him, "And don't touch the grips on the clubs or any part of the cart they rented."

"Oh," the young man said. "I'm afraid the clubs and the cart have been wiped down. That's one of our juniors' jobs, but I'm the only one who handled the card."

"Good. One of our people will come by shortly to go over everything. Hopefully your junior was a bit sloppy that day."

As soon as he'd hung up, he told Burns to get the forensic team over to the golf course and when all possible prints were lifted, run them through Canadian and American ID services.

After hanging up, Derron hesitated for a moment and wondered if he should have told Coswell about chastising the two for hitting into them. But Chief Ward had said he'd handle it himself. Better to leave it alone.

10

Heather was disappointed. Ernie was pleasant enough over coffee at the Wheatsheaf, but her probing was getting her nowhere. A half-empty cup and an uneaten piece of pastry across from him meant that Blakemore had bolted just before she arrived. The reason must have been acute for him to have abandoned the pastry, but Ernie wasn't talking.

Not wanting to waste time when a potential news event was about to unfold, she contemplated her choices. Cutting short her chat with Ernie was easy. In fact, he seemed mildly relieved when she made her excuses. But tracking down Coswell was a different matter. She called Frayley at the *Star*.

"Well, Babe," he said over the phone. "What've you got for me?"

"A problem," she said and proceeded to tell him about her frustrated attempt to get details of the seawall sting.

Frayley thought for a moment.

"Our best bet is to follow Coswell and Burns. They'll be in position well before Blakemore starts his run and there are only two ways into the park from the city, Georgia Street and Beach Avenue. If I park at the Rowing Club, I can cover the Georgia Street entrance. You go to Second Beach. They'll have to drive right past you to get into the park from there. Whoever of us sees them, phone the other and follow them in."

"What about just waiting for Blakemore? It'd be easy to pick him up before either of those spots."

"And do what? Run along behind him? No, we're best to rush in with the troops when the whole thing goes down. The three seawall murders took place between eight and nine. I suggest we get set up around seven."

"Gotcha," Heather said. "Meanwhile let's both keep an eye out for Coswell. If we can keep a tail on him, it'll save a lot of boring waiting time."

"Never boring, Heather. Look at it as an opportunity for some creative thinking."

***
***

Vancouver Islanders, gazing across the Strait of Georgia on a clear summer's day, witness a man-made atmospheric phenomenon. Each workday, the City of Vancouver emerges pristine in the early dawn and individual high-rises stand out in the first eastern rays of light. By seven, however, a purplish, grey-green haze smudges the skyline and spreads along the Sunshine Coast to the north. It settles a bit during the day when thousands of automobiles are finally parked adjacent to workplaces, but at three-thirty in the afternoon the haze builds again when the homebound rush begins and doesn't subside until dark.

Blakemore's eyes and nose were acutely aware of this phenomenon. Both ran profusely as he jogged down Beach Avenue to Stanley Park. He tried to regulate his breathing, recalling that the only place in Bear Creek with air like that was next to a smoldering slash pile. The flak vest (Coswell insisted he wear it) chafed under his running shirt, and the Berretta pea-shooter jammed over his left tit made it even worse. What did work well was the rear-view mirror clipped onto his baseball hat, which gave him a surprisingly clear view behind.

As he passed Second Beach and headed to Ferguson Point, he noticed that the seawall traffic had thinned out. Most, in fact, was coming towards him as fellow joggers, walkers, and the like hurried home, the Leighton murder perhaps in many of their minds. By the time he came alongside the Teahouse, there was virtually no one in front of him.

He gazed enviously at the restaurant, imagining the diners tucking into their desserts. He knew Coswell and Burns were there, ready to rush in behind him, but also probably digesting a delicious meal they'd sat down to in advance. He tried to concentrate on keeping up his pace even though his legs were already aching. Siwash Rock looked a long way off.

He'd gotten about halfway down the straight stretch of seawall when he became aware of a forest trail that emerged on his right and then paralleled the wall for a hundred metres or so before vanishing back into the woods. Burns was right. This was a perfect spot for an ambush. He tried not to stare at it as he ran, trusting that the city policemen had it well covered. His aching legs and laboured breathing no longer bothered him, over-ridden by the wave of adrenalin that surged through his body.

But nothing happened.

Siwash Rock came and went, and he was still alone on the seawall. He stopped running and stood motionless, his senses hyper-acute. Sounds were all distant: traffic moving through the Stanley Park Causeway, marine vessels coming and going under the Lion's Gate Bridge, aircraft descending to YVR....

The smell of seaweed wafted up from below and he contemplated for a moment how effectively that would disguise the early stages of body decay. He looked over at the forest edge and could see no movement, although the light had faded to such a degree that individual trees were blurred into a dark green band.

***
***

The parking lot at the Ferguson Point Teahouse was not a happy place at this moment. Burns leaned against the squad car, radiophone in hand.

"Nothing. Not a damn thing. Our killers obviously took the night off."

"Bugger," Coswell said. "What a colossal waste of time. But I'm not all that surprised."

"About what?"

Both men turned at the sound of a familiar voice. Frayley and Heather emerged from the shadows.

"Frayley!" Coswell said. "How the hell did you get here?"

"Drove here, like you. Just taking my junior reporter out for a treat," he said. "But now that we're all here, what's happened to Blakemore?"

Coswell glared at Heather who stood defiant beside her boss.

"Told him the whole damn thing, didn't you?"

"I warned you not to keep us out in the cold."

"Good point," Frayley said. "Now what's the scoop?"

Coswell sighed and admitted to them that his plan had

failed. He also implored them to be kind in their reporting of the incident, suggesting they write in merely general terms so as to avoid scaring off the suspects.

"Why not report the whole thing?" Heather said. "Even if you haven't caught them, they'll think twice before killing someone else if they read that you're getting this close."

"Crazies aren't that logical," Burns said.

"I agree." Coswell said. "And it could be on your conscience if anything goes wrong because of what you write."

Feeling he'd done all the warning he could he turned to Burns, who was still holding the radio phone.

"Tell Blakemore to come in. We don't want him risking his neck any longer. If the killers are further on, we're not set up to apprehend them."

Burns did as ordered but omitted one key command: defining exactly *who* was to notify the big corporal.

***
***

Blakemore was in a quandary—what to do now? He really didn't have any specific instructions at that point and cursed himself for not insisting this eventuality be covered. The adrenalin rush had worn off and he was aware again of the tiredness in his legs. Returning to the Ferguson Point area could blow his cover, if indeed that still existed. He pictured a concentration of police vehicles parked there and officers buzzing around.

He remembered from Coswell's map that there was a bridle path through the park paralleling the causeway. If he could get onto that, he would have a shortcut to Beach Avenue and the West End. All he had to do was turn directly east from the seawall into the forest, cross two dirt trails, one paved road and he'd be on the bridle path. He started off.

Light was really fading now and when he entered the tracts of forest, he was surprised to see how dark it had become. The odd street light on the paved section helped. He felt better crossing there, but was soon plunged back into the gloom as he searched for the bridle path.

When he finally reached it, the sudden transition from soft forest floor to gravel path almost caused him to trip, but he recovered quickly and began to jog again. Car lights from the heavy traffic on the causeway flashed through the trees, giving him some light but not enough to see the trail clearly. A few stumbles forced him to slow to a walk. He was making progress, though, and the welcoming glow from the high-rises in the West End beckoned.

But another source of light appeared behind him and it was not in the least welcome. He turned around and looked back. Shapes weren't discernable, but the headlights of two cyclists speeding toward him were unmistakable, the beams bouncing along the path.

He dived for the bushes, struggling to pull the Beretta from its holster. A squeal of handbrakes and the skid of the tires in the gravel reverberated as the riders slammed to a stop and dismounted. Their headlamps remained on — two perfect targets. Blakemore, gun finally in hand, got ready to squeeze the trigger.

"Corporal Blakemore. Is that you? Are you all right?" Then, in a flash of insight that probably saved his life, the speaker added, "It's us, Vancouver Police."

Blakemore gasped.

"Jesus! Bike cops. I thought you were the killers. I goddamn near shot the both of you."

Two headlamps converged on the Beretta in Blakemore's hand.

"My God," was all that one man could say.

"We were just delivering Sergeant Burns' orders," the other said. "You're to come in. We saw you leave the seawall and figured you were headed here but we had to loop way around to get our bikes onto this path."

The first rider, having regained his composure, pulled out his shoulder radio and called Burns.

"Message delivered," he said. "Will escort Corporal Blakemore to park boundary."

"Tell him he's an incompetent asshole and damn near got you killed," Blakemore shouted, but the officer was too quick on the "off" button for the invective to go through.

***
***

Ernie leaned his elbows on the balcony railing and gazed down at Stanley Park. He was worried about Paul Blakemore, probably on the Siwash Rock stretch by now, open to the assassins while Coswell and Burns were safely ensconced at the Teahouse like two tiger hunters waiting for the sacrificial goat to be attacked. But his thoughts weren't entirely on that scene. Something Paul had said in the Wheatsheaf was nagging at him.

The mention of a letter from the California Governor's office had evoked a name: Tommy Carlyle. He thought back to a time shortly after he'd moved to Vancouver from Bear Creek.

As a complete newcomer to the city's gay scene, he was on the outside looking in until Bruce Leighton saw him at that bar on Denman Street, alone and a bit depressed. He remembered gazing wistfully at the happy, boisterous crowd, Leighton the obvious centre of attention. When Bruce sent someone over to invite him to join the group, his social life blossomed. That someone was Tommy Carlyle.

But now he had an uneasy feeling as he tried to better re-call the man. Something was amiss, but it was lost in the memory of the multi-directional conversations that were typical of Bruce's gatherings. He vaguely remembered dis-cussing failed gay relationships with Carlyle, who was par-ticularly vehement on the topic, but not wishing to dwell on something so gloomy with all the fun going on around him, he'd moved away from the man at the first opportunity.

Only later did he learn that Carlyle was high up in Cali-fornia State politics as an administrator in the Governor's office, a bizarre situation since the present governor made no bones about his dislike for the gay community.

"Bizarre:" the word that Paul Blakemore had used to describe the West End murders.

11

Sitting beside Sergeant Burns in the back pew of St. Paul's Anglican Church, Coswell smiled to himself. On the way over, Burns commented that he and his wife were married at St. Paul's twenty years ago. Coswell imagined how tradi-tional that ceremony must have been compared to the go-ings on at Leighton's funeral.

The dress was anything but somber; colour and flam-boyancy prevailed. One mourner came in drag: high heels, a scarlet, hip-hugging sheath, and enormous gold hoop earrings.

The priest, clad in traditional Anglican ecclesiastical fin-ery, was a pleasant surprise. He imparted a lightness to the occasion quite unlike anything Coswell had ever heard before at a funeral. The odd religious comment emerged, but mostly the service was a cheerful commentary on Leighton's life and accomplishments. Coswell suspected that Leighton hadn't been a religious man and the priest, out of respect, resisted the temptation to preach doctrine to such a large audience.

With the faint hope that their two suspects might have shown up like arsonists returning to the scene of the crime to double their pleasure, both officers looked around till their necks hurt, but there was no sign of them.

Coswell was happy to see Ernie and Blakemore sitting side by side in a forward pew, further "proof" to anyone watching that they were, indeed, a twosome. The post-ceremony reception, to be held at Ernie's, would further reinforce the link and establish Blakemore as a potential target. That, of course, assumed that the corporal's cover hadn't been blown. Security would have to be tightened up, though. He didn't want a repeat of the Stanley Park fiasco.

As he sat listening to the priest, it occurred to him that he hadn't seen two other individuals at the service either — Heather McTavish and her boss, Frayley. He wondered if they'd weaseled their way into the reception, but then squelched the thought. Ernie wouldn't want two news-hounds poking around his grieving friends.

***

The reception was an invitation-only affair, but from Blakemore's vantage point, it seemed as though half the West End's gay population was there. He'd managed to squeeze himself into position beside one of the hors-d'oeuvres tables, but had a problem out-reaching two rotund creatures on either side of him who pounced on the delicacies as if they were starving. After a few collisions, the pair introduced themselves as Bernie and Tony. Actually, Tony did the introductions; Bernie never left his mouth unoccupied by food long enough to speak.

"You're Ernie's latest, aren't you?"

"He's had others?" Blakemore said. Growing up in the West End, he'd learned the language game from masters of gay repartée.

"Oh, that's just an expression, silly," Tony said. "Ernie's new down here, and of course I wouldn't really know all about his love life. He's awfully cute, though, and I'm sure he's had many offers."

"Ernie's sincere. He doesn't sleep around."

"Oh, my. Aren't you the touchy one?" With that, he leaned forward and spoke to his partner. "Bernie, give it a break. Tony wants to circulate. Come."

While the two muscled their way through the crowd, Ernie came over and spoke to him.

"I hope those dreadful gossips didn't give you a bad time. No one believes a word they say, so fresh meat's a treat for them. They've taken over from Roger and Frank, God rest their souls, but in a vicious way. Roger and Frank were harmless; these two are mean, especially Tony."

"Why were they invited, then?"

"They own the barge where Bruce's office is, along with numerous properties in the West End. Leaving them off an invitation list, if your business is anywhere in urban Vancouver, could be fatal."

Blakemore decided not to relate his conversation with Tony, but remembered that Roger and Frank were the body-building florists, murdered in their apartment.

"How fatal? Any connections with the West End victims?"

Ernie laughed. "No. Tony and Bernie murder only with words. You can scratch them off your suspect list, believe me."

Blakemore wasn't about to scratch anyone off his list until the murderers were identified, although he had to concede that the two porkers probably weren't physically capable of doing the West End killings. They were, however, rich enough to hire a killer, and some gossips, in his experience, were borderline paranoid schizophrenics who so believed their own poison that hatred boiled over in the form of physical action.

When Ernie moved off to tend to his duties as host, Blakemore decided he'd better earn his pay and start pumping for information on the killings. Tony seemed his best bet and so he went looking for him. He also felt he should soothe any bad vibes from their initial conversation, if for no other reason than to maintain Ernie's good status in the business community. He didn't have to go far. Tony and Bernie had found the source — the kitchen where the food trays were being filled.

"Hey, Tony," he called out. "I understand from Ernie that you and your partner have your fingers on the pulse of the real estate business in this neighbourhood."

Again, Tony took up the conversation while Bernie continued to eat.

"You can say that again. What we don't know isn't worth knowing. Why? Are you in the market?"

"I wish," Blakemore said. "I've just moved here from the interior and I can't believe how high the rents are in Vancouver, especially in the West End. The place I'm in right now is a real hole. I'd like to get something better."

"You're not living with Ernie? Do I hear a platonic relationship? That's just too, too un-gay."

"I don't like to rush into things. I think there should be a breaking-in period — both parties independent, so to speak, until we're sure."

"Oh, how old-fashioned," Tony said. "You sound like a virgin."

Blakemore winced. He could just imagine the gossip building in Tony's mind, but he pushed on, and took a shot in the dark; maybe the portly duo owned the building where the double murder took place.

"Wouldn't *you* like to know?" he said. "But what I'd really like to find is a sitting job, like Ernie has. I know it's an awful thing to ask, but any chance Roger and Frank's apartment's vacant? I read about their deaths. It must be hard to rent a place where there were such gruesome murders, but it wouldn't bother me any and I'd pay you the rent I'm putting out now."

"You're right," Tony said. "You'd think the building was a sleazy East Side drug house judging by the total lack of response we've had to our ads. We don't let to just anybody and the press has our usual renter types scared off, thinking they'll be murdered in their beds by the crazies who did Frank and Roger in." Then, after a short pause, "Just how much are you paying in rent right now?"

Without the faintest idea what the Force was paying for his room, he pulled a figure out of the air.

"Six hundred dollars a month."

"God," Tony said. "It must be a cubby-hole. Roger and Frank's apartment rented for three times that."

"My goodness," Blakemore said. "Their business must have been very successful."

Tony's voice dropped to a whisper.

"Just between you and me, they made dinky-do out of

selling flowers, not enough to support their grand lifestyle. I think they sold something else that grows in pots, if you know what I mean."

Blakemore let his jaw drop.

"Really! They were into selling drugs? Maybe I'd better think twice about my offer. I don't want any crazed addict banging on my door in the middle of the night."

Bernie interrupted, pausing in his feeding frenzy long enough to reassure Blakemore that Tony was way off the mark.

"They did no such thing," he said. "Roger's parents were moneyed. He inherited a bundle when they died. The flower shop was just a hobby. Frank's contribution was just a pretty smile, but that's another story."

"Then why do you think they were murdered?"

"Wackos," Bernie said. "Wackos don't need a reason."

At that point he didn't know whether to believe either man. It seemed odd that the two didn't have the same information. After all, they were partners.

"Call me tomorrow if you're still interested," Bernie said, handing him his card. "Maybe we can work out a deal."

The reception was to be over by six, but with so much food and good wine, the last guest didn't leave until almost eleven. Ernie collapsed into a big leather chair.

Blakemore recounted his conversation with Tony and his partner.

"I can't help you there, Paul," Ernie said. "I don't collect gossip and I didn't know Frank and Roger's backgrounds terribly well, but they seemed like nice honest people to me."

"Seemed...." That was another word that bothered him. Gossip or no, he'd pass that on to Coswell, unaware that the very next morning the inspector would have received far more significant information.

***
***

Burns was already at his desk when Coswell swept into the precinct at 0800.

"Lingered over my pancakes and coffee this morning, Sergeant," he said. "But I'm glad to see you're up and running. What's new and exciting in the investigative world today?"

"We got a name," Burns said, his face expressionless. "Maybe two. Forensics lifted nice sets of prints off the golf clubs. Lucky for us, the washer boy didn't do a good job on the suspects' loaners."

"You've already run them through the system?"

"Yep. Things move fast in this electronic world. The FBI got back to me right away."

"Well? Let's have it. You should be jumping up and down, for Christ's sake."

Burns suppressed a smile. Holding the floor over Coswell was a rare treat.

"The first name's Bobby Deavers. He has a record, assault, weapons charges and a DUI, all when he was in his twenties. Nothing since."

"Why the FBI interest?" Coswell said. "None of that sounds Federal to me."

"He's a member of a Ku Klux Klan type organization out of Texas called the Knights of the True South, an ultra-secret bunch that the FBI hasn't had much success infiltrating. Deavers is one of the dumber ones — got the club logo, crossed six-shooters, tattooed on his arm so he stands out like a neon sign. His buddy, a Charles Thornton, has no rap sheet but they've been seen together at gun shows the Feds keep an eye on, so he's likely a member too. Sacramento, California's listed as their last known whereabouts."

"I take it they hate everybody who isn't a white, Anglo-Saxon, Baptist, gun-loving heterosexual," Coswell said.

Burns nodded.

"You got it. Knocking off gays is right up their alley and they'd be good at it. They're both ex-military. Special forces."

"Wonderful. Two killing machines with warped minds," Coswell said. "Okay, let's get them. What've you done so far?"

Burns had done everything. APB's were posted; the suspects' photos were distributed to all police units; the border station personnel on both sides were alerted. It was just a matter of time until they were apprehended. Coswell prayed that no one would be hurt in the process.

12

The Orcas Bay Café, an all-night diner in the tiny US-Canada border town of Blaine, Washington, had been blessed recently by the arrival of a new group of regulars who met there at night over coffee and donuts. The usual late hour customers were truckers passing through, state troopers, and the border guards on breaks, but this recent influx of business was novel.

The newcomers, dressed in Macs and windbreakers, blended in with the locals, but were different in one noticeable regard. They all carried sidearms and a quick peek into their various pick-ups revealed twelve-gauge shotguns racked beside the gearshifts. These were the new Minutemen, a quasi-vigilante group, sworn to patrol the northern border of their great country and keep out the terrorists who came down from Canada they said, "like shit from their geese," to quote one of the group founders.

These men were not popular with the state police, who didn't appreciate their territory being infringed upon, but the customs officials were a different matter. They welcomed the Minutemen and sympathized with their cause, knowing all too well how easily the border stations could be bypassed, sometimes only a kilometre or two away. They cooperated as often as they could. Tonight was typical: a senior customs officer entered the café and headed straight for the back table. He sat down and, in a low voice, spoke to the men.

"Got something for you boys that just came over the wire."

He pulled out a copy of the APB posters that Burns had organized.

"These two are wanted real bad," he said, "judging by the fact their photos were hand-delivered by a couple of Mounties this afternoon. They wouldn't say what the two are wanted for, but they gave us the 'armed and dangerous' warning. I'll bet they're a couple of drug dealers."

"Why do you think we should get involved?" a man said. "The cops can hold the border stations okay."

"One of the Mounties, kind of aside-like, told me these two most likely would cross somewhere between border stations and if I knew anyone who might be patrolling along there, I should clue them in. He didn't mention the Minutemen, but I'm sure you're who he meant. I guess they're in the same boat as us, too much territory to cover with too few men."

The waitress, on her way over to the table with a fresh pot of coffee, was taken aback by the sudden scraping of chairs as the men rose and went out to their vehicles.

"I'm staying, Betty," the customs man said. "Sorry to break up the party, but I'll have some of that coffee for sure and couple jelly donuts. Going to be a long night."

***
***

Sam Colyer spotted it first, a vehicle crawling along Zero Road on the Canadian side of the boundary directly in front of him. He'd drawn the best station for the night: the very end of Pott's Road, a dirt strip that that led to a home-built bridge straddling the border. In less complicated times, the farmers on either side regularly crossed there to help one another and share machinery. Although the bridge hadn't been used for decades, its solid timber construction survived the years and could still support the weight of a vehicle. If one could locate it along the heavy tree line, a quick, illegal crossing was a cinch.

Grey's farm abutted the US side of the bridge. Old man Grey himself had welcomed the Minutemen when they first came to the community, and promptly gave them permission to use his property as an observation post.

Colyer spoke into his radio phone, keeping his eyes on the creeping headlights.

"Slow-moving vehicle sighted, proceeding east on Zero Road," he said in a calm monotone, but then a flash made his heart jump.

"Yes!" he shouted. "A torch light swinging this way. They're looking for the bridge. Come on over, the party's on."

He was disappointed for a moment when the lights passed the bridge, but the vehicle soon halted and backed up. Colyer got out of his truck, pulled the shotgun from its rack and waited. He could hear the rest of the men arriving behind him, shielding their pickups' running lights by driving in perpendicular to the farm buildings. Within minutes they were beside him, on foot, guns drawn. At a signal they all moved down to the bridge.

"If they cross in the vehicle," one of the men whispered. "Take out the tires, but wait until they're all the way across. We don't want them escaping back into Canada. Keep down. They're probably armed. They can't see us but they can fire at shadows. I'll do the bull-horn. Don't take the buggers out unless I say so. Now all quiet."

The vehicle turned off the highway onto the verge of the bridge and stopped. The headlights went off and two men got out, flashlights in hand. After a brief pause and a low murmur of conversation, the men set off across the bridge, apparently abandoning the car.

The duo had crossed and were within yards of the waiting Minutemen when searchlights flashed on. Almost simultaneously, two shots rang out. The fugitives were bathed in light. One stood frozen in position; the other just managed to pull his pistol, a futile gesture. The firestorm that erupted riddled the men with bullets and twelve gauge shot pellets. Their bodies slumped to the ground.

A squeal of car tires pierced the air from across the bridge. The "abandoned" vehicle suddenly backed onto Canada's Zero Avenue and sped off, using only its running lights until it was almost out of sight.

The Minutemen appeared out of the darkness, their faces

grim. They looked down at the corpses. Sam Colyer broke the silence.

"Jesus!" he said. "What the fuck happened?"

"Wonderful, wonderful, wonderful," Mayor Schmidt said. He beamed at Coswell sitting in one of the two leather chairs across from him. Chief Inspector Ward, seated in the other chair, merely nodded his approval.

"Commendations all around, I hope, Chief Inspector," Schmidt continued. "And don't forget that Blakemore fellow. He's a fine policeman and with a little practice he could be a good golfer."

Coswell should have been as happy as the Mayor but he wasn't. The two men slain by the Minutemen had never officially moved out of the suspect category, and even if they were the killers, it was unlikely they'd acted alone. Someone had prompted them and that someone hadn't completed his objectives, whatever they were.

But Coswell's two superiors were deaf to his concerns. As far as they were concerned, the matter was closed.

This air of bliss extended to the Main Street Precinct. Inspector Marsden retook command and Burns, perhaps the most delighted of all, rejoined his city police cronies and bid adieu to Coswell and the RCMP.

One man's bubble popped, however, when Blakemore walked into Coswell's office. The inspector wasn't clearing out his desk as expected. Instead, he was leaning forward, hand under his chin, tapping a pencil on the metal top. A feeling of dread abruptly reversed Blakemore's joie de vivre. He sat down across from Coswell.

"I can go home to my wife now, right?"

"No," Coswell said. "We need you now more than ever. Think about it. What have we got on these two? Absolutely nothing. Forensics drew a blank on the West End victims — no prints, no DNA, zilch — and there aren't any witnesses. If those two were still alive, we wouldn't have a hope in hell of pinning anything on them."

"They've got to be the perps," Blakemore said. "Why else would they have run like that? The killings must be over, don't you think?" He realized he was almost whining.

"Possibly. But you're thinking like Ward and the Mayor now. Where's your sense of justice? We owe it to the victims to prove these guys were the murderers, and if they weren't acting alone, there's another perp out there who's dangerous as hell. And don't forget that somebody drove them down to the border. Was he an innocent taxi driver or part of the gang?"

The string of rhetorical questions ended with a terse summation:

"Those goddamned American cowboys have set us back a ton."

Blakemore slumped in his chair, and then straightened.

"Why's Burns not here? Don't tell me he's been pulled."

"'Fraid so. It's just you and me now — and Ernie, of course. Just like old times."

"And Ward?"

Coswell leaned back, put his hands behind his head and took a deep breath.

"I've decided to leave him in his euphoric stupour for the time being. He's given me no directive one way or the other which leaves us free to do our job. Don't worry about yourself. I'll take the flak when it comes. You're just following orders. Mine."

Resigned to his fate, Blakemore remained silent for a moment, reluctantly refocusing on the case.

"What about ballistics? Can't we match the dead border guy's gun with the slugs dug out of the West End victims?"

"We'll try, of course," Coswell said, "when and if the Washington State boys cooperate. But I think the actual murder weapon's been dumped up here somewhere, somewhere far away from where the bodies were found. Ordering a search for it would be a waste of time."

"What's your plan, then?"

"We're going to have that meeting with Ernie. There are plenty of gays in California for those guys to murder, so why did they come to Vancouver? Why were they directed here? Ernie's a resource. He knew the victims and he has a much better overview of the gay world than we do. Let's use him."

"I hope you have something specific in mind," Blakemore said. "Ernie's been wracking his brain as much as the rest of us. He wants it all over too."

***
***

Coswell waited twenty minutes before he drove to the gallery to be certain Blakemore had ample time to get there first. When he arrived, the starving artist was minding the front again, occupied with an older couple who were contemplating a large seascape. Seeing Coswell enter, he excused himself and quickly ushered the inspector through the gallery and into the back room. If he was curious about the meeting, he didn't show it, returning immediately to his customers without comment.

Blakemore and Ernie were picking at the remains of lunch scattered on the coffee table: ends of a baguette, a variety of cheeses, fruit and a half empty bottle of red wine.

Coswell spotted the familiar striped label the moment he walked through the door.

"Is that a Blue Mountain Pinot Noir?"

"It is," Ernie said and poured him a glass. "We haven't left you much to eat."

"There's plenty left to clear my palette," Coswell said, plunking himself down on the chesterfield within easy reach of the table. Between sips of the wine and swallows of bread and cheese, he carried on a running commentary.

"This is a wonderful vintage. Blue Mountain does a lot of good things but this is their best. How did you manage to get some? I thought restaurants scooped it all up."

"An advantage of being gay. We have connections everywhere."

"That's exactly why I'm here, your connections, and I don't mean the vintners, although that would be of interest too."

He set his glass on the table, sat back, and turned his attention to Ernie.

"First of all, I want to bring you up to speed. I don't think the death of those two cyclists should end our investigation. As I've said to Paul, there's a matter of closure here, to say nothing of the possibility there'll be more killing. It's my belief that we've interrupted a series that's not yet complete and there are more targets — you, Ernie, being one of them."

He paused to let the effect of his words sink in and then continued to press his argument.

"California's popping up way too often in this investigation ... the two suspects, their letter of introduction, and all this worry about Mayor Gryndon's visit."

When the inspector finally paused for breath, Ernie spoke.

"Whose name was on that letter of introduction to the Balmoral golf course?"

Ernie's question surprised Coswell, who had to admit that the golf club employees were the only people who had actually seen the letter.

"Why?" he said, and listened as Ernie told him about Tommy Carlyle, the California governor's aide, who'd been one of Bruce Leighton's groupies.

"Hmm. Very interesting. Aside from you, there aren't many of Leighton's group left. You've got to wonder about the last survivors, eh? I'd like to have a talk with your Mr. Carlyle."

"Can you get funding to go down there?" Blakemore said. "If Burns has been pulled off the case, it doesn't sound like the higher-ups are interested."

"I found a higher higher-up. The Attorney General himself has taken an interest and phoned me right after the Mayor appeared on the early news. I voiced my concerns to him."

"Robert Gillings? I'm impressed," Ernie said. "I wonder what drew him into the mix. A chance to stick it to the Mayor, maybe? It's common knowledge he and Schmidt detest one another. Gillings and his provincial government buddies have canned a few of the Mayor's pet projects, like the safe shoot-up centre for addicts and his move to have marijuana legalized."

"What will Ward think of all this?" Blakemore asked. "You can't keep it from him and he's not likely to miss his chief homicide officer disappearing for a few days."

"I've left that up to Gillings," Coswell said. "I'm sure he'll put it tactfully to our glorious Chief Inspector."

14

Heather had just finished typing up the column for the evening edition of the *Star* when Frayley walked into the office.

"About time you showed up," she said. "This might be the last newsworthy article on the West End murders and it needs to be good."

"Ah, my little chickadee," Frayley said. "It does my heart good to feel wanted. You need a little copyediting from the master, do you?"

"Probably not. But your name's going on this thing too so you'd better read it. Where the hell have you been anyway? I had to do a phone interview with Coswell, which was less than satisfactory. I guess he was punishing me for showing up uninvited at the Stanley Park debacle."

Frayley ignored her question. He picked up the article and read through it.

"This is good reporting," he said when he'd finished. "But I see that Coswell's guarded statement about 'individuals of interest' isn't exactly the rosy one that the Mayor just gave on the early news. Didn't you catch it?"

"No. I was too busy trying to get this in on time and don't tell me you want me to change it to parrot the Mayor's comments."

"You should have heard him, Heather," Frayley said. "He all but said that the case was closed and the streets of the West End and Stanley Park were safe again. He also went on about the upcoming visit of the Mayor of San Francisco, our world-class city and all that. Your article's going to pee on his parade. Coswell's right, of course. This case is far from being settled, but I don't know if it's worth alienating City Hall to make a point."

"You're kidding, right? You, the king of shit-disturbers, backing off?"

Frayley sighed.

"Heather," he said. "I've just come from our revered chief editor's office. Someone from way up there in the owners' box has leaned on him, and he, of course, leaned on me ... hard, and I'm just too old to find a new job."

She sat very still for a moment, emotions welling up. Disillusionment first, then anger. Finally, she got up to leave.

"Write what pap you want, then," she said, glaring at him. "But leave my name off it."

"Don't be mad, Babe," Frayley said. "I did manage to get you a plum assignment."

She paused at the door.

"The Governor of California is coming up to Vancouver Island on a fishing expedition. The yacht he's going on is already at Campbell River and he's due to fly in next weekend. Rumour has it the trip's to compete with the San Francisco Mayor's visit. In fact, he's arranged to have a helicopter bring press people to the yacht for interviews and photo ops."

Encouraged by Heather's apparent interest, he hurriedly continued.

"Mary Carpenter, our celeb writer, was supposed to go but she's terrified of flying in a helicopter, so I told the editor that you'd make a great substitute. He agreed."

Heather's anger drained. She turned to face Frayley.

"Thanks," she said. "But I'm still mad at you."

"Disappointed, I'm sure," Frayley said and then, when she

turned once more to leave, called after her.

"Oh, and by the way. I've been informed Coswell's going to be there, too. You'll probably be on the same helicopter flight with him."

She looked back at him. His face revealed nothing. What the hell was going on in that diabolical old brain? Was he giving her tacit approval to continue digging into the West End murders? She decided that he was. Her step was light as she headed down the hall. *The old bugger*, she said to herself.

***

Coswell decided to arrange his own flight to San Francisco and was duly shocked at the charges for short-notice bookings. He'd already splurged on his choice of hotel. The twinge of guilt heightened when a call came through to him from headquarters minutes later. Jane's mellow voice informed him that Chief Inspector Ward wished to speak to him. He braced for the reprimand.

"Got a new job for you," the Chief Inspector said in his usual voice of authority, decibels more than necessary. "California's Governor Kruger is coming to Vancouver the same time as Mayor Gryndon. Our Mayor Schmidt has suggested that you be in charge of security for them both, and I agreed. Jane will fill you in on the details." To Coswell's great relief, Ward didn't bring up the subject of his San Francisco junket.

Jane's voice came back on the line.

"Lucky you," she said. "I'd kill to meet the Governor. He's a hunk."

She gave him the dates of the visit. He was happy to see that he could make the San Francisco trip and be back in time for his new security duties. He didn't relish all that time in the air, but he had to do it.

"Enjoy San Francisco, by the way," she said. "You naughty boy."

Ouch. Somewhere down the line Ward would make him pay for getting trip funding from an outside source.

Carlyle wasn't the only reason for his trip. He also wanted to check out the "California connection," as he'd called it, particularly Sacramento, the last known US whereabouts of the two dead suspects, and Gillings had arranged for him to meet with FBI personnel in San Francisco. It appeared that the US Federal Agency was interested in the case, no doubt stimulated by Gillings himself.

And lastly, although not a conscious part of his decision-making, was the delightful prospect of spending three days in his favourite city in the whole US of A.

Vancouver is a beautiful city from the air with its clean beaches, busy sea traffic, and the magnificent Coast Range Mountains as a backdrop, but flying into San Francisco has its own unique scenery: the Golden Gate Bridge, of course, and an equally busy waterfront, but the vibrancy that emanates from below grabs the tourist. One can hardly wait to land and bask in the atmosphere. Coswell was no exception.

The mundane police cruiser that met him at the airport didn't dampen his enthusiasm a bit. He'd been to San Francisco a number of times before and loved the place. Even the street people seemed less down and out, almost happy in their concrete environment. And the restaurants ... dozens and dozens of great restaurants serving wonderful California wines. He'd booked two nights in the Harrington Arms, a small, traditional hotel in the city centre that did everything first class, including express check-in, chocolates on the pillows, and complimentary champagne in a cooler beside the bed. The room rate was atrocious but Coswell didn't care. The luxury could very well be his last.

The check-in at the Harrington was indeed express, taking only minutes. His bag melted into the hands of a bellhop and the concierge assured him that he would book the inspector into the restaurant of his choice for his evening meal. Satisfied, Coswell returned to the police cruiser waiting outside and was whisked off to the San Francisco Hall of Justice where he was to meet an FBI agent sent up from headquarters in San Diego.

The station seemed more like Grand Central than a police establishment, with people moving everywhere, most in civilian dress. The officer who greeted Coswell, however, was in uniform. She was a cheery, unbelievably tall redhead with crimson locks barely contained within her regulation cap. She approached with outstretched hand. He was sure she was over six feet tall and from his five feet nine vantage point, her eyes were a long way up. Captain's bars glittered on her shoulders.

"I'm so pleased to meet you," she said in a voice that was so nice it tingled. "I've admired the Royal Canadian Mounted Police ever since I was a little girl and I'm just thrilled to meet a member in real life. I'm Cindy Forsythe," (not *Captain* Forsythe, he noted).

For some strange reason the image of Nelson Eddy popped

into his mind and he looked to see if she was squinting at him, perhaps leaving her glasses somewhere, but her green eyes were open wide and the niceness flowed unabated.

"Your request for information must have been a dandy to have one of our esteemed FBI people come all the way up from San Diego to meet with you," she said, and then added, "My chief feels the SFPD should be in on the discussion, by the way. I've been assigned the task and I'm looking forward to being in such esteemed company."

A hint of mischief tugged at the corners of her mouth.

The meeting took place in Cindy Forsythe's office, a room spacious beyond anything Coswell had ever seen allotted to similar-ranking officers in Canadian police forces. The furnishings, too, were impressive: a large, solid oak desk with an orthopedic chair, a small settee against one wall and two visitors' chairs that were actually comfortable compared to the hard wood things Ward had in his office.

When Coswell and Cindy arrived, two men were already seated, one lolled back on the settee and the other in a chair that he'd pulled away from the front of the desk and pushed up against the wall opposite. That left two seats, Cindy's behind the desk and the remaining chair directly in front of her.

The man on the settee rose immediately and introduced himself, extending his hand.

"I'm Frank Miller, FBI, and my saturnine friend over there is Quentin Whitfield, CIA."

Whitfield didn't get out of his chair; he merely nodded. Coswell shook Miller's hand, nodded back to Whitfield, and proceeded to pull the exposed chair back towards the door.

"Better we sit in a circle, eh?" he said. "That way we can all see one another."

Cindy smiled, and spoke to Whitfield.

"What brings you here, Quentin?"

Quentin Whitfield was part of New England's version of royalty. His blue-blood family bankrolled his Harvard education, obtained an articling position for him with one of Boston's most prestigious law firms, and were broken-hearted when he said he wanted to be a cop. They settled on the CIA as the only dignified form of copship and were mildly relieved when he was assigned to the distant West Coast. Cindy Forsythe and Frank Miller gave tacit approval for him to take over the meeting.

"We're more than a little interested in your investigation, Inspector Coswell," Whitfield began. "Unknown to you, I'm sure, you've stumbled into a much bigger picture than just your murder cases in Vancouver."

Coswell didn't appreciate the words "stumbled" and "just" but he listened with growing fascination.

"After the 9/11 disaster, Washington decreed that all US agencies — us, the FBI, state and local police forces — work in much closer cooperation in order to detect clandestine operations happening country-wide. While each works in its own jurisdiction, there's considerable overlap, hence the dictum to get together whenever possible."

Coswell, amused that his Vancouver investigation was drawing attention from all levels of the magnificent American Justice System, listened to Whitfield drone on.

"While our agencies have been coordinating, we fear that the organized fanatics in our society are doing the same. Gone are the good-old-boys' meetings in the woods; these people are communicating now with up-to-date technology."

He leaned back in his chair and gazed up to the ceiling as though he were receiving a divine message.

"Yes, the extreme right in this country is on the move — the Ku Klux Klan, the Minutemen, vigilantes in every little hick town — all dangerous and lawless people, in my opinion. They believe legitimate law enforcement agencies have lost control and intend to correct that situation by any means necessary."

Cindy and Frank Miller were looking slightly bored. They'd obviously heard the speech before, but Whitfield went on.

"So far, these organizations have been local and acting independently, but if they ever unite under a national leadership, I can tell you they'll take over the country and the United States will go so far to the right, it'll tip over."

Coswell wondered just how far that change had gone already, given the extraordinary measures that had been put in place since 9/11. Perceiving the USA as the land of the free was now a big stretch.

"What has been particularly alarming," Whitfield continued, "is a rash of situations like yours that have surfaced all across this country: a plot to murder a visiting Imam in Philadelphia, a Chicano senator in Texas who's championed amnesty for illegal aliens believes he's being stalked, and most recently, the Memorial Day slaughter of the young men in Washington who urinated on the Veteran's monument. All of these happening so close together suggests to us a grander plan than just sporadic local flareups."

Miller finally interrupted the monologue. "All right," he said. "Enough of the history lecture. Tell the inspector where he fits in all of this."

Whitfield came close to sneering at Miller.

"That's the trouble with you FBI people," he said. "You've got ants in your pants. Jump before you get the whole story."

"And the CIA, of course, never makes that mistake," Miller said.

Cindy put a quick end to the sniping.

"Gentlemen, gentlemen," she said. "You are not offering sterling examples of cooperation with that kind of talk. Let's get back to business."

"Oh, all right," Whitfield said, and then spoke directly to Coswell "You, Inspector, could be smack in the middle of what we feel is a major operation of the group I just described."

"The Ku Klux Klan?"

"Not specifically," Whitfield said. "But individuals of that ilk. Your two deceased suspects were members of the Knights of the True South. That's a group with a wide range of members, from grunts like them to intellectuals and politicians, possibly at the very top level of government."

Coswell began to feel uneasy. Where was this leading, so far as safe old Vancouver was concerned?

"Frank and I have studied this latest incident carefully," Whitfield continued. "I apologize, Cindy, for not bringing you on board sooner but we wanted to be sure. Until recently, your fair city has not been involved."

"You're starting to lose me," Coswell said. "Just what does this grand organization of righteous zealots have to do with us exactly?"

Miller cut in.

"Your Attorney General, Robert Gillings, contacted our office. He feels, and we tend to agree, that your suspicion of a larger motive for the recent murders of gay men in Vancouver is well-founded. That, and the fact that Mayor Gryndon of San Francisco, a confirmed gay, is about to visit your city, is too much of a coincidence to ignore."

Cindy almost jumped out of her seat.

"Doesn't involve my fair city?" she shouted. "What a couple of horses' asses you two are."

"Now, now, Cindy," Miller said. "We just got that report, and the likely site of an assassination is Inspector Coswell's city, not yours. Mayor Gryndon is quite safe in San Francisco."

That was too much for Cindy.

"And I shouldn't worry that he might be killed somewhere else?" she fired back. "Well, to hell with both of you. My chief is going to put a stop to that trip, pronto."

"Brilliant idea," Whitfield said, "Don't you think we've tried that already? Gryndon told us to go to hell. Apparently the Mayor of Vancouver has assured him he'll be as safe as a bug in a rug."

Coswell hoped the fact he was in charge of the San Francisco mayor's rug wouldn't come up. Fortunately, it didn't.

Miller quickly changed the subject.

"What do you make of the Washington State Police report?"

"That the Minutemen insisted the first shots came from *behind* the border-runners," Coswell said. "And they reacted on instinct? I believe them. Many of those men are ex-service, trained to return fire with fire. Not unlike a lot of us, I think."

All three nodded in agreement. Coswell continued.

"I think the driver of the car that dropped them off knew exactly what was on the other side of that bridge, and literally triggered the action. Someone wanted those two permanently shut up and I believe it was done to protect a larger operation. If I had the opportunity, I'd interrogate the hell out of every official working that Blaine border station.

Maybe one of them is an extreme right-wing sympathizer and helped set up what turned out to be an ambush."

"I did suggest that possibility to the Washington State Troopers," he added.

"You can be sure we'll follow up on it," Whitfield said.

The meeting ended with Coswell promising to keep in touch and they, in turn, assuring him he would be kept in their loop.

"Give me a minute," Cindy said after Miller and Whitfield left. "I'm going to zip down to my locker and change into something more comfortable for travelling."

Coswell sympathized. He wished he were wearing something other than the new suit and tie he'd felt appropriate attire for a visiting RCMP inspector.

***
***

Captain Cindy Forsyth drove the entire way to Sacramento. Fortunately I-80 has virtually no curves to speak of, and with the words of Miller and Whitfield still ringing in his head, Coswell's brain was completely detached from his stomach, thereby averting any motion sickness. The speed to which Cindy pushed her '96 Dodge Viper and her propensity for weaving through the long lanes of traffic served as added diversions.

"Not issue, this car, I gather," Coswell said.

"No. It's mine. Cost me a bundle, but if I'm going to drive, I want to enjoy it."

She noticed his shoulders pressed back into the seat. "I'm not making you nervous, am I?"

"Of course not," he lied. "I like speed, but aren't you worried about a ticket? That can be embarrassing, you know."

She pointed to a flashing light on the dash.

"State-of-the-art radar detector."

As they sped past the exit to California Rte. 37 (the road to the Napa and Sonoma Valleys), he looked forlornly to the north and the names of vineyards danced in his head: Robert Mondavi, Clos du Bois, Chateau St. Jean, Stag's Leap....

Cindy interrupted his daydream.

"I wonder why they picked me to go with you to the Capital. Not that I'm complaining, mind you."

Coswell wasn't complaining either, glancing at her elegant legs and the creeping hem of her skirt as she cranked the Viper through its gears.

"Probably because you'll look less threatening to the Sacramento people than the Federal types. I think a foreign cop like me is pretty benign, too, so you and I should be a good team. We'll milk them for all they're worth."

"Them? Do you have anyone else in mind besides the Governor's aide?"

"No one specific, but I think some names will come up after we interview Carlyle."

The average driving time from San Francisco to Sacramento is an hour and a quarter, but forty-five minutes after leaving the Bay Bridge, the Viper passed over the Sacramento River and down the off-ramp that swung under I-5 and into the capital city.

Parking wasn't a problem, although it did entail a two-block walk; not a real effort for Coswell ordinarily, but keeping stride with Cindy made for an uncomfortable pace. He started to pant and hoped she wouldn't notice, but he didn't have to worry. She was a born-in-California girl, proud of her home state, and pointed out the sights.

"Have you ever seen a State Capital as magnificent as this? I think it's prettier even than the White House."

Although his straining lungs were hampering full appreciation of the view, he had to admit it was spectacular. They'd almost reached the end of a lush park when the building suddenly loomed above them, framed in giant oak trees. The black dome appeared first and then the white double rotunda below it, dazzling in the forenoon sunshine.

But as they approached the main entrance, the magnificent view was marred by the presence of uniformed guards at every door; a grim reminder of the security necessary to safeguard this historic edifice.

After passing through two security checks and, given further directions, they finally arrived at the reception desk for the Governor of California himself.

A woman was stationed there, middle-aged, meticulously dressed, who radiated an aura that suggested her sole purpose in life was to keep the public hordes from her boss and his aides.

Coswell took over at this point, feeling that his facile charm was needed to get past this potential obstacle.

"And how are you this lovely California morning?" he started off, handing her his card. "We'd like to speak to Mr. Carlyle, please. We don't have an appointment, but if you'll tell him we're here, I know he'll want to see us. I'm looking after the security for your Governor Kruger when he comes up to Vancouver next week. You might also mention to him the name Bruce Leighton, someone he will definitely remember."

The woman jotted Leighton's name down on a memo pad.

"I'll call this through for you," she said. "Why don't you look around for a few minutes?"

There wasn't much to see. The hall consisted primarily of

cold marble and the ceiling was finished with bland plaster, a duplicate of any modern office building. A few uninteresting pictures hung down the long corridor.

"This is crap," Cindy whispered. "Wait till you see the old building. It's beautiful."

It was fortunate that there was nothing of interest, because within minutes Tommy Carlyle stepped out of a doorway at the end of the hall and walked briskly towards them. He could only be described as diminutive, and at a distance, one would have taken him for a slim boy dressed in a business suit. Only when he neared did the grey in his temples and the creases of age become apparent. His expression when he first appeared reflected annoyance, but that quickly changed to a professional smile as he approached, hand extended to Coswell.

"Welcome to California, Inspector," he said, then turning to Cindy, "And your lovely friend?"

"Captain Cindy Forsythe of the San Francisco PD," Coswell said, and just managed to catch the slight hesitation when Carlyle shook her hand as well.

"Forsythe," he said. "Any relation to the revered Judge Wendell?"

"Yes," she replied. "The judge is my uncle."

Coswell was duly impressed. In the late nineties, Judge Wendell Forsythe made big news when he presided over one of the most sensational trials in California history: the murder of an aging Hollywood icon by his crack-addict daughter and her boyfriend. The defense had won a change of venue from Los Angeles to San Francisco, claiming local bias. Forsythe's outstanding performance during that trial had fast-tracked his ultimate appointment to the Supreme Court of California.

"Please come down to my office," Carlylé said, and then to the receptionist, "No calls, Katherine."

Carlyle's office was generous for an aide, Coswell thought, or maybe everyone in the US Public Service had big offices. The furnishings were modern in the minimalist style. The only colour in the room came from a vase of flowers on a stand by the window and the California State flag hanging behind the desk.

Pleasantries over, and all seated, Carlyle's tone changed.

"Bruce Leighton's name is what got you shoehorned into my very busy day," he said. "I'm aware of the tragic circumstances of his death ... and the others, of course. We were all best of friends many years ago. I did my pre-law at your university."

Coswell wondered why the man hadn't chosen a more prestigious US college for his early studies. What drew him to Vancouver, a Canadian city that probably half of the American population didn't even know existed?

"I'm truly sorry I couldn't attend his funeral; duties held me here. But to get to the point: why have you come to see me?"

"A letter of introduction for a Bobby Deavers and a Charles Thornton. Do either of those names mean anything to you?"

"Never heard of them. What sort of introduction, and why ask me?"

He said that smoothly, without a trace of pretense.

"They're suspects in a multiple murder we're investigating in Vancouver. The letter in question bore the seal of the Governor of California. They presented it at an exclusive golf course in the city. The signature at the bottom was illegible but the title above read Chief Executive Assistant."

Coswell watched Carlyle's face carefully but all he saw was genuine surprise.

"That's absurd. First of all, no one in this office would use our stationery for such a purpose, and to a golf course? That's ridiculous. But in this day of computer reproduction, I suppose anything's possible. Forgery is no longer an art, it seems."

Coswell persisted. "But if the original did come from this office, forgery or no, there appears to be a connection, if you see what I mean. We were also told that the last known whereabouts of the two men was here in Sacramento."

"I see. You think they may have worked in this building — janitors or cleaners with access to stationery?"

"A possibility," Coswell replied.

"I'll have that looked into for you but I doubt we'll find those names. Anyone applying to work here, even in the most menial of jobs, is screened extensively. A criminal record would be a red flag. They simply wouldn't be hired."

Coswell moved on to his next line of questioning.

"Have you heard of an organization called the Knights of the True South?"

"Of course. Is that what your suspects are all about? Well, in that case, you've come to the right place. Off the record, I can tell you that bunch of Texas yahoos that Governor Kruger brought with him when he took office are probably all card-carrying members. They give Republicans a bad name."

Their conversation was abruptly cut off when the door burst open and Governor Adam Kruger himself charged into the room. He was the epitome of the tall, lanky Texan, but had an aggressiveness of manner more akin to a trader on the floor of the NYSE.

Coswell wondered if the room was bugged.

"What's this 'no calls' bullshit, Tommy, my little caballero?" Kruger said, and then seeing Cindy, added, "Afternoon, ma'am."

Carlyle introduced everyone, obviously irritated by his boss' presence. The "caballero" appellation had stung.

"RCMP, eh?" Kruger said, pumping Coswell's hand with political gusto. His speech, it seemed, consisted of rapid-fire sentences with a paucity of verbs. "Admirable bunch. Old-fashioned discipline. Way it should be."

Carlyle cut in.

"The Inspector will be in charge of local security for the Vancouver Conference on Urban Renewal," he said. "You'll recall that you've decided to speak at the closing banquet there along with Mayor Gryndon."

The sentences lengthened.

"Yeah, yeah. Don't nag me. Leaving the best damn salmon fishing on the Pacific Coast to break bread with a man I can't stand is something I don't need to be reminded of."

Kruger returned his attention to Coswell.

"When are you headed back to the Great White North, Inspector?"

"Soon," Coswell said. "In fact I'm scheduled to fly from Vancouver to Campbell River to coincide with your arrival."

"Hell, man," Kruger said. "Come with me. My wife's made up some charity thing she has to attend just as an excuse not to come. I've got an empty seat on the executive jet." And then without waiting for a reply, he turned to Carlyle. "Tommy, you fix it."

Katherine, the woman from the reception desk, appeared at the open door.

"Governor Kruger," she said. "Your driver's waiting."

"Okay, okay. Everybody nags me. Now I forgot why I came in here. It'll come to me though. See you later."

"Ma'am," he said, nodding to Cindy on his way out the door.

All three were speechless. Carlyle broke the silence.

"God, but I hate that man. If it weren't for the jail time, I'd save everyone a lot of trouble and assassinate him myself."

That statement, in Coswell's estimation, moved Carlyle well down the suspect list; the man was too honest.

"Why do you stay?" Cindy asked.

Carlyle sighed.

"There are some outstanding people working for the public good in this office and they need support. Fortunately the governorship term is finite, but the core group will remain and there's hope. A new star is rising and I want to be here when he becomes the next governor. California will become a much better place, for all classes in our society."

"Mayor Gryndon?" she asked.

"Mayor Gryndon," he confirmed.

Aside from ordering a search for Deavers and Thornton in the personnel files, Carlyle really had nothing more useful for Coswell's investigation. The aide hadn't been back to Vancouver in over a year and his awareness of the Knights of the True South unfortunately didn't extend to naming names.

Carlyle walked with them to the hallway that led into the old part of the Capital before he said goodbye. He told Coswell he'd phone the Harrington Arms and leave the details regarding his flight with the Governor, although the time of departure had already been set—eight A M Sunday. That still gave Coswell two nights in San Francisco and the bonus that he'd save the provincial taxpayers the cost of a return flight to Vancouver. The moans from the bean-counters would be a little muted at least.

"I love both your cities," Carlyle said, a note of wistfulness in his voice, "and when I get a chance, I'll visit."

After thanks and assurances all round, they parted.

***
***

Coswell actually enjoyed Cindy's guided tour, despite the fact that his only interests in life, outside work, were good food and wine, but Cindy's enthusiasm was infectious. The building was magnificent, from the basement rotunda with its famous murals, to the third floor hall and the portraits of past governors. The only negative, as far as Coswell was concerned, were the stairs, particularly at the pace that Cindy kept up. She didn't miss a room. By the time they returned to the Viper, he was exhausted.

"Home, James?" Cindy said after she settled in behind the wheel.

"Not yet. We've got an address to look up: 400 block Eleventh Street."

Cindy looked over at him.

"A little Canadian detective work," Coswell said. "Deavers and Thornton were ex-US Rangers. I figured an army unit like that would have an old boys' newsletter of some sort, the Esprit de Corps, if you will. Actually it's called *The Ranger Register*. I got an old Vietnam vet classmate of mine from university to finagle their mailing list for me."

"You actually got their address," Cindy said, "and you kept that information all to yourself, you naughty boy."

Coswell was beginning to warm to the "naughty boy" label. Inspector Ward's secretary, Jane, had called him the same thing. Obviously he was managing to give the two women a tickle.

"Yep," he said, "435 Eleventh Street. It's just a few blocks north."

The house was in the old downtown area of Sacramento, a fixer-upper adorned at some time in the distant past with an ugly green paint, now badly faded, and topped with a multi-patched roof nearing the end of its days. A long, steep set of front steps led up to a small porch. Coswell forced his aching thighs to climb them. No one answered his knock at the door. He noticed Cindy stayed behind him at the bottom of the steps ... routine police procedure.

He also noticed there were no freebie newspapers or store flyers lying around, the usual porch debris after a long absence. The two men had probably been in Vancouver for a few weeks at least. Someone was removing the junk mail for them.

He debated which neighbour to approach first, but was saved the trouble by the appearance of an elderly gentleman wearing coveralls who strode across the lawn from an adjacent residence.

"Can I help you?" he asked, suspicion written all over him. Nothing better than a neighbour for a watchdog, Coswell thought. Cindy answered the man.

"Looking for Bobby and Chuck."

Smart, Coswell said to himself, using the non-cop approach. Most Americans he knew were terrified of getting involved in anything as messy as murder.

"Calls himself Charlie," the man said, his suspicion mounting. "Guess you don't know them too well."

Coswell took over. He spoke as he descended the stairs.

"She doesn't," he said. "I'm the one who knows them.

They said they were going up to Canada for a bit but I thought they'd be back by now."

"Yeah, I did too, but I'm not complaining. Steve gave me a check for two month's rent in advance just in case they were delayed. They're the best damn tenants I've had in a long while. It's hard to get good ones in this neighbourhood."

Coswell's heart jumped. Steve — a third man!

"You know, I never met Steve," he said. "Was he army too?"

"I didn't know any of them were army until I picked up that *Ranger* thing off the porch. Bobby and Charlie seemed to spend all their time at the golf course or riding around on those fat-tired bikes you see everywhere nowadays. Steve's the only one who works, it seems ... government job, I think. Anyway, as I said, they're good tenants and I ain't nosy."

He'd be the only neighbour in the world who wasn't nosy, Coswell thought, especially since he managed the place and probably had access to it during the day when the men were out.

"Well, we're just passing through," Coswell said. "Tell the boys we called, will you? I'm Mark and this is Cindy."

They got back into the Viper and Coswell gave a cheery wave as Cindy pulled out into traffic.

"Bingo," he said. "Who do we get to mine the gold back there?"

"Miller. Whitfield will just piss off the locals."

***

The drive back to San Francisco took only forty minutes; rush hour traffic was coming the other way.

"It would probably be best that you be the one to pass on to your FBI colleague what we found out," Coswell said, trying not to look concerned as Cindy sped by yet another string of cars, foot to the floor.

She smiled. "I agree. Being upstaged by an alien will undoubtedly bruise his Federal ego."

"Do you think he'd be further insulted if you told him to be certain to get Steve's last name off the rent checks?"

"Yes, and I'm going to enjoy doing so. And don't you worry, I'll have that name and the biggest dossier I can put together on our boy Steve ready for you before you fly out with the Governor. After all, if Steve's in Vancouver, you're the one who's got to find him."

Coswell thought for a moment.

"You might as well go all the way and suggest, when they get his full name, that someone look hard through the Capital staff personnel and see if they can find an ID photo. That would be wonderful."

"If he was on staff at the Capital we'll have more than an ID photo," Cindy said. "They'll have done a complete check on him right back to his army service record. Maybe he shared a common background with Deavers and Thornton."

He liked this woman and he'd made note of the fact that she used her maiden name. He wondered.

"Have you made plans for dinner tonight? It's almost six o'clock and I have a reservation for one at Lance Town's restaurant that can easily be changed to two."

"My, my, you must be on one super-generous expense account."

"A small token for the amount of help you've given us," Coswell said.

"I think it's you we're going to thank if there is a plot against Mayor Gryndon and you manage to foil it. But I'm going to take you up on the offer anyway. It's not every day

I get to dine at San Francisco's top eatery. Besides, we're both dressed okay for the place and I'm starving. How about you?"

"Famished." The donuts he'd managed to swipe from the station coffee room while he waited for her to change were a poor substitute for an adequate lunch.

When he discovered that her apartment was literally en route to the restaurant, he insisted she park her car there and they'd taxi the rest of the way.

"I want to do California wines this evening," he said, "and it'll be nice not to drink alone for a change."

If Cindy wondered about his drinking alone, she didn't say anything. She insisted, however, that FBI agent Miller be informed of their Sacramento revelations before they did anything else. She made the call from her office and suggested Coswell use the phone in the staff room to notify Lance Towne's establishment of the reservation change.

His restaurant call took only seconds; the donuts were all gone. She was just hanging up when he walked into her office.

"How did he take it?"

"He's going to phone Whitfield, despite my request to the contrary."

"Perhaps it's for the best. After all, we're supposed to be cooperating."

"Right," she muttered.

***
***

The Harrington Arms obviously had some clout in the restaurant booking world. They were seated at a table nestled into an intimate corner made even more private by the strategic placement of leafy potted plants.

He studied the wine list while Cindy looked over her menu.

"I never look at a menu without a glass of white wine in my hand," he said.

Their waiter, who'd just appeared, overheard the comment and made a suggestion.

"Our sommelier has just opened a Jordan '05 Russian River, which is available by the glass this evening."

Coswell liked that; the wine was an expensive vintage not ordinarily sold by the glass and their man was going to let them in on it, although he had to concede that their less than Armani apparel might have prompted the information. Cindy picked up on that as well. After Coswell accepted the special Chardonnay offer and the waiter hurried off to get it for them, she glanced down at her dress.

"The big budget items in my life are a car fetish and the ridiculous rent on my apartment. Clothes are way down the line. I spend most of my time in uniform anyway and the majority of the rest in jock outfits, so I don't see the point in maintaining an upscale wardrobe."

"Ditto," he said, "except my big two are food and wine."

They were silent for a few minutes while they studied the menu.

Coswell already knew what he wanted, but didn't wish to admit he'd pulled up the restaurant's menu on the internet before he'd flown out of Vancouver. Cindy took a few moments to decide.

When the waiter returned with two glasses of the Chardonnay, Coswell relayed Cindy's choices to him and placed his own order.

"You can bring the appetizers now," he continued. "We'll finish our Chardonnay with that and I'd like a bottle of the

Poet's Leap Riesling to have with the entrées."

"Very good, sir," the waiter said, using the continental form of "It will be done," rather than the usual American, "Excellent choices. I'll get the chef on that right away."

"Whoa," Cindy said. "A glass, and then a bottle of wine? I might look like there's a lot of me to absorb that much alcohol, but I don't have a high tolerance, probably because I work out a lot."

"Don't worry," Coswell reassured her. "The secret is the food. A sip of wine, a bite of something and lots of conversation. One thing compliments the other. Any toxic effects are neutralized that way."

Cindy laughed. "I'll give it a try."

The Jordan Chardonnay was superb. Coswell sipped the buttery liquid.

"I wonder what the Feds are doing tonight," he said. "Discussing matters intently over an Arby's beef dip, do you think?"

"Not Whitfield. He's first class all the way. I'm surprised he's not here, but Miller I can see at Arby's."

"Will the dynamic duo want to meet with me before I go back to Vancouver?" Coswell asked.

"Without a doubt. Miller made that perfectly clear when I was on the phone with him back at the station. Don't take this personally, but you really are an alien and they'll want to give you a lot of coaching. Hope you're up to it."

"I can tell you, Cindy, I haven't gotten where I am today by being deaf to suggestions. My mind's never totally made up until I'm absolutely sure of the answer, and in this case, I'm a long ways from it."

"You must have a working hypothesis, though."

Their appetizers arrived at that point and Coswell had

difficulty concentrating on her question. With a mouthful of the most wonderful preparation of fois gras he'd ever eaten, Cindy's voice seemed far away. He managed a second forkful before answering her.

"Yes. As I told you and the G-men this morning, I think the West End killings and the ambush of the killers at the border are all part of a plot aimed at a significant target, possibly your mayor. The enigma is the third man. Was Sacramento Steve the driver of the car at the border? Is he the ultimate hit man or just a gofer? Who else is involved? I don't know the answer to any of these questions; what I do know is we have to find answers quickly. Mayor Gryndon arrives in Vancouver a week from this Saturday."

He returned to the fois gras with a vengeance, after a gulp of Chardonnay. Cindy ate more slowly and was still deep in thought.

"I don't quite see the purpose of your trip to Governor Kruger's fish love-in."

"Orders," Coswell said. "Apparently the security people for the Governor are concerned about the quality of what we've arranged in Vancouver. They want a detailed briefing before the big man arrives in the city."

Cindy smiled. "Gryndon's the one in real danger and Kruger needs reassurances. That's a hoot. When it comes to balls, I think our mayor has him beat, hands down."

"Well, in truth, your mayor's security people have been on our backs as well, for over a month now. Kruger's crowd is more recent."

After they'd finished their main courses, the waiter appeared to take their plates away, placing a dessert menu on the table as he did so. Coswell reached for it and found what he wanted. When the waiter returned, he ordered.

"A baked chocolate soufflé pour deux and a flute each of your Anderson Valley Ermitage champagne."

"Nooo," Cindy said.

"Yes," Coswell insisted. "We can't have chocolate without champagne. It's a sin."

She giggled.

Coswell's alcohol tolerance had been honed over many years and he barely felt a buzz from the evening's wines. Not so with Cindy. Her eyes began to glaze over. Mercifully, the taxi ride from the restaurant to her residence was so brief she managed to stay awake ... barely. Coswell instructed the driver to wait while he escorted her to her apartment.

"T'rific evening," she said, fumbling with her keys. "But I'm completely bombed. Bedtime. See ya tomorrow. Thanks."

Coswell gently pulled the door shut after she'd gone in. The automatic lock clicked into position. He returned to the cab and headed back to the Harrington Arms.

He'd done okay. Cindy had enjoyed their date and she wasn't just being nice.

He was in the mood for a nightcap. A cognac, perhaps ... a Remy Martin.

***
***

Coswell felt exhilarated. He'd wakened at six, showered, shaved, and breezed out the front entrance of the Harrington Arms for a morning constitutional: a three and a half block walk to Sears, the place to eat breakfast in downtown San Francisco. He arrived at the restaurant early enough to get a seat and order one of their famous waffles with a double side of eggs before the usual lineup formed. The last half block of his walk was uphill; quite steep, he thought, thereby justifying the caloric intake (despite the previous night's meal still trying to work its way through his digestive tract).

He lingered over a second coffee and read the newspaper he'd picked up outside his hotel room door. He wondered at what ungodly hour some unfortunate must have delivered it. By the time he got back to the Harrington it was just seven-thirty.

The concierge called to him from the reception desk. "Message for you, sir."

Coswell marveled at the man's memory. He'd barely spoken to him when he'd checked in.

"You're to call a Captain Forsythe. Here's her number."

He called her from his room and, to his surprise, she was bright and alert. He commented.

"I thought you might at least have had a teeny headache this morning."

"Maybe a little one when I first woke up," she admitted, "but eight hours of dead sleep and a three-mile run have me wide awake."

"Too bad I didn't know that," he said. "We could have done Sears together this morning. I've just gotten back."

She laughed. "Orange juice and champagne with scrambled eggs? No thanks. Coffee's all I need this morning and I've had two already. Miller left a message on my answering machine last night. For some reason I didn't hear it ring, but he and Whitfield want to meet with you and me in my office again at eight. Are you okay with that? I'll pick you up."

"Ready and waiting," he said.

***
***

When Cindy and Coswell entered her office, Whitfield and Miller were already there, sitting side by side on the two chairs this time, leaving the settee for him. As before, Miller did the greeting,

"That was fine work you two did yesterday," he said. "But we have considerable follow-up information that I'm sure will interest you both."

That approach amused Coswell; like the Feds had won the day, eh? He merely smiled, but Cindy responded sharply.

"Lucky you got pointed in the right direction, I'd say."

Miller bridled. "I said 'great work'."

Coswell leaned back. He sensed a long-winded report coming up.

Miller began.

"Steve Carson is the name of third member of the group and he did serve concurrently with the other two in the US Rangers. They enlisted together in their home town, Bakersfield, Texas. Nothing outstanding, either good or bad, showed up in their military records. The Sacramento police had nothing on them either, not even a speeding ticket."

Whitfield gazed out the window, apparently bored with the proceedings.

Miller continued.

"Carson got a job at the government buildings in Sacramento as a janitor and is presently on three weeks' vacation leave. None of his co-workers could tell us much about his private life; he was a man of few words, it seems. But I did get his picture from the personnel files along with details of his weight, height, and so forth."

He handed those to Coswell and then looked in Whitfield's direction presumably to get his input, but Whitfield remained silent.

"And that's it?" Coswell said.

"What else can we tell you?" Miller answered, surprised at the inspector's reaction.

"A lot," Coswell said. "Did you check out the references on Carson's job application? There must have been something in addition to his military record. What did he do in his off time? Those three would've kept up their shooting skills, I'll bet. Did you canvass the local gun clubs, shooting ranges and the like? And golf, I'm told, really gets people talking and revealing their personalities. How did they behave at the courses they played? Were they part of regular foursomes?"

He turned to Whitfield.

"Is Carson also a member of that Knights organization? I'd be surprised if he wasn't. Tom Carlyle remarked that the Governor's staff was riddled with them. Surely you must have some names. Did our three mix with them anywhere — bars, golf courses, gun ranges? Did you question the security staff that'll be coming up to Vancouver? I'd hate to think you missed out on that one."

Cindy's eyes were wide open and her mouth slightly ajar.

"What the hell *did* you guys do in there?" she said. "Don't tell me you dropped the ball."

Whitfield couldn't remain silent any longer.

"We had limited time. Miller and I left the locals to it and I'm sure they'll get to all your questions. But something's come up which I think tempers the situation considerably."

They all looked at him.

"I've just received some very pertinent information from the Washington State Police. It appears that one of the border victims was carrying a backpack filled with a lifetime's supply of cocaine hidden in water bottles."

Coswell seethed. That information should have been sent

immediately to him, not to the CIA, and the condescending tone of Whitfield's voice added to his irritation.

"Your suspects may be no more than a couple of druggies shopping for supplies in Canada where cocaine's cheap and a lot easier to obtain than in this country. And even if they were the men who killed your Vancouver gays, and I wonder about that, they probably did it just for sport, not as part of an assassination plot."

They all waited for Coswell's response. He looked directly at Whitfield.

"Accepting that explanation, in my opinion, would be a big mistake. I'm certain those two men were involved and not because they were on some psychopathic rampage. I firmly believe that they were given a list and deliberately sought out their victims. Someone directed those murders and that someone is still in business."

Cindy was mesmerized. Coswell continued his argument.

"No, there's a plan behind all of this, so far a successful one, and no matter the motive, gay men are the target. It's simple logic to assume that North America's most prominent gay politician, Mayor Gryndon, would be the ultimate prize and a laid-back city like Vancouver an irresistible opportunity."

"I can sympathize with your reasoning," Whitfield said, not quite hiding the sarcasm in his voice. "You've proceeded along that line to a point at which it would be difficult to turn back."

"Embarrassing, you mean. No, if you could assure me that I'm wrong, I'd be only too happy to abandon all of this. But, quite frankly, I'm not impressed with your side of the investigation so I'll continue with mine."

Cindy left no doubt as to her feelings in the matter.

"And I hope you will. Any possibility of harm to Mayor Gryndon, no matter how slim, must be taken seriously."

Whitfield sighed. "As you will. But I must get on with other matters. I'll wish you good luck and goodbye, Inspector."

With that, he got up and left, leaving an uncomfortable silence in his wake, finally broken by Miller.

"Son of a bitch. He could be right. But listen here, Inspector, the FBI at least will continue to cooperate with you. I'll make sure of it."

He took out his wallet, extracted a card and wrote a number on the back.

"This will get me any time, twenty-four hours a day. Not many people have it, but don't hesitate to call if you need something."

Coswell thanked him, adding that he'd appreciate all of the Sacramento information sent directly to him when it became available. Miller agreed and promised to add the Washington State Police findings as well.

"You know," Miller said, as he got up to leave. "It's strange that the Washington State guys were so slow getting that cocaine tidbit down to us. You've got to wonder about a conspiracy, but that's Whitfield's job. If he misses it, he'll be sent back east with his tail between his legs."

Coswell warmed at the thought.

After Miller left, Cindy stared at Coswell for a moment.

"You're really something," she said, and then returned to business. "Now, I've got to spend the day catching up and I'm sure you'll want to enjoy the city in the brief time you have left, but I've got an invitation for you tonight. My uncle's hosting a small gathering at his home this evening and I'd really like you to meet him."

Judge Wendell Forsythe. Coswell couldn't believe his luck.

He'd probably be the only RCMP officer to ever meet the man. The name-dropping back in Vancouver would be wonderful.

"I can pick you up at your hotel at six-thirty," she said, "and ferry you to and from his place. I'm not drinking a drop of alcohol ever again, or at least not tonight, so I can drive. He lives in Cow Hollow, which isn't far away. Dress is casual and don't feel insulted when he turns the hockey game on. He's an absolute sports nut."

Hockey? In California? Coswell had no interest in sports, including hockey, and marveled that a Canadian game would be popular so far south.

"Oh," Cindy said as an afterthought, "Don't eat beyond lunch today. Uncle Wendell will have his usual mountain of food to pick at."

She told him to help himself to the phone in her office. She had to leave immediately for morning roll call.

The moment she left, he dialed the Chief Inspector's office in Vancouver. Jane's voice came on the line.

"Inspector Coswell. How nice of you to keep in touch."

"Jane, my dear," he said. "I need a couple of favours. Would you call this number and have Corporal Blakemore phone me at my hotel in exactly thirty minutes?"

"And favour number two?"

"Don't tell Ward you've spoken to me and don't show him the fax that you'll be getting shortly. It's for Paul Blakemore. He'll pick it up."

There was a moment's silence before she replied.

"I meant it, you know. You are a truly naughty boy and I hope you don't get us both into trouble.'

"I promise," Coswell said. "Bye."

16

If it hadn't been for Ernie, Paul Blakemore would have said to hell with Mark Coswell and snuck back to his wife. The inspector gave him an impossible task just before he left for California.

"Find out where those two lived," he'd said. "It had to be in the West End and when you find the place, look for a third man, the guy that drove them to the border. He's still a potential threat, or at least a lead."

Blakemore brooded. The two suspects were obviously not members of the gay crowd and to canvass the hundreds of apartment buildings in the area would be daunting to an entire police force, let alone one man. He corrected himself — actually two men. Ernie was still with him and had promised to spread the word among his West End contacts.

But what word? Two bike riders with satchels and sunglasses, one pair with stars and stripes? Not much to go on.

All of this rumination was taking place in the Wheatsheaf, Blakemore's new home away from home. He was now on a first-name basis with most of the staff. He'd contemplated keeping up with the running, but it was just too painful, so he resigned himself to gaining a few pounds. He needed some reward for doing a boring job.

Jane's call brought him back to earth — more orders from Coswell.

He cursed and grumbled all the way to his jeep two blocks away — mid-morning parking near the Wheatsheaf was always a bitch. He sat and waited impatiently for the thirty minutes to go by before dialing the number Jane gave him. The Harrington Arms switchboard operator put him through immediately to the inspector's room.

He got no further than "It's Paul," before Coswell cut him off.

"I want you to go down to Ward's office and get Jane to give you the fax I just sent up. There's a photo of a Steve Carson on it who I believe is the third man you've been looking for. That should fast-track finding the guy. But stay back. So far we've got nothing on him so all we can do is set up surveillance."

"Have a heart," Blakemore pleaded. "I can't do that alone, even with Ernie's help."

"You won't have to. I've just spoken with Gillings. Take the fax down to Main Street and show it to Burns. He's back on the case as of now. You'll have all the manpower you need."

Blakemore was speechless.

"And one last thing. Phone Zach Benson at the hospital forensic unit and tell him we really need him to tie those two into the West End killings more than ever. The FBI will be sending DNA samples from both Deavers' and Thornton's bodies. I've got an in with an agent down here."

"When are you getting back to Vancouver?"

Coswell outlined the change in plans and his flight with the Governor to Vancouver Island.

"Now I have to go. I'm dining with Judge Wendell Forsythe this evening and I have a lot to do before then. If anything comes up while I'm still here, phone me at this number. Otherwise, I'll call you from Vancouver Island when the Governor's plane comes in sometime on Sunday. Bye."

Blakemore glared at his cellphone and muttered:

"Governor Kruger, Judge Wendell Forsythe, posh hotel,

dinners in San Francisco and all I have is the West End, the Wheatsheaf and Ernie."

***
***

Deep in the windowless bowels of Vancouver General Hospital, Zachary Benson toiled at his equally tedious job. Blakemore's call was unsettling. Zachary's boss, Peter Mueller, and his forensic unit had moved on to other tasks and dragging out all the West End data again would be time-consuming. He hated to ask Mueller to do that, but he felt an obligation to Blakemore, if not Coswell. Blakemore had saved Heather's life in Bear Creek.

The Chief of Forensic Pathology was surprisingly agreeable.

"I never feel right when we don't supply an answer in cases like these," Mueller said. "With modern equipment, that should be a rare occurrence and now that we're to be supplied with good DNA material from the two suspects, all we need to do is find a match in the evidence bags. Go to it."

There were slim pickings in those bags. All Zachary had, really, was a piece of carpet from the apartment where the double homicide had taken place. The city forensic team had actually cut out a square directly beneath the head of the one victim who'd shown signs of struggling, but analysis drew a blank.

That left Zachary with only one option: a search for that tiniest of clues, skin cells adherent to the fibres.

He'd recreated the killing in his mind: the victim's face pushed into the carpet, immobile until he heard his friend shot, then reacting violently in an attempt to shake his assailant off. The killer probably grabbed a handful of hair to subdue him, but there was a good chance the hand slipped or was driven into the carpet by a violent twist of the victim's head dislodging skin cells in the process. All Zachary had to do was find them.

He was looking for specific leaves on one tree in a forest. The metaphor was discouraging, but he continued to look down his microscope, examining every fibre. He'd begun at the periphery of the patch, knowing the centre would be saturated with the victim's cells, and reasoned that the first skin cells he saw working in from the outside edge could be from the killer.

One hour later he was exhausted and had a slight headache from the bright field light and the continuous focus of his eyes. Dust mites, most still alive, were an annoying distraction. He'd started his search arbitrarily from the right edge of the square and found skin cells, but not until he'd almost reached the central area. All belonged to the victim.

He decided to take a break before examining the opposite side. The weekend was coming up and Heather was flying out early Sunday morning to Vancouver Island. Since weekends were the only quality time they had together, he'd promised they'd do dinner out after they both finished their day's work. Unfortunately, when they'd sped off in the morning the responsibility of booking the restaurant wasn't made clear and he'd lost track of whose turn it was to do that.

"Hey, handsome," Heather said when she heard his voice. "Nice to know you can tear yourself away from those dead bodies long enough to think of me and call."

"I think of you constantly," he said, "even though your pals Blakemore and Coswell have dumped another load of work on me."

Zachary regretted that statement the second it left his mouth.

"Really," she said. "Have they got a new case so soon?"

He was trapped.

"Er, it's just a sort of clean-up from the West End stuff...." he said, a feeble attempt to put her off. He could almost feel the energy rising on the other end of the line.

"Zachary, my love," Heather cooed, "You know you can't keep anything from me and you really shouldn't. We need to have an open relationship."

He gave in and told her everything Blakemore had passed on to him.

"Now don't you worry about any repercussions, sweetie," she said. "I protect my sources with my life. We'll have a nice chat at dinner this evening. By the way, where are we going?"

"The Kettle of Fish. I need some brain food."

Coswell, not exactly certain what Cindy meant by "casual," decided that leaving his tie off was as casual as he should dare. After all, an occasion involving a member of the Supreme Court of California had to have some element of formality to it. The reference to a televised hockey game threw him a bit, but he rationalized that he could quickly doff his suit jacket if shirtsleeves were the order of the evening.

He was relieved when Cindy drove up wearing designer jeans and a sleeveless blouse, the only element of adornment being a single-strand pearl necklace.

"And what did you do with your time today?" she said when he got into her car.

He smiled, remembering what he'd said to Blakemore.

"Professionally speaking? Aside from a phone call this morning, I've done absolutely nothing. Pleasure-wise, I've had a wonderful day. You were an inspiration yesterday, Cindy, with your whirlwind tour of the Capital, climbing all those stairs, and I wakened this morning with an urge to exercise. The brisk walk to Sears for breakfast just whetted my calisthenic appetite so I actually worked my way down to the Ferry Market building, on foot all the way."

Cindy was impressed. Even downhill, that was quite a distance.

"I did stop for a leisurely lunch at the Ritz-Carlton and lingered at the terminus of the California cable car line to listen to the street musicians. The Ferry Market was definitely worth the trip. I had a drink in the Market Bar to restore my bodily fluids and people-watched for a while. I was shocked how quickly the time passed and sadly had to take a cab back to the Harrington so I could get ready for this evening."

Cindy smiled. His continuous walking couldn't have been more than fifteen or twenty minutes at most, and he probably had a nap when he got back to his hotel.

Cow Hollow turned out to be an upscale neighbourhood between Fort Mason and the Presidio. Coswell, in his perusal of the real estate section of the morning newspaper, discovered that a mere condominium in the area went for over a million dollars.

Cindy parked in front of one of the more impressive units on Chestnut Street. She read his mind.

"He bought here when prices were sane," she said. "If he

ever needs to sell this thing he'll be able to afford the best nursing home in California."

But ostentation doesn't mean safety in a big American city; Coswell noted the wrought iron security gate and the speaker attached to it.

Cindy pushed a button and a voice came on.

"Yes?"

"Pull up the drawbridge," she said. "It's me."

"Me, who?" the voice said.

Cindy turned to Coswell.

"He always does this, the old wag. He knows darn well who it is."

"Open the gate you old fart," she shouted.

"Oh, it's you, Cindy."

A snicker accompanied the release of the lock.

Wendell Forsythe met his niece with a giant hug at the door. He wasn't much taller than Coswell and his head barely cleared her chest. Hug over, he turned and extended his hand.

"Inspector Coswell," he said. "I'm so pleased to meet you. Cindy told me the famous Royal Canadian Mounted Police were sending down one of their finest to shake up the local constabulary. The case you're on sounds fascinating. Come in. You must tell me more about it."

The condominium was typical of many in the Bay Area, with the lower level dedicated to garage and storage. A long flight of stairs led up to the living quarters, a huge open space with living room, dining area and kitchen all on one level. Forsythe didn't stop there, but turned instead to another set of stairs.

"We're headed for the den," Cindy said. "I don't know why he even furnishes anything else. He lives in that damned room."

Her uncle heard the comment.

"That's all a bachelor needs," he said. "The rest's all for show, except for my bedroom in the loft."

When Coswell saw the den, he understood. The room took up the entire level, bathed in light from floor-to-ceiling windows that overlooked the Bay. Bookshelves, filled with hardcovers ranging from P.D. James to William Shakespeare, lined every other wall. There wasn't a law tome in sight.

A treadmill and a weight apparatus occupied one corner of the room, but the rest was furnished with big, comfortable leather sofas and chairs facing a giant TV screen. Between it and the seating area, a low table laden with bowls and dishes of finger food beckoned Coswell.

"Make yourself comfortable, you two," the judge said. "And help yourself to the nibbles while I roll out the drinks. Kevin just phoned. He and Carl will be over shortly. They both had some interview to do."

In answer to Coswell's puzzled expression, Cindy explained.

"Kevin's an old friend of mine from college days. We were both on the varsity basketball teams. Carl's his hockey player buddy."

Forsythe snorted.

"Now there's a description of omission if I ever heard one. Kevin Slater is the centre for the Seattle Seals of the NBA and Carl Neufeld's a veteran defenseman for the NHL Minnesota Blades. Kevin should also be Cindy's husband but she's too stubborn."

Cindy laughed.

"It's good you're a judge," she said. "You have absolutely no tact."

Having surprised Forsythe by declining a Canadian beer, Coswell was deciding between the excellent California Chardonnay and the Yakima Valley Pinot Noir when the tallest man he'd ever seen bounded up the stairs and strode into the room. He was blond, with pale skin, almost albino, and had striking azure blue eyes.

"Cindy, my love," he called. "Come give Kevin a hug. It's been too long."

Cindy got up and on this occasion was embraced by a man who made her tall frame appear normal.

The second man arrived at a more leisurely pace. He had a physique completely different physique from his friend: dark, short and heavily muscled. Both men moved with the confident grace of athletes.

Forsythe made the introductions all round and then let them choose their seating while he took drink orders. Coswell settled on the Pinot Noir; Kevin and Carl accepted the Canadian beer; Cindy requested a Perrier with lime.

"Don't ask," she said to her uncle. "I sinned last night at Lance Town's."

Kevin and Cindy carried on a two-way conversation, the uncle cutting in from time to time, but Carl remained silent, regarding Coswell with disquieting intensity. During a brief lull in the conversation, he finally broke his silence.

"Your name rings a faint bell, Inspector," he said. "I have a good friend in Vancouver who's actually house-sitting an apartment I own there. His name's Ernie Downs. We played Junior A hockey in Saskatchewan in our high school years. He joined the Mounties while I slogged it out on the rink, but he's out of the force now and runs an art gallery in the city. Do you know him?"

Coswell almost choked on his wine. The fact that Ernie even knew a hockey player, let alone took part in the sport, particularly at that level, was a shock.

"I know him well," he managed to reply. "In fact, we worked together on a big case not far back when he was stationed in southeastern BC We still keep in touch."

"Ah, that's where I heard your name. He told me all about that investigation. A deranged Vietnam vet was the villain, I recall. Ernie spoke highly of your investigative skills."

Coswell was impressed by how articulate the hockey player was, a large cut above the grunting clichés that were the norm in TV interviews.

"Ernie was just being kind," Coswell said. "He and his partner were the real keys to cracking that case."

Coswell now took centre stage. The others wanted an account of the Monashee murders as well. That quickly led to questions about his present investigation. He gave a brief summary and then let Cindy tell them about the Sacramento field trip. She did so, carefully avoiding any mention of the concern for Mayor Gryndon.

Judge Forsythe seemed particularly amused by the exchange with Tommy Carlyle.

"Ah, little Tommy," he said. "A five-foot and not much else bundle of ferocity, the likes of which have rarely been seen in the California courts. He'd argue that night was day and persuade the jury to believe it if you let him get away with it. A ruling-a-minute kind of guy, but I loved sitting his cases. He sure as hell kept me awake."

Coswell was curious.

"Why did he leave what sounds like a successful law practice to become an aide to the Governor? Sounds like an awful comedown to me."

"The Josh Gryndon affair, most likely. That's old gossip now but at one time those two were an item—an inseparable item. When Josh started his rise up the political ladder, Tommy literally cleared the way for him, taking a long sabbatical from law to do it."

Seeing Coswell's empty wine glass, he paused for a moment to refill it before continuing.

"They were a magical pair. Josh could stay on the high road and Tommy did all the dirty work, so to speak. He was a master of organization, but by the time the falling-out came, Josh could fly on his own. Tommy just disappeared, ultimately popping up in the Governor's office. I think he just wanted to get away from San Francisco and I'm sure the Governor welcomed him with open arms, or at least a firm handshake."

A man with that intensity, wronged? A huge motive for murder. Carlyle had been written off way too quickly.

The hockey game brought an end to conversation. The judge, Kevin, Carl, and to Coswell's surprise even Cindy, became engrossed in the contest. He took full advantage of their diversion and consumed a goodly portion of the "nibbles" without anyone noticing.

The game turned out to be a rout. The San Jose Sharks were leading the visiting LA Kings by four goals by the end of the first period. Conversation started up again, and to Coswell's delight, it was not devoted exclusively to sports. All present, including Carl, had university degrees and the topics of discussion ranged from politics to fine dining in San Francisco (a subject the inspector managed to sneak in). It was almost midnight before the group broke up.

Goodbyes and thank you's said, Kevin and Cindy led the way down the stairs followed by Coswell and then Carl. As they parted to go to their separate cars, Carl spoke softly to Coswell.

"You'll keep a special eye out for Ernie, won't you? He's the class of that Leighton bunch, for sure. It's too bad about the murders but if anything ever happened to Ernie ... that would be a tragedy."

Before Coswell could reply, Carl turned and walked quickly to catch up to Kevin. They got into a sporty convertible and sped off. He watched the car disappear around a corner and realized he had another name to add to his list.

"Well, did you enjoy the evening?" Cindy asked as she expertly navigated the Viper through the narrow side streets on the way to the Harrington Arms.

"Immensely. Good food and great company. I really like your uncle and I envy your relationship. My uncles considered me the runt of the litter and generally ignored my existence."

"That's too bad because the older touch is a real comfort at times. Uncle Wendell has shored me up in some pretty shaky situations."

She said that with a wistfulness that made Coswell wonder.

"Did you get the private joke, by the way?" she asked, brushing away the momentary lapse in her cheerfulness.

He shook his head.

"That I should be married to Kevin?"

"That was a joke?" Coswell said.

"Actually, I should have said it was a private joke between Kevin and me. Uncle Wendell has no idea. Kevin's gay."

"And Carl?"

"Gay too. They're long-term partners."

Coswell was glad the interior of the car was dark. He was rarely caught that surprised.

"Our secret, of course," she said.

"Of course." He knew that the two men would be forced by tradition to stay in the closet so long as they were in the public eye. A gay mayor was acceptable. A gay basketball player and especially a gay hockey player? Probably not.

But why? What the hell was the difference, and who the hell should care? Then he thought of the West End killings. Some people did care.

***
***

For once in his life, Coswell almost enjoyed being in an airplane. Aside from the vacuum in his stomach when the Governor's Lear jet powered to its cruising altitude, the rest of the flight was smooth and steady. The passenger cabin had been custom designed with four seats that rivaled the leather ones in Judge Forsythe's den, arranged two facing two with a small table in the middle. To Coswell's surprise, he and the Governor were the only passengers. He expected at least a couple of security people.

"How do you like my little plane?" Kruger said.

"Cozy," was all Coswell could think of to say. Not much to describe a few million dollars worth of aircraft, but the Governor seemed satisfied with his response.

"Way I like it. Detest that thing the President flies around in — too big and too accommodating. Privacy's the word when I travel. Away from the hordes for a while."

"I can sympathize with that," Coswell said, "but where are all your security people?"

"Flew out last night. Commercial airline. Rest assured, they'll be waiting for me when we land on Vancouver Island.

Usual procession of black limos to where the boat's docked."

The word "boat" reminded Coswell that he needed to make a suggestion.

"Perhaps I could have my session with them at the airport and just hop over to Vancouver from there," he said. "That way I could get right at setting things up for you when you come over next weekend."

"No way. Today's Sunday; God's day. You need to be fishing. Talk security while we drag our lines for salmon. I like good company and you'll be the only Canadian on board, besides a few pesky reporters—necessary evil, no fun. You look like a fun person. Also, it'll make your security responsibilities feel more personal."

Coswell wondered what there was about his appearance to evoke the impression of "fun."

"Have to do a bit of work," Kruger said, "before we pick up Brian. Help yourself to the reading material. Stowed under the table here."

"Brian?"

"Brian Sterne. My fishing buddy. Owns the boat we're going on. We'll drop down and pick him up in Seattle."

With that, the Governor opened a brief case, put on a pair of reading glasses and began going over a bundle of files, completely ignoring his guest.

Brian Sterne. Probably the Brian Sterne of Silicon Valley fame, Coswell thought. The man was a reclusive billionaire who'd invented some security program indispensable to business computers. He wasn't quite in Bill Gates' league but he was well up there. To be buddies with an extrovert like Kruger seemed strange.

The landing in Seattle was smooth, but the hard braking necessary to bring the jet to a stop gave Coswell's stomach a flip. Sterne arrived at the airplane, whisked out in a glorified electric golf cart. Kruger barely had time to tuck the folders he was reading back into the briefcase before Sterne climbed the stairs the co-pilot had lowered for him.

Brian Sterne was the most nondescript individual imaginable. His was the face drawn by a police sketch artist that could be a million men. Coswell mused that he'd be a great bank robber; no one would remember him. Even his attire was neutral: fawn Chinos and an olive green golf shirt buttoned to the top.

He sat down and quickly fastened his seat belt. Kruger did the introductions while the pilot taxied the Lear to the designated runway for take-off.

It was a relief to Coswell that all he had to do was return the other man's nod. Sterne appeared as much ill at ease as he was until the plane finally leveled out.

"God did not mean us to fly," he said.

"He didn't mean us to float on the water either," the Governor said, "on something the size of that yacht."

It's too bad God hadn't put his foot down on both methods of transportation, Coswell lamented to himself.

The conversation picked up with the Lear in cruising mode. Coswell's curiosity was satisfied when Kruger gave a summary of his friend's life.

"Brian and I go way back," he said. "All the way to our Texas Baptist roots. Brian's daddy was a genuine preacher. Mine just acted like one. Both were salt of the earth, eh Brian? Capital "R" Republicans. Americans all the way, with a bit of westward leaning, I have to add."

Coswell wondered whether a true Texan ever leaned far outside his state's border.

"When it came time for our university education, west was the only direction our pappies looked: Palo Alto, where that old Republican giant, Leland Stanford, founded the best damn university in the whole of the United States. None of the Ivy League bullshit for us, eh Brian?"

"Amen," Sterne said.

"We've come a long way since we dangled our lines for bass in those ole fishin' holes. Remember those days, Brian?"

"Blissfully," Sterne said with a sigh. "But salmon fishing in Canadian waters isn't to be sneezed at."

"Amen to that."

An image leapt into Coswell's mind of a front porch somewhere deep in the heart of Texas with two good old boys massaging one another.

On his way to meet Ernie again at the Wheatsheaf, Blakemore's cellphone rang; Zachary Benson was calling from the forensics lab.

"Paul. I'm grinding my way through this DNA search and so far all I've found is victim's cells, but I'm still looking. Those samples from the dead suspects, by the way, haven't shown up here yet. If I do find some of their DNA, I'm going to be awfully frustrated if I don't have the material on hand to do a match. Where are they?"

"I don't know. Maybe it's the weekend thing, but I'm

surprised. I got the distinct impression from Coswell that the FBI types were really going to facilitate all this."

"Well, hopefully they'll get here soon." Zachary said, and then, after a pause, "My conscience won't let me go, Paul, if I don't 'fess up to a little slip I made when I spoke to Heather earlier this morning. I'm afraid she knows you and Coswell are still pressing on with the case."

Blakemore stifled a curse but there was no use giving Zachary hell. Heather would have dug the information out of someone sooner or later.

"Don't worry about it," he said. "And I'll get Coswell going on those DNA samples as soon as he gets back."

He switched the phone off and foolishly hoped that Heather was occupied with other stories.

***
***

He could see her red hair from the street, sitting across from Ernie at what Blakemore now considered his personal table in the Wheatsheaf. He was annoyed at the expression on his former partner's face, which he interpreted as a slight tinge of guilt for giving out too much information. He'd spoken to Ernie on the phone right after Coswell's call from San Francisco, and passed on all that the inspector had told him. Now he regretted doing so.

He picked up his coffee and pastry and joined them at the table.

Heather greeted him. "Mr. Meter-reader. So nice to see you. How's business?"

"Boring," Blakemore said. "Absolutely brain-dead boring. I wish I was back in Bear Creek."

"I guess," she said. "That's a good place for brain-dead all right."

Her joshing ceased abruptly.

"Now let's cut the bullshit. What are you up to? There has to be one helluva good reason you're still under cover, and don't tell me it's because Coswell forgot to take you off." Then as an afterthought, she added, "Where is your fearless leader, by the way? He doesn't answer his phone, although I've discovered that doesn't mean a lot."

"Out of town on official business," Blakemore said, and, preempting her next question, "and it's none of your business where."

He was pleased; his partner hadn't spilled the beans.

Heather turned to Ernie.

"Will you tell your rod-up-his-ass partner here that withholding information from the press will result in a lot of printed speculation, which will cause a lot more trouble than if he keeps us informed?"

Blakemore spoke to Ernie.

"Will you tell this vulture from the press that she has no right to this information and I am not supplying it no matter what she says?"

Ernie couldn't keep himself from laughing.

"This is just like the good old Bear Creek days," he said. "But you'll remember, Paul, when Heather was brought in up there the case progressed quickly."

"This is different. Up there she knew the victim. Down here she's not involved in any way whatsoever."

"Sorry," Ernie said to Heather. "The vault door appears to be slammed shut, but maybe if you'll be a bit patient, things will change."

Heather thought it over. She hoped Ernie's comment meant he was going to work on Blakemore, but it didn't matter. According to her boss, Frayley, she'd be seeing Coswell in a day or so anyway, and the inspector might be a little more giving.

"Oh, all right," she said. "But I've cooperated once already with you guys and I don't think you're being fair."

Blakemore turned his concentration to his coffee and pastry. Ernie gave her a surreptitious wink. She smiled, but as she got up to leave, snarled at Blakemore.

"Thanks for nothing, you stubborn old bugger."

The only indication the corporal had even heard her was the slightest hint of a frown. Ernie suspected the word "old" did it.

After Heather pulled away from the front of the bakery, Blakemore and Ernie got down to discussing Coswell's latest revelations.

"Did he say anything about his interview with Tommy Carlyle?" Ernie asked.

"Not a word. Like I told you, he's got that third man thing stuck in his mind."

As the two conversed, a Vancouver City Police cruiser pulled up in a loading zone directly in front of the bakery. Sergeant Burns eased his big frame out the passenger side; the driver remained in the vehicle. Ernie saw them first.

"Uh, oh. Your city police buddies have just arrived."

Blakemore glanced over to the door.

"Yeah. That's Burns. I told him to meet me here. This is leveler ground than that downtown precinct, I can tell you."

The sergeant didn't come over to their table directly. Without Coswell present, he held rank and damn well planned to be comfortable. Coffee plus pastries equaled comfort.

Blakemore leaned over the table and spoke to Ernie in a low voice.

"You haven't had the pleasure of meeting our oversized colleague yet, have you? He's a real bundle of joy."

Ernie watched Burns slowly advance, coffee in one hand, pastries in the other, his face expressionless and making eye contact with no one. Paul's sarcasm appeared well-founded.

Blakemore made the introduction: "Sergeant Burns," he said. "Sorry I don't know your first name, but meet Ernie Downs."

Ernie sensed he was not in for a handshake and he was right. Burns did look at him, but only nodded. Ernie nodded back, giving him the biggest smile he could muster. There were times he envied some of his more flamboyant acquaintances, who would have grasped Burns in a big hug and gushed appreciation for all his work on behalf of their departed friends. The look on the sergeant's face would have been worth the effort.

"You got the file?" Burns said.

Blakemore handed it over. Two swallows of coffee and a big bite of pastry later, Burns opened the file, still chewing, and examined its contents.

"What great ideas does your inspector have for us to locate this guy ... in a city of one and a half million people?"

"He didn't say," Blakemore replied. "I guess he figured you'd have the answer. This is your territory, right?"

Ernie was enjoying the exchange. He suspected the sergeant and Paul were equally matched heavyweights in the thick skin department, but was surprised when Burns turned his attention away from Blakemore and began to question him.

"What can you tell me about Chris Reikel, Bruce Leighton's almost widow?"

Ernie's mind raced. What on earth had prompted a question like that? The homophobic overtones were obvious, but there had to be substance behind it.

He answered directly.

"An okay guy, perhaps a bit of a mother hen, certainly so far as Bruce was concerned. Obsessive-compulsive, fastidious, but warm and loving. They had a great relationship. But your 'almost widow' comment puzzles me. Were you just being facetious?"

"No. Reikel's last comment to Coswell and me when we interviewed him was that the two of them were going to get married."

"And it's legal now in this province," Ernie concluded for him. "But what has that got to do with Bruce's death?"

"He's kind of the last man standing in Vancouver of Leighton's group. Besides you, of course," Burns said. "That makes him a suspect, who, by the way, everyone seems to be ignoring. Maybe Leighton was having second thoughts about the marriage thing. That would provide two heavy motives: a jilted lover and loss of future income. We've discovered Reikel didn't have a pot to pee in, money-wise. Leighton was the total breadwinner."

Blakemore finally spoke.

"I know he was one of your friends, Ernie, but Burns has a point, and if you think like a cop, you've got to agree."

"All right," Ernie said. "I'll think like a cop." He sat back in his chair and crossed his arms. "Bruce Leighton was an athlete, but Chris is so out of shape he couldn't mug a ninety-year-old granny. So what would he have to do? Hire killers, obviously. But with what? You've already discovered he has no cache of funds anywhere, and I don't think killers-for-hire work on a contingency basis. And why would he kill all the others? No, I think you can take Chris off your list."

All three men were silent for a few moments. Ernie, particularly, was deep in thought, triggered by something Burns had said.

Blakemore finally broke the silence.

"I guess that sends us back to Coswell's assassination theory, the whole series of killings just a giant con to get us to let down our guard on the ultimate target."

"Do you really believe that?" Burns said. "It's just too far-fetched. You couldn't even sell that to a B movie producer. No, a local vendetta's what we should be looking for, in my opinion. I think all of those West End victims got themselves killed because they severely pissed off the wrong person or persons."

He was warming to his own theory.

"That's why Chris Reikel came to my mind and I wasn't kidding about the jilted lover motive. Maybe he suspected his love was sleeping around with the others and had the lot of them murdered to get revenge."

"So you think there's a chance the killing might be over?" Blakemore said, forgetting that Ernie could have been part of the sleeping around.

"Yes, I do and I don't think we need to be worrying about some assassination attempt on the Mayor of San Francisco."

Blakemore suddenly felt a kinship with the sergeant. He liked the man's no-nonsense, logical thinking, much like his own. The fact that Blakemore wanted to go back to his wife and stop this undercover stuff probably coloured his feelings.

Ernie wasn't so impressed.

"You are going to look for this Steve Carson, though, aren't you?"

Blakemore sighed.

"I don't have any choice. I'm under orders."

"Me, too," Burns confessed, equally disgruntled.

This lack of enthusiasm did not sit well with Ernie. They needed a boost.

"I've got a suggestion for you that might speed things up."

They both looked at him and Ernie almost laughed at their quizzical expressions. They looked like two bears at feeding time.

"I've noticed a column called Crimestoppers that appears once a month in *The Star* where photos of wanted individuals are printed. I understand it's been very effective."

"It has," Burns said. "So you think we should stick Carson's mug there? What excuse will we put under it. Suspected West End murderer? Mayor Schmidt would kill us if we did that."

"No," Ernie replied. "I'd put all three faces there—Carson, Deavers and Thornton—with a simple statement: 'If you have seen any of these men please call whatever number.' You don't have to say why."

"When does that Crimestoppers thing come out next?" Blakemore asked.

"It could be real soon," Ernie said. "We have an in at The Star, remember?"

"Oh, shit," Blakemore said. "Heather."

Canadian Forces Base Comox on Vancouver Island is the home of 19 Wing, a maritime patrol, search, and rescue unit. Helicopters and the big, lumbering Auroras are the usual aircraft using the runways, but Comox is also a favourite destination for fighter pilots — both Canadian and American — logging hours. Civilian air traffic flies into the base as well but somehow the staff in the air control tower keeps it all straight.

While the Governor's Lear Jet circled, Coswell looked down and saw a row of US Air Force F-15's lined up single file at the end of the main runway. They took off, one at a time, gathering speed, hovering just above the runway until they reached the end, and then powering straight up, each doing a 360° roll in the process before turning south to their base in California, a manoeuvre referred to as "the salute" to their Canadian hosts. Coswell marvelled that any human stomach could survive such an insult.

The limousine ride to Campbell River, twenty miles north, proceeded without a hitch, primarily because Coswell directed the driver to take the central highway (straight as a die) instead of the scenic but tortuous shoreline route. Twenty-five minutes later they pulled up in front of a yacht so big Coswell thought Sterne must have rented a cruise liner.

"It's two hundred and eighty feet," Sterne told him. "She just fits in this facility."

The security men got out of the limo first. The small crowd that had gathered on the dock stood behind a rope barrier set up by the yacht's crew. Coswell and Sterne got out next and walked quickly to the gangway while Kruger followed at a more leisurely pace, waving to the bystanders, his bodyguard pressed close beside him.

On board the yacht, the press were relegated to one end of the lower deck where chairs and a microphone had been set up. Sterne obviously wanted nothing to do with that scene.

"Come with me, Inspector," he said. We'll go up to the lounge and let our esteemed Governor do his thing. The press is already assembled and I'm sure you have as much love for talking to them as I do."

"Too true," Coswell said, resisting the urge to say "amen."

As they climbed the stairs to the next level, he looked over and saw Kruger and his security men make their way to the assembled reporters. A flash of red in the crowd caught his eye. Heather? Possible. She'd be brazen enough to ask for the assignment. He hoped Frayley wasn't with her; one of those two was bad enough.

Coswell had pictured the ship's lounge as a small room with portholes, fixed seating and hanging lockers containing wine bottles. The room he entered rivaled the entire lobby of the Harrington Arms, elegantly furnished with white leather chesterfields. On one wall stood a functioning soapstone fireplace.

Sterne sat down, put his feet up on a coffee table and waved Coswell to an adjacent seat. A steward appeared.

"Bring me a double Glenfiddich," Sterne said. "I've got to get that sardine can of Kruger's out of my system. My plane's a 737, which is a considerably more comfortable, but every so often I have to humour the man and fly in his Lear."

The steward turned to Coswell.

"And you, sir?"

"I'd like a glass of white wine," he said, and when the man didn't move, added, "A Meursault if you have it."

"We have it," Sterne said. "Bring the Lafon Les Charmes, '99."

Without a word, the steward hurried out of the room. Coswell rarely drank Meursaults because of their exorbitant price, but on this yacht he felt he might as well ask for the best.

When it came, one swallow let him know he was drinking something very special. It wasn't till he returned to Vancouver and looked it up that he discovered its cost: three hundred and fifty dollars a bottle.

Sterne opened the conversation.

"I'm curious, Inspector, as to how one goes about protecting someone like Governor Kruger in your city, especially at a banquet where there'll be a great many guests?"

"It's pretty cut and dried," Coswell said. "There are only so many ways harm can come to him: a knife, a bullet, a bomb or, rarely these days, a liquid or gas poison. We start by setting up a perimeter, leaving a large cushion around the man. That keeps the close range assassin at bay."

He took another sip of the wine before continuing.

"The long range sniper is a tougher problem. We routinely sweep adjacent buildings, as well as carry out a room-to-room search of the speaking venue. We also try to keep our charge away from windows or spaces that give an opportunity for a long shot. The limo that brings the Governor to the centre is bullet proof. "

Sterne was listening with great interest and encouraged Coswell to go on.

"Our greatest resource is the picture ID that everyone must wear to get within the perimeter. Our men, as well as the hotel security people, are trained to watch those very closely. Finally, you'll notice a wall of human flesh around your friend—his own security guards."

Sterne thought for a moment.

"What about the kitchen staff, the cleaners and so forth?

There's no way you could check out all their backgrounds. One of them could be a fanatic."

"We don't check them all, that's for sure, but we do get a list of the recent hirings and temporaries. Those we do investigate."

"Well, it sounds as though the Governor is in safe hands," Sterne said. "He's probably more at risk right now with those press hounds grilling him."

Coswell laughed. If they were all like Heather, that statement wasn't too far off-base.

***
***

The subject of that thought was not a happy lady. She'd just listened to a briefing that made her blood boil. The Governor's entire visit was to be a feel-good affair, no subject raised that might embarrass the great man. Reporters were warned that featuring Brian Sterne in any of their articles would be severely frowned upon and a tour of his yacht out of the question. A challenge to Heather. A plan began to form in her mind.

Kruger was handsome, she had to admit, and his pearly-toothed smile charming, but he breezed through the press conference with a barely hidden air of impatience. She made her move.

"Mr. Governor, Mr. Governor," she stammered, jumping up from her chair with her hand raised as though she had to go to the bathroom.

"Yes, ma'am," Kruger said, flashing another of his patent smiles.

"I'm, uh, Heather McTavish, from the, uh, *Star*, and I'd like to, uh, ask you ..." She stopped short, feigning panic and held her breath, which she knew would make her face red.

"Yes?" Kruger said. "What would you like to ask?"

"I forgot," she said and plopped down on her chair, casting her gaze woefully at her feet.

The conference ended and the reporters filed along the deck to the gangway. Heather sat glued to her chair. A few of her colleagues shot puzzled glances at her as they left. Kruger had disappeared up a flight of stairs to an upper deck but just before doing so, he spoke briefly to one of his security men.

The man came over to Heather.

"I'm so embarrassed," she told him. "Don't worry, I'm leaving, but I'd like to let the others get a ways ahead."

"The Governor has requested that you join him in the lounge," the man said.

She was going to try a semi-swoon, but realized she'd be wasting her efforts on this guy. His facial expression hadn't changed from the moment he came over. He might as well have been a robot. She followed him up the stairs, saving her performance for the Governor.

***
***

Kruger burst into the lounge and, seeing Sterne and Coswell with drinks in their hands, shouted to an invisible steward, "Bring me one of those scotches, my man."

Sterne laughed. "Definitely not the wine," he said, and noting Coswell's puzzled expression, explained, "The Governor hates the stuff, don't you Adam?"

"Embarrassing, especially now I'm a Californian," Kruger admitted. "Bad experience when I was a kid. Never got over it."

"Now on another subject," he said, sliding onto one of the chesterfields. "There's the cutest little reporter out there who I just had to take under my wing. Poor thing's stage struck. Froze right up during the question period. Got the look of a sweet Texas farm girl—red hair and freckles. Touched my old heart she did, so I invited her up. Don't be mad, Brian. She's really a darlin'."

Sterne rolled his eyes. Coswell almost choked.

The security guard held the lounge door open and Heather entered.

"Ms. McTavish," he announced.

She stood for a moment, gazing around the room, her mouth appropriately agape. Coswell was impressed with the performance: little innocent peasant girl set before the king. Kruger jumped up and went over to her.

"Mr. Governor, your honour," she said. "I don't know what to say, but thank you, thank you. I was so embarrassed out there and I really wanted to ask you some questions."

She was talking so fast, she almost ran out of breath.

"The *Star* paid for me to come here and I so wanted to do a good job. I'm a junior reporter and I haven't had much experience with important people like you and Mr. Sterne...."

"Now don't you worry little lady," Kruger said, placing his arm over her shoulders. "You can just relax. Now, I want you to meet Brian Sterne and this here's Inspector Coswell of your own RCMP."

Heather pushed forward and extended her hand to Sterne, who barely touched it, looking a little stunned by the whole performance. Coswell couldn't wait for his turn.

"Nice to see you again, Heather," he said, grasping her hand in a firm grip.

Her eyes flashed momentarily in a silent plea for him go along with her charade. He debated with himself. He couldn't let her get away with it, but a complete squelch would cost him in the long run.

"Heather's just being modest," he said. "For a rookie reporter she's done pretty well in Vancouver. She's got a great boss: Harold Frayley. Perhaps you've heard of him."

Kruger shook his head.

"I have," Sterne said. "He's been following the recent gay murders in your city. Those cases have even hit the Seattle dailies. Now that I think about it, I believe I saw your name on some of those articles, Ms. McTavish."

"Mr. Frayley is so generous that way," Heather said.

Sterne was obviously not falling for Heather's tactics but Kruger seemed oblivious.

"Well you just go ahead and ask me your questions," he said. "But first let me get get you a drink. What's your poison?"

"I rarely drink alcohol," Heather replied. "But perhaps a bit of white wine if it's not too much trouble."

"Nothing's too much trouble on this ship, eh Brian?"

The steward appeared immediately.

"The Meursault would be a good choice," Coswell offered, draining his glass. The steward left and returned in seconds with two fresh glasses of the wine, removing Coswell's empty in the process.

Heather took a sip. Her eyes widened and then she took a more substantial mouthful.

'Rarely drinks alcohol' my ass, Coswell said to himself.

He watched Sterne's face—eyes narrowed, a trace of a frown on his forehead as Heather began her interview.

"It was so good of you to invite reporters over when you're on vacation," Heather said to Kruger. "I wish our leaders were more generous that way ... and the police. It's not easy putting out a daily column that catches our readers' interest."

Coswell winced at the backhand comment but had his eyes on Sterne, whose body language at the moment was not friendly. She seemed to sense that, and directed all of her attention to Kruger.

"Mr. Frayley told me that you were also taking time to come over to Vancouver and attend the closing ceremonies of the Pacific Urban Renewal Conference. I think that's very big of you. Mayor Gryndon's going to be there, of course, but that's on an official basis. Part of his job, really."

The butter was going on so thick that Coswell had to suppress the urge to cough.

"Me and Josh Gryndon ain't exactly buddies," Kruger said. "But we stand together when it comes to what's good for California. 'Politics make for strange bedfellows' is an old saw that would apply here, wouldn't you say?"

"Bedfellows," he repeated, and then roared with laughter. Wiping tears from his eyes, he said, "Now don't go quoting that, little lady, or I'll be thrown out of my gun club."

The humour was lost on Sterne. He was staring intently at Heather.

"My friend, Adam, is generous with his remarks, at times to a fault," he said. "I didn't catch the nature of the article you were sent over here to write. Harold Frayley's a crime reporter. Why would his department be interested in an interview with the Governor of California?"

Heather didn't skip a beat.

"Actually I'm just filling in for our paper's celebrity columnist; she couldn't come. But now that I'm here, I would like to ask the Governor's opinion on a few crime-related matters. I know he's a champion of 'the legal system our fathers knew,' a direct quote, I believe."

"You bet that's a quote," Kruger said. "And I'm damn proud

of it. Move the moral fibre of the USA back to what it was fifty years ago. Presto, tonne of today's problems, fixed."

"That would be about the time bus segregation became illegal in the United States," Heather commented.

"Well, around about then," the Governor said. "But definitely before crazy ideas like legalizing pot-smoking, shooting-up in public places, plea-bargaining killers from the gas chamber, and most ridiculous — two homos getting married in a church."

"Oooh," Heather cooed. "You're not going to like Mayor Schmidt. We don't have a gas chamber but the mayor's pro all the others."

"Who the hell is Mayor Schmidt?"

"He's the Mayor of Vancouver, Adam," Sterne said, "your host at the conference."

"Oh, shit. I'll be sitting between a couple of queers. Got to get that changed."

"Very funny, Adam," Sterne said, then turning to Heather, "The Governor is a terrible joker, but sometimes his comments are taken out of context. I hope you won't do that. This is really an off-camera conversation, don't you agree?"

Heather didn't miss the tone.

"Of course," she replied. "I consider it a privilege to have the opportunity to even be here. Mayor Schmidt isn't gay, by the way. He has a wife and two children."

Kruger was finally sensing something amiss.

"Enough of this interviewing," he said. "Let's get you some up-close and personal stuff. We're going fishing and you, my little darlin', are coming along."

20

Forensic investigation is often a painfully slow process, gathering tiny bits of information and piecing them together. The field draws the most compulsive of scientific minds, toiling in their laboratories at a deliberate pace, oblivious to the impatience of those awaiting results.

Zachary Benson, however, had worked as a country coroner and sympathized with the difficult task the police faced in murder cases. He responded promptly whenever he could and, unlike most of his colleagues, enjoyed rubbing shoulders with the officers as the cases progressed.

Returning to his search for DNA samples on the carpet from the apartment murders, he finally hit pay dirt; tiny fragments of skin carefully teased from the nylon fibres contained DNA that belonged to neither victim. A killer had left a trace.

All he had to do now was match it to its owner. He put a call in to Blakemore.

"Success at long last," he said, "I found a second DNA in that rug sample. Now I *really* want those suspect samples or a lot of hard work goes down the drain."

"That's fantastic, Zachary," Blakemore said. "But there's nothing I can do about those until Coswell gets back. I hope the Washington State cops aren't jerking us around."

"Why would they do that?"

"Maybe they're embarrassed by a bunch of rednecks taking over law enforcement in their jurisdiction and snuffing out a couple of important leads in a murder investigation.

They probably want the whole thing to be written off as a couple of druggies bumped off, bad guys getting what they deserved. Who cares?"

"That's stupid," Zachary said. "I'd think cooperation between neighbouring law enforcement agencies would be a given."

"Ah, the view from the ivory tower."

"Screw you."

Blakemore laughed. "That's certainly not ivory tower language, but okay, I'll try to get through to Coswell. He'll get the ball rolling for sure. And ..."

"And what?"

"And thanks, by the way. You've done great work."

"No problem," Zachary said, slightly mollified.

Halfway through dialing Coswell's number, it suddenly occurred to Blakemore that maybe the DNA samples had been sent and were sitting on Coswell's desk at the Main Precinct. He hung up and punched in Burns' phone number. The sergeant was not enthusiastic.

"I'm not going to open his mail. I've got no authority to do that."

"Oh, for Christ's sake, Burns," Blakemore said. "Take some initiative. Go look for it."

There was a pause while the sergeant went into Coswell's office and picked up the extension.

"The only thing I see here is a parcel from the San Francisco Hall of Justice."

"That's it," Blakemore said. "The Washington State people obviously sent the stuff there instead of directly to us. They probably think the only forensic equipment we've got up here are hand-held magnifying glasses. Now, you don't have to open it; just take it over to Zach Benson at the General."

"You giving orders now?"

"Oh, don't be like that, for God's sake. Coswell will be pissed off at us both if we don't facilitate that analysis. Besides, aren't you a little curious to know if our border runners really were the West End killers?"

"Okay, okay," Burns said. "I've got to go out anyway and check on the search for your third man, Carson, which, by the way, is using up a lot of good police time."

Satisfied that he'd gotten that dig in, he added, "I did manage to get in touch with Heather McTavish just before she left for Vancouver Island. She's going to push her boss Frayley to have a special edition of Crimestoppers put out with our boys' pictures in it. Hopefully that'll help things along."

"It has to," Blakemore said. "The way we're going now, it will take us forever to find them."

21

Coswell made one last desperate attempt to get his security meeting over with as close to dry land as possible. The moored yacht was acceptable, remaining rock-still in its enormity, even in the wakes of passing vessels. Bobbing about in a small fishing boat would be a different matter.

"Oh, live a little, Inspector," Kruger said. "Have some fun. Besides, my chief of security and his number one man are coming with us. Your meeting can wait till we're done fishing. Let Vancouver look after itself for a day. Besides, it's Sunday. Nobody's supposed to be working."

The fishing boat turned out to be a forty-foot launch ingeniously tucked into a compartment just above waterline.

Passengers got into it from the lower deck and when all were aboard, a series of hydraulic arms swung the craft out and then gently lowered it to the water.

Two men wearing ship's crew uniforms manned the boat. Kruger's security men sat up front with the driver, Heather and Coswell were seated in the middle, and Sterne and Kruger were ensconced in swivel chairs at the stern.

Mercifully, the ride out to the fishing grounds didn't bother Coswell. The powerful boat raced out into the strait on a steady plane. He glanced over at Heather, or what he could see of her, dwarfed in a life jacket, her eyes barely peeking over the top.

The two crewmen were enjoying their jobs. They wore big smiles and attempted to make conversation above the noise of the motor. In contrast, the security men sat rigid as a pair of sphinxes. Coswell couldn't help but wonder if they were members of the Knights of the True South, and if so, how similar fundamentalists were in appearance — stern, unyielding. Definitely not fun people.

The boat slowed down. The deckhand peered at what looked like a computer screen, but turned out to be an electronic fish finder. So much for the mystique of the sport, Coswell mused.

Kruger and Sterne let their lines out; the boat slowed to trolling speed. Within minutes both men got a strike. The driver kept the boat perfectly aligned to avoid tangling the lines while his partner leaned over the side, ready with a huge scoop-net.

Kruger pulled his catch in first, a twenty pound spring salmon. Sterne's fish had more fight in it and ten minutes elapsed before the deckhand could manoeuvre the net under it. Another salmon, slightly larger than Kruger's.

With the action over for the time being, Coswell became aware of the swells that were lifting the boat and then sliding off, taking his stomach with them. He was going to be ill, no doubt about it.

"Hey there, Inspector," Kruger said. "Come on over here and have a go. They're biting for damn sure. Brian, let the little lady take your seat."

"They don't have fishing licenses," Sterne said.

"Oh, bugger the licenses. They're not really fishing; they're just holding our rods while we take a rest."

Refusing wasn't an option.

They switched places. Coswell found himself staring over the back of the boat, holding the biggest fishing rod he'd ever seen. He'd done some spin-casting for trout as a boy but found the big reel on Kruger's rod clumsy. Heather, on the other hand, settled into her chair, let the line out and adjusted the tension on the reel with surprising dexterity. He copied her.

Having his mind occupied with the fishing rod stalled the wave of motion sickness, but when the lines were set and the trolling speed resumed, the swells began to set his stomach in motion again. He was thankful in a way that he was at the stern of the boat. Barfing over the back would be a lot less embarrassing than heaving over the side, where his vomit might splatter unfortunates downwind from him.

His reel screamed.

In a flash, the nausea disappeared.

"Good God, man!" Kruger shouted. "You've caught a whale. Keep reeling. Don't give him any slack."

Coswell wound furiously but the fish continued to run.

"Turn up the drag," Kruger said. "Or the bugger will strip off your line."

He took his hand off the reel handle and cranked up the drag wheel, but too much. The rod almost jerked out of his hand, but he held on. The fish broke the water. He gasped.

It was huge!

Everything went out of his mind: his motion sickness, the West End murders, the security assignment and even his food fantasies. There was nothing but him and that giant fish. Thirty minutes went by as though they were seconds. The fish made run after run but gradually his frantic reeling and the constant drag on the line brought it to the boat.

When he saw its back just a few feet away, he was so stunned he released his death grip on the rod, but the deckhand was quick. He scooped under the creature just as it was about to swim away.

The fish was so heavy, Kruger had to reach down and help pull it aboard. The deckhand slammed a billy down on its head and, when the spasms stopped, slid the creature out of the net.

"Jesus," Kruger said. "That's a fifty-pounder if it's an ounce. Congratulations. Great job bringing it in my man, great job."

"Horseshit luck," Heather grumbled. But the bite continued and in a few minutes her line was hit. The fish wasn't as large as the others, but she played it for all it was worth. By the time it came alongside, the salmon was totally exhausted and scooping it up was no problem.

"Just your size," Kruger said. "A nice firm ten-pounder."

Damn. She wanted to release the thing and try for a bigger one. The small size comment stung. She'd trolled for salmon many times when she lived on the West Coast and knew what she was doing. It burned her to think Coswell had out-fished her, the fluky bastard.

Kruger's respect for local fishing laws returned; since four salmon were the daily limit, there wasn't any point staying out longer. Coswell was delighted. He'd caught the fish of a lifetime and been out on the ocean without barfing. It was his day.

His good mood carried over to the security meeting on board the yacht. He left Heather to continue probing Kruger and Sterne in the lounge, while in a smaller salon he met with the two security agents who'd gone out in the fishing boat with them.

He needed to be in a good mood. Ferring and Ales were the agents' names and Ales was in charge. Coswell picked up on the man's attitude immediately: an arrogant son-of-a-bitch much like the CIA agent, Whitfield.

Both men scrutinized Coswell's portfolio, which itemized Kruger's every minute in the city from the helipad to the convention centre and then to the airport. Routes, entrances, exits, seating arrangements at dinner, positions of security men, all carefully drawn out.

If Coswell thought he was going to be complimented for his plan, he was wrong. Ales merely grunted.

"You can pencil in Ferring and me," he said, "on either side of the Governor at all times, including at the dinner."

"You mean right at the table?" Coswell said. "That would look weird."

"I don't care what it looks like. That's where we'll be."

"Seated?"

Ales gave him a disgusted look. "We never sit," he said.

Coswell shrugged his shoulders. He knew there was no use arguing; the guy had the mindset of a mule. He handed him the portfolio.

"You can keep this. I've got copies back in Vancouver."

"Under lock and key, I hope."

"Of course," Coswell lied.

Ferring, the other man, never said a word during the entire briefing. If anything, he looked even more sullen than Ales. Couple of assholes, Coswell said to himself. He hoped they wouldn't cause trouble for his own staff.

The meeting over, Coswell returned to the lounge. As he made his way along the outer deck, he heard the unwelcome sound of a helicopter warming up. Looking towards the stern where the Governor had held his press conference, he saw the infernal machine. His worst fears were met when he entered the lounge.

"You're going to have a beautiful flight back to Vancouver," Kruger told him. "Great scenery and a lovely lady at your side."

A helicopter ride with Heather McTavish ... wonderful.

22

Sergeant Burns' hours of tedium came to an abrupt halt with two phone calls, one right after the other. The first was from Zachary Benson at the Vancouver General Forensic Unit.

"That DNA info you just brought over to me?"

"Yeah?"

"Ran it up against the skin cells I got off the apartment victim's rug."

"And?"

"I hate to tell you this, but it doesn't match either of your suspects, Deavers or Thornton."

Burns barely heard the rest of Zachary's message.

"Blakemore's cellphone's off-line. I figured you'd be just as good anyway. You are all working together, aren't you?"

"Absolutely," Burns said, recovering from his surprise. "I'll pass this information on right away. And thanks, by the way, for doing that analysis so quickly."

He hung up and couldn't repress a feeling of triumph. Coswell's assassination fantasy had just been dealt a big blow. He was looking forward to the afternoon meeting.

The good feeling, however, was tempered by the second call. One of the city police constables in the West End was patched through.

"Got a good citizen ID on that Steve Carson person you want," the officer said. "A guy who lives in the same apartment building recognized him and the other two from the pictures in the morning *Star*."

Burns almost yawned. Hooray, he thought, we're going to catch another druggie.

"Okay," he said. "But don't move in. The inspector just wants him watched. Draw straws and let the loser do the surveillance. The rest of you go back to doing real police work."

He could hardly wait to speak to Coswell. Shadowing drug suspects was the RCMP Narcotics Squad's responsibility, not city police. He smiled to think that maybe Blakemore would get the job. He didn't seem to have anything else meaningful to do.

★★★
★★★

But Burns resolve faded when Coswell arrived at the Main Street office. The inspector looked awful, like he had a bad case of the flu.

"I don't know why every goddamned helicopter pilot thinks his passengers are all interested in the bloody scenery and has to twist the cursed machine around to give everyone a special view."

"Bit hard on the old stomach, was it?" Burns said, enjoying the fact that the mighty Coswell actually had a human frailty.

"You're damn right it was, and that friggin' red-headed vixen encouraged the bugger to do a fly-past over the whole West End, including Stanley Park. I think she knew perfectly well I was uncomfortable."

"Must have been a beautiful view, though."

Coswell glared at him and he regretted the comment. Blakemore's slightly late arrival saved him.

"Where the hell have you been?" Coswell said, seizing on an outlet for his ill humour.

Blakemore snapped back, "Trying to get through rush hour traffic in that dinky Hydro pisspot."

Coswell settled down and listened to both officers' reports. Blakemore essentially had nothing of note, but Burns' news about Zachary's DNA discovery was another matter.

"Great work," Coswell said. "Now we're moving."

Burns was stunned. Coswell should have been deeply disappointed, not elated.

"Steve Carson, the third man, that's who held the apartment victim down. I wondered when he'd come into the picture. He's as much a killer as the other two. In fact he's probably the leader and went to the apartment because it was a trickier job than the park killings."

Blakemore and Burns struggled to grasp this latest brainwave.

"Now," Coswell said, directing his question to Burns, "How have you set up the surveillance?"

Burns stuttered, "Uh, I have a constable sitting outside the apartment block."

"A constable!" Coswell shouted, "And I suppose he's in a cruiser with his lights flashing. Where's your brain, for Christ's sake? Get two detectives down there that know how to tail somebody and make sure they look as un-coplike as possible."

Blakemore felt a twinge of sympathy for Burns, but he'd learned the hard way that straying too far from Coswell's line of thinking was a mistake. The time had come, however, to clarify his own position.

"And what's my job now?" he asked, hoping he'd be given something more exciting to do than pretend he was a meter reader.

"You're going to find out if Carson's still there," Coswell said. "I want you to think up some reason the power needs to be checked in that penthouse. Get the manager to let you in. Now, both of you get going. We've got exactly five days till Gryndon and Kruger roll into town for the banquet."

Blakemore followed Burns out to the squad room. The sergeant was seething.

"He wants to know what's in my brain, but I tell you, someone should have a look into his. He's jumped to a conclusion about the third man being a killer, and this assassination thing's become a damn obsession with him."

Blakemore nodded.

"I agree, but Coswell didn't make inspector by being a fool. He must know something we don't."

"Possibly," Burns said. "But I still think he's barking up the wrong tree. I'll get going on that Steve Carson surveillance but I'm not giving up on finding the real perp in these murders. The widow Reikel is still a person of interest in my books. Maybe assassins do work on a contingency basis these days."

***
***

From his office, Coswell watched the two men as they talked. He didn't need to hear them; their facial expressions relayed their doubts.

He wasn't keeping anything from them. He realized his theory was based on conjecture but in the past he'd rarely been wrong when he followed a hunch this strong. Steve Carson, the third man, was vital, not only to solving the murders, but in aborting an attempt on the San Francisco mayor's life; he was sure of it.

***
***

He tried to rationalize away his worry. The exterminations had served their purpose: ridding the world of a few contemptibles and sending the investigators on a false trail. The problem of Deavers and Thornton being ID'd was nicely solved at the border and even though the police were on to Carson, the man was still in place, his cover arranged. But where was he? Why hadn't he checked in?

And then he began to relax. Carson was a pawn. There were more powerful pieces standing by ready to be moved when needed. The mission would succeed; nothing could stop it, not even the clever Inspector Coswell. God was in command and God's will would be done.

He sipped the Macallan and chuckled at the memory of the doleful Scot who had handed over the six bottles as though he'd sold the family farm.

He leaned back in his chair and let the mellowness take over. His mind drifted.

"*Vesti la giubba* ..." The familiar strains brought him back.

He reached for the remote and turned up the sound. Domingo's voice rolled over him. He listened in ecstasy to the heart-rending aria.

"Gospel!" his father had bellowed. "Give me some gospel or some wholesome country. None of that wop-wailing crap."

He could smile now, but he remembered the embarrassment when, as a young freshman, he had blurted out his discovery—San Francisco Opera. It was silly to continue hiding his love for this wonderful music, but he did, playing it only when he was alone. His father was long dead, but his voice lingered on, as did the derision from his down-home friends. But somehow the listening pleasure was heightened by treating it as a forbidden fruit, as forbidden as the others in his private world.

***
***

Chris Reikel was in tears again. He'd told himself not to open the photo albums, but he couldn't help himself. Bruce Leighton smiled out at him, page after page of happy memories. "You have more pictures of me than my mother has, Chris darling," he'd said, and laughed. "You're preparing for the day when we sit side by side in our wheelchairs and need the photos to remind us of what we were."

Growing old together. That reassurance had enveloped Chris like a warm blanket and he so needed it. He could never completely trust the unbelievable luck that someone of Bruce Leighton's charm and genius had chosen a nobody like him for a mate.

His reverie was broken by an obnoxious buzz from the intercom.

The squeaky voice of Jake, the concierge, came over. "The police are here again to see you. Shall I send him up?"

Chris' annoyance changed to curiosity. Why did the police need to talk to him again? He had nothing more to tell them, but perhaps they were bringing him news. Maybe they'd caught Bruce's killer.

He peered through the peephole when he heard the knock, mindful of the warning he'd been given about unexpected visitors. Frank and Roger lost their lives opening their door to the wrong people.

The man certainly looked like a policeman: clean-shaven, neutral, slightly bored, a Vancouver Police baseball cap on his head. A loss of style, in Chris' opinion, from the traditional. His badge shone from the wallet he'd flipped open and held in front of the peephole. Chris released the latch and let him in.

In a moment, he knew he'd made a mistake.

Why was there only one man? Police usually worked in pairs. The uniform was right, dark blue, and he did have a pistol strapped to his belt, but one item was missing: a bullet-proof vest. All uniformed officers wore those now, even the traffic cops.

Chris lunged for the door, too late. The man grabbed the back of his shirt and pulled him away, reaching at the same time for the short night-stick hanging from his belt. Chris spun around and managed to dodge the first blow. He screamed, not in fright now but in rage. This was Bruce's killer. He attacked, clawing at the man's face, but his efforts were in vain. The night-stick landed with a sickening crunch on his temple, shattering the bone and bursting an artery in his brain. He fell lifeless at his assailant's feet, his pupils dilating in death.

The killer worked quickly. He glanced in a hall mirror to see if his victim had drawn blood with his pathetic attack. Seeing none, he pulled on plastic gloves and proceeded with his task.

***
***

A look at the apartment block's intercom board reminded Blakemore how much the West End had changed since he lived there. In years past there would have been a name beside each apartment number, but no more. Only the manager's suite was listed. He pushed the button and when a man's voice answered, went into his act.

"Pacific Hydro here. I've been sent to check on the electrical drain from one of your units."

"The meters are in the garage," the voice said. "And you guys have your own keys."

"It's not that simple," Blakemore said. "I need to see the apartment."

There was a pause, but momentarily the man appeared at the front door and let him in.

Blakemore glanced around the lobby. The place was upscale, with elegant chairs on the carpet and expensive artwork on the walls. The manager, too, wasn't the usual grumpy, slightly seedy individual one imagined doing such a job. This man was young, clean-cut, and wore Levi's jeans and an open-necked, designer shirt. A single gold ring dangled from his right ear.

"It's those guys in the penthouse, isn't it? A grow-op, right?"

Blakemore was delighted. Obviously he didn't need to dream up anything to get into the apartment; the young manager was doing it for him.

"Our meter has recorded an unusual power demand from your penthouse," he said. "It could be just a system malfunction."

"I'll bet. I was suspicious of those three the minute they moved in. One month's rent up front—in cash no less—and two of them rode around on bicycles. I've been going to check the apartment, but quite frankly they frighten me. They're three cold fish, I can tell you."

He excused himself for a moment to check whether or not the car driven by one of the men was in the garage. He returned promptly and declared that all was clear.

"The other two keep their bikes in the apartment, would you believe?" he said. "But I haven't seen them around for a few days."

They proceeded to the elevator and were whisked non-stop to the penthouse.

A steel door with the ubiquitous security keypad marked the entry to the apartment. The manager pushed the door buzzer, waited a minute, and when no one answered, punched in a series of numbers that released the lock.

"Master code," he said. "It overrides the renter's number but does record my entry. I'll leave a note saying why I came in."

Blakemore's heart began to beat faster as the door swung open, his hand on the Beretta hidden in his workshirt, ready to jerk the young man out of the way if trouble loomed. But his worry was unnecessary; there was no one home.

"Pigs!" the manager said, looking over the mess, empty beer cans, pizza cartons, magazines scattered about. He sniffed the air. "But they didn't smoke, thank God. I'll have to pay for cleaning but at least I won't have to fumigate the place."

Agitated, he hurriedly inspected each room and lastly, the balcony.

"Well, that's a relief," he said. "No grow-op. I wonder why they refused the maid service. For the few extra dollars it would have cost them, they could have lived in some semblance of order."

His relief was short-lived when it suddenly occurred to him that the mess lacked one sure sign of male sloppiness: clothes strewn about.

A quick check of the bedroom closets and bathroom cabinets confirmed his suspicion; the renters had pulled out.

"Lovely," he said. "Now what do I do? The rent's paid up till the end of the month so I can't just assume they won't be back. You'd think they would have told me something, but who knows these days."

Blakemore didn't want any of that room touched. A forensic crew needed to go over it with a fine-tooth comb. While the manager was doing his inspection, Blakemore opened the breaker panel in the hallway (having been told its location by the hydro office) and when the manager returned, he pretended to be examining it.

"No problem here," he said, "but I have a suggestion. If I shut the power off in the basement, they'll have to get hold of you to get it turned back on. That way you'd know when and if they return. Leave them a note to that effect. Blame Hydro for the inconvenience. Shutting the power off would save you some money, too ... help pay for the cleaning later."

The manager readily agreed, scribbled a note, and taped it to the door when they left.

Confident that the young man would leave the apartment untouched now that it was supposedly to be without power, Blakemore hurried out to his vehicle, glancing around to see if he could spot the surveillance team Burns had set up. A cable TV service truck was parked across the street with no one in the cab, but perhaps the team was in the back, broiling in the heat.

He phoned Coswell.

"I didn't think Carson would hang around," the inspector said when Blakemore gave him the news. "If he saw his puss in the morning paper, he'd have had a big incentive to split. Actually, I suspect he moved out even earlier. If the powers that be picked him to set up the other two, he must have been the brains of the trio and knew it was too risky to stay there."

"If you were so sure of that, why did you give Burns such a bad time about the surveillance?" Blakemore asked.

"I've detected a slight lack of enthusiasm in our Sergeant Burns and I need him to suck it up a bit. I think that little chastisement was worthwhile, wouldn't you say? When you make sergeant yourself, you'll find out that handling your own men can be tougher than solving cases. Little techniques like that help."

Blakemore didn't argue, but his last conversation with Burns made him doubt the inspector's wisdom, at least in the sergeant's case.

"Anyway," Coswell continued. "You've done a good job. I'll get a forensics crew over there right away. Might as well use the city bunch. No use overworking our men if we don't have to."

As if the city crew had nothing to do, Blakemore mused. The inspector would not be remembered with fondness in the Main Street police station.

"Now, I want you to get back to Ernie. See if he's dug anything up. Also, don't forget he could still be a target with

Carson running around. Make sure he's aware of that. In fact, I want you to stick to him for the next few days."

Blakemore frowned. From his point of view, a one-night visit with his wife seemed a better suggestion, but he stopped short of making it. Instead, he slammed the little Suzuki into gear and headed off to Ernie's gallery. It was just about closing time and a cold beer with his former partner would ease some of his frustration.

✳✳✳
✳✳✳

Heather tramped into the *Star* office. Fraley was at his desk.

"How did it go, Babe?"

"I enjoyed the flight," she said, "the booze and the entertainment, but I can tell you, celeb reporting is a big bore — too restrictive."

"Entertainment?"

"Yeah. Tippling with the gov and his billionaire pal, and would you believe? Salmon fishing with Coswell. The lucky bugger actually caught a bigger fish than I did. I got back at him, though. I think he suffers from motion sickness so I had the helicopter guy do lots of dipsy-doodles around the harbour. The good inspector was looking a might green. Too bad he didn't barf, but oh, it was real close."

"You're a mean broad," Frayley said. "Did you get some good stuff for Mary's column?"

"Enough for her. She likes bubbly things so I gave her details of Sterne's yacht and the fishing expedition with him and Kruger. That's a lot more than the rest of the press crowd got. They had to settle for a lecture, a few toss-offs from the Governor and numb bums from sitting on hard deck chairs at the back end of the boat."

"You're not writing the column?" Frayley said.

"No and I don't care. I'd probably sneak in some innu-endos about Kruger's right-wing attitude that our revered Chief Editor would throw out anyway. Let Mary do her thing. She's a nice lady."

"'Nice' is not you," Frayley remarked. "But I do have some news you can get your teeth into."

He paused, tantalizing.

"Well, let's have it then, for Christ's sake," Heather said, "and I wish you wouldn't do that. I hate to beg."

He laughed. Crime reporting had become a lot more fun since his fiery partner joined the Star.

"I got those pictures inserted into a special edition of Crimestoppers for you and guess what?"

"There you go again. What?"

"There's a stakeout set up at an apartment block in the West End."

"A stakeout? What for? Those cyclist guys are dead. I thought it was just a plea for information on them. What didn't Burns tell me?"

"There were three men in the group."

Heather's eyes widened.

"Burns didn't say a word to me about a third man," she said. "Was it the driver who took them to the border?"

"Yeah, but my informant tells me the scuttlebutt is the third man is more than just a driver."

"Wow!" Heather said. "Another killer. We could be look-ing at extra innings is what you're telling me. That's great. How are we going to handle this?"

"Like we did before. I'll ride Coswell and Burns. You work Blakemore and his pal, Ernie Downs. We're going to get this story, Babe, and it's going to be a big one. I smell an-other Webster award. We'll share, of course."

"Of course," Heather said, wondering how big her share would be.

★★★
★★★

Burns, already in a bad mood from Coswell's scolding, did not take kindly to the reception he received when he approached the concierge at Bruce Leighton's apartment building.

"What is this, a St. Patrick's Day parade?" the man said. "I should just leave all the doors open so you can walk in and out of poor Mr. Leighton's apartment, bothering Mr. Reikel. Really! You people have no mercy."

"What are you bitching about?" Burns said. "Two visits don't rate as an imposition and besides, Chris Reikel wasn't exactly calm and collected when we came last week, so we went easy on him. We need a more detailed report."

"Why didn't the officer this morning get all that?"

Burns froze for a second and then barked to one of his constables.

"Have all exits sealed off — *now*."

The concierge stepped back, startled.

"And you," Burns said, "are going to get us into that apartment as fast as your lily white legs can carry you."

The man stabbed frantically at the Leighton apartment intercom button, calling out Reikel's name as Burns' big fist grabbed him by the collar.

"I said move it. You're not going to get an answer on that thing."

The man whimpered: "Shouldn't you have a warrant or something?"

The expression on the sergeant's face was all the answer he needed.

"What do you think?" Burns said as he and Coswell surveyed the Reikel crime scene. The sergeant was feeling decidedly more contrite now with his suspect lying in a crumpled heap at his feet.

"Too obvious," Coswell replied. "There's way more disruption here than you'd expect from a tussle that looks as though it never got out of the foyer. Clothes pulled from drawers, things moved around in the kitchen, pictures tilted … what grab-and-run thief does something like that? Especially after he's just killed somebody."

"Yeah. Thieves kill by accident usually, even the druggies. They might go for the wallet and small valuables, but getting the hell away would be a big priority after a thing like this, I agree."

"I'm going to turn your question back on you," Coswell said. "What's your thinking right now?"

"Not a helluva lot, I'm afraid. I showed Steve Carson's picture to the concierge—waste of time. Said the guy looked like a cop in uniform with a gun. His face didn't even register."

"Well, cheer up," Coswell said. "This time we have a fresh body that the fishes haven't been nibbling on and our forensic team is going to have first crack at it. Look at the scuff marks on the floor. I think our Chris fought back. Mueller and his team will have a field day."

"You think it was Carson, don't you?"

"Yes. I do indeed, and you know what?"

Burns shrugged his shoulders.

"I'm getting very, very worried."

Blakemore waited in the back room while Ernie dealt with a couple of gallery patrons. He amused himself by leafing through some of the art magazines, hoping to find a luscious nude to ogle. He really had to get back to his wife soon.

Ernie eventually came in and opened up the bar.

"You should have helped yourself," he said.

"I don't like to drink alone. In fact I don't like to do a lot of anything alone."

"Missing Barbara, eh?" Ernie said, pouring Blakemore an ice cold beer and himself a glass of white wine.

"Here's to that," Blakemore said, lifting his glass.

They were silent for a moment, enjoying the cold drinks. Ernie spoke first.

"Anything new at your end?"

"A local ID'd the third man, Steve Carson," Blakemore said. "Your Crimestoppers suggestion did it. The three of them were renting a penthouse in the West End but Carson's flown the coop. Coswell wants you to be aware of that. You could still be a target."

Ernie mulled that over for a moment.

"You know," he said. "I think I've dug up a possible motive for all these killings, but the attempt on my life, if it truly was one, doesn't fit."

"A motive? Jeez, let's hear it. I hope it's better than Coswell's assassination thing. Killing five men as a diversion so someone can do in the Mayor of San Francisco is just too weird."

"I think the original hate motive is correct. The only thing that hasn't been explained is why those specific men were targeted."

"I'm all ears. Why?"

"All the victims had taken out marriage licenses."

Blakemore exhaled in surprise.

"Yessirree," he said. "That would do it all right. Hate crowd tinder, for sure. How did you find out, Ernie?"

"Sources. Sometimes the gossip mongers can be useful."

Blakemore recalled old stuff-his-face Bernie and his malicious partner, Tony, the two gays he'd met at Leighton's wake — Ernie's sources, no doubt.

"There's one big question, however," Ernie said. "Is Steve Carson going to carry on killing now that his two partners are gone?"

"Probably not. I think the three of them just came up here to stock up on cocaine and as a diversion decided to teach us Canadian liberal perverts a lesson by bumping off a few gays. How they found out about the marriage angle, I don't know. Maybe they came across a like-minded informant in the Registry office."

"A good suggestion, Paul. Perhaps you could get Burns or Coswell to look into that."

"Better Burns," Blakemore said. "Coswell's tuned in to another wavelength. He thinks Carson deliberately set Deavers and Thornton up to be shot by the border people. But why not consider he was just dropping them off? After all, he hadn't been ID'd at that point and he was free to return to Vancouver, maybe to score more cocaine."

He leaned over and topped up his beer.

"You know," he continued. "The more I think about this, the more logical your hate theory gets. When I look back, that bike messenger type came into the Wheatsheaf when you and I first met there. Seeing you give me a big hug and blow me a kiss could have disgusted him enough to add you to the list, regardless of our marriage status."

Their speculations ended abruptly when someone entered the gallery, triggering a loud *beep*. Ernie glanced up at a small monitor. Blakemore hadn't noticed the device before, but despite the small screen, he recognized the visitor instantly: Heather the Horrible.

"Well, isn't this my lucky day," she said, when Ernie called her into the studio. "Two for the price of one again."

Blakemore rolled his eyes.

"Oh, goody, here's our second bonus from the Crimestoppers ad."

She gave him a disdainful look.

"Please don't thank me," she said, "even though I *was* the main facilitator. Worked too, didn't it? Now, how about answering a few questions? I think you owe me."

Blakemore resumed drinking his beer.

"I gather the third man you and Burns cleverly slipped into Crimestoppers without telling me wasn't home when you went looking for him. But surely to God with his picture in the *Star*, and presumably in every city cop's hands, you should be able to pick him up pretty damn quick."

"How did you know I went looking for him?" Blakemore asked.

Heather cursed herself. Blakemore caught her slip. Frayley's informant, the coroner's driver, gave her that information after he'd chatted up the city constables.

"Sources," she replied, ignoring the corporal's accusing glare. "Anyway, what are you going to do now with this Carson guy running loose? Could there be more killings?"

Blakemore replied so quickly that Heather was sure it was a tacit signal to Ernie — *stay out of the conversation.*

"Carson will probably run back across the border now that his cover's broken. You're right that it's just a matter of time till we pick him up and I'm sure he knows that. Doing a killing on his own would be stupid at this point. I don't think we'll see any more."

Heather remained silent for a moment. Blakemore's explanation sounded a bit too glib. While she was thinking up another question, her cellphone rang. It was Frayley.

"I'm right outside Bruce Leighton's apartment. His mate Chris Reikel's just been beaten to death. The assumption is that it was a robbery gone bad, but Coswell's arrived on the scene and I think it's more than that."

There was a pause. Heather could hear a commotion in the background.

"Got to go, Babe," Frayley said. "The coroner's just come out with the body. I'll see where they take it and if it ends up at Vancouver General, then Reikel's murder isn't a simple mugging; it's tied into the West End killings."

And then, as though he'd just thought of it, he added:

"Your man Benson will likely be in on the autopsy. Maybe you could get him to share his findings with you ... unofficially, of course."

Heather felt a twinge of guilt. She really shouldn't pump Zachary, but a resource was a resource. She'd be discrete, of course. At the moment, though, this news would definitely liven up the conversation with Ernie and Blakemore. She watched their reactions when she related Frayley's phone call.

Ernie was speechless, Blakemore vocal. "Holy shit," he said. "The list goes on."

But, momentarily, his policeman's logic clicked in.

"How do they know it wasn't just a botched robbery?

Coswell could have been called simply because Reikel's part of his West End investigation."

Heather glanced over at Ernie. He was paying no attention to their conversation.

"Poor Chris," he said. "Poor little Chris."

Realizing Ernie was too distraught to answer any questions, Heather turned back to Blakemore.

"But if the body does end up in the Vancouver General forensic unit, surely that's significant."

"Yeah," Blakemore said. "And it'll mean that Coswell must have spotted something. Damn. That'll just reopen the whole can of worms, and you, Ernie, have to be super vigilant again. With one more hate killer left out there, you're still at risk."

He thought for a moment.

"And you know what else? It puts another dent in Coswell's assassination theory. If the mysterious plotters had the first murders done and the two bike killers axed to get our guard down, they'd be pretty damned stupid to commit another one now."

"Assassination?" Heather said, eyebrows arched.

Blakemore winced.

"Whoops. Somehow I thought you knew about Coswell's fantasy that all these killings are part of a plot to assassinate the Mayor of San Francisco when he comes up here on Saturday. Damn. Coswell will have my head if he thinks I told you."

"Don't sweat it," she said. "I won't say anything, but it's not exactly a quantum leap of intelligence to put a series of gay killings and the gay San Francisco Mayor's visit together. No newspaper is going to touch it, though. Imagine, 'Mayor Gryndon at risk during Vancouver visit.' That's pretty low-brow press even for the sensationalist rags of which the Star is definitely not one."

Blakemore breathed a sigh of relief. He shuddered to think what would have happened if she'd decided to run with the story.

"I guess Coswell isn't content with the mundane," he said, "and that's probably why he's an inspector. Impresses hell out of the brass with his original ideas. The rest of us work on the 'common things are common' approach to most crimes; very boring."

Heather didn't find Coswell's theory as unlikely as the others did and if he was right— bonanza. That would be a story to guarantee another Webster Award for Frayley and a big boost up in the journalistic world for her.

She made her excuses and headed off to find her boss.

***
***

Coswell and Burns watched the coroner's wagon pull away with its grisly cargo. There'd been a bit of a scene when Frayley arrived from the Star demanding a statement, but he'd backed off after a short briefing emphasizing the robbery-murder explanation. They were both disconcerted, however, to see him jump back into his car and follow the coroner's vehicle.

"He smells something, the old bloodhound," Coswell muttered. "We won't get off so easy the next time he corners us."

Burns nodded and then asked, "Now what do we do? Wait for the report?"

"No. We're going to Carson and cohorts' apartment. Let's see what your forensic people have found."

Despite Coswell's belief in the superiority of Peter Mueller's lab, he was impressed with the city police forensic staff, who were methodically going through the suspects' apartment. Their leader, a young man with "MAYFIELD" stenciled on his uniform, met him and Burns at the door.

"Booties, gentlemen," he said, "and please don't touch anything."

They pulled on the paper shoe covers and followed Mayfield into the apartment.

Three technicians were going over every inch of the place, zip-loc bags and test tubes in hand. One was enthusiastically wielding a miniature duster checking for prints.

"The bathrooms have been a goldmine," Mayfield said. "We have toothbrushes, drinking glasses, even an empty contact lens case to analyze — DNA samples virtually everywhere."

"That's great," Coswell said, "and I'd appreciate it if you could get those over to the Vancouver General Forensics lab as quickly as possible."

Mayfield frowned.

"We're perfectly capable of doing that work in our lab downtown."

"I'm sure you are. But everything with these West End Cases is being centralized at Vancouver General."

"So I've heard."

The bitterness in Mayfield's voice prompted Coswell to respond with something positive. Team pride was important in maintaining dedication.

"I have a challenge for you, though," he said, "and solving

it will be as useful, if not moreso, than forensics on the corpse."

The young man perked up. Even Burns looked interested.

"Only one of the three occupants of this apartment has been using it over the last week and he's the one we want. He knows we have a photo of him so he's likely changed his appearance. I'm willing to bet the contact lens case is his. In our photo, he's wearing glasses."

"Why would he forget his case?" Burns asked.

"Probably because he rarely wears the lenses and was in a real hurry to exit the place."

"The challenge," Coswell continued, "is to find any-thing else you can—traces of hair dye for instance, signs he shaved off the mustache he was wearing when his photo was taken—those sorts of things."

"No problem," Mayfield said.

Coswell handed him his card.

"Call me the moment you get anything, day or night."

After the technician hurried off to resume his work, Burns and Coswell made a quick circuit of the apartment.

Burns spotted it first.

Tucked down at one end of the counter in the kitchen was a combination phone-fax-copier-answering machine. He called Coswell over.

"I think I've just found our own goldmine," he said. "Carson must have really been in a hurry if he left this behind."

"Or too dumb to know it could hold evidence," Coswell added.

They both stood over it, blessing their good luck.

"Go check with the young boss out there and tell him I want this thing cleared right now," Coswell ordered, and then as a second thought, added, "Actually you'd better bring him in here. I don't know about you, but I'm not a whiz with these things, and I'll bet our boy Mayfield is."

Coswell was right.

"That's been dusted and swabbed. It's okay to touch it," Mayfield informed them. "But what do you want me to do?"

"Squeeze every bit of information out of this machine that you can."

Mayfield looked the device over for a moment.

"You'd have to take it to an expert to do that properly, but I can tell you a few things."

Watching the digital display panel, he pushed a series of buttons.

"The obvious, of course, is that there are no messages, either outgoing or incoming. If there were, they've been erased. But these machines are all about memory and this one is top of the line. Let a good computer technician at it and I think you'll get a lot of information."

"Our computer men are all in Ottawa," Coswell said. "Sending it back there's too big a delay in this case. What's local, Burns?"

"Corporal Jones, an egghead who accidentally became a cop. He's in charge of our electronics division and he's really good. If there's anything worth retrieving from this thing, Jones'll get it."

"Then bundle it up, my good man, and off to Jones it goes," Coswell said, heading for the front door, leaving Burns to tote the machine.

They had one important stop to make, however, before delivering their precious find.

23

Zachary Benson blessed the administrators of the Vancouver General Hospital for allotting a separate room to forensic autopsies. Although Zachary enjoyed the banter from his fellow pathology residents in the large, multi-tabled general autopsy theatre, forensic work required continuous concentration. Every inch of the corpse might give an important clue in a criminal investigation, whereas a general autopsy was much more routine — cause of death, state of organs and so forth. There was time to let the mind wander. There was no margin for mind-wandering in forensics.

"What's your read on the head trauma?" Mueller said, watching Zachary meticulously scrape material from under Chris Reikel's fingernails and place it on glass slides.

Zachary examined the wound with a gloved finger, carefully feeling the depression over the temple. His answer was cut off by a knock at the door.

"That's Inspector Coswell and Sergeant Burns," Mueller said. "They wanted to be present for this one and I told them to come ahead. I hope working with an audience doesn't bother you."

Zachary laughed. "No. In fact it brings back memories of a certain coroner's job I did in Bear Creek with the locals breathing down my neck."

Both Coswell and Burns had seen dozens of autopsies in cases far more gruesome than Chris Reikel's. They barely gave the body a glance as they mounted the steps to the small observation gallery behind the head of the table.

"Afternoon, doctors," Coswell said as he sat down. "Anything you can tell us yet?"

"Dr. Benson, over to you," Mueller replied, smiling.

"We haven't opened the skull yet," Zachary said, "but I don't thing there'll be any surprises. The blow to the right side of his head fractured his temporal bone which, in turn, probably lacerated the middle meningeal artery and perhaps deeper vessels. In short, gentlemen, his brain got squished by blood pumping out of his arteries like a garden hose gone mad."

"Not completely clinical," Mueller interjected. "But certainly makes the point."

"Any idea what the murder weapon could have been?" Burns asked. "We didn't find anything at the scene."

"I was just trying to figure that out when you arrived," Zachary said. He returned to palpating the fracture site and after a moment gave his answer.

"A cudgel with a rounded end, I'd say, an inch and a half in diameter."

"A cudgel?" Burns asked.

"Like a miniature baseball bat," Zachary replied.

"A policeman's nightstick," Coswell said. "Remember, the concierge thought the visitor was a cop. He didn't mention a nightstick but the man's gun probably drew most of his attention. It always does."

"Yes," Zachary agreed. "It could have been a nightstick. Bring me one and I'll test it for fit."

Coswell laughed. "How about it, Burns? Did you save your old one when you made sergeant?"

"No, I turned it in."

Coswell looked at him sharply. The tone in that answer was far too serious for something meant in jest. What was going through the sergeant's mind? He'd quiz him about it later.

"I'm sure the victim put up a fight," Zachary went on. "Look at these two fingernails."

He lifted up the corpse's right hand to demonstrate the nails — one broken off and the other turned back.

"There's also something under three of the nails of the left hand that's not dirt. I'll bet it's skin. I picture the man clawing at his attacker, missing with his right hand and breaking the nails on rough clothing. The left hand caught flesh, I'm sure of it. No blood, mind you, but I don't need blood if skin cells are available. We can do a DNA match if you can supply us with a sample from your suspect."

"I've got a first-class technician sending that over to you, probably as we speak," Coswell said, delighted with the findings.

"And," he remarked with a sly grin, "I guess our murderer was left-handed."

"Very good, Inspector," Mueller said. "Victim facing attacker and blow to the right temple equals left-handed, I agree."

Coswell turned to Burns.

"Steve Carson is left-handed. It was in his military records."

***

Burns kept silent on the drive back to the Main Street Precinct, but Coswell was having none of it.

"All right, Burns," he said. "Let's hear it. You've got something stewing inside and if it has anything to do with this case, I want to know about it."

Burns paused, organizing his response.

"A Glock pistol and a policeman's nightstick — both standard city police issue. I know you can get a badge facsimile at any novelty shop and, believe it or not, the police force sold VPD insignia hats for a couple of years as fundraisers. But the pistol and the nightstick?"

"Our force did the same thing," Coswell said. "We even sold T-shirts with the RCMP crest on them. But a Vancouver cop mixed up in all this? I don't think so. How the hell did you get off on that tangent?"

"I don't know. I was day-dreaming about the bicycle patrol a while back and there is the odd bigot amongst us, I have to admit."

"Reasonable thinking in the beginning, but not now," Coswell said. "The nightstick was probably a fish bonker from a sporting goods shop and the Glock either stolen or smuggled across the border. No, I'm sure we're on the right track and we're within a hair of confirming it all. Mueller's lab and your computer geek are going to do just that — trust me."

"I hope you're right."

Coswell pulled the squad car into the precinct parking lot and popped the trunk latch — his contribution to transporting the heavy fax machine into the station.

***
***

Corporal Jones was sequestered in a windowless room deep in the bowels of the Main Street Precinct, adjacent to stores and the evidence room. He looked out of place in his uniform, surrounded by computers and electronic equipment of all sorts. He barely looked up when Burns and Coswell entered.

"I'm just about done," he said, staring at a large monitor

in front of him. The phone-fax machine from the penthouse was pushed to one side.

All visitors were forced to stand; Jones occupied the only chair in the room.

"Okay. Gather round and I'll show you what came out of that thing," he said, nodding to the fax machine. "I've transferred all the data onto my PC."

With a click of the mouse, a series of phone numbers appeared on the screen, each with a date and time beside it.

"First of all, there were no outgoing calls. This machine was used solely in a receiving mode. The incoming calls were all from Washington State."

He highlighted three of the numbers.

"These were faxes. The first one came in, as you see, three weeks ago. Here it is."

To their astonishment, a double click of the mouse caused an entire fax to appear on the monitor. It was a list of three addresses, one in Vancouver proper, one in North Vancouver, and the last in Richmond, near the airport.

"All private residences," Jones said. He clicked the print icon and handed the copy to Burns.

"The second fax was sent two days later."

A list of names and addresses appeared, Bruce Leighton's and Chris Reikel's names at the top, the rest of the West End victims below. Ernie Downs' name was not on the list.

"And this was the final one that came in just last week."

"My God!" Burns said.

On the screen was a complete architectural schematic of the Vancouver Convention Centre.

"Believe me now?" Coswell said.

Ignoring the impact of his findings on the two officers, Jones continued.

"I've taken the liberty of identifying the point of origin of the fax calls. They came from three separate shops in downtown Seattle, all Internet cafés."

After handing printouts of each screen to Burns, he brought up the phone numbers again.

"These other numbers are interesting. They're from public phone booths on the upscale side of Lake Washington. All except this one, which came from Redmond, Washington, also a public payphone."

Coswell looked at the date.

"That's the day before Deavers and Thornton got blasted at the border."

"Well, that's it," Jones said. "If you don't have any questions I have a pile of stuff to do here."

"You're a genius," Burns said to him. "I don't know how the hell you did it but thanks a heap."

"You don't want to know. Not everything I do is legal."

As they left, Coswell stopped at the door and turned around.

"I've just had a thought about those private residences," he said. "Could you check into the Federal Gun Registry and see if a Glock nine millimeter pistol lives in any one of them?"

Jones typed in a series of commands and then, after pausing a moment to study the results, typed in another series before printing out the results. A single address appeared with a list of weapons that included a Glock semi-automatic and sundry ammunition.

"I cross-referenced it with our B and E reports. This home was broken into the same day the first fax was sent. All of the residences had identical security systems in place and the owners were either at work or out of town. It doesn't take a particularly talented hacker to get all that information. I'll bet he even supplied a floor plan of the house so the system could be disabled."

"Terrific," Coswell said. "The only thing they couldn't get locally would be the silencer, and smuggling a small thing like that across the border would be a snap. It'd fit into a potato chip can."

Coswell led the way back to the squad room, nattering out loud.

"This thing's planned like D-Day, Burns, and the generals are on the other side of the border. Tracking them down will be damn near impossible. They're sure as hell taking great pains to hide their tracks — pay phones and drop-in fax centres, for Christ's sake. I'd love to get my hands on Carson and squeeze their names out of him, but we can't get side-tracked. Our first priority is to prevent an attempt on Mayor Gryndon's life."

"By doing what?"

"Getting him to cancel his visit. The floor plan of the convention centre sitting in that fax machine virtually confirms there'll be such an attempt and he'd be damned stupid to offer himself up as a target. I'm calling Bob Gillings."

Burns whistled. "The Attorney General? Won't that get you into a barrel of shit with your boss and the Mayor? That's really going over their heads."

"When it's war and you've got a cannon you use it, regardless of the recoil."

***
***

The recoil came faster than expected. Immediately after Coswell spoke to him, Gillings contacted Mayor Schmidt, who promptly called a meeting in his office at City Hall.

It was Jane, Chief Inspector Ward's secretary, who notified Coswell.

"What have you done now?" she whispered into the phone. "The Chief Inspector is livid. He's ranting about being kept in the dark and getting ready to have your head on a platter. You'd better get your story straight fast because you're to meet with him and the Mayor in the Mayor's office in thirty minutes. Good luck. It's been nice knowing you."

She hung up before he could ask if Gillings would be there.

***

Vancouver City Hall was built as a make-work project in the early 1930s. Its architecture marked a transition point between the ornate Art Deco style and the more austere modern era. Despite the economic depression of the day, the interior of the building boasts sumptuous marble and gold leaf ceilings.

Coswell noticed none of this as he passed through the polished brass entrance doors and headed for the elevator lobby. The brass continued: the elevator surrounds, the doors and a great cast directory on one wall. The Mayor's office was on the third floor.

His secretary waved the inspector straight in. The look on her face — pinched and unsmiling — wasn't exactly reassuring.

The Mayor, seated at his desk, was also not smiling. Ward, standing by a window, fixed Coswell with a withering glare.

"Have a seat, Inspector," the Mayor said, gesturing to a chair facing the desk. "I've just found out from Robert

Gillings, and I emphasize the word 'just', that you have new information regarding the visit of Mayor Gryndon from San Francisco. I thought you might share it with Chief Inspector Ward and me."

The sarcasm wasn't lost on Coswell. He realized that Gillings probably relished hitting Schmidt over the head with the latest revelations concerning the danger to the San Francisco mayor. He could also imagine the shit that Ward took as it ran downhill and now it was his turn, but he'd prepared his defense.

"It appeared to me,' he said, "that the Attorney General and I were the only ones who seriously considered an assassination plot after the two suspects were gunned down, and since I didn't have anything more than my suspicions until now, I didn't feel it necessary to bother either of you."

Ward turned red in the face and looked like he was going to explode. Schmidt cut in before he could do so.

"Point taken, Inspector. We were perhaps a bit carried away by our optimism when the two killers departed the scene," he said and then, glancing at Ward, "An understandable error for some of us."

That set the Chief Inspector off.

"I don't know what in hell you thought you were doing running up and down the coast wasting taxpayers' money and not keeping me informed," Ward said, his face beet red. "I ought to bust you to sergeant, for Christ's sake."

"Now, now," Schmidt said. "That would upset Robert Gillings. Not a wise move. Besides, Inspector Coswell was acting in good faith, I'm sure, and it appears he's averted a potential disaster. In fact, the more I think about it, a commendation may be in order, certainly not a demotion."

Coswell wondered when his chief last had his last blood

pressure checked. A single artery in his temple was pulsating with alarming clarity.

"That aside," the Mayor continued. "I want to be absolutely certain of the danger before I contact Mayor Gryndon in San Francisco. Cancelling his visit for this very important international conference is not a trivial thing. We want to be an attraction for world business, not some hick city that can't offer decent security."

If possible, the artery on the side of Ward's head became even more prominent.

"I think it was just bad luck this happened here," Coswell said. "It could have occurred in any other convention city, including San Francisco, and I'll bet they'd warn the Mayor away exactly as we're doing."

"I agree," Schmidt replied. "But I can tell you, Americans look at our law enforcement system up here as inefficient, leaky and a magnet for criminals. God knows, that security staff in San Francisco has been on my back from day one."

Coswell wondered for a moment why the Mayor dealt directly with the security staff, but then realized that Schmidt wouldn't want some blunt policeman's report scaring Gryndon away.

"Unfortunately," Schmidt continued. "The US media spread that message around the world. Very damaging to those of us who are trying to promote our city."

"It's not law enforcement that's the problem," Ward cut in. "It's the damn laws and the politicians who make them."

Schmidt frowned at him. The "politician" comment hit a nerve, but he said nothing and sat quietly as the inspector delivered his report.

"Good job," he said, when Coswell had finished. "Now, I want you to sit here while I contact Mayor Gryndon. Be ready to answer any questions that come up from him or his staff." He buzzed his secretary on the intercom.

To Coswell's relief, the call went through quickly; Ward's glare was beginning to get to him. Schmidt opened the conversation with the Mayor.

"I'm sitting here with Chief Inspector Ward of the RCMP and one of his senior officers. They've just briefed me on a very serious situation concerning your upcoming visit to Vancouver."

He did a good job relaying Coswell's report, omitting nothing. When he was finished, a brief pause ensued while Mayor Gryndon replied.

Schmidt handed the phone to Coswell.

"He wants to speak to you."

Coswell took the receiver, barely hearing Schmidt hiss to Ward, "It appears that Mayor Gryndon knows more about your inspector's activities than you do."

"My spies down here have told me all about you, Inspector," were Gryndon's first words. "I didn't hear your name mentioned in Mayor Schmidt's report just now, but I know you're the one responsible for rooting out those thugs."

"Thank you," was all Coswell could think to say, guessing that it was Cindy Forsythe and perhaps FBI agent Miller who were the "spies."

"It's me who should thank you," Gryndon said. "I do appreciate the warning, but I'm coming anyway. I'm a man of my word and I've committed to attending the Urban Renewal conference — a subject that's near and dear to me. And to admit I've been scared off by an assassination threat? No way. That's bad PR for me and your city."

"I think the danger is more than a possibility, Mr. Mayor,"

Coswell said, "and the PR on our end would be far worse if something happened to you."

"Again," Gryndon replied. "Thanks for the warning, but I'm proceeding as planned. I have a heads-up for you, though. I'm afraid that you'll soon be inundated by my security people and probably some reinforcements from the FBI and the CIA."

Great, Coswell thought. They'll all be coming — Miller, Whitfield — and then a pleasant feeling swept over him. Maybe Cindy Forsythe.

"It was nice talking to you, Inspector. Now let me speak to Mayor Schmidt for a moment."

Schmidt took the phone. He got to say just three words while Gryndon dictated his wishes:

"Hello."

"Done."

"Goodbye."

Ward and Coswell stared at him when he hung up, a stunned look on his face.

"He's coming, regardless, and he feels reassured that you, Inspector Coswell, are in total command of all security."

Coswell felt his sphincters tighten. Ward's choking didn't even register.

✳✳✳
✳✳✳

The beer had whetted Blakemore's appetite and with a few broad hints, he finagled a supper invitation from Ernie. He also wanted to see the West End penthouse again. Checking it over at Bruce Leighton's wake had given him an idea, reinforced the moment he walked through the door, once again struck by its opulence.

"Wow, this is really a palace," he said, gazing around the

room. "It seems a shame that you rattle around in here all by yourself. Maybe you should get a roommate."

Ernie laughed. "Like you, for instance?"

"Not permanent, but if Coswell continues to ignore me, I'd be a lot more comfortable here than in that bachelor dump they've rented for me. I'd still be doing my job — you're supposed to be bait and I'm your guardian."

"Interesting proposal, ignoring the deeper meaning of the word," Ernie said.

They were interrupted by a telephone ring. Ernie picked up an extension in the kitchen. The surprise in his voice when he answered drew Blakemore's attention.

"Well, for heaven's sake, it's been ages. Where are you?"

There was a silence as Ernie listened to a lengthy explanation.

"I've got a better idea," he replied at last. "Jump in a cab and come over to the apartment. I'm just getting dinner ready for myself and a good friend. We'd love to have you join us and, no, it would not be an imposition."

Ernie hung up the phone and stood over it for a moment before turning to Blakemore.

"That was Tommy Carlyle. It seems the Governor wants him up here to rewrite his conference speech. He's become a little nervous about his ignorance of Canada and doesn't want to embarrass himself with Mayor Gryndon performing at the same function. Tommy at his side apparently will alleviate his concerns."

"Another player returns to the game," Blakemore said.

***
***

Burns was sitting in Coswell's Main Street Precinct office when the inspector returned from his city hall meeting.

"Your phone's been ringing off the hook," he said. "Are you ready for the list?"

"Give it to me. It couldn't be any more stressful than my meeting with Ward and the Mayor."

Burns looked as though he was more interested in hearing about the meeting than delivering messages, but proceeded to reel off the calls.

"Mayfield, the forensics guy, phoned first. They pulled the P-trap off the bathroom sink and examined all the crap. He gave me a lot of details I didn't really need, but basically Steve Carson has shaved off his mustache and darkened his hair up with Grecian Formula something. There weren't any eyeglasses in the apartment so he might be switching back and forth with his contacts."

"Did you get that to our poster people?" Coswell said.

Burns nodded and continued with the list.

"Dr. Benson phoned next. He did a rush job on the DNA and you were right; everything matched: the skin cells in the carpet from our double apartment killing, samples from the suspects' penthouse, and best of all, the crud under Chris Reikel's fingernails. Carson's our man, for sure."

Burns took a deep breath, but before he could continue Coswell began firing orders.

"Okay. Here's what I want you to do. Get those posters out fast and have every man, woman, dog, and horse at your disposal issued with copies. I want everyone to concentrate on a five-block radius around the convention centre. He has to show his face somewhere. Barbers, corner stores, news vendors, restaurants, coffee houses, bars, hotels — the works. I want this guy's portrait etched into everyone's brain."

"Damn, that'll take the whole force."

"Whatever," Coswell said. "If you get any flak, let me know. The Mayor and even the Attorney General are in on this. They'll want nothing held back. For the next forty-eight hours, this is your only assignment."

Burns shook his head. Things were getting heavy.

"Now, before you get going, was there anything else?"

"Yes — three more calls. One from a Quentin Whitfield saying he and Agent Miller will be in Vancouver tomorrow and want to meet with you. Another from Cindy Forsythe, who said you'd know who it was and please call her. Here's the number." Burns glanced at Coswell to see if there was a reaction.

"Get on with it," Coswell said. "She's a San Francisco cop."

Burns looked disappointed.

"The last call was from Harold Frayley. He wants an interview ... again."

Coswell had no problem deciding which call he would answer first.

The number Cindy Forsythe had given Burns was her cellphone. She answered on the second ring. Coswell felt a warm glow as he heard her voice.

"God, you sure know how to get things going down here," she said. "I've just spoken to Miller. He and Whitfield are on their way up to Vancouver. But the reason I called is to update you on the Sacramento investigation. I'm sorry I took so long, but you wouldn't believe the foot-dragging that goes on in our Capital City. The red tape is a foot thick everywhere, including the local police department."

Coswell nodded in silent sympathy. Bureaucratic obstacles were the bane of efficient policing.

"Anyway," Cindy continued. "Steve Carson is a shooter all right. According to the Sacramento Gun Club's records, all three of the men were active in silhouette target competitions with semi-automatic pistols."

"What were the silhouettes? Human torsos?"

Cindy laughed.

"No. The targets are miniature steel animals. Sheep, bears, turkeys, that sort of thing. Carson was the best of the bunch, although Deavers apparently was also good. Thornton was a poor third. The sport's really popular nowadays, I gather, especially with the ex-military crowd."

"Anything on their social life?" Coswell asked.

"That was interesting. The officer who went out to the club couldn't get any further than the manager, who seemed to think that members' privacy was sacrosanct. He produced competition results and so forth, but nothing personal. I can push him with a warrant if you think it'd help."

"Whatever," Coswell said. "But I do want you to find out for me which of the Governor's security staff are members there, especially those who might've shot in the pistol competitions with our suspects. I need those names as quickly as you can get them to me and if you can tie them all into the Knights of the True South, that would be a super bonus."

Cindy gasped. "You think the Governor's staff is involved in this? I know Kruger detests Gryndon, but to have him assassinated? You've got to be kidding."

"Just covering all bases," Coswell said, a pattern growing in his mind.

"Well, here's a last little tidbit for you. Carson had a membership at a place called the Sacramento Pipeline, which is a hangout for climbers where they practice on artificial rock walls. You'd better make sure he doesn't pull a Spiderman routine on you."

He thanked her for the information and promised he'd keep her informed as the situation evolved.

Despite Tommy Carlyle's small stature, he impressed Blakemore as someone to avoid in a fight, either verbal or physical. A hint of terrier resided beneath his urbane exterior.

The dinner conversation flowed smoothly, even though most of it was between Carlyle and Ernie. Blakemore, content to listen in, knew that his former partner was subtly probing, delving into his suspicion that the Governor's aide might be involved in the West End murders.

"It seemed to the group up here that you dropped off the edge of the world," Ernie said. "We thought you might have touched base with us somewhere along the line."

Carlyle sighed. "The political world has an insatiable appetite for one's time, I'm afraid. I was actually shocked when your Inspector Coswell showed up at my office and made me realize how quickly the years pass."

Odd comment, Blakemore thought. The shock should have been on hearing that his former friends had been murdered, but perhaps the Sacramento papers carried the story. He was waiting for Ernie to drop the Chris Reikel bombshell, an event too recent for Carlyle to have gotten the news.

"Yes," Ernie said. "And with Chris gone now, you and I are the only ones left."

"Where did Chris go?" Carlyle said, with no reaction

other than curiosity, and when Ernie told him, his jaw dropped.

"Oh, my God, Ernie," he said. "What's happening around here?"

"Paul?" Ernie replied, leaving the answer to his ex-partner.

Blakemore weighed his response carefully; Carlyle could be acting. After all, he was a politician ... and a lawyer.

"Hate killings," he told Carlyle, "done by three ex-US Rangers who came to Vancouver from Sacramento looking for drugs and while they were here decided to amuse themselves by killing prominent gays. Two of the men were caught and the third's on the run, probably back across the border by now."

Satisfied that Carlyle seemed to be accepting this, Blakemore went on:

"I believe we owe you a debt of gratitude. Your personnel department gave us an ID photo of one of the killers, a Steve Carson who worked as a janitor at the Capital. We've sent that photo out in an all points bulletin to city police and RCMP. We'll soon have him in custody too, if he's still in Canada."

"Ah, I see," Carlyle said. "A janitor. That would explain the mysterious letter of introduction to the golf course. I'm not familiar with that name, but you can be sure our stationery will be monitored more closely when I return."

Smooth, Blakemore thought. Too bad he didn't have a picture of Carson to show Carlyle just then. Facial response to a photo was difficult to fake.

Ernie took over.

"The banquet at the convention centre isn't until Saturday, Tommy, and I'm organizing a happy hour tomorrow right here. Paul's coming, of course, and there'll be a couple of friends from San Francisco. I'd really like you to come."

"I wish I could, Ernie," Carlyle said. "But Kruger's changed his plans again. He's not flying over; he's coming with Brian Sterne on the yacht instead. They're sailing to Vancouver from Campbell River tomorrow morning and parking at the cruise ship dock beside the convention centre."

Blakemore wondered if Coswell knew about that.

"I have to lock myself in the hotel room," Carlyle went on, "and rewrite that damned speech so it's ready for the big man's perusal when he arrives. I doubt if he'll let me out of his sight after that, but thanks anyway for the invitation."

"If you can get away," Ernie said. "Don't even call. Just come on over. You're welcome any time."

The evening ended at that point and Carlyle said goodbye. Blakemore noted there was none of the typical gay hugging; a subtle coolness had marked the entire get-together. Ernie called a taxi and went down to the foyer with Carlyle to wait for it.

As soon as the apartment door closed, Blakemore phoned Coswell. He had an excuse now and was fed up with being ignored. To his surprise, Coswell wasn't upset about the Governor's change of plans.

"Actually it's going to make my life easier. Kruger can literally walk directly to the convention centre from the boat. That'll free up more men to escort Gryndon when he comes in from the airport Saturday morning. Now tell me your reading on Carlyle. I'd almost forgotten him."

"I haven't had a chance to discuss it with Ernie yet. He's downstairs right now seeing him off in a cab."

"Well, talk it over and get back to me if the two of you think he's a player. I've got to go. Your assignment remains unchanged. You stick with Ernie until this is all over. Carson's still on the loose and it doesn't appear that this guy, Carlyle, can be eliminated as a suspect."

"Bugger," Blakemore said as he was cut off and heard Ernie re-enter the apartment.

They looked at one another and both shrugged their shoulders.

"I don't know," Ernie said. "I just don't know."

Blakemore lamented. That wouldn't give him a return call to the inspector. And then he recalled the happy hour invitation.

"Who's coming to that?" he asked.

"Couple of jocks," Ernie said. "You'll like them."

"Jocks?"

Frayley was pacing the floor when Heather walked into his office, but the scowl on his face lightened when he saw her.

"Hey, Babe," he said. "I hope you've got more to show for your day than I have. I followed the coroner's wagon to Vancouver General Hospital and when I was sure the stiff was being deposited there, I tried to get back to Coswell, but the man disappears like the Scarlet Pimpernel."

Heather sympathized with his frustration.

"Join the crowd. But I've got something that might cheer you up. When I was talking with Blakemore and Ernie Downs, they let slip the fact that Coswell's convinced there's going to be an assassination attempt on Mayor Gryndon. At the moment, it appears Coswell's the only one who thinks so, but if he's right, we've got a sensational story about to drop in our laps."

Frayley whistled.

"Coswell's a clever bugger," he said. "He'll be a winner either way. If there isn't an attempt, it's because our fearless inspector scared the killer away and if there is, he's a genius. No wonder he's risen up the ranks."

"How are we going to handle our end?"

"We'll run with the assassination thing. If it fizzles, we still have the West End murders story. It's only a matter of time until they catch the third man and when they do, we'll squeeze a good column out of him. Meanwhile we need to be ringside with Gryndon. You catch him at the airport and stay with him. I'll get us into the convention centre and we'll take it from there."

"Sounds good to me," Heather said. "I don't think there's anything more to get out of the two Bear Creek Mounties anyway and finding Coswell's too time-wasting. Besides, he has to appear on the scene when Gryndon arrives. We'll corner him then."

She could feel the excitement mounting and knew Frayley was feeling the same — the old lion moving in for the kill.

***

Coswell arrived late at the Main Street Precinct on Friday morning after a poor night's sleep. Nightmares from eating a late supper, and anticipation that he'd be called with news that Carson had been found, made him toss and turn until the early hours.

The Tim Hortons coffee wasn't doing its job and he cursed himself for stopping there instead of at Starbucks, where he could have gotten a decent double espresso with a kick to it. Damn those donuts—the Lorelei that drew him in.

To add to his misery, Burns had come and gone from the office, presumably to check on his street patrols. He'd left two messages, one that Brian Sterne's yacht wasn't due in until late Saturday morning, the day of the banquet. That, at least, was a relief. But the second message started his head throbbing. Miller and Whitfield were coming to the precinct at nine, less than thirty minutes away. Lovely, he thought; a shitty coffee and donut for breakfast and now a couple of US Feds. Well, at least it was on his turf this time.

***
***

Coswell watched with amusement as the two men made their way through the squad room, Whitfield looking like he'd stepped in something smelly, and when they saw the cubbyhole he'd been assigned, the surprise on both their faces tickled him to the core.

"Welcome to my humble abode," he said. "Have a seat and make yourselves comfortable." He took diabolical pleasure in knowing that the chairs had the comfort of Presbyterian church pews.

"May I get you a coffee?" he said, pointing to the communal urn in the squad room, but no way were the two agents chancing its tarry contents.

"No, thanks," Miller replied. "We've just had breakfast."

If Coswell thought Whitfield might have been a bit sheepish about his abrupt dismissal of the assassination theory, he was wrong. The CIA agent immediately went on the offensive.

"Let's get to it, then," he said. "What have you got for us?"

Coswell suppressed his immediate desire to tell the man to go pee up a rope.

"I think it would be more appropriate for me to ask what *you* have for us," Coswell said. "I spoke to Cindy Forsythe yesterday and she was helpful, but I gather there was some stonewalling at the Capital."

Miller, noting the tension, tried to be a mediator.

"Right," he said. "I went over the material from Sacramento. What would you like to know?"

"The gun club that Carson and his buddies belonged to is of special interest to me. I suspect that many of the Governor's security people belong to it as well and I'd like to know if the names Ales and Ferring are amongst the members."

Coswell enjoyed seeing the two agents straighten in their chairs.

"I'd also like those names looked for in your list of known Knights of the True South in the Sacramento area. In fact, I'd like to know all the Sacramento names that are on that list."

Miller looked at Whitfield for a response. The CIA man's eyes were narrowed and a deep frown creased his brow.

"What's the inference here? Are you pointing a finger at the Governor? That's ludicrous."

Time to play hardball, Coswell decided.

"Yes, I am looking at the Capital and I've more than enough to support that view. Now, are you going to get me that information, or not?"

Miller cut in again.

"I think we've gotten off on the wrong foot here," he said. "Quentin and I've come to help, not hinder your handling of the situation. But you'll have to admit that implicating the Office of the Governor of California in something this nefarious is quite a stretch for us."

Whitfield rolled his eyes. Miller continued.

"But you've been right so far in your suspicions, and if that information is of use to you, you'll have it. Won't he, Quent?"

Whitfield gave a Gallic shrug.

"And while you're at it," Coswell said. "I want to know if the Governor's aide, Thomas Carlyle, has had any unusual contact with Washington State and the City of Seattle in particular."

"Jesus!" Miller gasped.

"This is getting just too ridiculous," Whitfield said.

Coswell leaned back in his chair and folded his arms over his chest.

"Well?" he said, gazing defiantly at the two.

"You'll have it," Miller said. "Now would you please fill us in on the reasons for all this? I know the time constraints you're under, but we're willing to do some of the legwork for you, especially with the American contingent."

Coswell barely managed to complete the briefing before Burns appeared outside the window. Coswell waved him in.

Introductions done, the sergeant gave his report.

"There's no sign of Carson, and we've combed that five-block circle with everything we've got. I don't think the guy's there. My bet is he's holed up in the suburbs, maybe even as far out as the Fraser Valley."

"Where's that?" Miller asked.

"Anywhere between the eastern border of Vancouver and seventy-five miles of farmland turned residential going east," Burns said.

"Public transit," Whitfield interjected. "Easy to cover. Just post men at the stations around the convention centre."

A logical suggestion by an American from a big city, Coswell had to admit, but Vancouver wasn't San Francisco or Boston; personal vehicles were preferred ten to one over public conveyances.

"If he's out there," Coswell said, "it's more likely Carson will heist a car and drive in. By the time it's reported stolen, he's into Vancouver and makes his way to the centre on foot."

The meeting ended with Whitfield agreeing to gather the information from Sacramento and tap into Carlyle's phone records. Miller would dig up as much information as he could on Ales and Ferring, the Governor's two security men.

When the agents had left, Coswell turned to Burns.

"Let's get out of here. The newshounds are prowling and I want to be in the field. We'll tour the convention centre and vicinity. If we really grind our brains into it, maybe we can predict what this bastard Carson might do."

26

Blakemore almost regretted staying overnight at Ernie's apartment. Although he slept blissfully, his host was up with the dawn, rattling around in the kitchen.

"Oh, did I wake you?" Ernie said with questionable concern. "I wasn't sure what time you had to be at work, but I've got coffee and scones ready. Juice is in the fridge."

Blakemore grumbled, "You are my work, Ernie; I'm being ignored for anything else."

"Well then, we both have the day off. I've got my substitute running the gallery, which leaves me free to get ready for this evening. You'll be a big help. This place is a mess."

Blakemore looked around. The apartment looked immaculate. Ernie didn't know mess. He was assigned the window cleaning while Ernie wielded the vacuum. Next, towel and linen changing, and then mirror polishing (Blakemore's job). At eleven, they broke for lunch: bagels, cream cheese, lox, and capers with a glass each of ice cold Riesling.

"You don't drink beer with salmon," Ernie informed him.

Blakemore felt that a nap was in order after lunch. The cleaning was physically exhausting and they'd wakened much too early. He knew that lying down on one of the freshly made beds was a no-no, but the big leather sofa in the living room looked inviting. While he was thinking about how to put this suggestion to Ernie, the phone rang. Ernie picked up the extension in the kitchen.

"Josh Gryndon. For heaven's sake, where are you?" There was a short pause and then, "Of course you can stay here tonight. In fact your timing couldn't be better. I'm having a small party this evening for Kevin and Carl. They've just arrived in town from San Francisco and they'll be delighted to see you. As you know, we can accommodate an army in this place. Come over as soon as you get in."

Blakemore was stunned; the Mayor of San Francisco was dropping by, for heaven's sake. Coswell would have a shit hemorrhage when he found out.

Ernie continued his telephone conversation.

"You couldn't stay in a safer place. In fact, I've got a genuine, live-in RCMP corporal babysitting me right now. He can protect us both. Great guy; you'll like him. He even does windows."

"Very funny," Blakemore shouted across the room.

Another pause while Ernie listened and then replied, "I can certainly ask him, but he might be a bit of a damper. He's sweating the whole security scene for the banquet on Saturday. Anyway, hurry over. We're looking forward to seeing you."

Ernie hung up the phone and flashed a big grin at Blakemore.

"What a party we're going to have. I need to cater in for sure, and I must do an inventory of the wine supply...."

"Whoa," Blakemore interrupted. "What's coming off here?"

"An event, my good friend, an event, and you're going to be part of it. Not everyone gets to be tête à tête with the Mayor of San Francisco."

Ignoring Blakemore standing flummoxed in the living room, Ernie began thumbing through a directory beside the phone. He paused for a moment to add:

"Oh, by the way, he wants Coswell invited for some insane reason. Are you going to phone him or shall I?"

Blakemore flopped down on the chesterfield.

"You order the food first and then I'll phone Coswell. I need a moment to prepare myself."

***
***

"Jesus H. Christ," Coswell screamed into the phone. "How the hell am I supposed to protect these people when they pop up out of the blue like that?"

Blakemore brought the receiver back to his ear.

"Actually, I think it was a smart move," he said. "The Mayor slips into town a day before he's expected and stays at a place that's pretty easy to secure. I'm here and I'm sure the man has a whole raft of security people with him. They'll guard every portal in and out of the building, no problem."

Coswell calmed down. Blakemore was right. Like the Governor, Mayor Gryndon had actually made his job easier: one less trip to the airport to worry about and more time to concentrate on the convention centre, the likeliest site for an assassination attempt.

Ernie's party was another matter. Chief Inspector Ward and Mayor Schmidt would expect him to be burning the midnight oil double-checking security at the centre and intensifying the hunt for Steve Carson. But what the hell, he'd go. After all Gryndon was the probable target. Meeting with him would be well within the call of duty and if the nibbles in Ernie's studio were any example of the food that would be served, to say nothing of the excellent wines, it'd be a shame to miss out.

"Cocktails at six," Blakemore pre-empted, expecting the inspector to yield to temptation.

"All right, I'll be there," Coswell said. "Don't let Gryndon out of your sight and be damn sure Ernie clears every guest."

Blakemore finally made it to the chesterfield; Ernie was in the shower. He closed his eyes and had almost fallen asleep when an unfamiliar sound caused him to waken with a start. Someone was fiddling with the front door lock!

He jerked to a sitting position and cursed himself for leaving the Beretta with his shaving stuff in the bathroom. He sat frozen, watching as the door swung open.

"Surprise! We're early." Two men entered carrying sports bags.

Blakemore's eyes bulged. From hours of watching sports

on television, he immediately recognized the faces. Ernie, the bugger, deliberately hadn't mentioned his invitees' last names—Kevin *Slater* and Carl *Neufeld*—sports stars extraordinaire. His mind was spinning so fast that he was speechless. The two men halted in the foyer, equally surprised to see him. Fortunately, Ernie came out of the bathroom at that point wearing a white terry cloth robe.

"Oh, you tempter, you," Kevin said, looking past Blakemore to Ernie, who rushed forward to greet his friends. Hugs all around and then they all stood back and looked at Blakemore. Ernie paused for effect before he introduced him.

"This is my friend, Paul Blakemore," he said. Nothing more.

Blakemore regained his composure. He sure as hell wasn't into hugging. He quickly extended his hand. The nuances of the moment were picked up instantly by the two athletes. They shook his hand and regarded him with puzzled expressions. Ernie finally relented.

"Paul's as straight as a poker, I'm afraid," he said. "But don't worry, he understands the scene. You can relax. Welcome home, by the way, Carl, your chamber awaits."

"You really didn't need to do that, Ernie," Carl said. "We're only staying the weekend."

As the two men hauled their bags up to the master bedroom, Ernie said to Blakemore, "Carl is the fairy godfather who owns this apartment and lets me house-sit."

Blakemore smiled. Only Ernie would get away with calling Carl Neufeld "the fairy godfather." In the hockey world Neufeld was known as "the Crusher," a Norris Trophy winner (best defenseman) and a man feared by every offensive player in the National Hockey League. Blakemore struggled with the gay image, but there didn't appear to be much room for doubt.

"Gay as his blades," Ernie said, settling the question. "And one of the sweetest guys you'll ever meet."

27

Coswell swore as he took yet another wrong turn in his attempt to make his way to Ernie's apartment through the maze of West End streets, a diabolical response by city planners to residents' complaints of vehicles speeding through their neighbourhood. Dead ends were created in what seemed a haphazard manner, effectively discouraging drivers from even entering the system, let alone speeding through it. Unfortunately, the blockages were mere extensions of the sidewalks, leaving frustrating drivers the temptation to motor right over them, Coswell being no exception.

He'd been able to see the apartment complex for some time but finally gave up trying to reach it by licit means and took the direct route instead, bouncing his car over the sidewalk divide. His feeling of triumph, as he drove to the front of the apartment, was short-lived; flashing red and blue lights appeared directly ahead of him.

The lazy buggers, he muttered to himself; they could fill their damn citation book and never take the cruiser out of park. He pulled over and stopped. Both doors of the vehicle swung open, but no one got out. Coswell's heart sank. These were Burns' men, loaded for bear and watching out for a potential hit on Ernie. He shuddered to think that one of them probably had the riot gun out of its rack while the other ran Coswell's plate through the console computer. He berated himself for deciding to drive his own car to Ernie's rather than taking a police vehicle.

Finally, both officers got out of the cruiser and approached his car. One maintained a stony face but the other, a corporal, couldn't help his wide grin.

"Good evening, Inspector," the grinning one said. "On your way to an emergency?"

Coswell was in no mood to be the butt of the Vancouver Police Squad's joke-of-the-night.

"All right," he said. "You caught me. Give me a god-damned ticket if you have to but I am actually on a case."

"Wouldn't think of it," the officer replied. "But we've got to keep up appearances. The locals love to phone in all these digressions. I think they sit on their balconies just waiting for people to jump those dividers."

Coswell mellowed out. These men were just doing their jobs.

"Any action over there?" he said, pointing to Ernie's apartment.

"Just the regulars coming and going," the corporal replied. "There were two suspicious individuals wearing sunglasses who went in about an hour ago, but our man inside let them go up so they must've had proper ID."

Coswell's mind flashed back to Chris Reikel's body lying in the foyer of his apartment. He pulled out his cellphone and dialed Blakemore's cell number. Seven rings later an automated voice answered suggesting he leave a message. Blakemore wouldn't ignore his call. What was going on up there?

"Did those individuals leave the building at any time?"

Coswell asked. "I presume you have all entrances and exits covered."

"Like a blanket. A cockroach couldn't move in or out of there without our guys spotting it. Why? Do you think those two are trouble? They haven't come out yet."

"Maybe," Coswell said.

He debated calling Ernie's phone but then decided the direct approach would be best. If anything had happened to Ernie and Blakemore, he wanted to trap the assailants at the scene of the crime. He commandeered the two officers and entered the apartment block. The policeman inside, acting as concierge, met them at the door. Coswell waved aside the officer's insistence that the IDs he'd checked were valid and ordered him to escort them to the penthouse.

When they stepped off the elevator and were all in position, guns drawn, Coswell signaled for the door to be unlocked. The "concierge" punched in a code and stood back. Coswell and the two officers burst into the apartment.

Fortunately, the only one to greet them was Blakemore lounging on the chesterfield, eating from a bowl of mixed nuts and sipping a glass of beer. Kevin and Carl were still unpacking in the master bedroom and Ernie had disappeared into one of the other bedrooms to dress.

Staring at three semi-automatic pistols pointed at his chest, Blakemore sat perfectly still and asked, "Was it something I said?"

Coswell was exasperated. "Why the hell didn't you answer your cellphone just now?"

"Whoops," Blakemore said. "It's in the bathroom with my shaving stuff. I forgot to clip it on. Has there been a problem?"

Coswell turned to the two patrolmen.

"Sorry, men. False alarm, but thanks for the backup. I'll take it from here."

They holstered their guns and left, gazing for a moment around the luxurious apartment. The big grin returned to the police corporal's face.

"You call if you need us for any more emergencies, Inspector," he said. "Have a good evening."

"Smart ass," Coswell said when the door closed. He turned to Blakemore.

"What the hell was I supposed to think? Two suspicious men wearing shades get past our man at reception and you don't respond to my call."

"Sorry. But all's well. They're two old friends of Ernie's come to stay a couple of nights. They're just putting their stuff away and Ernie's changing. How about I get you a glass of wine?"

The mood shifted.

"What's cold?"

The party got going quickly after that. Blakemore was relieved to learn that Coswell had already met the two athletes, which effectively diverted attention away from him as the conversation moved quickly to BC wines and Vancouver restaurants. Blakemore was soon bored; he wanted sports talk. Josh Gryndon's arrival came as a relief.

The San Francisco Mayor was buzzed up through the intercom at the reception desk. Ernie had left his name there earlier in the day. He was alone, carrying a single garment bag.

"I sent my security men off to a hotel," he said. "But they'll probably leave one poor soul sitting with your receptionist in the lobby all night. Would you be a good guy, Ernie, and smooth that over with him? My people can sometimes be a bit difficult."

Coswell intervened.

"I'll do that," he said. "The receptionist is actually one of our men."

"Inspector Coswell, I presume," Gryndon said, reaching out to shake his hand. "Hurry back. We have a lot to chat about."

Coswell headed to the elevator while Ernie introduced Blakemore. He noted that Gryndon merely gave a familiar wave to Carl and Kevin.

***
***

It was fortunate that Coswell did go down to the reception area. Gryndon's man and the Vancouver officer were not seeing eye to eye. They were arguing over a gun.

"I don't want anyone that close to me packing," the officer-receptionist said. "He can sit there, but not with a sidearm."

Coswell looked at Gryndon's man. From the expression on his face, surrendering the weapon wasn't an option, but his own officer had a point. While he tried to come up with a Solomon-class decision, a familiar figure came in the front door: Tommy Carlyle, who looked as surprised to see Coswell as the inspector was to see him.

"The party's just getting going," Coswell said quickly. "You go on up and when I've settled a little problem here, I'll join you."

He spoke to the officer behind the desk.

"Take Mr. Carlyle to the elevator and express him up, will you?"

What a stroke of luck, he thought—Carlyle and his

former lover, Gryndon, together in the same room. Even the best of actors couldn't disguise murderous feelings face to face like that.

He dealt with the gun standoff quickly. When the Vancouver officer returned from the elevator, Coswell spoke to him in a voice that boomed throughout the foyer.

"If he has a legal permit on him that says he can carry a weapon in Canada, you'll just have to put up with it. If he doesn't, then you confiscate the damn thing and he doesn't get it back till he gets a permit. Any problem, you call in the officers just outside, but I'm sure an individual intelligent enough to be chosen as a security officer for the Mayor of San Francisco wouldn't cause an international incident."

He barely glanced at Gryndon's man as he brushed past him to get back to Ernie's apartment and watch the action. In the few seconds it took for the elevator door to open, he looked back and was satisfied to see the gun being handed over.

The atmosphere on Coswell's return to the apartment was decidedly strained, despite a valiant attempt by Ernie to defuse the situation by chattering non-stop. Carlyle and Gryndon were standing, facing one another. Coswell hurried up the steps to the mezzanine lounge where the group had congregated. The look from Carlyle made his stomach flutter, but Gryndon welcomed him back with gusto.

"Ah, the good inspector. I must bend your ear," he said, and then to Ernie. "We're going to retire to the den for a short conference. Carry on without us for a bit, will you?"

Coswell noted Gryndon's familiarity with the apartment. Obviously this wasn't the mayor's first visit there. He wondered how much of the man's background Ernie had withheld. He'd discuss that with him later.

The den looked more like a library to Coswell, completely lined from floor to ceiling with bookshelves. A ladder that moved on rollers along a track gave access to the books on the very top. Titles were eclectic: cars, mechanics, sports, music, mysteries, history, classics and every sort of reference material, including dictionaries in four different languages.

Gryndon saw him looking at the books.

"Not what you'd expect in a hockey player's apartment, eh? There's a lot more to Carl than appearances suggest. He's highly educated—no thanks to the institutions he attended. The US college scholarships he won were really a sham. They wanted his brawn, not his brain."

"When does he get time to read any of this?" Coswell said.

"In the offseason, mainly. You might be interested to know that he plans to be a writer when he hangs up his skates."

"You mean he spends all summer here? I wonder why Ernie didn't mention that."

"Carl is a very private person. I imagine Ernie was just respecting that."

And worried that I might blab all over town the fact that Carl Neufeld is gay, Coswell concluded.

They sat down on two of the old-fashioned arm chairs, perfectly comfortable for their intended purpose: reading. Elegant floor lamps stood on either side.

"Now," Gryndon said. "I'd like you to elaborate a bit more on this plot to do me in that Mayor Schmidt seems so worried about. He was quite clear about the assassin, but totally vague about the reasons or persons behind such a plot. I'd like to know it all and since it's my neck on the line, I think I deserve full disclosure."

Coswell took a deep breath and then told him everything, all his suspicions and the investigation up to the present, including his meetings with the US Federal agents and his trip to Sacramento. Gryndon was shocked.

"The Governor? Tommy Carlyle?" I don't believe it."

"You don't have a policeman's mind," Coswell said. "We're trained to be suspicious, especially when motive seems so obvious. Those men around the Governor, in my opinion, have an extreme right-wing attitude that makes them excellent soldiers in the army of the Knights of the True South. To them, killing gay men would be a service to mankind."

"All right. I can see your reasoning there, but Tommy?"

"Most common motive for murder in the whole world: loss of personal dignity. I'm aware of your past relationship and I believe your breakup must have been acutely embarrassing to him, probably the reason he never returned to his circle of friends in Vancouver. Instead, he became isolated in the redneck world of Sacramento politics, and isolation, I can tell you, often leads to paranoia. And in the right person, murder."

That statement hit hard. Coswell decided he'd better temper his suspicions a bit.

"He did say the reason he was working for Governor Kruger was to hold the fort for you, for when you become the next Governor of California, and that you'd be a boon to everyone. But that could have been a smoke screen."

Gryndon sat pondering for a full minute before he spoke.

"You're wrong about the Governor. Kruger thinks I'm the best thing that ever happened to him, politically speaking. He's sure that his anti-gay stance makes him popular with the majority of voters in California and having me as possible opposition to him in the next race gives him a shoo-in. No, he's the last one who would want me killed."

Coswell watched Gryndon struggle with the concept of Tommy Carlyle wanting vengeance.

"We had bitter words, Tommy and I, that's true. It was over nothing, really. We were both exhausted from tough campaigning and we'd been too close in the pressure cooker for too long without relief. Sadly, we're both adept at using language as a weapon and the wounds went both ways — deep."

He was silent again and stared off into space for so long that Coswell began to feel uncomfortable. He decided to ask the obvious question.

"Do you think he could be the one behind all this?"

Gryndon looked at him for a moment and to Coswell's absolute amazement, replied, "I'll ask him."

"Uh, I don't think that's such a good idea," Coswell stammered. "He's not likely to admit it and I think it would be better to just let us keep a close watch on him."

"No. I think we should settle this now." And before Coswell could object any further, Gryndon rose and strode out of the room, the inspector scrambling after him.

But the Mayor was a master politician and didn't, as Coswell feared, blindly confront his former lover. Instead, he melded into the conversation Blakemore had managed to steer to the topic of sports. Gryndon, surprisingly, proved to be both a basketball and a hockey fan. He joined right in.

"California — home of champions: the Lakers, the Forty-Niners, and, give them a few more years, the San Jose Sharks, future Stanley Cup winners."

"When pigs fly," Carl said.

Tommy Carlyle quietly sipped what looked like a scotch straight up. Coswell wondered for a minute if Blakemore had actually been clever enough to start the sports talk to give the aide time to calm down, but then dismissed the thought. Blakemore had the finesse of a rhinoceros. Ernie, however, was a different matter. As soon as he saw Gryndon and the inspector come out of the den, he hurried into the kitchen and began transporting tray after tray of food to the big dining room table.

"All right," he announced. "Everyone up. It's buffet time. Fill your plates and find a comfortable spot to eat. I suggest the balcony, but anywhere else is fine."

Coswell took the "fill your plates" suggestion literally. Ernie had gone tapas — chicken, beef, goat, prawns, squid, sausage, vegetarian, cheeses, pita bread — mouthfuls of exquisite taste after taste.

Everyone did go out to the balcony to enjoy a rare event in Vancouver: summer weather showing up the first week of May. A few clouds dotted the horizon, promising a spectacular sunset.

Gryndon, plate in hand, manoeuvred himself so that he followed Carlyle outside. The aide chose a chair at the extreme left end of the balcony and when he sat down, Gryndon was right beside him. Coswell edged as close to them as he could, telling himself to keep his ears open and not get lost in the orgasms of taste. Unfortunately he couldn't hear the two conversing. They spoke in low voices and were completely drowned out by Kevin, who was enjoying himself exchanging repartees with Carl. The latter had commented that the view to the North Shore mountains in the changing light could be compared to "a Tony Onley canvas evolving."

"Carl's such a snob," Kevin said. "When these North Dakota boys come off the farm and get educated, it goes to their heads. Who the hell is Tony Onley?"

"Was," Carl replied. "He's dead — killed in a plane crash. But he left behind a marvelous legacy of work, west coast scenes like the one we're seeing now over the North Shore, soft lines and colours with the wonderful blues and reds blending into each other, shifting from three to two dimensions as the sun sets...."

"Ernie. Make him stop," Kevin said. "He's putting me to sleep."

"That from a man whose highest aspiration is to play with big round balls every day," Carl said.

The voices to Coswell's left were becoming even softer and then, out of the corner of his eye, he saw Gryndon's hand reach across and lightly touch Carlyle's arm. The aide's face, which had worn a sour expression from the minute he'd arrived, slowly broke into a shy smile as he looked toward his former partner. That look said everything—forgiveness, fondness, relief. Coswell didn't need Gryndon to tell him; Tommy Carlyle was off the suspect list. Paranoids driven to murder were never in a forgiving mode.

Summer ended Saturday morning. Coswell wakened at six to the sound of his alarm and the pounding of rain against the bedroom window. Wonderful, he thought, a day for everyone to stay inside and curl up with a good book. He hoped Mayor Gryndon and Governor Kruger would do just that. The longer they stayed in secure quarters before the banquet, the better.

He lay in his warm bed for a few luxurious minutes, delaying the shock of bare feet on cold floor. Wall-to-wall carpeting was included in the purchase price of his apartment, but he'd turned it down. Childhood memories of his obsessive mother's screaming vacuum cleaner and her constant admonishment not to spill had created in him a total aversion to all things carpet.

The thought of his departed mother caused a pang of remorse as he rose and surveyed the mess he'd managed to create in less than two weeks, since Iris Chew had last straightened it all up. He could almost feel his mother's displeasure emanating from her grave and he'd have to take even greater pains to avoid Iris. The obvious solution, tidying some of it up himself, never entered his mind. He preferred to feel guilty.

After a shave and a lingering hot shower, he wrapped himself in a towel and returned to his bedroom to search for the new suit he'd bought for his San Francisco trip. He glanced longingly at his usual rumpled attire strewn about the room, but the banquet necessitated formalwear. To his relief, the suit was actually on a hanger along with the tie and the only white shirt he owned that had a collar that didn't choke him. A sniff of the armpits sent him back to the bathroom for another slather of Old Spice, but all in all, he felt he'd be presentable.

He whipped off the damp towel, flung it over a chair and dressed quickly.

Despite the early hour there was already a lineup at the Robson Street Starbucks, but nobody dawdled. It took only minutes before Coswell, latte and slice of banana loaf in hand, settled into a cozy corner. He scanned the morning *Star* and noted that the crime column for the day was dedicated to home invasions — nothing on the West End cases for a pleasant change.

He pulled out his cellphone and dialed Blakemore's number. It was time to get the security going on Mayor Gryndon. He could have waited for a more reasonable hour, but rousting Blakemore gave him a modicum of sadistic pleasure.

"I hope I didn't wake you," Coswell said when the corporal's sleepy grunt came across the connection and, not wanting to get into a lengthy conversation, gave the orders for the day:

"You've got a new assignment. I want you to switch from Ernie to Gryndon. Keep that Beretta handy and stay with him until I meet you at the convention centre. I'll take over from there. Don't leave with Gryndon until I tell you to, and when you do, keep in constant touch with me. Use your cellphone. I'll keep the line open. Any questions?"

Blakemore's brain was too numb to think of any. He hung up and listened for signs of life in the apartment. Hearing none, he rolled over and went back to sleep.

Coswell phoned Burns next, but that call was unnecessary; the sergeant was already up and preparing to leave for work.

"Big day," he said. "You really didn't think I'd sleep in, did you?"

"Just checking. See you at seven thirty?"

"Roger."

That settled, he swallowed the last of his latte and headed off for the Main Street Precinct.

***
***

The drive from Robson Street to Hastings and Main cuts across morning rush hour traffic and is a relatively short distance. Rain, however, especially the first rain after a dry spell, causes havoc in the city. For a population that's rained upon the majority of the year, such chaos is puzzling, but it invariably occurs. It took a half hour for the gridlock to loosen enough for Coswell to get through and by the time he made it to the station house on Main, it was almost eight o'clock. Burns was already there, along with Miller and Whitfield.

"Sergeant Burns was kind enough to have a cruiser pick us up when we phoned," Miller said. "Getting a cab on a rainy morning in this town is a real problem."

Burns sat with a smug look on his face.

"All right," Coswell said. "I might as well brief the lot of you at once."

He looked at the two agents.

"But first, what have you two got to report?"

Whitfield started off. "It wasn't easy getting that phone information. Those bastards in Sacramento think they're a law unto themselves. I actually had to threaten bringing Washington down on their heads if they didn't co-operate. Anyway, Carlyle did not make any calls to Seattle either from his office or his apartment."

"You did better than me," Miller said. "It appears that you can't get a job at the Capital if you're a known member

261

of any radical group, right wing or not. If any of those men are Knights, then they're on the secret rolls, and to date we've had little success breaking into them."

He got up from the hard metal chair (probably to let some blood back in his ass, Coswell speculated) and continued his report.

"Kruger's two bodyguards, Ales and Ferring, are also ex-US Rangers, but they were Intelligence Corps officers. It's unlikely they had anything to do with Deavers and Thornton or even Carson, except maybe at the Sacramento Gun Club. They were members there, too, but so are a lot of the Capital staff. Let's face it, Americans like to shoot guns."

"Did you get anything more on Steve Carson?"

"He's not one of the known Knights either, but being a Texan and running with Deavers and Thornton makes me think he must be one. I suspect he's at a pretty low level though, but you can't be sure. A custodian's job is good cover. He'd be free to move a lot more easily than someone close to the Governor."

Unless the Governor himself was part of the Knights' hierarchy, Coswell thought.

"If there's anything we can do for you, Inspector," Miller said, "just name it. We're planning to stay until the Governor and Mayor Gryndon are on their way back to California."

"No, even if by some miracle you could identify Carson's masters," Coswell said. "I don't think the man can be called off. He's in a mission-to-be-accomplished mode and I doubt he's in contact with anyone. I'm afraid everything's in our court right now."

Whitfield got up from his chair.

"Good luck, Inspector. We'll be in touch."

Coswell's mind buzzed while he waited at his desk for Burns to return from the briefing room, where he'd gone to organize his men. He'd thought of sending a limo filled with security men in suits to the front entrance of the convention centre and then sneaking the Mayor by a yellow cab to the service entrance, but somehow he suspected the Mayor wouldn't go along with it. Blakemore, however, was a different story; he could be added to Gryndon's security.

"Go rent yourself a tuxedo," he told Blakemore. "If I can't get you a seat at the banquet, you can pose as a waiter. I want someone in that banquet room I can get to move quickly if need be. That someone is going to be you. Tell Gryndon I've ordered you to be a chaperone. If he gives you any trouble, phone me. Also tell him to send all his security staff down here to get their ID passes, along with yours. When the lot of you get out of that limo, I want Gryndon to be so hidden, he'll look like someone in the middle of a rugby scrum all the way to the banquet room."

"What about the press?" Blakemore said, thinking of Heather McTavish. "Gryndon's a politician. I've never seen one pass up an opportunity to speak or get his picture taken."

"Tell him this one's different. I don't care if Christ's waiting there to talk to him; he's not to stop for anyone."

The protocol for Gryndon now settled in his mind, Coswell turned his thinking to Governor Kruger. The man was coming to the conference essentially to pump up his own image and Coswell knew just who would fit in well with that attitude: Vancouver Mayor Schmidt and RCMP Chief Inspector Ward. The press would swarm on them like bees to honey and they'd love it. That would clear the way for Gryndon to be whisked into the centre with minimal attention.

A brief phone call to the Mayor's office settled the matter quickly.

"Great idea," Schmidt said. "I'll call Chief Ward and we'll go down to the yacht and welcome the Governor to Vancouver. In fact, it would probably be sociable of us to escort him to the banquet. After all, he is the ranking politician."

Right, thought Coswell. And Kruger's movie-star persona would garner a wonderful photo op: Schmidt, the Governor and Ward in full dress regalia, standing on the deck of Brian Sterne's yacht. Front page in every daily from Prince Rupert to San Diego.

Burns didn't even get a chance to sit down when he returned from the briefing room.

"We're off to the front, my good man," Coswell said. "We don't have a moment to lose."

The Vancouver Convention Centre has one of the most spectacular settings in the entire world. Its signature five sails give it landmark status rivalling the Sydney Opera House. Add the Pan Pacific Hotel rising at one end, the cruise ships docked alongside, the skyline of the West End, the North Shore Mountains, and the lush green of Stanley Park ... visitor and citizen alike are awed.

To Coswell, however, this lovely complex was a nightmare.

An endless stream of humanity moved through the buildings and adjacent walkways with few restrictions, typical of Vancouver's people-friendly civic areas. His self confidence waned. How could he ensure anyone's safety in that massive space?

The city police were already at their posts. Their number visibly impressed Coswell, and Burns took pride in that. He took even more pride when they went inside the centre to inspect the RCMP contingent — all four of them. Coswell was furious.

"That old son of a bitch. He expects me to protect one large duck in a virtual shooting gallery and he gives me four men, barely enough to cover the entrances and exits to the banquet hall with no one to patrol the other floors."

"You have Blakemore and me, too," Burns said.

"No. I want you to command the perimeter and be instantly available to any of your men if they see something. Blakemore will be in the banquet room with me. We'll just have to hope that's enough."

He spoke briefly to the four RCMP constables.

"We're going to sweep this place three times. Right now, at 1400 hours, and twenty minutes before our dignitaries arrive. Let's get on with it."

And sweep they did, from bottom to top, at a pace that surprised (and winded) Burns. Coswell missed nothing. He peeked into kitchens, washrooms, closets and noted all personnel en route.

"Memorize everything," he told the men. "After a while, you won't have to look at the details, you'll see a pattern and when it's broken, it'll be obvious to you. And believe me, our man Carson is going to break that pattern somewhere. Don't miss it."

Satisfied that everything had been covered, he gave final instructions.

"We'll spread out for the next sweeps. Anyone who shouldn't be in the building won't be able to dodge us all that way. You keep in touch by radio. We're all on the same frequency. Report anything suspicious, and I mean *anything*. Questions?"

One constable raised his hand. Coswell made note of his name: Easton.

"What are your orders if the man resists or runs?"

Coswell looked hard into the young man's eyes.

"You neutralize him, permanently if necessary."

Burns blinked. He'd never heard that order given before. In the city police, there might be tacit approval to shoot someone, but rarely verbal.

"All right, men," Coswell said. "Go to your posts. I want every exit and entrance of the banquet hall covered. Easton, you're in charge. I'll pick you all up again at 1400. Stay alert."

***
***

Heather was on the phone in the newsroom of the *Star* trying vainly to contact Coswell. She got the usual "He's out of the office at the moment but leave your number and I'll have him call you" response. She was angry and ready to take out her hostilities on the poor switchboard woman when Frayley burst into the room.

"I did it, Babe. I got us into the convention centre."

That surprised Heather. She assumed the political news crew would cover the event, and unless an editor could be convinced a murder was sure to happen, the crime columnists had no business being there.

"I told our esteemed editor that you and I were going to do a piece on the security that's been laid on for Kruger and Gryndon—the cop's point of view and all that."

"Like a human interest thing? I'm surprised he bought it. Sounds pretty dull to me."

"I think he's feeling a little guilty about buckling under to Mayor Schmidt's position when those two border runners were killed."

"Why didn't you just tell him about the possibility of an assassination with this Steve Carson guy on the loose? Now that's a story."

For a moment Frayley looked uncomfortable.

"He'd have canned it right there. 'Vancouver the safe' is the message our leaders want issued, and even if an assassination attempt actually occurred, I think the story would be stifled."

"They'd have a lot of trouble stifling Gryndon's dead body, if the attempt was successful," Heather said.

"True, Babe. And you and I'll have ringside seats—the scoop of the decade."

"Sometimes your ghoulishness scares me," she said. "You wouldn't really sell your mother for a story, would you? I've heard rumours."

"It would depend how good the story was."

***

The second sweep through the convention centre went well. Constable Easton took control of his little group and no one questioned his leadership. All Coswell had left to do was coordinate the arrival times of the Governor and Mayor Gryndon.

He'd given Burns a list of the reporters allowed up to the

banquet room, with strict orders that they were to follow directly behind the Governor's party. When everyone had entered the building, he expected that most of the residual press corps would then disperse from the main entrance, leaving the area relatively quiet for Gryndon's arrival.

It was two-thirty. Coswell had three hours before a final sweep through the centre. He'd promised the banquet co-ordinator that Kruger and Gryndon would be in their seats by six-thirty. The Governor would make a few remarks first, followed by Gryndon, who was the main speaker of the evening. Dinner would be served immediately afterward.

In truth, Coswell had no intention of keeping his promise; a ten or fifteen minute wait for Gryndon's arrival wouldn't hurt anyone and could even be a bonus. Security aside, Gryndon would probably enjoy the late, grand entrance he'd make and the Governor would have more time to spread his Texas charm around before the competition moved in.

Burns, who'd memorized the catering wagon's schedule, suggested to Coswell on their return to the main entrance that they take a coffee break.

"For heaven's sake," Coswell said, "it's only a couple of hours since lunch. You couldn't possibly be hungry."

"I ate lunch early," Burns grumbled, and then, brightening, said, "They've got Vibeke's pastries."

Coswell, being more than a little familiar with the Kitsilano Queen of Danish goodies, succumbed.

Seated on the steps of the convention centre, munching their sinful pleasures, the two men went over their security strategy for the umpteenth time.

"I can't think of anything more we can do," Coswell said. "The only place I can see a shooter having an opportunity to even get a peep at his target would be at the sit-down banquet. Gryndon will have a wall of bodyguards around him coming and going and I'm not planning to let him stop anywhere en route. A clean shot under those circumstances would be virtually impossible. No, I think we have to keep our eyes open the widest in the banquet hall."

"My men have all the entrances and exits on the ground floor covered, plus a picture of Carson burned into their brains. I think we have an excellent chance of stopping him before he gets anywhere near the banquet floor."

"I hope you're right."

Feeling much better after the danish and the mutual assurances, Burns headed off to do yet another round of his troops, while Coswell went for a walkabout. The clouds had cleared and the May sunshine was warm. He was surprised how much he'd enjoyed the perambulations in San Francisco, even while struggling to keep pace with long-legged Cindy Forsythe. He postulated that the increased blood flow to his head sharpened his senses and his mental acuity. At this point in his career, he needed as much of those as he could muster.

He made his way along the cruise ship docks and saw that Brian Sterne's yacht with the Governor on board hadn't arrived yet, Kruger likely making the most of his Campbell River fishing trip.

He continued until he reached the concourse that led ultimately to Gastown. When he'd rounded the end of the Pan Pacific Hotel, he gazed across Burrard Inlet to North Vancouver and the mountains behind, the familiar peaks of the two Lions now visible as the clouds blew east. He stood for a moment, leaning on the iron railing, and took in the view.

Much as he hated being on boats, he was fascinated by them and watched with interest the comings and going of the tugs, the freighters, and the little Seabuses that cross Burrard Inlet every fifteen minutes connecting the North Shore with downtown Vancouver. One was heading to the dock almost directly in front of him and he followed it as it passed by the huge waterfront derricks that marked the shipping port of Vancouver. He imagined the passengers disembarking and walking down the long passageway that led them to the Skytrain station, the city's LRT, and the escalators to the street.

And then a startling revelation came to him: Seabus passengers could also continue through a series of underground and covered walkways connected not only to the Skytrain and the street, but also to the Pan Pacific Hotel, the cruise ship terminal, and the convention centre. North Vancouver would be a perfect place for Steve Carson to hole up. He could travel the whole route on foot and be lost in the mass of humanity that moved with him. Coswell pulled out his cellphone and called Burns.

"We've got to get a man covering down there. I'm willing to bet that's how Carson's going to arrive."

"Okay," Burns said. "I'll make sure everyone's been fed and hit the outhouse, and then I'll send a couple of uniforms over. They'll be able to watch the Skytrain station as well. That weakens us a bit at the convention centre but I agree it would be nice to nab the guy before he even gets to the centre."

"Plainclothes men would be better," Coswell said. "Uniforms will spook him. What about getting a couple of your detective buddies from the precinct to help out?"

"Ask Inspector Marsden? You've got to be kidding."

"Point taken. Okay, uniforms it'll be. I haven't got time to jump through any hoops right now."

Heather and Frayley stood at the top of the stairs at the convention centre's main entrance and gazed down at their colleagues amassed below them — reporters, journalists and cameramen.

"What's with this 'Urban Renewal' that's so bloody important it draws all these people?" Frayley said. "Media are here from all over. I saw one from Chile, for God's sake."

"If you think that's impressive, you should look at the list of delegates inside," Heather said. "Urban core-rot seems to be happening everywhere. I overheard one man use the expression 'Walmart vacuum effect' — businesses all getting sucked out to the 'burbs."

"Yeah. I can see that would raise hell, especially with tourism. Why travel if one city looks just like another? Not much character in a shopping mall."

Heather looked around and tried to spot Coswell, but he was nowhere to be seen. She thought she saw Sergeant Burns in the mob at one point, but the curse of being so short allowed her only a glimpse.

"I'm going down there," she told Frayley. "I can't see a damn thing from up here."

"Be my guest," he said. "I'm not moving. My days of enjoying a media scrum are over. I'll follow in behind when the smoke clears. While you're down there, keep your eyes open for an old buddy of mine, Sam Spencer from the *Tacoma Review*. His editor might have sent him up for this. If you do see him, tell him where I am. He might not be on the list to go upstairs and I don't want to miss him."

Heather smiled, knowing that Frayley had probably tried to browbeat the list out of Coswell or his delegate, but obviously hadn't succeeded. She'd try to charm it out of Burns—a nice Brownie point for her if she could manage it.

Getting to the front of the media horde proved more difficult than she expected. A territorial instinct prevailed, causing some of her colleagues to object vociferously when she pushed her way past them. She snarled back and held her course until she finally elbowed aside the remaining wall of human flesh to reach the very front of the pack. The fact that she didn't present much of a barrier to anyone's view likely explained why she wasn't immediately hauled back.

Her timing was fortuitous. Burns crossed literally right in front of her and rushed down to a yellow cab that had just pulled up to the curb. A man with a camera bag slung over his shoulder, wearing a hat and dark sunglasses, got out. The cabbie, having received his fare and realized he was in forbidden territory, sped off with a squeal of tires. The new arrival barely had time to turn around before the sergeant was in his face.

"What the hell do you think you're doing? And how did you get past the road block back there?"

"I showed them my press pass," the man said. "My flight was delayed and I'm late. Sorry if I've caused any problem."

Burns, his face hard as stone, inspected the picture ID that dangled from the man's neck. Without the slightest change of expression, he pulled a notebook from his back pocket, flipped it open and scanned a list of names.

"First off," he said, "that ID wasn't issued here and the name we have for the *Tacoma Review* is a Sam Spencer. Your tag says Richard Ardmore."

"Oh my," the man said. "This was all so last minute, but they told me everyone would be notified. Mr. Spencer is ill and I've been sent in his place. I figured my Washington State press ID would suffice until I could get a local one issued, but I guess there's no time."

Burns concurred in no uncertain terms.

"You're certainly right about that. I'm afraid you're shit out of luck and here's what you're going to do. You'll walk back that way and find yourself a bar where you can watch the whole thing on the news channel and write your story there."

"Oh, dear," Ardmore said. "But wait."

He rummaged in his camera bag and pulled out a small piece of paper.

"This is the phone number of the Chief Editor of the *Review*. Please, use my cellphone and call him. This assignment's a big one for me and I just can't blow it."

Heather, who was standing literally beside the two men as they conversed, felt a wave of pity for the reporter. She suspected he was a rookie just like her and, besides, he was representing Harold Frayley's old buddy.

"Aw, give the poor guy a break, Burns," she said. "Make the call. Nothing's happening around here yet anyway."

Others had heard the exchange as well and added their voices to Heather's. Baiting a city police sergeant was a welcome diversion from the boredom of waiting.

"He's just trying to do his job," one of the voices said.

"Suppression, that's what's happening," from another.

There were scattered boos.

It was Burns' turn to be flustered. Begrudgingly, he took the phone that Ardmore held out to him and dialed the number. The conversation was brief. Ardmore was Gordon Spencer's replacement, confirmed.

"All right," Burns said. "I notice your newspaper's on the admit list for the banquet, but I want to see you with that group at all times and I'll tell you just how to do that." He pointed to Heather. "Just stick with the redhead here, the one with the big mouth."

Heather gave Burns a big smile.

"You're such a sweetie," she said.

He was about to say something to her but changed his mind when he saw Coswell appear at the entrance doors. He rushed over and began an animated discussion with him, repeatedly looking in Ardmore's direction. Coswell followed his gaze and looked as though he was going to come over, but was distracted by a sudden pressing forward of the media horde. They'd spotted Governor Kruger, Mayor Schmidt and Chief Inspector Ward, surrounded by security men, making their way on foot from Brian Sterne's yacht to the convention centre along the dockside avenue.

Heather was almost pushed over by reporters, mics thrust forward, streaming past her in their haste to intercept the Governor. Ardmore, she noticed, was one of the mob. *Eager beaver*, she thought.

"Not down there with the rest of the pit bulls, Babe?" Frayley had appeared at her shoulder.

"I'm above all that," she said, nose in the air. "I just do exclusives."

"Well, let's head over to the entrance then. We can jump right in behind the big man when he goes upstairs."

"Good idea. Your man, Spencer, by the way, is sick. The *Review* sent a junior named Ardmore in his place. He's getting into the banquet room, though. Your friend must be a somebody, all right."

"Ardmore? Never heard of him," Frayley said.

They made it to the entrance doors just in time. For a man who ordinarily enjoyed lingering in the limelight, Kruger moved quickly. His smile brightened a bit when Heather managed to catch his eye and give him a little tinkle wave. He winked back.

The mob came to a halt at the entrance doors. The Governor and two of his security men passed through, followed by Schmidt and then Ward. Coswell, Burns, and two uniforms formed the barrier. The sergeant, list in hand, began admitting those reporters allowed up to the banquet floor. Heather and Frayley were first; the rest followed, spread out much more than Coswell had intended. The jostling of those left outside slowed the procedure. He decided to go on ahead and leave Burns and his man to check the rest of the reporters through.

Heather was almost trotting to keep up with Kruger, and Frayley's wheeze gave her some concern; someday he'd have a heart attack, rushing like that. When they reached the doors of the banquet room, Kruger and his group were let through, but a uniformed RCMP officer stopped everyone else. He had a list in his hand identical to Burns'.

"There are three vacant tables to your left as you enter the room," he told them. "Please get settled there immediately. That will be the designated press area and you must remain there."

"What if I have to have a pee?" Heather said.

"There are washrooms at this end."

They filed in. The delegates were already seated and Heather estimated there were probably a hundred or so. She and Frayley grabbed chairs closest to the aisle, facing the podium. The room wasn't particularly large; tables were set quite close together. Four or five had been placed end to end to create a huge head table, likely to accommodate as many as possible who could later boast that they'd dined elbow-to-elbow with Governor Kruger and Mayor Gryndon. Access to the kitchen was across the room from the press area through the swinging doors. On one side of these stretched a long serving table; on the other, an enormous bar.

Kruger handshook his way up the aisle and then along the head table, his two security men never more than a few feet away from him. The glad-handing slowed him down and he'd barely sat down when Gryndon made his entrance. The Mayor avoided the handshake routine by walking quickly and waving to the crowd instead. Unlike the burly pair of guards with Kruger, only one man accompanied Gryndon, a tiny fellow who, to Heather's surprise, took a seat directly across the table from the Mayor rather than standing, as Kruger's men did.

Vancouver Mayor Schmidt and Chief Inspector Ward and their wives sat on either side of Gryndon and Kruger. The rest of the table's occupants were conference dignitaries and their spouses. The chair opposite the Governor was vacant, but not for long. Coswell breezed right past the press table and made his way to it.

"Good evening, ladies and gentlemen." A grey haired man in a tuxedo had moved to a microphone near the end of the head table. He gave a few words of welcome and then introduced the two distinguished guests, beginning with Governor Kruger who "kindly cut short his vacation to say a few words to the conference participants."

Kruger made the most of his time at the podium by extolling motherhood issues: conservation efforts, personal freedoms, and the great friendship between the two countries, especially regarding the West Coast. He scattered a number of right-wing catch-phrases through his speech—"the principles of our forefathers," "the traditional family," and "laws for the majority"—most of which went over the heads of those listening, few recognizing the rigid thinking behind the statements.

Coswell paid little attention to the talk. Burns, in his last-minute report to him, had let drop the fact that earlier in the afternoon the uniforms at the Seabus terminal noticed a suspicious individual who'd emerged from the disembarking walkway and made an abrupt stop when he saw the officers. Before they could approach him, he moved quickly to the stairs and vanished into the crowd heading to the street.

This, combined with the *Tacoma Review* reporter switch, nagged at him. Was this the change in pattern he'd warned everyone else to look for and he'd missed it?

He waited until Kruger finished speaking and then, during the applause, quickly got up and went to the entrance doors. He'd had only a few moments to speak to Blakemore after Gryndon had arrived at the centre, and other than a general "You're the ranking RCMP officer besides me right now, so I want you to take control of our men outside the banquet room," there hadn't been time to give him any specifics.

He couldn't avoid eye contact with Heather and Frayley on his way down the aisle. A quick nod was all he planned to give them, but something caught his eye — an empty seat at the far end of the press table.

He stopped short. Heather was closest to him.

"Who's missing over there?" he said, pointing to the vacant chair.

Heather and Frayley turned and stared. They hadn't noticed it; the show was in front of them. Heather realized the significance first.

"Oh, shit. Ardmore's not here. That seat must be his."

She tried to rationalize:

"Maybe Burns held him up downstairs. They didn't exactly hit it off when the guy pulled up in a taxi."

Coswell bolted out the door, almost running over Blakemore.

"Whoa, Inspector. Did you eat something that didn't agree with you?"

Coswell had his cellphone out and started talking immediately to Burns stationed at the main entrance.

"Did you let that *Tacoma Review* reporter past your checkpoint?"

Coswell's face blanched when Burns informed him he had.

"Oh, my God," he said, turning to Blakemore. "Carson's in the building."

He needed only a few seconds to decide what to do. He started with Burns, who was still on the phone.

"I want you to leave a single uniform at each post. Take the rest and work your way up here to the banquet room. Examine every nook and cranny, but tell your men to be careful. I don't want anyone shot, unless it's Carson. Blakemore's with me up here. He'll sweep in the opposite direction, but he's going to have to do it by himself because there's only enough of my men to cover the banquet hall doors."

Blakemore, justifiably concerned that he might get shot in the process, was about to tell Coswell to mention that possibility, but, too late, Coswell broke the connection.

"When you cross paths with Burns and his men," he said to Blakemore. "I want you to continue to ground level. If Carson has found a foolproof hiding place, maybe he'll expose himself when the first wave of police goes by. Keep your weapon handy."

"What are you going to do?"

"I'm going back inside to stick with Gryndon. I've got a good view in all directions from there and I can act quickly if anything looks like it's going to develop. Now keep in constant touch with me. I have an earphone that I'll connect to my cell. Pass that on to Burns when you see him, too. I forgot to mention it."

***
***

Mayor Gryndon was at the microphone. Most of his talk revolved around urban renewal and quickly won over the crowd. He knew his subject and his remarks were often interrupted with applause. But the scrappy politician in him emerged from time to time.

"My honourable colleague, Governor Kruger, has spoken of forefathers, family values, and laws for the majority. I'd like to comment on that."

Kruger gazed straight ahead but there was a slight narrowing of his eyes as though he were waiting for the other shoe to drop. It did.

"But who were our forefathers, the early European settlers?

That's a pretty small group. Look at the population of America today: Afro-American, Hispanic, Middle Eastern, Caribbean. In Canada, the Indo-Canadians and Asians. Many of them will be the forefathers of generations to come and we must recognize that. And family values? I challenge you to name any one of those cultures that doesn't have family values equal to any other."

Kruger began to look uncomfortable. He tried to fix Tommy Carlyle with his gaze, but Tommy's eyes were directed only at Gryndon.

"Laws for the majority. That's how a democracy runs, right? But what defines majority? Is it what the media tells us? Our politicians? And who amongst us doesn't fall into a minority group in some way or another? Think about it. Isn't there something unique about you, or are you just one of a great homogeneous mass?"

There wasn't a sound to be heard in the entire banquet room; even the servers were hanging on Gryndon's words.

"In my opinion," he went on. "Laws should never be made to bully even the smallest segment of our legitimate society. We need order, yes, but not dictates that shackle us. The eighteenth century — the century of the forefathers of whom Governor Kruger speaks — is over two hundred years gone. That small handful of men did write tolerance into their laws but the tolerance we need in our world today is far, far greater. Remember that when you go back to your cities. Buildings alone won't achieve your urban renewal goals, but if you add the tolerance that I've described, you'll succeed. Make your downtown cores friendly to all citizens and they'll return in droves."

The applause was deafening; everyone stood up. Coswell held his breath — even a gun without a silencer would be muffled in all that noise. But to his great relief, the grey-haired gent quieted the crowd down and announced dinner. The serving people sprang into action.

The choice of main course was either beef or wild salmon.

"I've got salmon coming out my ears," Kruger told the server. "I want a slab of he-man beef — medium rare."

Gryndon's eyes twinkled.

"I'll have the meat too," he said. "As long as it's Alberta beef. That Texas stuff is like old shoe leather."

The waiter assured him the beef was from Alberta.

"Then I want it true he-man style: rare and still quivering."

***
***

Blakemore was in no hurry. He took his time checking out the corridor surrounding the banquet hall, stopping and chatting with the four Mounties at their posts. He'd been able to see into the hall when Coswell came out and noted a vaulted ceiling with exhaust vents going straight through the roof, negating the opportunity for an overhead shot. Shooting from within the hall meant certain capture.

No, he thought, Carson's only chance to nail Gryndon would be when the Mayor left the banquet hall.

The next level down, he decided, would be the safest place to intersect with Burns. He reasoned that the sergeant had the manpower and with a little luck he'd flush out Carson before they even reached that floor. Also, should Carson get past Burns and come running towards him, the stair railing would serve as cover. Besides that, Blakemore had the advantage of surprise. And if the man wasn't found, then he could shout down to Burns' crew when they appeared, thus safely revealing his position. Congratulating himself on his brilliant thinking, he stopped halfway down the stairs and sat down on a step to wait.

31

For the most part Coswell loved his job, but there were times when it interfered with his joie de vivre — particularly when dining. He'd expected the usual uninspired fare served at most banquets he'd ever been to, but the urban renewal people were treated to a real feast.

There were no wine decisions to be made; the sommeliers had done that for them. All award-winning BC vintages: a lovely Wild Goose Pinot Gris with the appetizers and a nicely oaked Golden Mile Cellars Chardonnay with the soup course. Those who chose the salmon for their entrée were poured a Nk'Mip Pinot Noir, and to Coswell's absolute delight, the beef was to be accompanied by the Jackson-Triggs' Okanagan Shiraz Proprieter's Grand Reserve, voted "The World's Best" at a London international competition.

His delight vanished when Ales, Kruger's chief security man, halted the waiter who was about to pour the first glass for the Governor.

"This one's been opened," Ales said.

"Yes," the waiter replied. "It's been breathing for exactly one hour."

"Sorry — procedure," Ales said. "We'll need another one that hasn't breathed at all."

No one objected. Everyone around Coswell was occupied in conversation, but he wasn't going to let that nectar disappear for possibly a lesser vintage and one that hadn't been properly prepared.

"For Christ's sake, Ales," he hissed. "Don't be an ass. Let him serve the bottle."

Ales spoke to the waiter.

"Go ahead. Serve it to the others. I'll go for another bottle which is to be exclusively for the Governor and Mayor Gryndon."

The waiter shrugged his shoulders and proceeded to fill Coswell's glass and then move down the table to the other beef eaters. The inspector sipped the magnificent red, and noted, with satisfaction, that most at his table had chosen the salmon entrée. With a little luck there'd be enough left of the Shiraz for him to have a second glass. He was even happier when Ales returned with the replacement bottle for Kruger and Gryndon—a good Cabernet, but nowhere near the quality of the Shiraz.

He taunted the security man. "Did you sniff the cork, Ales? It takes an expert to open a good bottle of wine properly."

Ales ignored him, and seeing the waiter occupied at the other end of the table, poured the wine himself for Gryndon and Kruger.

***
***

Blakemore's impatience grew. The city police were taking an inordinate amount of time to do their sweep. When they finally appeared, he shouted down to them.

"Hey, Burns. Did you stop for supper or what? It's been twenty-five minutes. My ass is numb."

To a man, Burn's crew jumped at the sound of Blakemore's voice and reached for their guns. Every man, that is, except Burns who walked to the bottom of the stairs and looked up.

"I might more appropriately ask what the hell you've been doing," he said. "There's been a lot of good leg power spent searching this goddamned place. We've checked every room, every garbage can, even the laundry chutes. Don't tell me we have to do your floor too."

"Nah," Blakemore replied. "From here on everything is secured by no less than four of Her Majesty's Royal Canadian Mounted Police, not counting me, of course. You can let down your guard."

"Well then, get your butt down here and help us sweep this floor. If this Carson guy hasn't fled the scene, which, if he's smart, he's done already, then he's a bloody magician fooling us with mirrors."

Blakemore descended the stairs and joined the crew. He was impressed at their thoroughness; Burns wasn't exaggerating. But they found no trace of Carson.

"Now what?" Blakemore said. "I'm getting hungry and with this penguin suit on I should be able to get into the banquet room and sample some of that upper crust grub. I'll sit in Ardmore-Carson whoever's vacant seat."

"Why not?" Burns said, in a loud voice. "We'll all try to get something up there. Let's go."

Blakemore's hopes were squelched when they reached the top of the stairs.

"Did you forget your orders?" Burns hissed into his ear. "You need to wait here ten minutes or so, then work your way back to the bottom floor, super-quietly. We'll follow you fifteen minutes later. Maybe Carson will poke his nose out. It should give us two good chances at him."

Damn, Blakemore said to himself, but he had no argument; Burns was right. Until Gryndon got back on his plane to San Francisco, Carson was a threat. He waited the ten minutes while Burns huddled with his men, then started down.

He wasn't as comfortable now, tiptoeing his way. Every sound he made seemed amplified in the empty corridors. He decided not to do a room check. No matter how quietly he opened the doors, Carson would hear him. No, his best chance was to spot him moving through the hallways, but when he reached the bottom floor, he'd seen and heard nothing. He was beginning to like Burns' suggestion that Steve Carson had split the scene, realizing how futile an assassination attempt would be with all the security that had been activated.

He contacted Coswell on his cellphone.

"Nothing here, Inspector," he said. "I think our man's left the building. We scared him off."

"Keep looking," Coswell said, barely audible.

The excitement of prowling the halls, believing an assassin might be lurking, wore off quickly. Blakemore was bored and hungry. Burns was taking forever again to make his way to the bottom floor. Probably rechecking the laundry chutes, he mused.

The thought of laundry chutes took Blakemore back to his high school days. He'd gotten an after-school job one year working in a hospital laundry and remembered the back-breaking work lifting wet linen out of washers into canvas trams and then pulling it all back out again to load into the driers.

Curious, he decided to check out the convention centre's laundry. The workers had left for the day and the door was unlocked (Coswell's orders). He went inside.

The room was larger than he had expected, almost as big as the hospital laundry. He gazed over the rows of hampers, lined with heavy vinyl rather than canvas, but otherwise identical to the ones he'd pushed around years before. He looked up at the ceiling and saw the ends of the big chutes, eight in all, positioned the whole length of the room. Laundry chutes required a straight drop, he recalled, or they'd jam up.

He hadn't bothered to turn on the lights. There was still plenty of daylight coming through the big windows; much more pleasant than the dungeon that had housed the hospital laundry. The biggest difference, though, was the silence. It was never silent when he had worked in the hospital. Driers, washers, mangles — a constant din. It began to grow on him, the silence, and he could feel a strange apprehension creeping over him as he thought of Carson again. This room would be a perfect place to hide out. He wondered how thoroughly the hampers had been searched.

He felt for the Beretta and was comforted by its touch.

Whoosh! Thump! A wad of linen crashed into a tram behind him. Startled, he jumped back directly against another tram and before he could catch himself, fell backwards into the soiled laundry. Cursing, he extracted himself, but as he raised himself up on his elbows, he felt a solid object beneath him. For a second he imagined he'd fallen on the assassin and the object was a gun. His heart pounded.

He jerked to a standing position, then realized how foolish he must look and was glad no one was around. Curious again, he turned back to the tram and rummaged through the laundry until he found the object, wrapped in a bundle of wet towels. When he unwound the towels, he was amazed to find a camera case, complete with camera inside.

He contemplated how it could have gotten there. Would any worker be so careless as to gather up a camera with the towels and toss the whole works down the chute? Not likely. His policeman's mind checked in. Thievery, that was the answer. Swipe the camera, disguise it with the towels, fire it down the chute, and then go down later and retrieve the prize from the laundry. Clever. He slung the camera strap over his shoulder and proceeded to the entrance foyer to wait for Burns. One of the city constables would be happy to investigate, he was sure.

***

Coswell shook off the mellow feeling creeping over him as the food and wine began to take effect. He chastised himself for being so weak. He should have abstained completely and eaten less, but temptation won again. He was disappointed, though, that the Shiraz never got back to him. Obviously he wasn't the only connoisseur at the table. He eyed the untouched glass of red sitting in front of Kruger. A total waste. Gryndon had done a much better job. He was well into a refill.

Kruger noticed Coswell's empty glass and deftly made a switch.

"Here," he said. "As you know, I can't stand the stuff. Enjoy."

And Coswell did. The Cabernet was quite lovely.

This extra glass of red wine, combined with Blakemore's report and the likelihood that Carson had fled, allowed him to relax. The mellowness returned. He hoped his judgment wasn't slipping, but logic told him all was well.

The earphone was bugging him. He pulled it out and turned on his cellphone's vibrate function.

The servers were clearing tables in preparation for the dessert course, whisking away soiled napkins and replacing them with crisp new ones. Bottles of champagne appeared at each table. Probably a number of toasts coming up, Coswell thought, and since his bladder seemed to have filled up all of a sudden, he decided to make a quick trip to the washroom. He crooked a finger at one of the servers.

"Is there a loo somewhere away from that mob of reporters?" he asked.

The waiter pointed past the end of the bar.

"The VIP washroom's in the corner over there," he said.

Gryndon, overhearing, leaned across the table.

"Are you having the same problem as me? My back teeth are floating."

Coswell nodded.

"Lead on," Gryndon said.

Both men rose from their seats as though a tacit command had been given. Two figures lurking in the perimeter of the room moved forward in unison and in seconds formed an escort: Gryndon's security. Coswell recognized the man who'd been in the foyer at Ernie's apartment building.

"Damn," Coswell muttered. "Now the whole crowd knows we need to have a piss."

Gryndon laughed.

"Welcome to the life of a politician."

One of the security men stopped them at the door of the washroom while the second man went inside.

"Hurry up," Gryndon said. "I haven't had to go like this since I was a kid."

Coswell sympathized. He wasn't doing much better. When the security man came out and declared the room clear, they almost collided in their haste to get to the urinals.

They stood in silence, enjoying the ecstasy of emptying their over-filled bladders. Coswell's phone was vibrating. He pulled it out of his pocket with a free hand, the other occupied in steadying his stream.

"What?" he said.

"Carson's in the laundry chute!" Burns shouted into the phone.

Coswell remembered from the sweeps: there was one in this washroom, right behind him. He looked into the mirror above the urinal in front of him. The door to the chute was slowly opening and the long, silencer-mounted barrel of a pistol appeared.

His sphincter went into spasm. The next moments went by in a blur.

The Mayor grunted when Coswell tackled him around the waist and hauled him to the tile floor. Urine splashed everywhere. Gazing from floor level, Coswell saw the entry door closing and pair of black shoes in front of it.

A man had entered the washroom.

Pffft! The unmistakable sound of a shot from a gun with a silencer. Coswell flinched, expecting the slam of lead into his body, but he felt nothing.

The black shoes weren't moving and a peculiar metallic sound reverberated as a body rattled down the chute to the laundry three floors below.

Coswell rolled off of Gryndon and looked up. Ales stared down at him, pistol in hand and a peculiar look in his eyes, not a look of concern, but rather of confusion and indecision. His gun, too, had a silencer in place and the bore was pointed right between Coswell's eyes. He had the unnerving feeling that Ales was going to shoot again, this time at him.

Blakemore brought the whole scene to a halt.

When he'd shown the camera to Burns and discovered its significance, he acted immediately. Shouting over his shoulder as he ran for the stairs, he told Burns to get through to Coswell on the cellphone. With an effort not called upon since his football days, he vaulted up flights of stairs two and three steps at a time, not stopping until he reached the doors to the banquet room. Constable Easton was stationed there.

"Don't let anybody out of here," Blakemore told him.

He stepped into the room and paused for a moment to get his bearings. He was distracted momentarily by a familiar red head just to his left. Heather got out of her chair and moved quickly to his side.

"Coswell and Gryndon are in the washroom over there where the two security guys are standing," Heather said, and then, looking towards the head table, "Oh, look, one of Kruger's men is headed that way, too."

She was about to start grilling Blakemore, but he broke away and proceeded up the aisle. He forced himself not to run, but moved at a brisk pace. As he approached the washroom, the man Heather had identified as one of Kruger's men was just going in. The heavy door swung shut behind him. Gryndon's crew, who'd let the man pass, closed ranks again, blocking the entrance.

Using his half-back's guile, Blakemore pulled his ID card forward from his neck to show them, gave a friendly grin, then lunged past, pushed the door open, and stepped inside. The two guards were right behind him.

He was confused for a second by the sight of Gryndon

on the floor in front of the urinals and Coswell kneeling beside him, apparently mesmerized by a tall man pointing a gun at his head. Blakemore acted instantly. He dove, elbows foreward, and hit the man just below the shoulder blades. He heard a thud and then the whine of a slug ricocheting off the tile floor, the wall and finally embedding in the ceiling. The gun clattered across the floor. The thud came from Ales' forehead when it smacked onto the edge of a urinal. He was unconscious, Blakemore draped across the back of his legs. Gryndon's men, guns drawn, rushed over to their boss, completely ignoring Coswell, who slowly rose to his feet.

"Good of you to drop in, Paul," he said to Blakemore, still lying prone on the tile floor. "Lend me your cellphone. I think mine's busted somewhere."

He casually zipped up his fly and spoke to Burns on the phone after Blakemore got up and handed it to him.

"We've just sent you a package down the laundry chute from the VIP washroom on this level. If there's any life in it, put on the cuffs. Otherwise, call the meat wagon and get it over to the morgue at the General. There should be a gun around him somewhere, too, so pick that up as well."

Everyone, with the exception of the unconscious Ales, stood and looked at Coswell.

"There's been an incident here," he said. "But I think, for the sake of calm, order, and the good name of our fair city, we should confine it to this room."

Gryndon grasped the situation immediately.

"I agree," he said, and then to his men, "Back outside you two, and pretend nothing's happened."

"What are we going to do about him?" Blakemore said. He'd knelt beside Ales and lifted the unconscious man's lids to check his pupils. "He's just knocked out, and if his skull's as thick as I think it is, he'll come to pretty soon now."

"Call Constable Easton in here and tell him to bring a set of cuffs," Coswell said. "Slap them on this bugger and the two of you stay with him till everyone's gone. Then I want him hauled down to the Main Street office. He's got a lot of explaining to do."

He handed Blakemore back his cellphone.

"What are you going to say to the Governor?" Blakemore asked. "He'll to want to know what's happened to his man."

Gryndon spoke up. "Don't worry. I'll look after that."

He took a moment to rearrange himself and checked his image in the mirror.

"I hope I don't smell like an outhouse," he said, "But there's enough perfume on Mayor Schmidt's wife to cover it up, I think."

***
***

The din of a hundred conversations and the clatter of dinnerware meant the bathroom ruckus had gone unnoticed by everyone except Heather. Even her boss, Frayley, was chatting away with fellow pressmen, but Heather's eyes were fixed on the head table and the washroom behind.

Enough men in that room now to have a poker game, she thought. What's going on? Gryndon's bodyguards were the first to emerge and they stood, as they had before, blocking the doorway, but then nobody showed for the longest time.

Champagne and desserts were being served.

Finally Gryndon, and then Coswell, emerged and returned to the head table. After they sat down, Gryndon leaned over and said something into Kruger's ear. The Governor continued to look straight ahead but his smile had slipped. Ales' partner, Ferring, who'd not budged from his post behind the Governor, turned and looked toward the washroom. He took a step in that direction but Kruger twisted around and froze the man in his tracks with a single command. Ferring returned to his post.

Heather was so intent on the head table that she almost missed the Mountie who'd laid down the rules to them when the press had filed in. He'd entered the banquet room and was quietly working his way around the perimeter. When he reached the VIP washroom, he spoke briefly to the security men before he pushed the door open and slipped inside. Heather's pulse began to race. A story was in the making, maybe the big one they'd hoped for.

***

There were a number of toasts, but eventually the evening ended. The head table filed out first. Heather noticed Kruger pause for a moment to speak to Coswell. She tried to intercept the inspector as he went by her, but he just gave her a quick smile and walked straight ahead. She didn't care; two Mounties and Kruger's chief security guy were still in the washroom. They had to come out sometime and she was going to be there when they did.

The question was, how? And then it occurred to her. Most of the security would be leaving with the VIPs. The women's washroom wouldn't be guarded. She had a hurried conversation with Frayley. His eyes got wider and wider when she told him what she'd seen.

"Way to go, Babe," he said. "Don't worry. I'll cover downstairs. Coswell will be so busy answering my questions, he'll totally forget about you."

She slowly edged her way along the wall, using the crowd as a screen. Everyone was standing now, waiting to exit. It took her only a few minutes to reach the washroom door and duck inside. As a further precaution, she went into one of the stalls and was prepared to stand up on a seat if someone came in to check the place. She noted the time on her watch and estimated it would take ten minutes for the room to clear. Then she'd start her vigil by peeking out the bathroom door.

★★★
★★★

The staff smoothly diverted the guests, including the reporters, along the third floor corridor to elevators that connected to the adjacent Pan Pacific Hotel. That left the way clear for the two notables to exit the convention centre through the main doors. Mayor Schmidt stayed with the Governor, but Chief Inspector Ward, who'd volunteered to escort the wives, followed the others to the hotel.

Gryndon and Kruger took separate routes to the ground floor entrance: the stairs for the Mayor's entourage and the elevator for the Governor. Coswell hustled after Gryndon.

"Back to Ernie's, I presume?" he said, when he got alongside.

"You're damned right. I must have a shower before I get on a plane, that's for certain. I stink. In fact, I think I'll delay my departure until tomorrow. Tommy's taking a ten-thirty flight out in the morning. I'm going to join him."

When they reached the entrance foyer, the scene outside was chaotic; the media had returned with a vengeance. Burns and his crew were valiantly trying to maintain order. Kruger was waiting with his group just inside the doors.

"Let's hit them together, Mr. Mayor," Kruger shouted to

Gryndon and that's precisely what they did, shoulder to shoulder, with Mayor Schmidt tagging behind. Coswell wondered at the friendly gesture, but thought perhaps it was a token of some sort of amends.

The crowd closed around the two men the moment they passed through the doors.

***
***

Frayley trailed the reporter contingent, who rushed out of the hotel back along the docks to the front of the convention centre. He had no immediate interest in Kruger or Gryndon. It was Coswell he wanted and he knew the inspector would be in the background somewhere near the entrance doors.

He was there all right, but had remained inside the building with Sergeant Burns. They were off in a corner, heads together, deep in conversation.

"We got the stiff out okay," Burns was saying. "He unfolded nice after he hit — flat on his back with the gun on his chest. There's a service entrance at one end of the laundry, so after all the pictures we left him in the tram and wheeled it straight into the Coroner's wagon. Piece of cake."

Coswell couldn't hold back a smile at the veteran cop's description of the body disposal.

"It was Carson, all right," Burns continued, "with a lovely hole through his neck. Killed instantly. Someone up there is a helluva shot. What's the story on that?"

Coswell described the events to him in detail, including his suspicion that Ales would have shot both him and Gryndon next.

"You think the Governor ordered all this?" Burns said.

"I don't know. That's still an open question, but I think

Ales was definitely part of it. There was no need for him to have a silencer on his gun, unless it was to finish things off if Carson missed. I think he came into the washroom, saw Gryndon and me on the floor and assumed the job had been done."

"And then deliberately eliminated Carson," Burns said. "And with no witnesses, Ales would've been the hero for killing the assassin — smart."

"Right. Their master was obviously taking no chances on Carson getting caught and singing. He was expendable. Nice organization, eh?"

"Yeah, and I guess we'd better keep Ales under close guard. He might be expendable, too."

Coswell agreed. He told Burns to intercept Blakemore and have him take their prisoner out of the building by the same route the coroner's crew had used to remove Carson's body.

"I'm going to stay here until Gryndon and Kruger are safely on their way and then I'll join you all back at the precinct. Keep Ales in an interrogation room, by the way, not in a cell."

Burns nodded but didn't move. In a voice mixed with awe and respect, he said, "You saved Gryndon's life. He'd be dead sure as shit's brown if you hadn't arranged to stay so close to him."

Coswell smiled. If only the sergeant knew how fluky that had been.

He was about to go outside but changed his mind when he saw Frayley prowling at the front door. He turned and hurried after the sergeant, joining him at the elevator.

"On second thought, Burns, I think I'll do my observations from the front windows on the third floor. I don't know why Frayley's hanging around the entrance instead of going after the VIPs and I don't wish to find out. He's probably got his antenna up from all the comings and goings on the banquet floor.

32

Heather was losing patience. The tables were all cleared and the cleaning crew had disappeared into the kitchen where the rattling of pots and dinnerware could be heard, but there was still no sign of Blakemore. Was he going to wait until everyone left the kitchen as well?

And then an unhappy thought occurred to her: maybe there was another exit out of the washroom and he was long gone. She decided to find out and was halfway down the aisle when the main entrance door swung open and Sergeant Burns marched in.

"What the hell are you doing in here?" he shouted. Coswell appeared right behind him. Out of the corner of her eye, she saw the door to the VIP washroom open a crack, then quickly close. She stood her ground.

"I'm not breaking any laws, and, besides, I'm a member of the press with a pass — see?" She lifted the ID tag from her neck and waggled it at them.

Coswell, annoyed as he was, couldn't help but admire the little imp, but what was he going to do with her? While he was trying to make up his mind, she laid it all out.

"I've watched the whole performance over there," she said, pointing to the VIP washroom. "There are two Mounties, one undercover, and the Governor of California's security man behind that door and I doubt if they're having tea. Something big's gone down and I want in on it."

She paused and fixed Coswell with her gaze.

"Or, I'll write something so full of innuendos, names included, that it'll curl what's left of your hair."

The hair comment hurt. Coswell was sensitive about his balding pate.

"Okay, Heather," he said. "I'll tell you what I'll do. You can come along with us, but I want you to promise me you'll not write any of this up without meeting with my superiors first. How about it? I think they call it responsible journalism."

"Is that like an 'informed public'?"

"How about 'interference in police business'?" Burns interjected, still frowning.

Coswell answered quickly, noting the rising flush on Heather's face.

"I think 'mutual trust' is the right phrase here. Cm'on, Burns, go spring Blakemore."

Burns' frown was nothing compared to the expression on Ales' face when Blakemore and Constable Easton led him out of the washroom. The man was absolutely livid and the huge bump on his forehead added to his fearsome countenance. His eyes flashed as he approached Coswell.

"You'll regret this like nothing you've ever done before," he said. "I should be commended, not dragged off like some criminal. Your superiors will hear about this, you can be sure."

Coswell was unfazed.

"You've just shot and killed a man. In this country that's a crime; a serious crime. Until we get to the bottom of it, you'll remain in police custody. You have the right to remain silent. Anything you say can —"

Ales lunged at him. Blakemore anticipated the move. He grabbed the back of the man's collar and jerked so violently, all Ales could do was let out a pathetic croak.

"The Corporal here is really your friend," Coswell said, not even flinching at the attack. "If he hadn't stopped you … Assaulting a member of Her Majesty's Royal Canadian Mounted Police is also a serious charge."

Heather had certainly flinched. Standing immediately beside the inspector put her in the line of attack. When Ales lunged forward, she jerked backwards, crashed into Burns and struck the back of her head against his solar plexus, winding him.

Ignoring the sergeant's gasps for air, Coswell walked past him and called a last order over his shoulder.

"Use the lock-up instead of the interrogation room if you need to. I'm going back to my observation post. We'll all meet downtown."

Coswell's coolness was external only; within, the incident with Heather had disturbed him. He'd been tiptoeing around the press from day one in the entire West End Murder investigation and he was tired of it. The little red dynamo had just brought it all to a head. It was time to unload some of this onto a higher-up, but who? Gillings? Schmidt? Ward? The Mayor and the Attorney General couldn't stand one another and Ward was still mad at him for going over his head. There'd be problems with any choice he made.

He continued to gaze out the big windows. Gryndon's limo, surrounded by an escort of motorcycle cops, had just left. Kruger was still in sight, proceeding the way he'd come, along the docks to Brian Sterne's yacht. The feeding frenzy of the media seemed to have abated and the

Governor was left in peace as he walked along, accompanied by his remaining security man, Ferring, a squad of Vancouver City Police, and the four RCMP officers.

Coswell decided to delay contacting anyone until he'd had a chance to interview Ales. Heather was in so far now, a little farther wouldn't make things much worse. He turned away from the windows and followed the corridor to the Pan Pacific Hotel. He could call one of the cruisers from there to drive him to the Main Street Precinct and avoid Frayley in the process.

***
***

The scene that greeted Coswell when he arrived at the station was not a welcome one: Frayley had joined Heather. The two were sitting in front row seats, looking through the one-way mirror into the interrogation room. He was surprised that Burns had let them get that far and regretted not giving more specific orders.

But they were a minor concern compared with what was taking place inside the room. Blakemore and Constable Easton were there, seated on chairs facing a table behind which Ales sat, minus the handcuffs. A tall, middle-aged man in a well-cut grey suit stood beside him, a man Coswell recognized: Roland Wells, one of Vancouver's top criminal lawyers. Wells was giving the two Mounties a piece of his mind, emphasizing his remarks by waving his index finger at them. Coswell blessed the fact that someone had turned off the intercom, but was not happy to see Heather scribbling notes at a furious pace. He hoped that lip-reading wasn't one of her skills.

He felt a tap on his shoulder and turned around. Burns was standing there, finger to his lips, gesturing for him to come back to the outer office. Fortunately, neither of the reporters had seen Coswell enter; their eyes were fixed on the drama before them.

"I figured there'd be no harm in letting them watch," Burns said. "But they ain't ever going to hear a word. The sound's staying off."

Coswell nodded his approval, then asked, "How the hell did Wells get here so fast? And on a weekend, no less."

"Beats me. Ales didn't make any calls.... The Governor, maybe?"

"No. Kruger spoke to me when we were filing out of the banquet hall and basically gave his permission to do whatever with Ales and he'd back me up. It could've been a smokescreen, but my instincts tell me he was sincere. He appears genuinely shocked by this whole affair."

"Who, then?"

"Ferring, Ales' partner. It had to be him, and I think he did it after consulting the master plotter."

Coswell thought for a moment and then made a decision.

"I want you to get hold of those two US Federal agents, Miller and Whitfield. Tell them everything that's happened and that I want them to pick it up from here re. Mr. Mastermind."

"I'm on to it," Burns said with uncharacteristic enthusiasm.

Coswell returned to the holding area, swept past the two reporters and ducked into the interrogation room before they could react. He was ready now to face Roland Wells.

"It's about time," the lawyer said. "My client should not have suffered any of this humiliation, let alone been kept waiting by a detective inspector."

Ignoring the implication that an even higher ranking

officer should have been in charge of a case that Wells had deigned to accept, Coswell replied.

"Sorry, but I was seeing to the body of a man your client mercilessly slaughtered less than two hours ago."

"Don't play word games with me," Wells said. "That man was a hired assassin. Mr. Ales literally stopped him from murdering the Mayor of San Francisco ... and you, for that matter. I should think that you'd be grateful to him for saving your neck, in more ways than one. The fact a killer managed to get that close to his target doesn't speak well for the head of security for the affair, that person being you, I understand."

"You understand a lot," Coswell said. "In fact, it's amazing you know so much about something that just happened." He turned to Blakemore.

"Have I missed out on an interview here?"

"Nope. Mr. Wells came in just a few minutes before you did and so far the talk's all been directed at Easton and me."

Wells didn't miss a beat.

"My client has loyal friends who contacted me with all the details. Now let's get on with this. Aside from his obvious innocence, you have absolutely no authority to hold Mr. Ales. He's part of a US diplomatic mission and therefore has immunity under international law."

"Except in the case of serious crime," Coswell responded, adding, "I'm quite familiar with international law."

"Are you really? Then make your charges and look the fool when they're presented to a judge."

"I think you're getting ahead of yourself, Mr. Wells," Coswell said. "We have the right to question your client here prior to laying any charges, but if you must have a reason up front, how about smuggling a silencer into this country?

I'm sure you're aware that silencers are illegal under Canada's gun laws."

Wells looked at Ales. Obviously, no one had passed this bit of information on to him.

"In fact," Coswell continued. "It's the silencer that has us most interested. Perhaps your client can tell us why he would need such a device."

A good lawyer is never blindsided for long and Wells, realizing the problem was more complicated than he expected, reacted quickly.

"My client is saying nothing until we've had a chance to confer and I wish to do that in complete privacy. This room, of course, is out of the question."

"All right," Coswell said. "I'll even save your man the embarrassment of sitting in a cell. You can use my office in the squad room. I can assure you it's not bugged, but you'll have to wait a moment or two while I arrange to have the way cleared."

He turned to Easton.

"Constable. Sitting just outside the door are two reporters, an older man and a red-haired woman. I want you to move them to the main lobby downstairs and stay with them. Tell them it's a matter of protocol — witness protection, lawyer's request, whatever. Promise them one of us will come down shortly for an interview. Don't take any guff from either of them. Be strong."

Blakemore chuckled as Easton left the room. "Good luck."

But any concerns that the constable would have a problem were ill-founded. Burns came into the room.

"You've got a keeper there, Inspector," he said. "Your man swept those two media types up like they were dust balls. I'm impressed."

"Good. Now I want you to take these two gentlemen to my office for their private discussion. When they're finished, bring them back here. We'll be waiting. I'm sure it won't take long."

Wells shot him a glance as he and Ales followed Burns out of the room.

Blakemore leaned forward in his chair.

"Do you think we have time to order in? I'm absolutely starving and I didn't get to eat a morsel of all that great banquet food, like some people I know."

"Oh, for Christ's sake," Coswell said. "You're always thinking about your gut. Surely the drama of the moment here is enough to suppress your appetite."

"Only seeing my wife would do that."

"God. You're just a bundle of primitive desires. Now, get your mind back on the case. While you were twiddling your thumbs in the VIP washroom, I assume you checked out the laundry chute. What did you find?"

Blakemore feigned hurt feelings.

"I was waiting for you to ask," he said. "I found out exactly how Carson got into position and how he planned to get out."

"Well?"

"Climbing rope and something called an Australian Stop Descender."

"What the hell is that?"

"It's a gadget that looks like a stapler. You clamp it to a rope and when you want to go down, you give it a squeeze and away you go."

"Don't tell me you were a climber," Coswell said, trying to picture the big corporal hanging from a rope.

"Nah. It was Easton who filled me in. Rock climbing's a

passion with him. He said that Carson could have slid down to the laundry in seconds and been out of the building in a flash."

"How the hell did he smuggle in all that rope? The chute must be fifty feet from top to bottom. Burns checked the guy in and he'd have noticed the excess baggage."

"Easton looked up the chute with his flashlight. He thinks there's a space just off the top, probably a big air vent. Carson likely planted all his climbing gear there days before all the security got laid on. I'll bet he even practiced a bit, rappelling down and checking how easily the door to the chute opened, getting his sight line and all that."

"How did he get up there to plant the gear?"

"According to Easton, going up that chute for an experienced climber is a piece of cake. He calls it a simple chimney ascent. Doesn't sound simple to me, but I guess those guys have legs of steel."

Coswell saw the whole picture at once: Carson entered the shaft from a second floor washroom. That level was used for small functions and was the least busy of the three floors. Planting his equipment would have been easy, and gaining access immediately prior to the banquet, equally simple. The straggle of reporters following Governor Kruger and his party wouldn't have paid any attention to one of their members heading to a washroom.

"You know," Coswell said. "That gives me an idea what the contingency plan was if Carson couldn't get into position. I'll bet there was a string or a length of fishing line attached to the rope at the top of the laundry chute so it could be yanked down from the washroom."

Blakemore nodded.

"Right. Ales shoots Gryndon, pulls the rope down, then

goes out and shouts murder. Everyone rushes in. It takes just a minute for some bright soul to open the door to the chute and discover the rope. Mad rush to the other floors and Ales is never suspected. Carson's marks are all over the chute so it'd be assumed he got away."

"Neat, eh?" Coswell said. "But you know, the biggest question of all is how on earth could they be sure Gryndon would use the washroom? He and I were the only ones to go there during the entire evening."

And then it dawned on him.

"Oh, shit. It was the wine. Gryndon and I were the only ones that drank out of the one bottle. Kruger didn't drink any of his; he gave it to me."

"A diuretic," Blakemore said. "Makes you go like a racehorse. My father-in-law has to take the stuff and when it kicks in, the old urinal better be close by. But how did the bottle get spiked? One of the waiters?"

Coswell knew precisely how the diuretic got into the wine and who put it there, but could he get the proof in time? He jumped up and headed for the squad room. Startled, Blakemore followed him.

Burns was sitting at his desk, idly staring out his favourite window. His daydreaming ended abruptly when Coswell and Blakemore rushed into the room. The inspector gave orders in midstride.

"Burns. I want you and Blakemore here to hotfoot it back to the convention centre. Take some uniforms with you. You're going on a bottle hunt. Paul will explain it to you."

He scribbled the name of the Cabernet on a notepad.

"Here's the label you're looking for. Hopefully it wasn't the house red for the evening and even if it was, I want every opened bottle of the stuff gathered up for our lab. If we can find the one Ales handled, and it has traces of a diuretic in it, then we'll have solid evidence against him."

"He was the spiker?" Blakemore said.

"No doubt about it. Now off you go."

He sat for a moment after the two men left. He'd been so preoccupied by the recent events that the full realization of just how close to disaster they'd come hadn't really hit him. It finally did, and he shuddered. It was only by the grace of God that it was the foiled assassin being hauled away in the coroner's wagon and not Gryndon.

And then he began to smile. It wasn't God and goodness. It was sin that had saved the Mayor. Coswell's sin: gluttony. If God was involved, the great Jehovah had one peculiar sense of humour.

He took a deep breath, slowly exhaled and then proceeded to his office where Ales and Wells were engrossed in their discussion. He tapped on the glass and went straight in. Both men looked up but the lawyer responded quickly.

"You've come at just the right time," he said. "I think we can settle this little matter quite easily. First, the silencer was a simple oversight. Mr. Ales often has the device in place when he practices shooting in areas where people are bothered by the noise of the weapon. He inadvertently left it attached when he flew up here and nothing was said by the Canadian border officials."

That was possible, Coswell had to concede. Ales undoubtedly had the necessary documents to carry the gun, and many of the Canada Customs people wouldn't know a silencer from a pogo stick. To them, the whole thing would just have been a gun.

"My client has agreed to have his weapon and that pesky silencer confiscated by you and he'll pay whatever fine he

owes for his infraction. We'll also waive any action directed at the RCMP corporal who virtually assaulted Mr. Ales,
causing him some bodily harm. In return for that generous
offer, my client is to be released from custody immediately."

Coswell felt a warm, fuzzy glow inside as he squelched
Wells' brilliant solution.

"I'm afraid a significant piece of information has surfaced which puts Mr. Ales in a whole new light. It appears
that your client is involved in a far more serious affair that
I'm not, at the moment, free to discuss with you until my
superiors have been informed. Mr. Ales will remain our
guest a bit longer."

That stopped Wells for a moment, remembering the silencer bomb that had been dropped on him, but then he
quickly went on the offense.

"That's absolutely ridiculous," he said. He put his hand on
Ales' shoulder. "Don't worry. I'll get a writ of Habeas Corpus together so fast it'll make the inspector's eyes spin. And
what's more, I'll present it to the judge on call this weekend
personally. You'll be out of this dump in an hour."

The moment the lawyer stormed out of the office, Coswell waved one of the detectives over and arranged for
Ales to be taken to a cell, ignoring the venomous look the
man gave him.

It was time now to contact a superior.

He decided that Gillings, the Attorney-General, would
be his best choice and managed to reach him at his home.
Gillings listened patiently while Coswell gave him a complete report, including the interview with Ales and Roland
Wells. When he'd heard it all, Gillings let out a low whistle.

"Great work, Inspector," he said. "I knew you were onto
something when I read your very first report on those West

End murders. It's always nice to be right, especially when some people we know aren't. You've saved a very important man's life."

Coswell wondered if Mayor Schmidt's and Chief Ward's ears were burning.

But the warm glow from Gillings' praise changed to a sinking feeling when the Attorney General paused briefly, obviously thinking of the best way to broach a difficult subject.

"But I'm going to ask you to step back for a moment, and look at the present situation from a pragmatic point of view."

Uh, oh. Coswell thought. Here it comes — the muzzle.

"Mayor Gryndon is unharmed and heading home. No one other than you and your colleagues are aware of what's happened. So far as Joe and Jane Citizen of BC are concerned, the Conference on Urban Renewal has been a resounding success and Vancouver benefited greatly from the wonderful publicity. The West End murders have been solved and the killers received the ultimate punishment. Everyone's safe again."

And with money flowing into their pockets from the convention, they probably don't give a damn that Ales would get away with murder or that some unknown person or persons orchestrated the whole thing. American wackos. Who cared, now that they were south of the border? Gillings was right, but it grated.

"I'm not going to give you any orders," Gillings went on. "I'll back you up no matter what you do. I just want you to think about it. I'm here if you need me."

Coswell hung up the phone and leaned back. He stared at it for a moment, and then he remembered Frayley and

Heather. He'd forgotten to mention them to Gillings. He reached for the phone to call him but then sat back again. Maybe there was another way to see justice done. He got up and headed to the main lobby, where Constable Easton was entertaining the two reporters.

Actually, only one reporter was being entertained. Heather was chatting with the constable (probably sucking out his brain, Coswell thought) but Frayley stood several paces away, his cellphone at his ear. Whatever his conversation, it ended with the inspector's arrival. He hurried over to join them. The joyous look in his eye did not bode well for Coswell.

"Ah, Inspector," he said. "I've just discovered the most amazing fact. It appears that a very dead body with a gunshot to the neck has been carted away from the convention centre this evening. I also gather that the corpse was quite fresh."

Coswell gave thanks for his procrastination in going after Frayley's snitch. The media were onto the story now and not because of any leak from him. He dismissed Constable Easton and invited the reporters back upstairs to his office. On the way, he planned his speech. When they were all settled and the office door closed, he began.

"I'm going to level with you, even though my neck is stuck way out. I really should be referring you to my superiors, but I'm not going to do that because I believe you'll handle the information I give you responsibly."

The look they gave him was reminiscent of National Geographic films he'd seen of lions waiting their turn to feast on the kill.

"The body you've just mentioned was the third man in the West End killings. He managed to get into a laundry chute and was about to shoot Mayor Gryndon, but one of Governor Kruger's security men dispatched him before he could."

"The guy you had in handcuffs with the big bump on his head?" Heather said.

"That was a misunderstanding. There was a lot happening in a very short space of time and since the Governor's man was holding the smoking gun, we weren't taking any chances. He was taken into custody. Unfortunately, he resisted this action to such a degree that we had to act forcibly."

"Is he still in custody?" Frayley said.

"Yes. There's a set protocol in a shooting like this, as you can imagine, but I'm sure we'll have everything cleared up soon."

The reporters looked at one another. Heather took the initiative.

"I think you're snowing us, Inspector. My guess is that you've busted this assassination plot wide open and the guy in the laundry chute plus his two buddies were just pawns. I also think that Kruger's man is a suspect in that plot."

Coswell feigned shock.

"Really, Heather. I don't know where you could get an idea like that; certainly not from me."

"Methinks he doth protest too much," she said to Frayley.

"Sorry," Coswell said. "But that's all I can give you. Anything more would have to come from higher up. Perhaps, though, I could make an off-the-record suggestion."

"What's that?" Frayley said.

"Mayor Schmidt might be your best bet. Everyone ultimately reports to him and any information he clears will have the official stamp that I'm sure your editor will appreciate."

"Okay, Babe," Frayley said. "Let's go. I don't think old Stonewall here is going to be of much more use to us. Schmidt might fill the air with bullshit, but at least he'll say something."

Heather lagged behind, pausing to give Coswell a dirty look and a parting shot:

"You're not getting off that easy. I'll be back."

Coswell smiled benignly. She'd be back, all right. He was certain that the minute Attorney General Gillings hung up the phone after hearing what happened at the banquet, he'd called Mayor Schmidt, who in turn would contact Chief Ward.

They'd all have pat answers prepared, but the very act of being interviewed would make them think hard about concealing the truth, particularly from Frayley, who had a nose for such tactics. Moreover, if Burns could get hard evidence to implicate Ales, and if the two US agents, Miller and Whitfield, came up with something as well, then it would take a high-level act of suppression to prevent the story from coming out.

And Coswell wanted the story told; Ales and his handlers needed to be brought to justice.

33

There wasn't a man on the Vancouver City Police Force happier in his job than Corporal Gary Stewart. Gary was a member of the motorcycle squad, a small, tightly knit group of officers with great pride in themselves and the classic Harleys they rode. He was also the leader of an even smaller group of elite riders who comprised the internationally known VPD motorcycle drill team. It was this latter unit that invariably supplied the escorts for visiting dignitaries.

Having seen Mayor Gryndon's limo safely to Ernie Downs' apartment, Stewart and his men had returned to the docks and parked their motorcycles adjacent to Brian Sterne's yacht. As they chatted to one another, a tall, blond man appeared on the ramp, paused for a moment to take in the scene below, and then quickly descended. Reaching the dock, he accosted the first officer he came to — Corporal Stewart.

"What are you doing here?" he demanded. "You couldn't have gone to the airport and back so quickly." And then, noting the corporal's surprise at being confronted, he lifted his ID tag into view. "I'm security for Governor Kruger and Mayor Gryndon. You were supposed to accompany the Mayor to the airport first and then come back for Governor Kruger. What happened?"

The man's tone of voice irritated Gary. He examined the ID tag with exaggerated care.

"Well, Mr. Ferring," he said. "I suggest you ask Sergeant Burns. He gave the order to escort the limo back to where we picked it up this afternoon and then return here to wait for the Governor who's flying out tonight, which I hope is damn soon because it's getting late."

Ferring's agitation worsened.

"Well this isn't good enough," he said. "I must speak to the Mayor. He can't just change plans like that without notifying us. Where did you take him?"

Gary became even more annoyed with the security man's attitude.

"Why don't you call him and ask?" he said. "I presume you have his phone number, what with you being his security and all."

Ferring ignored the remarks and looked over the corporal's head at a limo parked further down the dock, the vehicle that had conveyed Mayor Gryndon and his two security men to Ernie's apartment. Without a word, he left the corporal and walked directly to the limo. A short conversation with the driver ensued and then, with a look of resolution on his face, he crossed the street and hailed a taxi.

"Obnoxious bastard," Gary said to no one in particular. "It pisses me off when guys like that get their way."

***
***

Coswell's phone was getting a workout. First, Miller called and told him that he and Whitfield were leaving first thing Sunday morning, driving to the border, starting their investigation there, and then working south to Tacoma and Seattle before flying back to California.

The next call was from Burns.

"Got bad news for you, Inspector," he said. "I'm afraid the bottle hunt isn't going to be worth doing. Would you believe that all commercial establishments must thoroughly rinse wine bottles before they can be returned for recycling? It has something to do with union workers and wasps, I believe. The odds of there being any drug residue in any of them is zero. I saw the rinsing machine and I can tell you it gives one helluva blast with hot water under pressure. Your Cabernet bottle is clean as a whistle."

"Shit," Coswell said. He waited for a moment, letting his

disappointment subside before he released his men. "Okay, that's it for tonight. Go home to your good wife, but tell Blakemore I want him to bunk in at Ernie's again. I don't care if Gryndon has two security guys looking after him and Carson's dead, I want Paul to stay with him till he gets on that plane tomorrow morning. He's leaving on a ten-thirty flight, by the way. After that we can all breath easy."

Coswell felt deflated. All he had on Ales now was the weapons charge, which certainly wasn't enough to hold him in jail, but he wanted another go at questioning the man before he left the country. The opportunity presented itself with the next caller: Judge Wheeler, the jurist who'd drawn weekend duty.

"You're generating a lot of work for me this weekend," the judge said. "Bob Gillings called me a short while ago and thankfully filled me in on the situation with your American detainee. Roland Wells, the arrogant SOB, had the audacity to show up at my house shortly after the call with a writ of Habeas Corpus for the same said prisoner."

"I'm sorry, your Honour," Coswell said, "but I had good reason for wanting the man held."

"I understand that, and I did help you out as best I could under the law. Holding him in your lock-up, though, is out of the question. You have to let him go, but I told Wells that his Mr. Ales was to remain in the city and present himself Monday morning at City Court regarding the weapons infraction."

That was certainly better than nothing, and Coswell thanked him profusely. Now he had to call Burns again.

"I know, I know," he said, listening to Burns grumble into the phone. "You're off duty, but I need one more favour from you before you tuck in. I have to release Ales, but

Judge Wheeler ordered him to stay in the city until Monday. I need a tail on him—a good one. Tell whoever you pick to phone and tell me when and where Ales settles down for the night and with whom, should there be someone."

"I suppose you want this tail on him until he leaves town," Burns said.

"Just until Mayor Gryndon flies out tomorrow. I know I'm probably the only one who's interested in pursuing this thing any further, but God will ultimately thank you."

"My boss, Inspector Marsden, sure as hell won't. But I tell you what I'll do. I'll get a man to start the shadow, but I want him relieved as soon as possible by one of your own men. How about Easton? He looks like a keener to me."

"No," Coswell said. "He and Ales were face to face too long in the washroom for him to be of any value. But I'll ask him to suggest one of the others."

In truth, the inspector wasn't going to be in any hurry to do that. None of the RCMP constables manning the convention centre were likely to be as skilled in surveillance work as Burns' man.

"Have your guy contact me directly," he told Burns. "No need for him to bother you, or anyone else for that matter."

The sergeant paused for a moment. He suspected he was being had, but was too fatigued to argue.

The last call on Coswell's phone was from Blakemore, who, despite his continuing assignment, was in a jovial mood. The sounds of laughter and the clink of glasses in the background suggested he wasn't the only happy one there.

"I've been instructed by no less than the Mayor of San Francisco to demand that you come over and join what I can tell you is one bang-up party. If you think the last one was some-thing, wait till you see what's been laid in for this one."

Coswell's depression lifted.

"I'll be there as soon as I've met with Kruger. He's flying out tonight on his private jet but he wants to speak to me before he goes. He cornered me after the banquet."

"Good luck," Blakemore said. "But there's lots of time. This shindig is going to go on into the wee hours of the morning. These gay types really know how to party."

He'd barely broken the connection with Blakemore when there was a knock at his office door. He thought it might be Burns' surveillance man, but a uniformed con-stable entered and told him he was needed down at the lock-up.

"There's a lawyer raising hell with the corporal on duty about releasing a prisoner. He's got a writ that's supposed to be an instant pass out of here, but the corporal's stub-born and won't do anything without your say-so."

Coswell followed the constable to the holding cells. The sound of angry words greeted them. Wells and the corpo-ral were having at one another. Coswell's arrival was a re-lief to them both.

"It's about bloody time," Wells said. "Will you tell this le-gal cretin that he's obliged to release my client post haste?"

Coswell spoke to the corporal.

"Bring prisoner Ales to interview room one," he told him, and before Wells could object, added, "along with the pa-perwork and his personal effects."

"What's this nonsense about paperwork?" the lawyer said. "Mr. Ales is not required to do anything at this point except leave."

"You're wrong. A man's been shot to death and the

paperwork involved with that is considerable, even though your client may be exonerated."

"You've had your question period already. That should be sufficient."

"Oh, I wish it were that simple," Coswell said. "But you of all people know how important it is to document everything. I'm afraid it could take some time."

"It's eleven o'clock. Be reasonable, for God's sake."

Coswell paused, pretending he was mulling over the request. After a moment, he brightened.

"I have a suggestion. If your client can delay his return to California, I could arrange to have everything done Monday morning."

"I'm in court all day Monday," Wells said, "and my client is in a hurry to get home. Surely you can cut this short somehow."

Tricky bastard, Coswell mused. He thinks I don't know that Judge Wheeler's already insisted that Ales stay over till Monday.

"Sorry," he said. "But it's not really necessary you be present for what amounts to a formality. Perhaps you could assign a competent junior or even an articling student to sit in on the interview."

Wells looked at him, suspicious, but the arrival of Ales distracted him. He asked for a few minutes of privacy with his client, which Coswell granted. Through the window he could see the discussion taking place; Ales listened intently as his lawyer spoke. The options were settled upon quickly and the inspector waved back in.

"My client will meet with you in this office Monday morning at nine o'clock sharp. Are you in agreement?"

"Sounds good to me," Coswell said.

While Ales was signing for his personal effects, he added, "The gun, of course, stays here."

"Of course," Wells said.

The two men left. Coswell called after them.

"Have a nice evening."

The squad room was empty and he wondered if Burns had sufficient time to organize the tail. Since he could do nothing about it at that point, he called down to the duty sergeant at the reception desk to arrange for a squad ride over to Brian Sterne's yacht. Unfortunately, he had to descend to the parking lot level in order to get his ride or he would have witnessed Wells, Ales and a third man conversing on the front steps of the main entrance.

34

The motorcycle squad, killing time by polishing their already spotless machines, was the only sign of life on the docks. No cruise ships were moored. Sterne's yacht sat alone, almost in darkness as though everyone had turned in for the night. Coswell made his way up the gangway.

A single crewman appeared out of the shadows, startling him.

"Christ, man, you scared the shit out of me. What's with the lights out thing?"

"We're getting ready to sail," the man said. He then spoke into a small, hand-held radio, announced the inspector's arrival, and listened as brief instructions were given.

"Follow me," he said and led Coswell to the fireplace lounge.

Kruger was alone, sipping a glass of scotch, the bottle on a table beside him. He didn't get up from his chair, appearing too comfortable to do so. He waved Coswell over to the chesterfield beside him.

"Getting the awful taste of that champagne crap out of my mouth. One goddamn sip of the stuff makes me ill. Toasts should be banned."

Coswell declined the offer to pour himself a glass. He didn't want to dull his palate before he got to Ernie's celebration.

"Brian's up in the wheelhouse. Stewards battening down the hatches, I guess," Kruger said, "which is good. We can talk openly."

The remark puzzled Coswell. Did Kruger wish to keep the incident from his bosom buddy? Strange. The Governor continued.

"First I knew anything funny was going on tonight was Gryndon whispering in my ear. Damn near crawled out of my skin. Said something about a shooting in the washroom. My man, Ales, involved. Play it cool. No messy publicity."

Smart, Coswell mused, "publicity" being the magic word to persuade any politician.

"I grilled Ferring but the bugger claimed total ignorance. Pretty damned amazing, being Ales and him go way back. Pleaded with me to let him go to the police station. Wanted to check on his buddy before we flew back to Sacramento."

Ferring on the loose! Coswell's heart gave a jump but then relaxed as he realized that neither Ferring nor Ales knew where Ernie's apartment was. Gryndon was still safe.

"Now fill me in," Kruger continued. "The plane's warming up, so make it quick."

Coswell's summary took less than five minutes, ending with the fact that Ales was staying over till Monday.

The Governor was speechless for all of two seconds before he reacted.

"My God. You sure about the pissing drug manoeuvre? That's way off the wall. A plot that tricky just to do some ·gay bashing? Like popping off Gryndon's going to end the practice? Too weird."

"Weird is the word all right," Coswell said. "But normal thinking doesn't hold here. Stomping on gay men gives these people some bizarre satisfaction, it appears. What prompts anyone to do that, God only knows — feelings of inadequacy, revenge for childhood abuse, desire to please someone they admire, or fear. Some, I suppose, see themselves as crusaders: ridding the world of evil, reveling in their cause...."

"Good soldiers. Fighting the foe. Loving the killing?" Kruger interjected.

"Exactly. Or the generals who enjoy ordering the killing."

The Governor thought for a moment.

"You think I might be one of those generals? You'd be wrong. Homosexuality's not a mortal sin to me. It's an aberration. I'm against legitimizing aberrations, but I'm not a fanatic about it. Murder's a sin, under any guise. Not something I'd condone."

"I believe you. But there are two men I suggest you talk to when you get back to California. One's an FBI agent named Miller and the other's Whitfield, CIA. The events here in Vancouver may be the action of a small group, but these men tell me there's growing fear in your country that a national movement's afoot that's so far right wing it could be labeled neo-Nazism with an evangelical twist."

"Ales and Ferring are part of it?"

"I've no doubt that they're part of this skirmish at least," Coswell said.

"Then what do you want me to do with them?"

"Be sure that Ferring flies back with you. I'll see Ales to the plane on Monday. After that they're not my problem any more. If I were you, I'd do nothing until talking to Miller and Whitfield and then I'd follow whatever advice they gave."

Kruger rose and stuck out his hand.

"First-class job, Inspector," he said. "I will follow your advice. But I can tell you, I plan to clean house pretty damned quick."

"Don't turn your back on Ales and Ferring in the meantime," Coswell said, shaking the Governor's hand. "Their mission failed and they might be feeling a touch desperate."

"Gotcha," Kruger said.

***
***

The police cruiser that brought Coswell to the yacht was waiting for him when he descended the gangway. Ferring was still in his mind.

As he got into the vehicle, he asked the driver, "Did anyone go aboard that boat after me?"

"One man, about ten minutes ago," the officer said. "Tall, blond hair, nice suit. Some guy called down to him from the top deck and he went up there."

Blond hair, suit — that was Ferring, but who was the caller? Brian Sterne?

"I was talking to Gary Stewart while I was waiting for you," the constable continued. "He's the corporal over there in charge of the motorcycle squad. Apparently this same individual came off the boat earlier, said he was security, and gave Gary a bad time about taking some VIP to the wrong place."

"Wait here," Coswell said. He slid out of the cruiser, walked quickly over to the motorcycle group, spoke briefly to Corporal Gary, and then proceeded to the limo. It took him two minutes in all to find out what had happened. He returned to the cruiser, steaming.

"That limo driver not only gave Ferring the goddamned address, he told him the pick-up time for tomorrow morning."

This revelation was lost on the poor constable.

Coswell's mind whirled. Was Gryndon still a target? His cellphone rang. It was Burns' man.

"Detective Plummer here. Thought I'd better tell you what's happened so far."

Coswell breathed a sigh of relief. Burns' surveillance man was on the job.

"The subject and his lawyer got into a cab after a brief conversation with a third man who was waiting for them outside the precinct — blond fellow in a suit," the officer said. "The lawyer got dropped off at Pacific Centre where he probably had his car parked. The cab then proceeded to the Bayshore Inn where the subject got out, paid his fare and went into the bar. I don't know where the third man went, but it looked as though he was waiting at the precinct for his own cab."

Coswell felt his heart quicken.

"Did the blond man pass anything to the subject?" he said.

"No. They just talked, but I was too far away to hear them."

"Is the subject in your view right now?"

The phone went silent for a moment.

"Yes, he's still at the bar, watching the widescreen TV. The place is packed. I'm talking to you from the lobby."

"Don't let him out of your sight even for a second. I want to know his exact whereabouts until Mayor Gryndon climbs on a plane back to the States."

"My shift ends at seven tomorrow morning, Inspector. Sergeant Burns told me you'd have relief for me before then."

"I'm working on that," Coswell said. "But if the relief man is a bit late, please hang in there. I'll be sure you're paid double time or get time off booked—your choice. Meanwhile, call me if anything comes up."

He hit the *off* button on his cellphone before the officer could reply.

The surveillance could have been called off, he had to admit. Ferring was momentarily flying out with the Governor and he hadn't passed over his gun, according to Plummer. Ales was weaponless and the chance of him getting one at the Bayshore Inn was a big zero. He contemplated calling the detective back, but then, with a shrug, tucked the phone away. In his experience, too careful was a lot better than almost sure.

***
***

Coswell was pleased to see the same city police officer doing concierge duty at Ernie's apartment, the result of a bit of leaning on the reluctant Inspector Marsden.

Gryndon's man was there, too, and gave the inspector a big smile. He pulled his jacket back to reveal his holstered gun.

"He's got a permit from the Mayor's office, no less," the disgruntled officer said.

"Don't worry," Coswell told him. "I'll be the last visitor

up there tonight and I doubt if anyone's going to storm the place. Why don't you guys play cards?"

Gryndon couldn't be in a safer place, Coswell decided. A bank of monitors at the reception desk showed every entrance, exit and even the underground parking lot. The guests upstairs were all known to one another and unless he'd made a terrible miscalculation, there wasn't a killer in the lot. Time to relax a bit. God knows he deserved it.

Unfortunately, the elevator hadn't even arrived at the ground floor before his euphoric bubble burst; Detective Plummer called back.

"I lost him," he said. "He told the bartender to watch his drink and save his seat while he went to the men's. It took me a while to get through the crowd so I could check on him and he managed to skip out a side entrance before I could get there. I asked the cabbies outside if any of them had just picked up a fare but they said no."

There was no use chastising the officer. A lone surveillance man was severely limited if the subject was really intent on losing him. Plummer had done the best he could.

"He's on foot, obviously," Coswell said, "and only half a dozen blocks from this apartment, which is 1050 Beach Avenue, by the way. You can try to spot him on the street, but I'll bet he's ducked into Stanley Park. The way here through the park isn't much longer and you'll never find him in there."

"I've already swept Denman," Plummer said, "and I'm criss-crossing my way down to Lagoon Drive. Unless he's using the trails, he has to take one of those streets and at this time of night there's not likely to be many pedestrians other than him."

"He'll be on the trails," Coswell said. "You can look a bit

longer but I want you to end up here and park close to the entrance. You'll be my eyes out there. I'll give Ales' description to the men inside, though, in case the bugger sneaks through the hedge or something."

"Right, Inspector. But you will remember my relief, won't you?"

"Top of my list, Detective."

Coswell returned to the reception area and briefed the two men regarding the Ales situation. Gryndon's security man remembered Ales from the banquet and was puzzled by Coswell's instructions, but didn't ask any questions. "Detain him," the inspector said. "With force if necessary."

As he ascended in the elevator, he told himself there was no way Ales could get at Gryndon without being apprehended. It was unsettling, though, that the man had deliberately eluded his tail. He was up to something.

Ernie answered the door to the apartment and Blakemore was right; the party was in full swing. Carl, the hockey player, sat at the baby grand, playing "Hey Jude," complete with improvisation that sounded professional to Coswell. Kevin and Tommy Carlyle stood beside him singing the lyrics in surprisingly good harmony. Gryndon was splayed out on a big armchair below them waving one hand in time with the music and holding a glass of champagne in the other. Blakemore was circling the food table, filling a plate with delicacies, his beer mug set aside so he could use both hands.

Everyone acknowledged the inspector's arrival but Coswell just gave them a wave.

"Don't stop," he said. "You guys have a great sound. Keep it up."

Gryndon, however, rose from his chair and came over to

the food table where Coswell had joined Blakemore.

"I highly recommend those smoked salmon things with the black stuff on top," Blakemore offered.

Coswell was surprised there were any left with the big corporal hovering over the table. Ernie had four bottles of wine open along with the champagne, and Coswell took a moment to decide on one. A single glass was all he was going to allow himself with the thought of Ales on the loose nagging at him.

"Glad you could come," Gryndon said. "I'm going out onto the patio for a breath of fresh air. Why don't the three of you join me? The music makers will probably follow us when they've run out of wind."

The unusually warm weather for May had persisted and despite the late hour, the temperature outside was a balmy twenty degrees. But Coswell paid no attention to the weather. His immediate thoughts were on the possibility of a sniper getting a shot at anyone stepping out onto the balcony. He rushed ahead of everyone.

"Hang back for a sec," he said. A quick inspection satisfied him all was safe.

The penthouse towered above all of the adjacent buildings; even if Gryndon hung his head over the railing, getting hit from that far below would be a miracle. He gave the all-clear and the rest filed out.

"You're still concerned?" Gryndon said.

"I'm afraid so," Coswell replied and proceeded to tell the whole story right up to and including the recent disappearance of Ales. Everyone was shocked. Blakemore broke the silence.

"Unless the guy's a suicide bomber, he hasn't got a hope in hell of carrying out anything with the security we've got set up. Christ — two men in the lobby and two and a half Mounties up here. How's he going to get anywhere near Mayor Gryndon? Also, my reading of Ales is he's an arrogant son-of-a-bitch who's so in love with himself he wouldn't risk getting caught."

"All true," Coswell said, "but remember how close Carson came to completing his mission and we had that place covered like a blanket."

"Yeah," Blakemore said. "But there were a lot more access points at the convention centre than here."

Coswell, however, was standing firm and said to Gryndon, "Until you're in the air to San Francisco, I'm not assuming anything."

"I appreciate your concern, Inspector," Gryndon said, "but I agree with Paul. I'm leaving from the foyer downstairs, flanked by security people, fifteen paces to the curb; getting into a limousine with smoked glass windows, surrounded by motorcycle police; and then being driven to the Vancouver airport. I don't think even a bolt of lightning could get me, let alone a single gunman."

"It's those fifteen paces that have me worried," Coswell said. "I'm actually going to have the limo back into the parking garage. You'll get in from the elevator there. That'll be only three paces, totally surrounded by human flesh."

Gryndon roared with laughter.

"If you ever get tired of your job up here, Inspector," he said, "come down to San Francisco and I'll hire you immediately."

The laughter drew the rest of the group from inside. They came out onto the balcony, fresh drinks in their hands, and for an hour the conversation and good fellowship flowed. Coswell excused himself at that point, saying he was heading home to get some sleep before returning for the Mayor's departure at nine. Ernie saw him to the door.

"And making a last inspection of the defenses, I'll bet," he said as Coswell pushed the button for the elevator.

"Obsessive behavior," Coswell said, "got me where I am."

Ernie reached out and patted his arm.

"Sleep well, Inspector," he said. "You've earned it."

35

It wasn't just a last minute walk-around that Coswell had in mind. When he was checking Ernie's balcony for the possibility of a sniper, the Sylvia Hotel across the alley caught his eye. The 1912 heritage building was the only hotel in the area. The rest of the buildings were apartment blocks. It gave him an idea which soon grew to a certainty.

He spoke briefly to the officer-concierge, reminding him not to leave his post, regardless of his shift time, until Mayor Gryndon's limo had pulled away. The Mayor's security man had already worked out a schedule with his partner so each would get some sleep before they accompanied their boss to the airport.

Satisfied, Coswell went out to the street. It took a moment before he recognized the city police ghost vehicle parked in the shadows between street lights. He was almost beside the car when the driver's window rolled down and Detective Plummer's voice emerged.

"Good morning, Inspector. Aren't you worried you'll break my cover?"

"Come with me," Coswell said. "I think I know where

your subject disappeared to."

They walked quickly over to the Sylvia Hotel and entered the small reception area. A thin, ascetic young man greeted them with a cheerfulness that belied the hour. Coswell introduced himself and produced his badge. Plummer did the same.

"We'd like to know if a single male requested a room here tonight somewhere between nine and eleven," Coswell said.

"Yes," the clerk replied. "A man came in just after nine, actually, and booked a room for a friend who he said would be arriving later. He brought the friend's bag and took it to the room after he paid for two nights in advance, in cash. The friend got here about an hour ago, picked up the key and went to the room."

"Would you describe the two men to us, please?"

"They were both big men. The chap who booked the room was tall, blond and reasonably polite. The second man was the biggest. Dark, with a personality to match and had a big swelling on his forehead, which might explain his rotten mood. He asked, or better said, *demanded* a seven AM wake-up call and a room service breakfast at eight. He said he was planning to work in his room all morning and didn't want to be disturbed. I don't know what kind of work he was going to do because the bag the friend brought was a small overnight case and I didn't see a laptop."

Plenty big enough to stash a gun in, though, Coswell thought.

"This man is of interest to us, as you can tell," he told the clerk. "We'd appreciate it if you can forget that we've been here — catch my drift?"

The man nodded.

"Detective Plummer will be doing surveillance in the

corridor of the floor the gentleman is staying. Do you have something comfortable he can sit in?"

"There are nice padded chairs just outside the elevator. Feel free to use one of them."

A worried frown appeared on the clerk's brow.

"There's not going to be any trouble, is there? Things like that just don't happen at the Sylvia. Perhaps I should phone the manager, although I hate to wake him at this late hour."

Coswell assured him that wouldn't be necessary and he needn't be concerned. The clerk continued to look apprehensive, but didn't make the call.

"Damn," Plummer said. "This assignment's getting more boring every minute."

Coswell took him aside.

"I know, I know," he said. "I'd do it myself, but the subject knows me."

Plummer didn't look a bit mollified.

"I'm going to level with you," the inspector continued, "I need you to hang around until just before nine this morning. That's when I'm certain the subject will come out of his room. He's already had a chance to case the apartment where Mayor Gryndon's staying from the park across the street, so there's no reason he has to leave the room any sooner."

"If you're so sure," Plummer said. "Why can't I knock off for a bit and come back then?"

"Can't take any more chances with this guy. Remember what happened at the Bayshore?"

"Okay, okay," Plummer said.

Having made his point, Coswell continued, "I probably don't need to tell you this, but the second you see his door open, have a newspaper under your arm and pretend you're waiting for the elevator to go down for a late breakfast."

"You don't," Plummer said. "And you also don't need to tell me to phone you as soon after that as possible."

Coswell grinned. "You're my man," he said. "And I will make it up to you for the overtime."

"Hmmph," Plummer said.

The sag in the detective's shoulders lessened a bit, however, when the night clerk offered to bring him coffee and Danish.

***
***

Coswell lay in his bed, eyes open in the darkness, his worries flitting through his mind. Eventually he decided he had done everything he could and fell into a deep sleep. Five hours later he awakened to his alarm and was instantly alert. He showered, shaved, and was off to his favourite Starbucks on Robson Street by a quarter to seven.

He'd tried having morning coffee in his apartment, even bought an expensive cappuccino machine, but it was a waste of money. He needed human contact: the coffee servers, the line-ups, the grumbling and the banter. In his darker moments, he'd analyzed this and realized that he feared loneliness. He wondered, too, if his inept housekeeping wasn't, in fact, deliberate, an excuse to flee to an organized, public milieu.

One grande double cappuccino, a token slice of banana bread and a giggle from the nose-ringed girl at the espresso machine once again did the trick. The morning brightened right up.

He decided he'd leave Burns alone on his day off and bug Blakemore instead. He dialed the corporal's cellphone number and waited for a reply. No answer. The bugger's turned the thing off, he thought.

He ordered a biscotti to go along with the cappuccino he had left, the banana bread having done nothing to curb his morning appetite. He regretted not waiting a bit longer to go to the Dutch House of Pancakes instead.

It took several tries before Blakemore finally answered his phone.

"Damn, Inspector," he mumbled. "Don't you have any pity for people who didn't get to bed until three in the morning? Everyone else here's still asleep."

"It's almost seven-thirty, Corporal, and the sun's been up for some time. Besides, it's a big day, especially for you, and I'm surprised you're not up and raring to go."

"Why is it special for me?"

"At 9:05 AM, you get to go back to your wife."

"Oh, really? I've almost decided I'd have a better life as a gay. It's been a long time and this environment isn't all bad."

"Well the face of reality is on its way," Coswell said. "I'm knocking on your door in ten minutes. Be sure you're there to let me in."

"Okay, but I'm going to go look for a coffee. You might have to knock a few times."

***
***

When Coswell arrived at the apartment, Gryndon's second security man had replaced the previous one. He looked bright and alert, but the concierge had faded. Coswell presented each with a Starbucks grande Dark French Roast. The concierge accepted his with the gratitude of someone being given the elixir of life.

Ernie was busy in the kitchen making omelettes. Kevin and Carl were still in bed, but Gryndon and Tommy Carlyle were sitting out on the balcony in their dressing gowns, sipping coffee and enjoying the view. Blakemore sent Coswell out to join them.

"I need another coffee," he said, "before I engage in any meaningful conversation. Those two are wide awake, though, so have at them. I'm staying here to help Ernie."

The omelettes were superb and somehow Ernie had rustled up hot croissants with herbed butter and a choice of preserves from the Granville Island Market. The coffee was Arabica, served in porcelain cups. Blakemore, of course, aborted his by mixing in a dollop of heavy, whipped cream and three teaspoons of sugar.

"Is there any Turkish blood in your family?" Coswell asked him. "That's just gross."

"Tastes good, though," Blakemore said.

"More likely pioneer blood in the corporal," Gryndon interjected. "Those people required more than a caffeine jolt before they set out on their rigorous work days. They needed those extra calories."

"Except he rides around in a goddamned Suzuki jeep all day and the most exercise he gets is walking up the ramp at the Wheatsheaf Bakery," Coswell said, "especially after we pulled him from the YMCA assignment."

"Barbara will straighten me out, when and if I ever get back to her," Blakemore replied.

"His long-suffering wife," Coswell explained.

At precisely eight-thirty, Coswell went down to the foyer to await Plummer's call. Fifteen minutes later it came.

"He's on his way, Inspector, going down the back stairs. You should see him pop out into the alley from the back exit any minute now."

To the astonishment of the concierge and Gryndon's

two security men (the second had arrived), Coswell bolted for the front door and made his way at a run to the side of the building facing the alley. He arrived just in time to see Ales dart across and work his way past the garbage dumpsters toward the laurel hedge that ran down both sides of the apartment property—an ideal screen. With a silencer mounted on the gun, the sound of the discharge wouldn't be enough to localize the direction of the shot and in the confusion, the assassin could retrace his steps and be back in the hotel in seconds. Perfect.

Coswell hid himself behind the dumpster and let Ales pass. When the man reached what was probably ideal position, the inspector tiptoed up behind him.

"Good morning, Mr. Ales," he said in a loud voice. The security man jumped.

"Going out for an early constitutional?" Coswell said in a cheery voice. "Very admirable, I must say. Wish I had gumption like that."

Ales turned and looked at him in utter amazement. Coswell went on with exaggerated enthusiasm.

"You'll have an added bonus today. Do you know that Mayor Gryndon stayed the night in this building and in a few minutes he'll be departing for the airport? If we're lucky we'll be able to give him a wave when he leaves. Famous man, as you know. I've heard it said that he's going to be the next Governor of the State of California. Remarkable, wouldn't you agree?"

They stood there, Coswell with a self-satisfied grin on his face, Ales stunned and confused.

They watched the limousine back into the underground parking, pause only for a few moments, and then drive out. None of the occupants were visible initially, but as it passed, a side window rolled down and a hand emerged, giving the thumbs-up sign.

Coswell waved back. Ales didn't move.

"See you tomorrow morning," the inspector said, and as he turned and walked around the hedge to the apartment entrance, called back over his shoulder: "And you have a nice day."

Plummer was standing at the front door when Coswell approached. Ales remained rooted where he'd left him.

"Detective Plummer," Coswell said. "A very, very, good morning to you. I know you want to get home, but I'd like you to come and meet some very fine people who have wonderful coffee and will make you an omelette to die for. Also, since you're off duty, a glass of champagne and orange juice would certainly be in order. "

He gave the same message to the concierge.

Ernie and Blakemore had already taken the elevator back to the penthouse and when Coswell and his troops arrived, the party was on again. The two city policeman didn't arrive back at their respective homes until noon, dog-tired and complaining to their wives about what a tough night they'd had.

It was over. Coswell should have felt satisfied and to a degree he was. He'd solved the West End murder cases and been right about the assassination plot. Ales and Ferring were unfinished business, but he'd do his best to squeeze the former at his interview on Monday.

His biggest disappointment was his inability to point a

finger at the masters — the generals who were pulling the strings. Everything had now slipped back across the border and his role was at an end. He'd had that same empty feeling when the Monashee murderer escaped years before and although he'd put on a show that he really didn't care, in truth he had, and continued to send bulletins to the Washington State Police reminding them the killer was still free.

Blakemore drove him back to the main precinct in the Pacific Hydro Suzuki, which Coswell had to admit was like motoring in a covered roller skate.

"Just drop me off," he told Blakemore, "and go home to your wife. Tomorrow's soon enough to get going on the paperwork, but I want you here by 0830."

Blakemore wondered at the precise time, but didn't need any coaxing. He was off like a shot the moment the inspector stepped out of the vehicle. Coswell smiled and for a moment watched him drive away before he turned and started up the stairs to the main entrance of the precinct station. He'd gone only a short distance when he heard a car door slam behind him. A familiar red head emerged and called to him.

"Inspector. What luck running into you like this."

Coswell sighed and watched her hurry towards him.

"You've got me when I'm down, Heather" he said, "But come on up to the office and we'll talk."

She trailed after him like an Irish setter following its food bowl. She'd been waiting over two hours for him to appear, having been told by the desk sergeant that the inspector usually came in on a Sunday when he was working on a case.

There was a single detective in the squad room sorting

through a stack of paper when they entered. He nodded to them when they passed his desk.

"Have a seat, Heather," Coswell said, "and tell me what you got out of Mayor Schmidt."

"We got an appointment to see him on Monday at City Hall, that's what we got. Deadlines don't mean anything to him. Sunday's his 'family time' he says, and he doesn't let anything interfere with it."

"Hence your lying in wait for me."

"Aw, be reasonable, Inspector. I've been a good girl for you guys in all of this and I do have to get something written up today for tomorrow's edition. Give me something I can use, for crying out loud."

Coswell thought for a moment.

"It's pretty simple. If you want to play the fearless investigative journalist, then print the whole story, and a good one it is, although you might consider its effect on the business community. On a personal note, the reporting of an incident that might embarrass the Governor of California makes me nervous. The repercussions from that could be fatal to a couple of careers, yours and mine, and I'm fond of mine."

"Point taken," Heather said. "But I think this story needs telling. You people did one fantastic job and I think the public should know about it."

She paused for a moment when a flash of insight hit.

"The Governor thing is about that security man, isn't it? The one you dragged out of the washroom. I never did buy that 'misunderstanding' line you gave us. He was part of the plot, wasn't he?"

"I believe he was, but I can't prove it right now and I don't know if anyone else can either."

He leaned forward in his chair, picked up a pencil and

began tapping it on the desk, struggling with a decision. Heather waited patiently. Finally he spoke.

"Heather. Ordinarily I'd give you the political shuffle just like the rest of them, but I have a bad feeling that some person or persons is going to get away with abetting murder and that doesn't sit well with me. I also think that a dangerous vigilante movement is well established in the United States and if it isn't already in this country, it's coming soon. I know people are sick of crime and what looks like a totally ineffectual legal system, but vigilantism is a bad alternative. The 'morally right' are dangerous people. They need to be held in check."

Heather perked up.

"I think the free press is the way to do it," she said.

"Maybe, but public opinion can be fickle. You'd be surprised how many people side with these 'righteous' views. I don't envy your writing an article that'll be persuasive enough to condemn the 'take the law into our own hands' people."

"Try me."

And Coswell did. He left nothing out, including the involvement of the two US Federal agents.

"They're really my last hope at exposing this whole network," he said. "But that's going to be a tough battle. It isn't just the public that's fed up. A goodly number of law enforcement officers are even more frustrated with the system. They actually sympathize with these radicals. I think the slow response from Washington State to our West End murder investigation is typical."

"I don't think killing gays appeals to sane people anywhere," Heather said, "and I'm going to make that a big part of my article."

She picked up her bag and returned to her car where she sat for ten minutes, furiously scribbling notes.

Coswell remained in his chair after she left and stared out into the squad room. Eventually he got up and slowly made his way to his car, a heavy fatigue settling over him. He wondered at his judgment in this state.

He needed to sleep.

***
***

Ales, accompanied by a young female lawyer, arrived in the squad room at nine AM Coswell was refreshed and ready for the challenge. He had his office all set up.

Blakemore led the two in. Coswell remained seated behind his desk, simply waving them to chairs positioned immediately in front of him. Burns slid into the room behind them and took a seat against one wall. Blakemore settled into a chair on the opposite side. Ales and his lawyer were surrounded.

Coswell introduced himself and his two officers to the young woman.

"Mr. Ales has met them already," he said. "Ms....?"

"Burton," she said. "Sarah Burton from Black, Black and Wells. I was given to understand that this session was to be brief—a mere formality. Why the additional troops?"

Her tone of voice, strong and confident, surprised Coswell. This was no articling student. Wells had sent one of his young guns.

"These officers were involved in all phases of the investigation and they'll help expedite proceedings," he said.

She frowned and glared at each man. Blakemore gave her an unprofessional wink.

Coswell opened a folder placed on the desk in front of

him and gazed for a moment at the first page of what appeared to be a voluminous file. In reality, there was only one page of print (the questions he wanted to ask); the rest consisted of blank pages. Abruptly, he shut the folder, pushed it away, and switched on a recording device.

"I think the best way to do this would be to have Mr. Ales, in his own words, give us his version of the incident that resulted in Mr. Carson's untimely death."

"Untimely?" Ms. Burton said. "The man was trying to assassinate the Mayor of San Francisco. I think the word 'timely' is more appropriate." She pointed at the recorder, "And turn that thing off. My client's not here on the basis of any charge other than weapons possession. You don't need a recording for that."

Coswell's intimidation tactics were getting him nowhere with either Ms. Burton or her client. The latter, who was subdued when he'd come in, appeared to regain confidence and gave his summary in a strong, steady voice.

"I saw the Mayor's security men standing outside the washroom while he was inside. That's poor procedure. I didn't want to waste any time speaking to them so I went straight in. The Mayor and you were down on the floor in front of the urinals, dead, for all I knew. I detected movement to my left; I saw the laundry chute door open and a pistol pointed in your direction. My action was instinctive. I drew my weapon and fired. It's that simple."

"You didn't recognize the victim?" Coswell said.

"Of course not. All I could see was the gun."

"Interesting. You managed to hit the man's neck with your shot, so you could see that much of him anyway. I'm also thinking that the chute door must have been open wide enough for the victim to get an adequate view of his intended target. Odd you wouldn't have seen his face, too."

"Like I said. Everything happened on instinct. I aimed at a form, not a face and anyway, what does it matter? The man was going to shoot."

Coswell paused, tapping his pencil on the desk. Sarah Burton was staring intently at him, poised to interject.

"You might be interested to know that the man you shot was an American who coincidentally works at the Capital in Sacramento, the same place you work. His name was Steve Carson. Perhaps you knew him?"

Sarah Burton glanced at Ales. He wasn't a good actor. His answer came too quickly.

"Never heard of him."

This was enough for Sarah.

"Okay, Inspector," she said, standing up. "I don't know exactly what you're trying to do, but it sure as hell isn't any simple formality. Unless you're planning to charge my client in this Carson person's death, we're through here. Judge Wheeler is hearing us at ten this morning and as soon as that's over, Mr. Ales is planning to get the earliest flight back to his home today."

Coswell smiled. He'd gotten enough to pass on to Miller and Whitfield, his two US Federal colleagues. They would no doubt pay a visit to the forgetful Mr. Ales as soon as he returned to Sacramento.

"It was nice meeting you, Ms. Burton," he said, rising from his chair. Blakemore jumped up and hurried over to open the door. The young lawyer swept out of the room, followed by Ales, head down. She didn't respond to Blakemore's wide grin.

Burns, who'd been a dispassionate observer, was the first to comment after the two left.

"Didn't look too cocky, did he?"

"He'll remember us, that's for sure," Coswell said.

***
***

Heather was fuming. She'd worked right up to the ten o'clock deadline Sunday night perfecting her article for the Monday edition of the *Star*. When she was satisfied, she'd emailed it to Frayley, her boss, for approval and followed up with a phone call.

"Go with it, Babe," he'd said. "You've done good and I can't make it any better."

In hindsight, she realized that he probably knew what was going to happen. The night editor, without a word to her, canned it. The banquet evening was front-page, but it was under Mary Carpenter's byline, the *Star*'s society writer, who'd endured the front entrance scrum. Photographs and a flowery description of the event made up the article which Heather had to admit was good work, but fluff compared to the exposé she'd hammered out.

Harold Frayley winced when he came into his office. A copy of the first run-off of the early edition lay on his desk and Heather stood beside it, tapping her foot.

"Done good, eh?" She picked up the paper and brandished it at him. "Not one bloody word of mine in here, not a bloody one."

The intercom saved him.

"Good morning, Mr. Frayley," a voice said. "Mr. Scholfield told me to ask you to come up to his office as soon as you arrived. I saw you come in. He sounded like he didn't want to be kept waiting so I'd go straight up if I were you."

"Roger, Dierdre my love," Frayley replied. He spun around

and departed his office posthaste. "Be right back, Babe," he said to Heather as he hurried off.

She pulled back Frayley's swivel chair and plunked herself down, exhaling with a disgusted "hmmph." Scholfield, the editor-in-chief, was probably about to read the riot act to her boss and tell him to rein in his junior before she ruffled any VIP's feathers. Well, she wasn't going to give up the Vancouver crime story of the year without a fight. She opened up the paper, found the crossword, and began to solve it. Frayley could run, but he couldn't hide. She'd be there when he returned.

She didn't have to wait long and the look on her boss' face when he returned confirmed her suspicions.

"Sometimes this is a dirty business," he said to her. "Scholfield wants the whole thing dropped."

She couldn't stay mad. Frayley looked ten years older and his sadness touched her. It wasn't his fault. She got out of his chair.

"We gave it a try though, didn't we?" she said.

He looked at her, tears forming.

"We did, Babe. We surely did."

She touched his arm as she left the room. He remained standing, watching her go. Little did he know that within that red head was a plan to get her story told, a plan that even the esteemed Mr. Scholfield couldn't stop.

37

Coswell accepted the series of commendations that came his way from Mayor Schmidt, Attorney General Gillings and even old high-pockets Ward, the latter suggesting he take a week off. He declined, saying that Blakemore was far more deserving of the R and R and one man off the small Vancouver homicide squad at a time was enough. The truth being that Coswell found vacation time a bore. Work was his life and he had no desire to be absent from it.

The West End murders and the assassination attempt on Mayor Gryndon were quickly being forgotten by the local police, but Coswell knew the investigation was still active — across the border. He'd called agent Miller, the FBI man, right after his interview with Ales. It took just forty-eight hours for Miller to get back to him by phone from Sacramento.

"Would you believe? Ales and his buddy Ferring have vanished and I mean vanished. Kruger fired them both the day Ales got back to Sacramento. They cleaned out their lockers at the Capital and haven't been heard from since."

Coswell wasn't surprised.

"Permanently shut up," he concluded.

"Probably — either cement boots or money and new IDs in some lovely country far away. We've checked everywhere, but no luck."

"Well, I guess that's it," Coswell said. "Dead end ... literally."

"Not on your life. Whitfield and I have discovered some very interesting facts. We want to meet with you, in Seattle."

"Seattle?"

"Yep. And it's already cleared through your Chief Inspector Ward. You're booked on a ten AM flight tomorrow. We'll pick you up at the airport."

Seattle: the source of the phone and fax calls to Steve Carson and his cohorts. Had the Federal duo broken into the plot masters' ring? Coswell felt his pulse quickening; this was more like it.

***
***

Their meeting took place at SeaTac airport in one of the vacated departure lounges. Miller started off.

"We wanted you here because your tips got us going in the right direction."

Coswell glanced over at Whitfield, but the man's face revealed nothing.

"We started with Ferring's cellphone call records. Getting them was a snap; the Capital boys all use the same company."

"Ah," Coswell said. "To answer the question 'How did Ales' hotshot lawyer, Wells, get hired so fast'?"

"Right. Like you, we assumed it had to be Ferring but there was no way he would have acted on his own. He needed direction and money on very short notice."

"And the call went in to Seattle again?" Coswell said.

"No. There were no calls whatsoever from Ferring's phone."

Miller explained.

"He must have received verbal instructions plus the money from someone on Brian Sterne's yacht."

Coswell nodded.

"Kruger or Sterne," he said. "There wouldn't have been time to arrange it any other way."

Whitfield finally stirred.

"Correct. And it's most likely that Wells was paid up front in non-traceable cash. Ferring wouldn't have had access to that kind of money."

It was slowly becoming clear. Coswell listened in fascination as Miller continued.

"The second question was 'How did Carson get a press pass from the *Tacoma Review* authentic enough to convince your Vancouver police sergeant?'"

Coswell flinched. The pass might easily have been a fake and it was only the phone call to the newspaper's editor that got it accepted, and the voice on the line could have been an accomplice, not the editor.

Miller read his thoughts.

"The call did go through to the *Tacoma Review*'s editorial office. Sergeant Burns has an excellent memory. He gave us the number and we traced it."

"The chief editor was in on the plot?" Coswell said, astounded.

Whitfield joined in.

"Denied everything. Made a big show of berating his secretarial staff about it but no one buckled."

"It did, however, keep us on track," Miller said. "A call to our research department turned up some interesting facts about the *Tacoma Review*. It's an ultra-right-wing periodical, the Republican voice in Democrat land, and guess who the very silent owner is?"

"Brian Sterne," Coswell offered.

Miller beamed. He was really enjoying his revelation.

"Right again, and you wouldn't believe how difficult that was to find out."

"The accomplice could have been one of the editor's staff, though," Coswell suggested.

"True. But Sterne's name kept coming up again and again. Bells started to ring."

Whitfield took over.

"The final, and most convincing part of our investigation was the interview with Governor Kruger."

"We flew directly to Sacramento, planning to corner Ferring and Ales," he said, "but the Governor knew within minutes that we were there and called us into his office."

Thanks to me, Coswell said to himself, remembering his advice to the Governor just before he left Vancouver.

Whitfield continued.

"He listened carefully to everything we said concerning our investigation, our suspicions about a covert network, and the fact that his men, Ales and Ferring, were part of it."

Miller cut in.

"Before going to the Capital, we went to the Sacramento Gun Club, acting on your tip that Ales was lying about not knowing Carson. Cindy Forsythe apparently couldn't get anything out of the club manager, but we got him to open up."

Coswell had no doubt about that. Whitfield would have scared the shit out of him.

"Not only did Ales, Forsythe, Steve Carson and his buddies often shoot together," Miller went on, "but they regularly socialized in the clubhouse."

Whitfield, looking slightly annoyed at being interrupted, resumed his discourse.

"We told the Governor that we expected to pay a visit to Brian Sterne in Seattle as soon as we'd had our go at Ales and Ferring. At first, he refused to accept that there was any possibility his friend could be involved in such intrigue, but Frank and I both got the impression there was a hint of doubt in his voice."

Coswell remembered feeling the same during his conversation with Kruger on Sterne's yacht.

"Eventually, he opened up," Whitfield went on. "Apparently Sterne was a pugnacious little bugger in his youth, despite being one of the high school nerds. To compound his aggressiveness, he couldn't tolerate anything that wasn't American true-blue and right in the eyes of God. I suppose he was a chip off the old block; his old man was a Baptist minister, but I think his son took the righteousness to another level. He was very right-wing noisy in college but mellowed out, it appeared, after he graduated. It's interesting that his success in the cyber-world is from fighting evil viruses and such."

"A religious fanatic with tons of money," Coswell observed. "Either build churches or pay to have evil erased from the world — a greenback superman."

"That's our working hypothesis," Whitfield agreed. "We think Brian Sterne is behind this whole affair. He has the money, the smarts and the fervour to carry it out. The big problem, of course, is how do we prove it? If Ales and Ferring don't miraculously reappear, who do we have to interrogate?"

"Brian Sterne himself," Coswell said.

Whitfield nodded. "We have an appointment to see him in his Redmond office at one o'clock, a half hour from now. Just enough time to drive there."

And no time for lunch. Coswell scurried over to the counter to buy a muffin to eat on the way.

***

The building that housed Brian Sterne's business emitted an aura of darkness. The exterior was clad in heavy, smoked glass that effectively concealed the interior. Entry was via an electric-locked door. The foyer was tiny, just enough room for an armed security guard and a receptionist, a dark-haired woman wearing a black skirt and high-collared white blouse.

The guard checked IDs before the receptionist directed them to Sterne's office up four flights of stairs. There wasn't an elevator in sight. As the three men ascended, they could see row upon row of cubicles on each of the floors lit only by computer screens and tiny backlights. Coswell estimated there had to have been a few hundred people working there.

A young man wearing dark trousers and a polo shirt with the top button done up appeared at the top of the last flight of stairs. He led them to a spiral staircase situated in the centre of the room. Climbing single file, they came to a small landing in front of a stainless steel door, reminding Coswell of a bank vault. When they were all gathered, the young man pressed a button and after a short delay, the door swung open.

"Come in, gentlemen." Sterne's voice emanated from somewhere within.

The room, like those below, was in almost total darkness, but slowly lit up as great hydraulic steel plates retracted above, allowing natural light to shine through a domed glass ceiling. Multiple computer stations, arranged in a semicircle, lined most of the periphery and in the centre sat a huge oval table made of black granite. Sterne was sitting at one end of it — in the only chair. The rest of the seating around the table consisted of curved benches made of the same granite. Individual pads were laid on each, but there were no backrests. The men stared at the structure.

"I designed it myself," Sterne said. "You wouldn't believe how efficient the meetings are in this room. I think the butt time on those cushions is thirty minutes for men and forty-five for women. I prefer to communicate electronically, but the occasional face-to-face conference is a necessary evil, I'm afraid."

Coswell almost laughed, but since Sterne hadn't cracked a smile, he suppressed it.

On the drive up from SeaTac, Miller and Whitfield, nominated him to do the bulk of the questioning. They reasoned that he'd had the most contact with Sterne up to that point.

A wave from their host directed them to the sides of the table instead of immediately adjacent to his chair. Coswell took a seat to his right and the two Federal men sat on his left. There obviously wasn't going to be any idle chit-chat. Sterne sat expressionless, merely nodding as the inspector introduced Miller and Whitfield.

"We're here on a follow-up of the events in Vancouver," Coswell began. "We think you might be able to help us with our ongoing investigation."

Sterne remained silent; the inspector continued.

"It appears that the Governor's two security men, Ales and Ferring, were part of a plot to assassinate Mayor Gryndon. Unfortunately, they've disappeared, leaving us with some unanswered questions."

Still nothing from Sterne and already Coswell was beginning to feel the hardness of the granite. He paused for a moment before continuing, as though he were formulating his questions ad lib. In truth, the list had been clear in his mind long before he arrived.

"We believe all of these men were acting on orders, carrying out a well planned operation planned by someone with considerable influence in the Pacific Northwest, someone with significant financial resources."

Sterne finally broke his silence with an icy comment.

"Someone like me, you mean."

Coswell feigned embarrassment.

"Sometimes this job is unpleasant," he replied, "but the truth is you were seen with the man, Ferring, on your yacht just after he supplied a considerable amount of cash to hire one of Vancouver's best criminal lawyers to represent his partner, Ales. Since the two were employees of Governor Kruger, one would think *he* would have been the person to arrange legal counsel, but my colleagues here tell me that the Governor denied doing so. You can imagine, then, our curiosity."

Sterne replied without a moment's hesitation.

"I did give Ferring the money. He came to me because he was afraid to approach the Governor, whose nose seemed to be completely out of joint about this affair. When they returned from the banquet, Adam cut Ferring cold and virtually dismissed him with a wave of his hand."

Coswell had no problem picturing that. Kruger, he could imagine, would not be nice when he was angry.

"I've come to know the two men, Ales and Ferring, quite well. This isn't the first trip we've been on with the Governor. We all have similar values and you'll have to do a lot of talking to convince me they were part of anything sinister. I like them, and as I'm sure you're aware, the amount of money that Ferring asked for was, to me, a pittance."

Whitfield could remain silent no longer. He sensed that Sterne was slipping out of their net.

"The assassin at the convention centre arrived with a press pass from the *Tacoma Review*, a newspaper which you own, I believe. Could you give us some insight as to why that might have been?"

Sterne laughed.

"I've no idea, unless your killer was inspired by the articles in the paper and wanted to pay some tribute. Editor

James is a fine Christian gentleman and isn't afraid to speak out against some of the Sodom-and-Gomorrah activities that taint our society these days. Surely you don't think he was involved? Ed James is a newspaper man, not some terrorist sympathizer."

He was smooth. Kruger said that he hadn't divulged a great deal of information to Sterne after the banquet incident. Ferring might have supplied some of it, but it was unlikely that the *Tacoma Review* press pass came up in that conversation. Sterne's response was just too pat. Someone either supplied him with the information or he was in on the plot from the beginning.

But they had no more questions; Sterne had stymied them.

"Good day, then," he said in response to their silence. The steel door opened and the young man entered. "See the gentlemen out, Jacob. We're through here."

Coswell stopped at the threshold and looked back. The steel roof was closing and the room was returning to darkness. He could barely see Sterne, who'd gotten up from his chair and turned to one of the computer stations behind him.

***
***

They did the post mortem in the same departure lounge at SeaTac. The ride back from Sterne's office was a quiet one, each man deep in his own thoughts.

"This guy's guilty as sin," Coswell said at last, sipping the Starbucks latté he'd bought the moment they arrived at the airport. "But you're only going to nail him one way, I reckon."

"What's that?" Miller said.

"Beat him at his own game — electronically. I'd tap everything you can: phones, hard-wired anything into his office, his home. I'd get the best computer brains at your disposal to hack into his system. If he is part of an elite network, he has to consult his confrères sometime."

"Wishful thinking," Whitfield said. "But I think Mr. Sterne has gone into safe mode and we're not likely to pick up anything soon."

"What about pushing the *Tacoma Review* staff again or passing Sterne's picture around the internet cafés where the faxes were sent?" Miller offered.

"We can try," Whitfield said, "but I think the Inspector here is right. We have to be patient. Fanatics like that can't stay inactive forever."

They shook hands all round and then Coswell headed for the Horizon Air check-in.

He was assigned a port-side window seat and as the 737 took off west over the ocean, he gazed south and thought of Cindy Forsythe. Maybe he'd reconsider Ward's vacation offer.

His stomach was grumbling but he wasn't going to contemplate eating until firmly on the ground in Vancouver. Perhaps he would see what Robert had going at Éclairage on West Broadway. He was rumoured to be doing some wonderful things with pork.

Heather perused her toes poking above the bubbles in her bath. Some of her best thinking took place in the tub and she let her mind soar. She'd taken the afternoon off, leaving Frayley to write whatever to appease the editorial bosses. A phone call to her publisher in North Vancouver set up a late lunch date with the manager, a shrewd lady who'd steered *The Making of a Killer: The True Story of the Monashee Murderer*, her first book, into print. It took an extra glass of white wine, however, and a lot of talking to finally get a tentative okay to proceed with this latest inspiration.

She got out of the bath, dried herself and put on her favourite terrycloth robe — her writing robe. Zachary had drawn late shift at the hospital again, which left her an entire evening free. She sat down at her desktop computer and switched it on. She hummed to herself as it booted up and when the icons appeared she double-clicked MS Word. At the top of the blank document page, she typed: "THE WEST END MURDERS — AN EXPOSÉ."

***
***

He wished that he could speak directly to Central, but a phone call was out of the question, they'd all agreed on that. Wiretapping appeared to be a carte blanche power the government wielded post 9/11 and no line was safe. The meetings they'd had in the beginning were rare now, the computer having taken over conventional conferencing. It was really too bad, because tone of voice and facial expression were so important in picking up the nuances in any personal communication. It was too easy to hide true feelings in text messaging.

He had reported to Central the moment he knew that Gryndon had returned safely to San Francisco after Ales' second attempt failed. But so far there'd been no reply and the session with Coswell and the Federal agents was unsettling.

He had to know where he stood now with the group. The

chat line, he felt, was his best move. His voice was weak as he dictated the codes to log on to his computer and his fingers felt clammy over the keys, waiting. Control responded with one word:

REPORT

No question mark. No please. No "how are you?"

He glanced over at his notepad. An hour's worth of scribbles and scratch-outs left a simple reply and he typed it in.

IN RESPONSE TO SALES STAFF INABILITY TO COMPLETE DEAL, THREE PERSONNEL TERMINATED. TWO OTHERS ON LEAVE — CONTINUE EMPLOYMENT?

The delay in reply was agonizing — a full five minutes. There was no indication that the others were online but maybe Central had called them to Washington. At that very moment they could be discussing his fate, up front and personal.

Finally a message popped up on the screen.

PERSONNEL SITUATION ALREADY DEALT WITH. YOUR INVOLVEMENT IN THIS MATTER NO LONGER REQUIRED.

His chest began to tighten and he could feel his pulse racing. The underlining of that sentence struck him like a hammer. Ales and Ferring were probably dead and he was being summarily dismissed. The message continued.

DECISION HAS BEEN MADE TO SHUT DOWN ALL WEST COAST OPERATIONS UNTIL FURTHER NOTICE. RISK-PROFIT RATIO TOO UNFAVOURABLE TO CONTINUE.

But what about him? What was he to do? Surely the funding he supplied made his continued presence necessary to the group. And then his heart skipped a beat as he realized how foolish he'd been to have agreed to the trusts. He stared blankly at the last message:

COMPANY HAS AGREED TO EXTENDED R AND R FOR YOU — ENJOY.

WILL CONTACT FROM THIS END RE FUTURE ASSIGNMENTS.

GAAAWU

No, his plan had been a good one. The failure wasn't his fault and even more important, he wasn't a risk. No way could the authorities link him to anything. The group was being unreasonable. He logged back in again. A sinking feeling in the pit of his stomach grew as the screen came up:

THIS PAGE CANNOT BE DISPLAYED

THE PAGE YOU ARE LOOKING FOR IS CURRENTLY UNAVAILABLE....

They'd changed the website! Central, the illiterate bastard, had got somebody to create a new website. He was cut off.

He reached for the phone and then slowly pulled his hand away. For a moment or two he sat motionless, letting calm return, and then grasped the mouse. He clicked his email service and then "addresses." He peered for a moment at the list until he spotted what he wanted and then clicked: PUGET SOUND PERSONAL SECURITY SERVICES. He manoeuvered the cursor to the automatic dialer icon and clicked once more before picking up the telephone. Leaning back in his chair, he watched the fish swimming so casually in his screensaver aquarium.

***
***

1 2 3 4 5 6 7
8 9 10 11 12 13
14 15 16 17 18
19 20 21 22
23 24 25 26
27 28 29 30
31 32 33 34
35 36 37 38

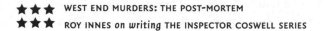
HOW IT STARTED

When my first crime novel, *Murder in the Monashees*, was published, it never entered my head to do a sequel. I'd already started two completely different works: a young adult mystery and a psychological thriller. Encouragement to pen a sequel, however, came from many quarters and so I set about writing *West End Murders*. I wanted to feature the characters that had gone over so well with readers of *Murder in the Monashees*, but I felt I needed something completely different to make the new novel work. I settled on a change of setting and placed the characters in the antithesis of outback Bear Creek, the metropolis of Vancouver. Once I'd done that, the writing moved along nicely. Scenes, plot, and new characters all just popped into my head.

THE STRUGGLE

Storytelling and good writing, unfortunately, do not go hand-in-hand. I've always struggled with the mechanics of the craft, and the more I delve into the subject and the more advice I receive, the tougher it gets. Some time ago I read a quotation in the *Globe and Mail* from Raymond Carver that describes this problem well:

Everything a writer learns about the art or craft of fiction takes just a little away from his need or desire to write at all. In the end he knows all the tricks and has nothing to say.

In all humility (I consider Raymond Carver the best word-smith of the twentieth century), I'd add one phrase to this: "...or is afraid to say it." Creating is one thing; exposing one's creation to the public is another.

The urge to perfect can slow one's writing to a crawl. Getting *West End Murders* ready for submission was a long, hard slog.

WHERE IS THE AUTHOR IN THE BOOK?

I'm everywhere, hidden for the most part, but there never-theless. Pure fiction, I think, is rare. An author's person-ality, life experiences, likes and dislikes form every page. When Paul Blakemore's name comes up on my screen, it's accompanied by an image of an old RCMP golf buddy, a Corporal Al. I vividly recall his quirks, his speech, his physical appearance, and I simply wrote those in. Sergeant Burns came easily, a policeman I've known since my youth. Even the minor characters are based on real people. I've distorted them all, of course; the real people are too real for the novel's purposes.

I do come to the surface in a number of places: Doctors Benson and Mueller reflect my own residency and my lat-er teaching years. Coswell's motion sickness is me all over and I curse the rocking conveyances just as he does. His gourmand tastes are mine as well — bringing up all those menus on the internet gave me great pleasure.

THE SETTINGS

This proved to be a minor problem. I worked in downtown Vancouver for twenty-five years but left there in the early nineties. The YMCA then was exactly as I described, but progress eventually won out and there is a posh new facility on the old site. The original y served my writing purposes much better and so I kept it. San Francisco, too, dates back. I haven't visited it for almost ten years, and I've never been to Sacramento. The wonderful world of cyberspace, however, enables me to be right up to date. Googling is as good as being there, visually speaking. The restaurant that Coswell took Cindy to has a virtual tour on its website. I actually panned right into the corner where the two sat.

I've changed the names of famous restaurants and chefs using plays on words or literal translations, a fun puzzle for readers who know the establishments.

I left the Sylvia Hotel unaltered. It truly is a piece of Vancouver history and I didn't want it confused with anything else.

The "salute" performed by the American jet fighter pilots over Comox is a real event, best seen while playing the adjacent golf course.

FORENSICS

As in *Murder in the Monashees*, I've used some poetic license here. The medical descriptions are accurate (my area of expertise), but the computer data sections are, for the most part, fiction. I'm not a Luddite in this field, but I'm far from expert. Guns I *am* familiar with, both as part of my hunting life and as a recreational target-shooter at the local gun club.

SPORTS

I've been a climber, albeit a rank amateur. My oldest son and my daughter are serious climbers, hence the "Australian Stop Descender." The golf sequence, though, is all me. I love the game and enjoyed getting the foursome together on the Balmoral, a fictional Vancouver golf course fashioned after one of the beauties on Marine Drive.

Stanley Park, its trails and the seawall, are more than a little familiar to me. I was a compulsive runner and put in many, many miles there. I altered the topography only slightly to serve the plot.

POLITICAL ISSUES

One critic wrote of *Murder in the Monashees* that I did not, in her opinion, develop adequately the issues brought up in the novel. She didn't specify which issues, but I presume she meant the environmental ones.

My answer to her is that I write novels like these solely to entertain, not to preach. There are many issues in *West End Murders* — gay rights, our justice system and right-wing fanaticism — but I use them for plot purposes only. If the characters expound on these from time to time, I let them do so, but it's they, not me, who bring them up.

HUMOUR

I admire authors like Jeffery Deaver who can keep the tension going from page one to the end without letup. Personally, however, I prefer a breather from time to time and humour serves that best, in my opinion. I make no apologies, therefore, for the comic relief scattered throughout *West End Murders*. I write what I like to read.

FICTION VS. FACT

The ranks of Lieutenant in the Vancouver City Police force and Chief Inspector in the RCMP are fictional. The actual ranking system in both forces is complicated, with terminology unfamiliar to the average reader: corps sergeant major, commissioner, superintendent, chief constable, etc. I acquiesced to TV conventions.

ERRATA

Real aficionados of crime writing love finding tiny errors and I'm sure I've unintentionally provided a few in *West End Murders*. Enjoy the hunt.

Pulling names out of the air is part of fiction writing and familiar ones come to mind first. None are intended to relate to actual people; they're just names. Occasionally embarrassing slips occur: I discovered, to my dismay, that there actually is an Inspector Ward of the RCMP and I don't know him from Adam. I hope he isn't a crime novel reader.

WHERE NEXT?

I'll finish the two novels I'm working on now, but I've rather enjoyed Coswell et al. again. I think next I might move them back into the bush, the Cariboo, perhaps. This time, Coswell will be the fish out of water. Blakemore and Burns joining him there could make for an interesting combination. I've just returned from a moose hunt in that region and have tons of background material.

Roy Innes is a retired eye physician and surgeon. His early penchant for the arts, buried for years in the world of science, was rekindled upon retirement. At that time, he enrolled in the Humber School for Writers program and, under the mentorship of literary notable Olive Senior, wrote his first novel, *Murder in the Monashees*, which was released in 2005 to excellent reviews. Equally at home in the city or the wilds, Innes is an avid hunter, a lover of classical music, and, belied by his skinny frame, a gourmand. He lives on BC's lush Gabriola Island with his wife, Barrie, and his daughter's cat.